Hunters' Island

Novels by Gordon L. Rottman

Tears of the River
Blazing Summer
The Hardest Ride
Ride Harder
Marta's Ride
Marta's Daughter

Hunters' Island

Beyond Honor

GORDON L. ROTTMAN

CASEMATE
Pennsylvania & Yorkshire

Published in the United States of America and Great Britain in 2024 by
CASEMATE PUBLISHERS
1950 Lawrence Road, Havertown, PA 19083, US
and
47 Church Street, Barnsley, S70 2AS, UK

Copyright 2024 © Gordon L. Rottman

Paperback Edition: ISBN 978-1-63624-070-1
Digital Edition: ISBN 978-1-63624-071-8

A CIP record for this book is available from the British Library

All rights reserved. No part of this book may be reproduced or transmitted in any form or by any means, electronic or mechanical including photocopying, recording or by any information storage and retrieval system, without permission from the publisher in writing.

Printed and bound in the United Kingdom by CPI Group (UK) Ltd, Croydon, CR0 4YY

Typeset in India by Lapiz Digital Services, Chennai.

For a complete list of Casemate titles, please contact:

CASEMATE PUBLISHERS (US)
Telephone (610) 853-9131
Fax (610) 853-9146
Email: casemate@casematepublishers.com
www.casematepublishers.com

CASEMATE PUBLISHERS (UK)
Telephone (0)1226 734350
Email: casemate@casemateuk.com
www.casemateuk.com

This is a book of fiction. Mentions of historical events, real persons or places are used fictitiously.

The letter from General Lee that Captain Young reads is from General Robert E. Lee's General Order number 16 issued on July 11, 1863.

"Some things end. But war never ends."

—*The Other Side of Dawn,* the
Tomorrow When the War Began series
John Marsden

Dedication

*To the soldiers, marines, sailors, and airmen
who fought in the Pacific War.*

Acknowledgements

A novel like this would not be possible without the help and advice of many, especially of those World War II Marine veterans who shared their stories. Many contributed minor "everyday" experiences that defined their not-so-routine days and nights, in particular William "Bill" T. Paull (10th Marines and Provisional Raider Battalion, 2d Marines) and James Broderick (2d Defense Battalion). A big thank you goes out to my many friends in World War II discussion groups for providing detailed expertise and advice. I am especially thankful to our local writers' group: Stan Marshal, Linda Bromley, Terry Davis, and Terry Miller. My longtime friend Steve Seale provided extensive and valuable advice on grammar and structure. Jesse Smetherman was invaluable for his firearms and ballistics knowledge.

This book would not have been possible without the aid of Akira Takawa "Taki" and his broad knowledge and expertise on the Imperial Japanese Army and Japanese society and culture.

Most of all I am indebted to my wife Enriqueta and our family for allowing me the time to craft this project.

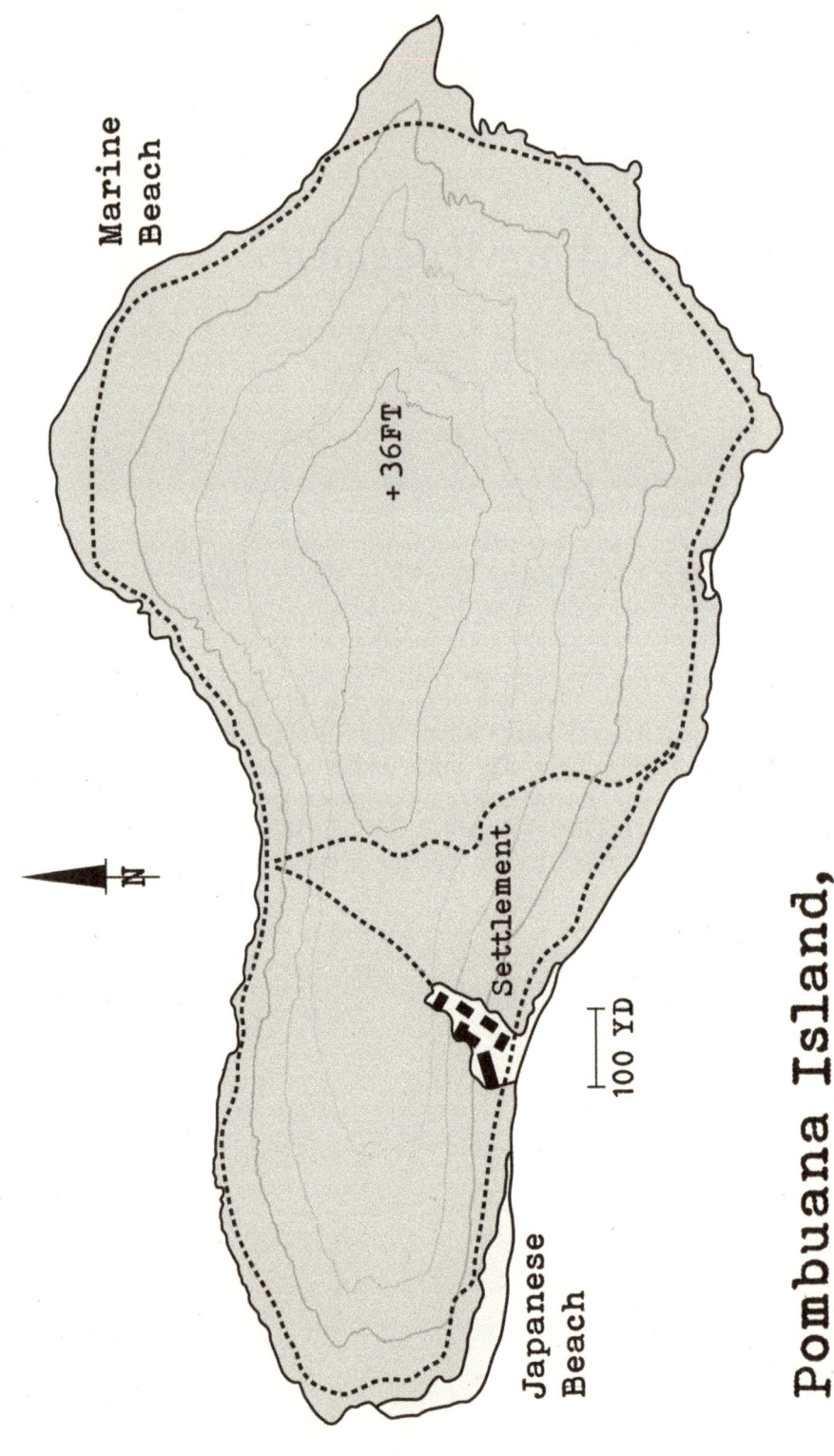

PART ONE
San Diego, California—"Dago"
and
Nagoya, Japan—*"Nagoya-shi"*

Chapter One

"As American as mom, baseball, and apple pie."

Henrik Hahnemann regretted what he was about to do, but he took the step off the road's frosted grassy shoulder and into the muddy field anyway. He tried not to think about last night's two hours of brushing and polishing to turn his scuffed work boots into his Sunday best. Now, with church over, the cycle began anew as he stepped onto the cornfield's stubble. He didn't need to be thinking about his boots, but about bagging supper.

The mud clumped thickly on his boot soles, good black Missouri River bottomland. Each step added another layer and more weight. The temperature was right at that point when the rising sun was defrosting the ground dirt, turning it into an adhesive muck. He'd scrape it off when he came across a stick. Henrik felt the tingle of the chilled December air, listened to the crunch of frozen corn stubble, and watched his puffs of breath as he trudged across the field. The brown whipcord coat and jeans over a wool union suit kept him warm enough.

Christmas was less than three weeks away, he thought, allowing his mind to wander and daydream about Christmas supper and gifts. Not that he expected much in the way of presents, but he knew Mama would do her best for the hallowed day's supper. Aunts, uncles, and cousins would stop by. Last year he and his younger brother and sister each received an orange from Papa. Mama had knitted a sweater and a pair of heavy socks for each of them. It had taken her all year and not because she was a slow knitter. Between washing, making clothes, tending the vegetable garden, canning, house cleaning, caring for three kids and Papa, cooking three meals a day, and all the extra things she did at St. Paul's Lutheran Church in Marthasville, she didn't have much time for working her knitting needles.

Henrik mentally shook himself and thumbed up the visor of his gray wool cap. Even with the snug knit earflaps, his ears were still cold. He'd better pay attention to the ground ahead as he neared the trees above the south pond. To his left was the fold of a low ridge, covered with leafless trees, a dreary image. This was the "warmest" part of the day, and the critters might be out. He lifted the butt of the J. C. Higgins 20-gauge shotgun into his shoulder. Like his boots, Papa had mail-ordered the single-shot scattergun from Sears, Roebuck & Company.

Twenty yards from the stand of scattered trees he halted and scanned the leafless brush and patches of brown weeds. This was a prime rabbit spot. No movement. Henrik was confident he'd hit a cottontail when it darted off through the sparse foliage. He'd had enough practice. Once he'd won a box of shotgun shells at the Warren County Fair for the 4-H project rabbit hutch he'd built. That had been a good deal; neighbors asked him to build five more hutches, and that brought his family a few more dollars. He'd gotten two dollars for each, except from miserly Mr. Dothage who had talked Henrik down to a buck eighty-five.

In *Field & Stream* Henrik had read about a fella up in New York who practiced rabbit shooting in an uncommon manner. He let loose balloons to be blown across the ground and blasted away at them. The article admitted the balloons were sometimes swept into the sky or popped in foliage. Henrik wasn't about to spend a penny for six balloons, and it didn't sound like it worked all that well. He had another idea. He opened up grocery sacks and let the wind catch them. They were heavy enough not to be blown off the ground—rabbits don't really hop all that high—and bags didn't pop. They bounded across the ground just as fast and erratic as rabbits. He spent ten of the valuable shells practicing on runaway bags. It was worth it, even if Papa was cross. As far as he was concerned that was ten real eatin' rabbits-worth of shells instead of paper practice bunnies. He'd granted that they'd been won by his son to do with as he pleased. It would have been a different story if they'd been a box of twenty-five shells Papa had spent eighty-nine cents on at Dickmann's Store. But Henrik could tell Papa was proud he'd used his noggin to improve on an idea. Mama though was put out with him "blastin' six perfectly good paper bags all to smithereens." They were invaluable to her homemaking.

Hardly thinking, he snapped the shotgun up and followed the bounding rabbit, leading it by some magically calculated interval, a skill he'd acquired when he started hunting at ten years of age. The gun punched his shoulder. The rabbit spun sideways as shotgun-blasted dirt and leaves leapt off the ground. It was a clean kill. Henrik knew Mama had heard the distance-muffled shot, signaling her to start the stew makings. The wood-burning stove was already heated. He could taste it now, potatoes, onion, cabbage, and carrots—she'd use the carrots sparingly to make them last the winter—boiled to the point where they dissolved in his mouth. It was worth being out here in the freezing air to wait for a meal like that … almost.

Two hours later he tramped up the road with his bulging game bag—really just a cut-down burlap feed sack with an old leather harness strap tack-stitched on. The whitewashed two-story house sure looked inviting with his nose, chin, and ears near frozen. His feet and hands were not much better off. Smoke wafted from the chimney, and the two dogs of questionable parentage ran excitedly about the fenced yard in expectation of his return. They'd soon be feasting on bunny innards. He'd never take Jake and Sue hunting as they'd range ahead, scaring off game. They were farm dogs meant to keep critters out of the garden, chicken coop, and feed barn.

Henrik wasn't looking forward to the remaining months of winter. Spring wouldn't arrive until mid-April. He'd already had enough of the endless chill, icy roads, snow drifts, breaking ice in the water troughs, and head colds and the fear of flu. He loved the outdoors, but he dreaded this bleak time of year.

On this chilly December Sunday of 1941, it was hard to turn his attention to the months ahead. There was his birthday in February, then his graduation from Marthasville High School in May. It seemed a long way off. He thought about the story he'd read in *Astounding Science Fiction Magazine* that Mr. Spencer, his science and math teacher, had lent him. "By His Bootstraps" written by Robert Heinlein was a time travel story. He didn't want to go that far into the future, 30,000 years. Half a year would do.

Henrik knew exactly what he'd find when he came through the door after shucking his muddy boots on the porch. Papa would be in his rocking chair, his stockinged feet propped up on a footstool before the crackling fireplace. There'd be *The Marthasville Record* newspaper or a third-hand farm magazine in his hands.

The first words out of Papa's mouth would be, "What'd you bag, son?"

"Two rabbits and two squirrels, sir," he'd respond.

"How many shells?"

"Four, sir."

"Four for four, good doings, son." Missing a shot was inexcusable. He knew one rabbit would be saved in the icebox.

Mama would be in the kitchen with Johanna helping her and wanting to hide so she'd not have to clean the game, a chore she detested beyond all others, except cleaning fish. He'd say, "I froze my hinny off to shoot supper and you're going to eat it too, so you can clean it." Mama would say something about his language. His fourteen-year-old sister would stick her tongue out, but she'd do the job, and do it good. She'd even pick out most of the lead shot. Ernst would be sprawled on the colorful rag rug woven from old shirts torn into strips. The twelve-year-old would have his nose in a schoolbook or geography book with the little globe near at hand. The radio would be playing one of the Sunday big band music shows: Glenn Miller, Benny Goodman, Tommy Dorsey, or Duke Ellington. Henrik knew "the Duke" was a black man. He'd seen some black people when he'd gone to St. Louis for the first time last year. He liked the Duke's style; it was more "jazzy." Mama wasn't too sure about what that meant.

Papa loved that radio, even though Mama had complained it was a vain, expensive contrivance. She'd never admit it, but she liked it too. When the men were out working, as she did her own chores, she'd sometimes turn it on and listen to shows like *Duffy's Tavern* and *Bringing Up Father*. Henrik was startled once when he found Mama tuning the radio herself. He didn't know she could do that. They'd gotten it just two years ago after the Missouri Power and Light Company ran a line out from Marthasville.

Having removed his boots, Henrik opened the door, eagerly anticipating the scene. Between the kitchen's woodstove and the front room's fireplace, the entire house would be toasty warm and filled with the aroma of the stew base, peas, cornbread, and cinnamon apple pie. Mama would rush Johanna to clean the game and get it into the pot.

That was not what Henrik found. Instead, everyone was clustered around the Sparton Model 1271 Console Radio. Ernst and Johanna were sitting on the floor, and Papa had pulled over a dining room chair for Mama. Papa was in his rocker, his hand held up shushing Henrik before he could ask questions. They looked as grim as they had two years ago when the war broke out in Europe—no, grimmer. They barely glanced at him and his bagged supper.

"What's going on—?" he started to ask, but sensed it was better to listen.

The radio was saying, *"Such an attack would naturally mean war and the President would ask Congress for a declaration of war. There is no doubt from the temper of Congress that such a declaration would be granted. The details are not available. They will be shortly when President Roosevelt will be giving out a statement."*

The unknown announcer's voice peaked. *"And just now comes word from the President's office that a second air attack has been reported on Army and Navy bases in Manila. Thus we have official announcements from the White House that Japanese airplanes have attacked Army and Navy installations in Hawaii and the Philippines. Hostilities are opening across the South Pacific and the situation is grave."*

Henrik felt a sense of unreality. He'd never heard anything like this before. Something gnawed in his belly. His gaze strayed to Ernst's prized world atlas spread open on the floor beside him.

"Secretary of State Cordell Hull has talked with the Secretaries of the Navy and War Departments. The Japanese ambassador and the special envoy are at the State Department engaged in conference with Secretary Hull. Their appearance at the State Department on this Sunday afternoon demonstrates the gravity of the situation. We will read the White House statement when it is released. We

return you to New York," the solemn radio voice announced. Somber music began playing and Papa turned down the volume.

Papa said, "Ernst, where's this Pearl Harbor?" Then he looked at Henrik, whose mouth was hanging open. "The Japs did an air raid on our ships in Pearl Harbor, son. Looks like we're getting pulled into a war after all."

"Pearl Harbor's right here," said Ernst excitedly, holding up the Rand McNally atlas. Everyone crowded around and looked at the string of islands comprising the Territory of Hawaii. "It's on this island—Oahu—and right beside the capital of the territory, Honolulu city."

"That's surely a long ways off," said Johanna. "Why's it called a territory?"

Henrik was surprised. His sister didn't ask questions like that. "It's like a state, right Ernst?"

"Yes, but the governor's picked by the President, not voted for."

Johanna looked a little confused with that.

"It's almost 2,500 miles from California," said Ernst.

"Show your Mama and Hansi"—that's what Papa called Johanna—"where these Philippines are."

"They're way over here," Ernst explained, opening the book to a page spanning the Pacific Ocean. "Seven thousand miles away. The Philippines are a lot closer to Japan than us. Must have been easy for the Japs to attack there."

Mama was peering at the maps; no doubt she didn't comprehend the distances. Her world was smaller. She said she'd only been to five counties in Missouri and nowhere beyond. The furthest she had ever been away from home was St. Louis just fifty miles to the east. "Thank the good Lord that Henrik isn't of age."

Of age ... of age for what? he thought. Then he saw the anxiety in her eyes. It dawned on him—*draft age*—striking him with a solid blow. He knew the draft had started last year because of the war in Europe. He'd just never thought it might be something that would touch him. Well, like Mama said, that was sometime away. A war might not even last that long.

But then he felt something else. His mind started spinning. *America's at war, like it or not. It doesn't really feel like it, but the President said we are. We are being attacked by the Japanese. Why? What did we ever do to them? They were the ones warring with China and killing them by the thousands. We weren't in the fight, but they sure as heck went out of their way to attack us and it sounds like a real sneak attack.* It was a lot to comprehend, when not a few minutes before his thoughts had been consumed by the prospect of rabbit stew.

He had to think about this. Too much was happening too fast. He looked at Mama, who was ready to break down in tears. That wasn't like Mama. This was a woman who'd butcher four hogs at a time and can a thousand quarts of fruits and vegetables in the spring and fall canning seasons, with Johanna's and Aunt Grace's help. Johanna was just looking confused. Ernst was absorbed in his maps, entranced by the geography of it all.

Papa took his mama's hand and patting it said, "Let's not worry on it now, Mama. We'll find out more about what's going on."

Mama suddenly stood, as imposing and strong-willed as ever. "*Henrik, was hast du schießen?*"—What did you shoot?

"*Zwei Kaninchen und zwei Eichhörnchen, Mama.*"—Two rabbits and two squirrels. Mama was always proud of his attempts at simple German.

"Hansi, you got verk to do," Mama said in her faint accent, and she disappeared into the kitchen. Henrik could hear her hand-pumping the cistern on the counter.

Johanna frowned but leapt to her feet. She was hungry too. Mama had her open a can of margarine, marking this as a special occasion. She tore open the paper packet inside and stirred the yellow dye powder into the pasty white margarine.

"The boys and I will stay here listening to the news," Papa said.

Henrik sat cross-legged beside the fireplace and broke out the gun cleaning kit. He'd clean it even if only a single shot had been fired. Ernst pored over his atlas, looking for every place mentioned on the radio. He decided to also clean the Winchester lever-action, their .30-30 deer rifle.

Reports trickled in through the afternoon. Official announcements were infrequent. Instead, they heard a lot of talk by smart-sounding people predicting what might happen. Papa explained to Henrik and Ernst that speculation and educated guesses were no different than rumors and gossip. Papa grew angrier, not at the commentators and lack of solid news, but at "those stinking lowdown back-stabbing Nips." They were hearing from the radio it had been a surprise attack and a lot of sailors and soldiers were killed, even some civilians. A lot of planes were destroyed on the ground and many ships sunk at anchor.

"And the little sneaks did it on the Sabbath," riled Papa.

***

Supper was a solemn affair. There was no retelling of Henrik's hunt, which Papa and Ernst always urged out of him. The women of the family would have been less than spellbound. Henrik guessed all the hunts sounded pretty much the same to them, except for the one last fall when he ran into a black bear up on North Ridge on Uncle Werner's farm. He didn't know which ran in the opposite direction the fastest—he or the bear.

Mama had added a lot to the supper prayer, asking that "our soldiers und zeemen be protected und that Gott vatch over this family und this great nation in the trying days that come." After the "Amen," she announced they would not speak of the war at the table, now or ever. But that was all Henrik and Ernst could think of. Instead, they had to listen to Mama and Papa *quietly* talking about *Onkel* Theodor, Papa's cousin in Germany. They'd not heard from him since a Christmas card four months after the war began in Europe in 1939. They had sent letters, but nothing more was heard from Uncle Theodor. Henrik's father had checked with the postmaster, and mail service still existed between America and Germany, but letters were slow crossing the Atlantic where they said a battle was on going between British convoys and U-boats.

Later he heard Papa on the phone talking to friends. One was Uncle Werner and another was Arthur Thimble who owned the town garage, an endless source of gossip, or as the men called it, "shooting the bull."

That night Henrik lay awake for a long time in his and Ernst's upstairs bedroom. He was covered with a sheet, two wool blankets, and a goose down quilt, but still felt cold. The radio announcers' voices bounced around in his mind. All those American boys being killed in a Sunday morning sneak attack and probably going to church. He wondered, *How do sailors go to church?* He felt offended and angry. His country had been dirty surprise-attacked. After playing recordings of the Lord's Prayer and the National Anthem, the radio station had gone off the air. They did that every night, but he'd seldom been allowed to stay up until ten o'clock, and never on a school night. The "Star Spangled Banner" had held a much different meaning to him. For once he couldn't wait to get to school in the morning to see what Buck and Lester thought, and Mr. Sprick too, the history teacher and coach.

Just as Henrik drifted off the phone jangled. It was impossible to make out whom Papa was speaking to.

I've got to do something... But being seventeen, there wasn't much he could. *Dirty Japs* was his last conscious thought.

***

"Are you boys awake?" asked Papa.

It was still dark at 5:30 a.m., their usual wake-up time, when Papa and Henrik fed the livestock, Ernst did the milking, and Johanna collected eggs before breakfast.

Henrik only mumbled, but then remembered what had happened.

"That was Mr. Hackmann called last night."

The Hackmanns were the nearest neighboring farm, and he was the school principal.

"He said President Roosevelt would make an announcement today and they will have a radio at the school."

Even though Papa didn't use the phone a lot, he seldom said much about what he talked about. He declared no one knew any more than they already did. The boys just didn't make phone calls to their friends. Each call cost money, even if a few cents.

And folks were making a lot of calls. There were three other families on their party line. Their code ring was three rings. There were a lot of one, two, and four rings as the others on the line called other folks. Out of courtesy one didn't stay on the line long.

The radio played the regular programs and commercials like every other day, but announcers talked a lot without saying much. Papa said they reported nothing new. "It's all just yakety-talk and rumors." Mama called newspapers *klatschblatten*—gossip sheets. The radio announced President Roosevelt would speak to the nation at noon.

"Think of that," said Papa. "The President can talk to everyone in the country at the same time. When I was a boy the only way to talk to everyone at once was to mail them all a letter."

Henrik couldn't wait for the speech. Maybe he could find out if there was something he could do. He bagged a squirrel and good-sized rabbit that afternoon. As he stalked them, he pretended they were Japs.

Chapter Two

"Should emergencies arise, offer yourselves courageously to the state."
Imperial Rescript on Education
October 1890

Obata Yoshiro knew his father had been up quite early. Father's friend, Mr. Iwanaka, had politely knocked quietly on the door sometime after 0500. Mr. Iwanaka worked the night shift in the Mitsubishi Aircraft Engine Works on the outskirts of Nagoya. They made fighter planes for the Imperial Navy, but he could not talk about it. Everything to do with the Imperial Army and Navy was secret.

Obata heard Mr. Iwanaka tell Father that when he turned on his radio for the morning *Nippon Hoso Kyodai*—Japan Broadcast News—it was playing military music. There were no announcements or commercials, just endless martial music. Father thought there would soon be an important broadcast, probably about the war in China. It was called the "China Incident," as though it were just some minor trouble in that strange land where the Emperor's soldiers were fighting communists, radical nationalists, and rampant banditry. That "incident" had dragged on for four and a half years. Japan had actually been conducting a creeping expansion into China since 1931. That is what Father called it. Ten years was a long fight, and the country was war-weary, according to Father. He could not say that publicly and cautioned Obata not to repeat it, even to his closest friends and relatives.

Obata tried to go back to sleep. He had a vested interest in what was happening in China, but he did not want to hear of it so early in the morning, especially on a school morning; a Monday at that. Before he knew it, he would be in the middle of it—the "Incident," whatever this one was.

He had received his "Notification to Report for Conscription Physical" this past May. Delivered in person by a rather elderly, but firm and abrupt 1st lieutenant, who emphasized there were no exceptions or excuses for failure to report. It is something that every nineteen-year-old expected. Mother had been quietly distraught, but dutifully kept a calendar counting down to the day Yoshio was to appear at the recruit depot in Nagoya over 300 kilometers west of Tokyo. When the day came, he endured the embarrassment of close physical examination accompanied by half-naked young men as self-conscious as he was. Obata knew that men rated as Class A and Class B1 would go to active duty. He shamefully hoped he might be rated Class B2 or B3 to receive a few months for the First and Second Period Examinations and then commit to seven years in the Reserve. A few weeks later the same stern officer delivered his "Notification of Acceptance for Conscription." He was rated Class A, meaning he was over five feet tall and in good physical condition. He had been surprised almost a quarter of the young men had at least early symptoms of tuberculosis, signs of beriberi, bad teeth, and poor eyesight. Many had never had eyeglasses. They were told that if conscripted they would be provided glasses. He attributed his health to the family's access to better food in the country and abundant fish from *Oji* Asahi's fishing boat, his mother's brother.

Yoshio would report in January to the army training depot outside of Nagoya for two years' military duty. He and his family viewed that duty with mixed patriotic pride and concern for his absence, as did friends, fellow students, and neighbors. It was a different matter when he lay on his sleeping mat at night or when he made the long morning walk to school. Then he was not so prideful. He was frightened.

He had heard countless stories of the horrors and miseries of the war in China. There were stories of raging Chinese attacks, more so than were admitted in the newspapers and on Nippon Broadcast News. All they reported were divinely inspired Japanese victories. There were stories whispered by veterans of the terrible food, disease, the foul weather with its endless heat and dust, and the cold, rain, and snow of the long winters. They mentioned the barbarous living conditions of the squalid Chinese masses. And the mud—they always spoke of the mud. He had seen returned soldiers on crutches, legless or armless or worse; silent, solemn young men who never spoke of their ordeals. They had been told not to, ever.

Obata had firm ideas of what soldiering was like; he had seen the movies, sometimes glamorizing war, sometimes showing the terror, and oftentimes the tedium. *China Night* was too much of a romance for Obata and was disturbingly scandalous. Adding to its sensationalism, it showed the courtship and marriage of a Japanese man to a Chinese woman, flagrantly violating the rules of racial purity…a Chinese woman, unfathomable to Father. He did not allow Mother to see it. Not unusual—he seldom let her see a movie, and his sister had never seen one. Obata could not comprehend it either. Why? Its scenes of the destruction of Shanghai were actually filmed there, and this had a tremendous impact on Obata's view of the war. It wasn't all honor and glory.

One of his favorites was *The Story of Tank Commander Nishizumi*, which he had seen last year. The calm, undemanding, and modest lieutenant constantly took risks that he could have ordered his men to undertake; instead, he chose to expose himself. He was devoted to protecting the men of his company and just as devoted to his beloved Nippon and the Emperor. While his leadership was inspiring, he died wading through a stream to test its depth so his tanks could cross, mercilessly shot down by a conniving Chinese solider. Nishizumi was declared a "military god" because of his soldierly qualities, which Obata very much admired.

Five Scouts was his favorite movie for its depiction of field life in China and the camaraderie between frontline soldiers. The scouts were sent on an ill-fated mission and while hopeless, they displayed a noble devotion to one another and the Emperor. They died in glory shouting "Banzai!"

These thoughts raced through Obata's mind. Sleep was impossible, and he knew he would soon have to be up and prepare for another school day. It was the eighth day of the twelfth month of the sixteenth year of the Showa Emperor, the Yamato year of 2601. On the Western calendar they used at school it was the eighth day of December 1941.

There was a quiet tap at his door, and it slid open. He had not even heard Father return from Mr. Iwanaka's.

"Obata, there will be an important broadcast in a few minutes," was all Father said. The wood-framed paper door slid closed.

Obata slipped on a *haori* jacket over his sleeping kimono went into the family room. A single oil lamp flickered. There was no electricity out here as in town. He straightened the open-fronted *haori*, which pleased him with its warmth. He found Father tuning the old battery-powered Imperial Phonoradio with its elaborately carved wooden facade. The solemn strains of the "*Kimigayo*" had just begun to play, the oldest and shortest national anthem in the world:

May your Reign
Continue for a thousand, eight thousand generations,
Until the pebbles
Grow into boulders
Lush with moss

Father and son stood with heads bowed. Obata noticed his mother kneeling in the kitchen door. Fumiko, his little sister, was still asleep. He saw Father's old watch with Japanese rather than Arabic or Roman numbers; it was 0600. A formal, stern voice began without preamble, an unnamed Imperial spokesman. It was, of course, not the Emperor or a prince or any known representative of the Imperial family. No one outside the Imperial Palace had ever heard His voice. Father and son sank to their knees.

"We, by the grace of Heaven, Emperor of Japan, seated on the Throne of a line unbroken for ages eternal, enjoin upon ye, Our loyal and brave subjects:

"We hereby declare war on the United States of America and the British Empire. The men and officers of Our Army and Navy shall do their utmost in prosecuting the war, Our public servants of various departments shall perform faithfully and diligently their appointed tasks, and all other subjects of Ours shall pursue their respective duties; the entire Nation with a united will shall mobilize their total strength so that nothing will miscarry in the attainment of Our war aims."

Obata did not move, but his heart raced at the immensity of what he was hearing. Once, he glanced up. Father was like a stone, showing no change of expression. Mother though had her sad eyes fixed on Obata. He lowered his head.

Then they heard the familiar voice of Prime Minister and Army Minister Tōjō. He stiffly read a short statement that the Imperial Japanese Army and Navy had commenced to do battle against America and the British Empire throughout the Pacific before dawn this day. The Empire of Japan was victorious and would prevail in this just war. Every Japanese citizen was expected to make sacrifices and do their duty to ensure total victory for the Emperor. There was no explanation as to why or if there was fighting going on right now.

The lively *"Gunkan kōshinkyoku"*—"Man-of-War March"—followed. Father turned off the radio to save the battery. The family bowed to one another. Silence descended, then after a long moment his father broke the hush. "Yoshiro, we know you will fulfill your coming duties and honor your family and the Emperor." They all bowed again.

"Now we must prepare for the new day of work and studies."

Mother backed out of the room still on her knees and went to the kitchen where rice was already steaming. Obata returned to his room and donned his dark blue *gakuran* school uniform in the gloom. He touched his collar, confirming the school's badge was still pinned on. He carefully folded his foot wraps into place so there would be no uncomfortable creases on the soles and pulled on his sandals. Emotions whirled through his mind: pride, sense of duty, responsibility, dread. He sensed mother's maternal fear. He was not so certain he could eat the coming meal.

Breakfast was unusually late. Mother had made extra effort; it was a special and memorable day. She could sense something grave had occurred, even if not fully comprehending the words she had heard. Besides the usual steamed rice, miso soup, seasoned dried seaweed and green tea, there were rolled omelets and fermented soybeans. Fumiko, his ten-year-old sister, sat silently. She would stay home learning how to eventually become a wife and mother. She too had heard the announcements from the kitchen, but he knew she had little understanding of what it meant.

Breakfast was quiet in the soft glow of a single oil lamp. It usually was, but today it seemed as dreary as a funeral. Obata noticed that Mother served the meal on her great-great-grandmother's honored serving dishes, something seen only for special events. He so wished to speak of the war with his father. He could understand his silence; they knew little. What was there to speak of? No doubt they would talk this evening as more official announcements were issued over the radio and the *Nagoya Shimbun* newspaper was out. Just as importantly, Father would have talked to his friends, neighbors, and the workers at his business, Nikko Special Glass Factory. Mr. Morioka, the work master, especially would have something to say, he always did. There was little doubt the war would be all that was talked about in school. He expected to hear further announcements there. Often official proclamations were heard in school before they were issued on the radio. He would be able to talk to his father about what he heard, just like an adult.

Because of the out-of-the-way location of their home—near the confluence of the Nikko and Shin Rivers flowing into Nagoya Bay—Obata walked alone to school for much of the way. He trudged along, following familiar rice paddy dikes. The temperature was just above freezing, and he was grateful there was little rain in December. No trees broke the stiff winds blowing off the bay. It was not until he reached the outskirts of town that he joined the growing clusters of blue-uniformed students with short-peaked black caps and their white book bags slung at their sides. Window lights lit the streets. The town had electricity, which came on an hour before dawn. The students were already talking about the war, exchanging rumors, and pronouncing their opinions of what would happen. Mostly they were repeating what their fathers and uncles had said based on the one broadcast they had all heard.

Obata's best friend Jiro ran to him, wide-eyed with excitement. They quickly bowed. "Obata, have you heard?"

Obata suddenly did not feel like talking about it. He only nodded his head. He had an uneasy sensation that he would be in the middle of it soon enough and talking about it seemed pointless and unnecessary.

"And you are going into the Army in a month." Jiro sounded excited for him.

He did not need the reminder. "As certain now as the Sun will rise and shine favorably on our Empire." It seemed the appropriate thing to say.

"Today you will be honored as a hero in school," Jiro proclaimed.

That made Obata feel better, even though he had done nothing to be proclaimed a hero and doubted he ever would. *A hero for what?* All he had done was sign a paper. He had not even taken an oath. That would only come when he completed his training as a soldier of the Emperor. A hero because he might die for the Emperor. There was no more honorable glory than that end, not that he looked forward to such a fate.

He let Jiro do the talking, as usual.

"Do you think I should volunteer now?"

"Wait for your Notice," said Obata. "It will come soon enough. That will let you stay and help your father take care of your mother. It will be a great burden on him without your help."

Jiro's smile turned into a long frown. That was a problem for him. His mother had a stomach cancer and was mostly bedridden. On occasion she had a good day and could even walk a little and take care of herself, to a point. A widowed aunt and her daughter had moved in with them and cared for his mother and Jiro too.

"Yes, perhaps I should wait for her…to…"

"That would be best," Obata said, clasping his hand on his friend's shoulder. "It would bring you honor to stay and help them."

They both knew that one's conscription could be deferred for up to two years owing to family hardships. They also knew that Jiro's mother might not last through the summer. July and August heat and humidity were ruthless. The past summer had been particularly hard on her.

After long moments of walking in silence, Jiro brought up something he had spoken of before.

"If I apply for a deferment then I could join the Air Defense Observation Corps—*Boku Kanshitai*. That would help me to prepare for military training by learning how to use a compass, binocular, and telephone. Can you imagine what it would be like to speak on a telephone? There is an observation post out on the point. Maybe I would be assigned there to search the sky for attacking enemy airplanes and report their numbers, direction, and altitude to the local army headquarters."

Obata knew that Jiro read much about the military. It sounded boring to Obata, endlessly sweeping empty skies with a binocular. "Maybe you would never see such airplanes," he said to Jiro. "I would think that the air forces of the Imperial Army and Navy would repel any enemy airplanes approaching the Home Islands."

"Maybe, but the Americans also have aircraft carriers," said Jiro. "Maybe they could sneak in close enough to attack us."

"Yes, but the Imperial Navy is supposed to intercept an invading fleet and destroy it in a decisive battle like we did with the Russian fleet at Tsushima in 1905."

Yashiro spoke of the Russo-Japanese War, the first war in which an Asian country, the Empire of Japan, defeated a modern European army and navy.

"Yes of course, but then one never knows in which direction the fortunes of war will fly," said Jiro. "The Spirit of Yamato—Yamato *damahin*—will always lead us to victory. I will visit the leader of the neighborhood branch of the Greater Japan Air Defense Association. My father knows him and can introduce me."

***

Obata's long morning walk was because his family did not live in town, but on a small rural farm plot. Rather than a neighborhood fire watch association consisting of the usual ten families as part of a block association, theirs was made up of fourteen adjacent farms near Nagoya Bay. The farm was not cultivated by his family since his father owned the Nikko Special Glass Factory. He viewed himself as a successful industrialist, not a mere farmer. The factory was essential for its fishing net floats and the special glass products they produced for the Imperial Army.

The shop used to make many styles of vases and lamp globes. Now they mostly made fishing net floats, some as large as 500 millimeters in diameter; larger across than his forearm and hand were long. The Ministry of Agriculture, Forestry, and Fisheries had decreed that fish harvesting be increased. Nets, glass floats, and ropes were in great demand. The Imperial Navy had priority on rope, and fishermen had to use smaller-diameter and lower-quality rope. Father had been concerned a few years ago that cork fishing floats were being imported from northwest Africa and southwest Europe. The Spanish Civil War and European political turmoil soon put a stop to that last source. Fortunately, traditional Japanese fishermen preferred the long-used glass floats.

Recently they had begun producing thousands of 100-millimeter-diameter glass spheres with small, short necks. The larger net floats were sealed and had no openings. As they were not much bigger than his balled fist, Obata wondered what these small spheres were for.

In the past workers were able to take home defective, but still useable, glass items. These spheres could not be taken from the shop no matter their defects. Flawed spheres were broken and re-melted. This seemed strange, but the spheres had been ordered by the War Ministry. They were secretive about everything, and one did not ask. But Obata still wondered about their purpose. They had rounded bottoms, not flat, allowing them to sit on a surface. Perfectly round spheres with a two-finger-tall neck with an opening he could barely insert his little finger into. Father said during a rare moment of speculation that maybe they would be filled with gunpowder and a time fuse inserted. A glass hand grenade? Low cost, but a glass grenade would be too fragile to carry in a war, he reasoned.

Their farm had been inherited from his mother's father. She was the oldest of three girls and there were no sons. If there had been sons, the oldest would have inherited the land even if younger than his youngest sister. A neighboring farmer leased their rice paddies so they would not lie unproductive, and his father fished. Obata's mother nurtured a small herb and vegetable garden for the family's needs.

Obata had been told the spherical fishing net floats the factory made were important to the fishing industry. The radio expounded food supplies were essential for national self-sufficiency and the defense of a small country surrounded by ravenously grasping enemies. This had been sternly taught to him by Oji Asahi. His uncle owned a 12-meter motor-sailer called the *Maya*—"Light Rain"—with a Ford inline four-cylinder motor. Obata had worked aboard the fishing boat every other week through summer breaks since he was fourteen. During his weeks ashore he read and studied for the coming school year. Fishing was hard work with long hours. Sometimes they stayed out overnight, and the boat had no sleeping accommodations. His uncle, the full-time deckhand, Isamu, and Obata slept on the deck wrapped in old wool blankets under what had once been part of a much-patched sail. When it rained or waves broke over the *Maya* at night they huddled in the small pilot house. They took turns manning the steering wheel to bear into the wind. The deckhand at that time furtively called the boat *Mika*—"Tree Trunk"—describing its handling on those wave-beaten endless nights. They ate cold rice balls with fish sauce and canned kelp. They had no means of cooking the fish they caught. They would not eat the catch anyway. They needed to sell the entire catch to the Nippon Taiyo Gyogyo Kabushiki Kabushili cannery—Nippon Ocean Fishing Company.

The little crew was perpetually wet and cold. Obata told himself that this would prepare him for the rigors of a soldier's life: the labor of hauling in and folding the nets, hand-working the bilge pump, caring for the fragile glass floats—actually sturdier than one would expect—picking through the flopping fish, throwing overboard the unmarketable, and shoveling out the slippery fish at the cannery's pier. He could repair snagged nets and splice ropes and knew lots of knots. The long hours beaten by the sun, rain, and wind hardened him. Not just physically, but spiritually, by exposure to the elements and mental toughness. He also learned about the gasoline motor and that might be useful in the Army. They were using more and more trucks and fewer horses and mules; a Nippon News weekly newsreel had reported. He also learned to keep a bearing when he steered and compensated for winds and currents. He knew he could be conscripted into the Imperial Navy instead of the Army. Fortunately, he had never registered as a fisherman. The authorities did not know. He had had enough of the sea. As the school emerged from its veil of mist, he thought that the Army itself might cause another change to his outlook.

***

Ahead they could see the silhouette of the two-story Western-style brick building, Nagoyakokusai High School. Against the lightening sky the tiled roof displayed Japanese influences. Its many windows were already glowing as hundreds of students assembled on the parade ground before the building. Inside the main entry was a display of Art Deco pottery made in Nagoya, a style blend of Japanese and European exoticized art.

By the time they reached the school many of the students stopped and gazed into the eastern sky behind them. Over the churning waves of the mighty Pacific Ocean the clouds had brightened into a glowing white on which the cherry red Rising Sun declared its splendor and might to shine down on the oldest and most glorious empire on Earth.

Obata and Jiro ran on the frosty ground the rest of the way to the school, anxious to learn about this new war. Both secretly hoped it might just be another "incident."

Chapter Three

> "LET'S GO GET 'EM!: Join the U.S. Marine Corps"
> Marine Corps recruiting poster

The stream was low, only inches deep. They used the flat sandstones set by Great Grandpa Hahnemann on the edge of the low-water wagon road-crossing. Henrik trudged up the steep mud-slick hillside, leading Ernst and Johanna toward town and school. It was only a mile and a half. From the stream it was another quartermile to school. The hill was so steep that sometimes Nellie and Flora could not pull a loaded wagon uphill. There were a couple of times the pigheaded mules refused to make their way down the slope when ice-covered, even if unhitched and leaving the wagon. Mama said, "They smarter than you men."

Mama had dished out an extra hearty breakfast—eggs over easy, thick-cut bacon, toast from a loaf baked yesterday with peach preserves, and fresh milk still warm from being squeezed out of Sarah by Johanna. Except for the flour, salt, sugar, and baking soda, most everything came from the farm.

Those thoughts were only passing. Henrik had the war on his mind. It was something bigger than anything he'd ever known. They'd heard little on the radio in the evening and the announcers must have said "Jap sneak attack" a hundred times. He had to do something.

Ernst shouldered the 20-gauge shotgun like a soldier and even mumbled with puffs of frosty breath, "Hut, two, three, four." Johanna, following Ernst, would shout, "Stop that, you're not a soldier, *du Satansbraten*." She sounded just like Mama when she called Ernst "you little devil."

They crossed a Marthasville oiled gravel back street, but East Main with the school had been asphalted years back. Usually everyone would be outside the two red brick buildings chattering, but the 7:30 a.m. chilly December wind had driven them inside. Henrik noticed for the first time the older grade school was a more faded red brick than the high school.

Henrik and a few other boys set their shotguns and .22s in Mr. Hackmann's cramped office. The boys would pot-shoot stew rabbits and squirrels on their way home. Henrik kept the shotshells in the shoulder bag Mama had made out of worn blue denim overalls. It was normal to hear the crack of gunfire after 3:00 p.m. from the woods and fields as boys headed home with freshly shot supper. Today there appeared to be more deer rifles than usual.

Johanna would pick up hickory nuts that she and Mama would crack on an old flat iron griddle. On Sunday Mama's friends would bring their own nuts and apples to peel. After much mysterious concocting they'd cook up pots of hickory nut apple butter and can it.

Everyone was in the auditorium, even the grade school kids in the old schoolhouse next door. The two-classroom building was for first to eighth grades. Ernst was in the sixth. Ninth-grader Johanna was in her first year in high school. That embarrassed Henrik at first, his little sister being in some of his classes.

Rumors he overheard said the Jap planes attacking Pearl Harbor came from aircraft carriers. Some were talking as if there was a danger of attack in eastern Missouri from Jap carriers. *Probably not*, Henrik figured. *If the Japs invaded, we'd be fighting them over California and not over the Missouri River.* Someone said Marie Sprik's mama had kept her home for the day fearing the Japs might bomb the school or the factory. Henrik thought the Japs would probably not be interested in blowing up Marthasville's only factory, the Harris Langebert Hat Factory, no matter how popular their Beaver Brand Hats were.

Most collected around the still heating up potbelly stove. Younger boys were sent out to the shed for more wood. Most of the girls—crowded out, and tired and fearful of all the war talk—had retreated to the grade school's little lunchroom and its stove.

Ernst said, "Those Zeros—whatever those are—can't fly this far," while showing some of the boys on the United States wall map how far it was from Missouri to California, some 2,000 miles. That's a far piece. Some young men of the town had traveled all that way and gotten jobs. America wasn't at war, but they were building airplanes and ships for the British.

A couple of other seniors—this year's graduating class numbered six—were saying they were going straight into the Army or Marines. It was Lewis Harman who wanted to be Jarhead, a marine. Buck Red said he was going into the Navy. He'd always wanted to see the ocean. Lester, he hadn't made up his mind one way or the other. "I'll wait," he announced. "I'll bet those Jap airplane carriers will be sunk by Christmas."

Henrik kept his mouth shut about it all. *He might be right*, thought Henrik. *The Japs will not go unpunished.* The war might be over before he could do his part. He kinda hoped not, but he knew he shouldn't hope for a longer war. *Do we even have our own aircraft carriers?*

Two of the seniors, Larry and Ronnie, were wearing khaki-green Boy Scout uniforms. The principal nodded, and they picked up the United States and Missouri flags from their stands and stood on either side of him. The boys fetching wood returned and the girls in the grade school building were called back. The other boys had donned Bull Dog pullovers—it was just a five-man basketball team, not enough boys for a football team.

Looking darkly solemn, Mr. Hackmann clapped his hands three times as the teachers lined up behind him. All of the ladies wore black armbands on their left sleeve as did Mr. Hackmann. Henrik would ask his mother to make the three of them ribbons. The auditorium was unnervingly solemn and quiet.

Sweeping his eyes over the forty-some-odd students, Mr. Hackmann quietly said, "We will now recite the Pledge of Allegiance." He turned toward the Star-Spangled Banner, placing his hand over his heart. "I pledge allegiance to the flag of the United States of America and to the Republic for which it stands…"

Mrs. Schäfer led them in the Lord's Prayer, their heads bowed, adding, "And protect our brave boys in uniform wherever they may serve defending us from our heathen enemies." The reading, writing, and spelling teacher was Pastor Schäfer's wife, the Lutheran minister.

Folding chairs hadn't been set up for an assembly, only those for the history class normally held there. The older girls sat on the chairs, and the boys and younger girls stood.

Mr. Hackmann gripped the edges of the podium. School assemblies were a rare thing. He never made long speeches. When he did, it might be in regards to Berry Sauer letting loose a dozen frogs he'd collected on the way to school, or Charley Burlier hiding Mrs. Storm's class notes hoping she'd cancel a test—she didn't.

He began in his quiet voice, "Young ladies, young men,"—he'd never called the students that, it was always boys and girls—"today the history of our country, of the world, will change. It is your duty as citizens of this great country to study harder, improve your grades, and help your parents in every way you can during the coming difficult times."

He glanced at his watch. "The President of the United States will be addressing the nation soon. We will have a radio in the auditorium and will assemble here at 10:15. Instead of noon as the radio said, we're an hour ahead of Washington here in Missouri." Please be patient and be attentive to your studies, especially homework," he added, to be punctuated by quiet moans. "And don't spread rumors, Tommy Perkins."

He turned and nodded to Mrs. Berker, "If you will."

The math and music teacher stepped forward, clearing her throat and holding a copy of *Songs of Freedom*. In her clear chiming voice Henrik had heard so often in church, she led the students and faculty in "The Star-Spangled

Banner," followed by "America the Beautiful." Before the students filed to their classes they gave the Bull Dog Growl, the school motto, with the girls giggling in the attempt at growling. Henrik felt pride and a lump in his throat, just a little one, the words "land of the free and the home of the brave" echoing in his mind. Yes, he had to do something more than be patient and attentive.

The teachers forbade any talk of the Jap attack. He could barely wait for 10:15.

***

As they gathered in the auditorium, Henrik noticed the big Ingraham wall clock said it was 10:18. There was a borrowed Motorola radio on the stage and a Philco in the back on a teacher's desk. Mr. Hackmann was kneeling before the Philco, slowly turning the tuning dial. Mrs. Storm was tuning the Motorola. Henrik had been one of the boys assigned to set up the folding chairs. With the radio tuning going on, everyone quietly took a seat. He was both surprised and embarrassed when Johanna sat beside him, her serious glance suggesting she was nervous and wanted to be near family. Ernst unexpectedly sat beside Johanna. They'd never before sat together during assemblies.

Mr. Hackmann usually demanded silence during an assembly, but this time he gave into all the talk and speculation—so long as the students kept their voices low. Most of the teachers congregated in the hallway, also quietly talking while awaiting the President's announcement.

"Is there going to be a war, Henrik?"

Johanna had a pretty round face, her cheeks reddened by the cold. *She looks so sad*, he thought. *Scared, actually.* "I hope not, Johanna." *I need to be honest.* "But I expect there will be one. That's all we heard last night on the radio."

"I don't understand all that radio talk."

"Me neither," he said, trying to lighten things. "I don't think Papa does either."

"Papa knows about everything like that," she said defensively.

"You're right; he just about understands it all."

"If everyone will take their seats, the President will speak soon," announced Mr. Hackmann. He looked back at Mr. Borgmann, who had loaned the Philco radio, but gave a helpless look and spread his hands palms up.

"Unfortunately," said Mr. Hackmann, "we can't tune one of the radios so the voices from both will not synchronize. That means it would sound like two people talking and difficult to understand."

Mr. Hackmann turned to the other radio, holding a microphone to his ear. He suddenly turned up the speaker's volume.

Students started at the sudden static burst followed by a solemn voice that increased in clarity, and suddenly there was F.D.R.'s familiar voice, but morose-filled.

"Yesterday, December 7, 1941, a date which will live in infamy, the United States of America was suddenly and deliberately attacked by naval and air forces of the Empire of Japan.

"The United States was at peace with that Nation and, at the solicitation of Japan, was still in conversation with its Government and its Emperor looking toward the maintenance of peace in the Pacific. Indeed, one hour after Japanese air squadrons had commenced bombing in the American Island of Oahu, the Japanese Ambassador to the United States and his colleague delivered to our Secretary of State a formal reply to a recent American message. And while this reply stated that it seemed useless to continue the existing diplomatic negotiations, it contained no threat or hint of war or of armed attack.

"It will be recorded that the distance of Hawaii from Japan makes it obvious that the attack was deliberately planned many days or even weeks ago. During the intervening time the Japanese Government has deliberately sought to deceive the United States by false statements and expressions of hope for continued peace."

Henrik realized then that they were in a war for sure.

The President went on. The scope of the war grew. He said the Japanese also attacked Malaya, Guam, Hong Kong, the Philippines, Wake, and Midway. Henrik didn't know where all those places were. He glanced at Ernst, who mouthed, *I'll show you where.*

Henrik remembered specific fragments of the speech:

"All measures will be taken for our defense. But always will our whole nation remember the character of the armed onslaught against us. No matter how long it would take us to overcome this premeditated invasion, the American people in their righteous might will win through to absolute victory. I believe that I interpret the will of the Congress and of the people when I assert that we will not only defend ourselves to the uttermost but will make very certain that this form of treachery shall never endanger us again. With confidence in our armed forces—with the unbounded determination of our people—we will gain the inevitable triumph—so help us God."

As the President spoke Henrik glanced around the room. Every student and every teacher had their eyes glued on the radio.

We'll never forget this day, he thought. "A date which will live in infamy," the President had said. He wasn't exactly sure what that meant, but he understood what "unprovoked and dastardly attack" meant. The speech had only lasted six minutes. Short for so much that would be forthcoming.

For a moment after Mr. Hackmann turned off the radio, it was as quiet as midnight in a church. Then students started whispering. Mr. Hackmann didn't follow up with his own words. He merely announced they would have an hour for lunch today starting now, and he went alone into this office.

Now what am I going to do about it?

Johanna was looking up at him. "Henrik, I'm scared. Are you going to go to a war?"

"I don't know."

On the following Thursday lunch hour Mr. Hackmann announced Germany had declared war on the United States and Congress immediately declared war on Germany and Italy. They learned what "Axis" meant and that the United States was now allied to the British, French, Dutch, and most other European countries, even if the Nazis had taken them over.

Henrik thought about their relatives in Germany—people he'd never met. No one in the family here had met them, but they were still family. What would happen to them?

There was talk among his friends about most of them being of German ancestry. They called this part of Missouri *Kleines Deutschland*—Little Germany. They were as patriotic as any American. They had heard of Germans—American born and raised—who had changed their names, dropping a second "n" off of their last name or dropping umlauts, the two little dots above certain letters.

***

Saturday, Uncle Werner took his two boys, Isaac and Richard, and Henrik and Ernst to the Calvin Theatre in Washington across the Missouri River. Although the movie house had opened in 1909, Henrik had only been to four movies. Everyone was pretty excited about the goings on or was just plain disheartened. *We're at war*, he mused, a phrase he heard often. Uncle Werner often went to the movie house, so Papa was satisfied his brother would let the boys see only suitable movies.

The featured film was *Tarzan's Secret Treasure* with Johnny Weissmuller and Maureen O'Sullivan. There weren't any farm girls like her around these parts, nor anyone wearing a swimsuit like hers. It was a pretty exciting plot, involving crooked scientists on an African expedition who discover gold. They captured Jane and Boy—Tarzan's family—to make him show them the gold's whereabouts. With the help of elephants, Tarzan rescues his family and foils the villains. Even with black bears in the Missouri hills, Henrik reasoned it was safer here than in Africa.

More fascinating to Henrik was the ten-minute newsreel titled "Japs Bomb U.S.A.!" Some people had paid ten cents instead of the full twenty-five cents to watch only the newsreel. It was exciting, but Henrik realized that there were no film shots of the attack or of any damaged American ships and airbases. There were some views of civilian homes burning and automobiles shot full of holes—the sneaky heathens. Most of what was shown were ships of the fleet and planes flying in formation probably taken on earlier exercises. One plane had British insignia.

Uncle Werner muttered, "Dang Brits got us into this declaring war on them Nazi Germans jus' because they attacked them Polacks year 'fore last." No doubt it was too discouraging to see sunken ships and burning airbases. It occurred to Henrik that there had been no mention of how many American ships had been sunk.

There was plenty of stirring music, and they saw the President's Pearl Harbor speech they had heard live on Monday. One thing of interest was a film of a two-man Jap submarine beached in Hawaii and the announcement that the crew had been captured.

It made him all the more want to right a great wrong.

They also watched a Tom and Jerry cartoon. Cartoons were new, and it was the first time Henrik had seen one. This one was in color—the first color film they'd seen. Pretty amazing.

They emerged from the theater to a chilly and gray day. People were talking in the small lobby and on the sidewalk. Uncle Werner steered the boys to Breamer's Pharmacy and Soda Fountain. In the winter they offered a swell hot cocoa. Ernst and Isaac were following, trying to produce Tarzan yells.

The shopkeeper's spring doorbell tinkled as Isaac held open the door for his elders. Henrik froze. At the magazine rack stood the last thing Henrik expected to see—a real life United States Marine.

Red-piped midnight blue coat, sky blue trousers with red strips, white belt, and dark blue cap with a bronze Globe and Anchor badge. His brown shoes were polished so dark they looked black. He must have been over six feet and fitter looking than Johnny Weissmuller. Hooked to his left arm was a good-looking redhead, light blue dress and dark blue coat.

The marine noticed Henrik staring at them and gave a grin and a nod, maybe thinking the dusky blonde-haired farm boy was gawking at his girl. It occurred to Henrik that her lipstick matched the red uniform trim.

Why not? he thought. He stepped forward like Papa had taught him when meeting a man, looked him in the eye, and gave a firm solid handshake. "I'm Henrik Hahnemann, sir."

The marine didn't seem surprised one bit. Looking him right back in the eye, he replied, "Sergeant Kliner. This is Miss Hudson," and nodded toward the girl. Henrik saw the three gold and red chevrons on his sleeves.

Henrik nervously shook her small hand. "Glad to meet you, ma'am." She giggled. She wasn't much older than Henrik.

"Let me guess, you want to sign up for the Marines?"

"I do. What do I need to do?"

"You think you're fit enough and tough enough?" He held a serious gaze.

"I guess I'll find out."

"He's a first class rifle shot," chimed in Ernst.

"I guess we'll find out," the marine smiled at Ernst.

There were a couple of silver badges on his left chest—marksmanship badges he knew.

"So how do I sign up?"

"Are you eighteen?"

"I will be soon."

"Have to be eighteen or both parents can sign a permission letter if you're seventeen."

He didn't see Mama and Papa doing that.

"I'm only sixteen," said Richard, for which he seemed to be glad.

"Here's something you can do. You can get all the paperwork done, take the physical, and just about the day you turn eighteen you can enlist."

"Where do I go to do all that?"

"You'll have to go to St. Louis, to the Navy and Marine Recruiting Station." He pulled out a notepad and wrote a phone number, address, and his name. He handed it to Henrik. "I work there. It's in the Federal Building, 1222 Spruce Street. You may be able to get a bus voucher from the Army recruiting station in your county seat."

"Thank you, sir." *That would be in Warrenton*, he thought.

The marine laughed, "Don't call me sir. I work for a living. There'll be a time when you have to call sergeants 'sir,' but not today."

Henrik didn't understand what that meant.

"The movie any good?"

"Yes, it is."

"Shall we?" he grinned to the girl. "I'll see you in St. Louis someday." He firmly shook Henrik's hand again.

"I hope so."

"Wow," said Eric.

"Are you really thinking about that?" asked Uncle Werner.

"Don't tell Mama or Papa, please. And you too Isaac."

"I'll not say a word," they both swore.

Henrik spent a whole dime for a copy of the December 15th *Life Magazine*. Papa would say something about frivolous money; a loaf of bread was eight cents. As it was, Papa read every one of its 150 pages. On the cover was a pretty girl. He'd expected a cover with a spectacular photograph from Pearl Harbor. Inside was an article titled "Japan Launches Desperate Attack on U.S." That was it—not a single picture from Pearl Harbor. Maybe such photos were military secrets. There were other articles about the Nazis and one on the Army showing off the "best tank in the world."

***

Henrik finished telling his parents about the movie. Papa obviously enjoyed his synopsis, asking more about the elephants, but Mama was quiet. He wasn't sure she'd ever seen a movie. He thought about the newsreel and figured Mama didn't wish to hear more about the war. He and Papa could talk about that later when they drank cocoa as the living room fire burned down. Ernst's first everyday chore was to stoke the fireplace and kitchen stove back to life.

What he did have to say would involve the war.

"Mama, Papa, this war…we don't know how long it will go on, maybe a long time."

"Now son, we don't have to talk about the war tonight. You boys had a special day and—"

"We have to talk about this, Papa. Sorry," he added, realizing he'd interrupted him. "I've thought about this hard. I want to make things right. The Japs attacked us without warning. They can't do that to this country, or any country. I mean, now we're at war with the Germans and the Italians too. They've got to be stopped somewhere," he finished.

His parents were staring at him, his mama in startled surprise, Papa maybe with a mix of pride, but surprise too.

Mama turned to Papa but didn't know what to say.

Papa straightened up, cleared his throat. "Well, Henrik, I understand how you feel and I'm proud of you for wanting to help clean up this mess that the politicians got us into. I was too young for the Great War, but what is it you want to do?"

"Join the Marines, sir."

"The Marines, you say?"

"Like those Marines fightin' in the Nicaragua?" blurted Mama.

"They came back from Nicaragua in 1933, Mama."

"Vell, vhere those *Teufelshunden* at now?" She still thought of the Marines as "Devildogs," the nickname given to them by the German soldiers they fought in France.

"I don't know, Mama. Maybe on their way to fight Germans or Japs." He realized he should have not mentioned he might be fighting Germans.

"Vhat they got against us *Deutsche*?"

"I guess because those Nazis say they want to take over the world, Mama."

"Must be them *Schwarzherzig*, eh, black-hearted Prussians," said Mama. "My Papa say they vere all vays pushy. That *schmuck* Hitler und his *kleiner Ganoven*, eh, smalltime gangsters, can't even run *Deutschland*." Mama would switch to German when excited.

"Son," said Papa, looking at him earnestly, "I can't stop you once you're eighteen, but I hope you aren't thinking to quit school on your birthday before graduating."

Henrik knew schooling was important to Papa. When he was a boy there wasn't a high school in Marthasville. He was mostly self-taught, and he and his brothers and sisters got some schooling from an aunt. Mama had only a fifth-grade education. Henrik would be the first Hahnemann to get a real high school diploma.

"I can wait until May, sir," he said.

He looked at the relief in his parents' eyes. He felt pretty grown up. He never liked letting them down.

***

On Tuesday Mr. Hackmann asked Henrik to wait a moment when he was picking up his shotgun from the office. After the other boys had left, he motioned for him to have a seat.

"Henrik, I heard you showed an interest in joining the Marines."

"Yes, sir." *Another talk to keep me here. He'll probably tell me, "The war effort needs farmers too."* He'd heard it so often he wanted to poke fingers in his ears.

"I received a letter today from the Missouri State Board of Education. They say that as of January 1, 1942, any student reaching his eighteenth birthday by that date and after with a 'B' average will be given the opportunity to take the High School Equivalency Test." He looked at Henrik. "Students passing with a score of 70 may be granted a High School Equivalency Certificate."

"That's swell news, sir. When can I take the test?" He surprised himself with an immediate response.

"Are you certain this is what you want, Henrik?" He held a pained expression for a moment. "I lost a brother and a cousin in the Great War."

"I'm sorry, sir, but yes. Our country's in trouble and I want to throw in and do something about it."

Mr. Hackmann nodded slowly. "Tomorrow I'll send a letter to the Board requesting the GED test." He took Henrik's hand and firmly shook it. "You'll do us proud, Henrik."

"I'll do my best, sir."

He wasn't looking forward to this evening's talk at home.

Chapter Four

> "*Fukoku kyōhei*—Enrich the country and
> strengthen the military."
> Wartime slogan

When Obata and Jiro arrived at the Nagoyakokusai High School they found most of the 800 students in the ground-floor hallways. They avoided the windswept courtyard but were not allowed to enter their classrooms until after the morning assembly, normally. It was cold in the hallways, but at least they were out of the brisk wind. Scratchy military music played over the loudspeakers and fortunately it was turned low. Everyone was talking and drowning out the solemn march-paced music.

Obata's friends did not know any more than he did. Most had heard the radio broadcast or told of it and that was all they knew—what the unknown announcer and Prime Minister Tōjō had bid. The rest was speculation.

The rumor most heard was what Father repeated daily—that the Americans had halted further shipments of oil, gasoline, scrap iron, and steel to Nippon because it was defending itself from radical nationalists and communists in lawless China. The Western nations' 90-percent embargo was strangling the Empire and preventing it from rightfully entering the modern world. Manchuria's iron ore and coal could not make up the difference. Obata knew all that denied fuel and steel would have gone into powering ships and building tanks, airplanes, and more fighting machines.

Gossip flowed like Friday night sake in a workers' *izakaya*. The recent tavern rumors included:

The Emperor had ordered the attack on the Americans and British and Dutch colonies to break their stranglehold on the Empire.

The Americans and the British were preparing to launch attacks against Nippon out of the Philippines, Australia, and Singapore.

Australian airplanes were reinforcing the Netherlands East Indies. The Dutch too, subjugating millions of Asians, were an enemy denying its plentiful oil and refineries to Nippon.

An American fleet was heading to Nippon and a British fleet was coming from Singapore.

American planes had been seen over Tokyo, with some claiming the Americans had been shot down and the few survivors chased off by the Imperial Army's Air Service. The Navy Air Service, ever in competition with the Army flyers, claimed the same.

The Russians were massing on the border of Manchukuo protected by Nippon, what most still called Manchuria.

The Japanese colonies of Korea and Formosa were in danger of invasion; Korea by the Russians and Formosa by the British.

To Obata the rumors reminded him that Nippon was surrounded by enemies and their colonies: America, Britain, Russia in Manchuria, the Netherlands, and their most ancient enemy, China. At least the French in Indochina had been neutralized when Nippon occupied the colony after the Germans defeated France a year and a half ago. That helped hold back the British from coming through Burma and Malaya from the British colony, India.

Most of the students were proud of what their country did to protect them. Some of the girls wept though. Obata could not understand why—fear, grief? One cannot comprehend girls. It occurred to him that if American planes were coming, the Mitsubishi Aircraft Works could be a target. He had a couple of friends who lived near the sprawling plant and he knew people who worked there.

Shouts from teachers cut through the chatter, calling the students to assemble on the parade ground for the morning meeting and the *tyourei*—the daily opening of the school ceremony—during which they would hear any additional official announcements. The usually quiet and orderly formation of students was anything but that, and the teachers struggled to restore order. In violation of rules, some students roamed about classrooms and others hung out of windows, calling to friends in other windows. The turmoil was unsettling in the otherwise stately ordered school.

As the students reluctantly gathered, rolling dark clouds flicked rain on them. It was not until someone started playing the *"Battota"*—"Imperial Army March"—that order was again established, teacher and student alike bolstered by the words, "We are the Imperial Army and our enemies are enemies of the Emperor."

Teachers in their suits simply took their positions in front of their grade and class groups and the students grew quiet, falling into formation as expected. The few girls formed a separate group off to the side with their matrons. They were taught in classrooms segregated from the boys.

The students lined up in a military formation, and the chanting and talking gradually fell silent except for the jaunty tune of the *"Battota"*—"Until our enemy is destroyed, forward, forward, one and all!" Even the boys in the rear of the formations ceased talking. Everyone wanted to hear what was happening.

The *tyourei* usually began with the *"Kimigayo"* national anthem and a short poem related to business, farming, fishing, the military, or simply one reflecting on nature. Any student needing a public scolding or who was to be presented an award, which was seldom, occurred at this time. When students were recognized, it was usually for a group effort rather than an individual endeavor. This too was the time new regulations were introduced. These seemed to increase weekly and mostly had to do with shortages of whatever there was not enough of in coming days.

Obata noticed that more loudspeaker arrays had been setup, "singing trees" they called them. He wondered if there was much to say about the war at this point. It had only been a couple of hours since it had been announced.

Jiro commented, "It may not be until tomorrow when the Emperor wins the war."

"You should not speak like that, Jiro. It is no joking matter."

"I am not joking; I am only praising the prowess of the Emperor's Army and Navy."

"You should be careful, Jiro-kun. Many do not think it is something to joke about."

"They are the same ones who do not think anything should be joked about."

"It makes no difference; they are the ones in power. I am surprised you even mentioned that, Jiro-kun."

"It is the way of our lives today."

The principal stood at attention and bowed to the student body who returned the greeting in long practiced unison.

"The Emperor has declared a state of war exists with the United States and the British Empire." The principal then proceeded to read the *Kyōiku Chokugo—The Imperial Rescript on Education*—signed in 1890. It was formally read to the student body on only four occasions each year. Fortunately, thought Obata, it was only 315 characters long. It articulated government's policy on the guiding principles of education, dictating such advice as, "So shall ye not only be Our good and faithful subjects, but render illustrious the best traditions of your forefathers." Many class hours were devoted to interpreting its principles and how they applied to the more earthly regulations governing public education.

Inspiring it was not, but it was a reminder to make every effort to excel for the Emperor and the Empire. Its reading was a means for the principal to reinforce his order, "Do not discuss the war, but study harder."

Loudspeakers or not, there were no other war announcements.

Instead, he feebly shouted three times, *"Tenno heika banzai!"*—May the Emperor live ten thousand years! All the students and faculty devotedly shouted in unison, throwing their arms skyward. The "singing trees'" screeching feedback was grating.

Expecting adjournment to classes, a man in a dark olive drab officer's uniform appeared from the shadows. Once close enough Obata realized the old and wrinkled man was Captain Yamamura. He walked with a limp. His red and gold collar patches bore three silver stars. Pinned on his left chest was the white-barred green ribbon of the Order of the Golden Kite, the red-edged white ribbon of the China Incident Medal, and the elaborate double crosses of the gold 1st Class Wound Badge—indicating a combat wound rather than a silver 2nd Class for debilitating injuries or illness. He visited the school frequently, mainly instructing the teachers in how to drill the students in marching about the school grounds. A few of the teachers had been in the Imperial Army themselves and did most of the actual drilling. The students almost universally hated this instruction. They also received some first aid training, which most thought useful. Captain Yamamura felt field sanitation training was more important, but the students hated it almost as much as drilling. His lectures on digging latrine pits and how to clean mess kits were the source of jokes. One of the worse classes the captain taught was a rambling lecture on the gasmask. What made it so loathed was that he had only a single mask to demonstrate to 800 bored students who could barely make out his muttered words or even see the mask.

***

Within days the Empire mobilized with all efforts poured into the new war with America, Britain, and the Netherlands. The newspapers and radio barely mentioned Australia, Canada, and New Zealand, which were considered as mere colonies of the vast British Empire. Thus, they too were called "British," including the colonies in Singapore, Hong Kong, and the South Pacific islands.

In a matter of days *tanka, haiku,* and other poetic forms were published in journals, magazines, and newspapers for political and propaganda purposes, blaming the enemy and encouraging popular unity: "Seize victory in war to seize a victory for the culture in the spirit of *Yamato*"—Nippon's ancient name, meaning "Great Land of Harmony."

Sumerogi no	Our Heavenly Emperor
Tataki norasu	Announces the war
Toki o okazu	At the same moment
Toyomi yuri okoru	We are jolted awake as

> *Ō-Yamato no kuni*   The Great Land of Yamato
>
> Kitahara Hakushū, Nippon's poet laureate, March 1942
>
> Kitahara Hakushū, *Bungei shunjū*

Obata stopped listening to the radio. "It is nothing but military and ancient traditional music, warnings the Americans or the British are coming, demands that we work harder and increase production, and to be on the lookout for spies, traitors, and slackers."

"And announcements our air forces have driven off American planes," muttered Jiro. He glanced around, ensuring no one was nearby. Some were questioning that claim. What planes?

"But listen to the victories, Jiro-kun," said Obata. "Victories are announced every day in the Philippines and Malaya."

That seemed true to Obata. Parts of the Philippines had been taken as had most of the British colonies in Malaya. Not only had they mostly destroyed the American fleet in Hawaii, but Japanese bombers had sunk two British battleships off Malaya three days after Pearl Harbor. The newspapers reported the day after that battle that a Japanese scout plane had dropped memorial wreaths to the lost British sailors and Japanese flyers. There had been eight American battleships at Pearl Harbor, but it was never reported how many were sunk. Obata doubted all eight went down as some claimed. There had been four American cruisers too, but nothing about them being sunk or any mention of the American aircraft carriers. There were four, some thought, but where? Nonetheless, the Americans and British had been deeply hurt and humiliated.

> *Ōbō Amerika*   Overbearing America
>
> *Rōkai Igirisu*   Underhanded England
>
> *Aware*   How sad!
>
> *Iki haji sarasu*   Now they face
>
> *Toki ni kimukau*   A life of disgrace
>
> Toki Zenmarō, poet and journalist, February 1942
>
> Donald Keene, *Sakka no nikki o yomu Nihonjin no sensō*

In the weeks following the declaration of war there was a sudden burst of activity at regimental district headquarters, which delivered batches of conscription notices to local police stations. A police officer or military affairs clerk in the more populous districts delivered them to the mayor's office. The notices were opened in the mayor's presence and delivered at night by police officers. Now that the war had started, it was apparent that reservists and conscripts had been called up in increasing numbers beginning the past July.

Scores of blue-uniformed police delivered Red Cards recalling thousands of reservists. Isamu, Obata's uncle's deckhand, was most annoyed when the pink envelop was hand-delivered by an arrogant policeman. The Red Card provided the report date and location and had a tear-off train ticket.

Isamu declared, "I should be given a deferment since I am a fisherman and fish-harvesting is crucial to feed the Empire."

Obata's Uncle Asahi said, "Anyone can learn to become a deckhand on this little boat. You proved that point, Yoshio," he chuckled. "If nothing else Isamu will more likely be assigned to the Imperial Navy owing to all his 'experience at sea.'" They were seldom out of sight of land.

Uncle Asahi was already asking around the waterfront, in search of replacements for both of them.

Ute to norasu	Commanded to shoot!
Ōmikotonori	The Imperial Edict
Tsui ni kudareri	Has at last been handed down
Uchiteshi yamamu	Shoot them down to the last man
umi ni riku ni sora ni	In the sea, on land, and in the sky
	Toki Zenmarō, poet and journalist, February 1942
	Toki Zenmarō, *Bungei shunjū*

Isamu was excited. "Obata-kun, I heard that 200 American Marines were captured in China at Peiping and Tientsin and another 150 on Guam." Almost in disbelief he said, "They surrendered without a fight. It looks like what Minister Tōjō says is true about Americans. They do not have the courage and honor to fight. They surrendered without drawing a sword and have dishonored their country. This war may be over before we have to don uniforms."

Obata did not think so, but it was wiser to say nothing. He thought that for someone so eager to see the Americans defeated, he was not as eager to fight them himself. "Did you know the Emperor renamed Guam as *Omiya Jima*—Great Shrine Island?" He was proud of that.

***

One evening, as they sat cross-legged on a reed mat facing the sea, Obata's father asked him to explain the rank insignia in the small chart he was given in school. Obata loved the view from the low bluff the house was perched on. The steel-gray sea rolled gently. He could just make out the misty shapes of three trawlers offshore flying gaudy flags signifying a successful catch.

"Yoshiro, you are about to undertake a great endeavor for the Emperor and the Empire," Obata's father said. He sat silently gazing out to sea, then continued. "I do not doubt you will bring honor to the family too."

"I will do my utmost to secure that honor. I will not fail you, Father." He felt sure of that for a moment, but something inside him questioned. *Can I? I have no idea where I am going, possibly across that unforgiving sea. What will I face? Will I return?*

All the posters, plays, movies, radio shows, motivational speeches, newspapers and magazines, and even leaflets bombarding him would not bring him home if fate was against him. He felt a nauseous ache crawl through him. *What would it do to Mother?* That worried him the most.

Ei-Bei o	The time has come
Hōmuru toki kite	To slaughter America and England
Ana sugashi	Oh, how refreshing
Shiten ichijini	The clouds in the four heavens
Kumo harwe ni keri	Have simultaneously cleared
	Saitō Ryū, retired general and poet, December 1941
	Donald Keene, *Sakka no nikki o yomu Nihonjin no sensō*

***

Obata's reporting date quickly approached. Mother had taken the trouble to pack a bundle of spare clothes, toiletries, his favorite bowl, a couple of his favorite books, a package of postcards, ink pens, and colorful postage stamps showing war workers and saluting aviators. She had not spoken to Father about this and was unaware that Obata could only bring a few toiletries and no spare clothes. She was disappointed when told he would have to leave most of it.

Father had bought him a small pamphlet with cartoon figures showing drill movements with rifles and pictures of soldiers' rank insignia and badges. Obata had marched and drilled in school, but never with weapons, until the day a shipment of five-foot bamboo spears arrived, and they started learning bayonet skills—lunge, parry, and thrust!

Mother surprised Obata with a belt of a thousand stitches. The *sen'ninhari* was a meter long, the width of a hand, white cloth with tie-tapes on the ends. She could have purchased one, but she had hand-sewed it and painted on the three black characters—"Triumphant Return." The real work was the red yarn stitches. Mother, one of his aunts, and little Fumiko had journeyed to town and neighboring farms, even the dockyard, in the chilly cloudy days, asking every woman to sew a red yarn stich to form the shape of a tiger for ferocity and straight border lines. He would wrap it around his waist under his shirt.

A pragmatic as yet not recalled reservist told him in the dockyard, "The belt's good luck is questionable, but it can be used to bind wounds and as a sling or tourniquet."

***

The day before departing home—perhaps for eternity—Obata's father presented him a small Rising Sun flag. Father's employees at the factory had inscribed the *hinomaru* good luck flag with their names. Most families with a son called to the Empire flew flags on their homes. Family, friends, and neighbors left small, inked wood panels at the Shinto shrine wishing the best for him.

It was known now that large numbers of young men had been called to the Emperor's service. A special train would arrive to convey them to the Nagoya garrison. Banners hung about the station offering congratulations, prayers, and good fortune.

On the day he was to report Obata put on his school uniform and cap. He hung the white school bag on his shoulder with the few items he could bring. Mother ensured he had his orders. She said little but prepared an abundant breakfast. She could not look him in the eye, and he sensed a great sadness. Fumiko clung to her mother's kimono. He squeezed her delicate hands before parting, and they bowed to one another. "I will write as often as I can, Mother."

Only his father accompanied him as they walked to the Utsumi Station. Before turning the corner Obata looked back to see his mother and sister still standing and already awaiting his return. They disappeared in the drifting mist.

"Your mother slipped in a couple of *norimaki*"—seaweed-wrapped *sushi*—"and some rice crackers."

It was a long walk in the dim light of a blustery dawn. Little was said. Obata wondered how he would feel two years from now as he came home. He hoped he would be walking unhindered. He remembered the silent crippled veterans he had seen so often.

Young men were gathering at the station. It was light enough now that the mist had burned away. Most were alone, some accompanied by their fathers and others by uncles. A few were surrounded by entire families, including children. They waved good luck flags and chanted military slogans and patriotic songs. Others joined in with the singers. Father laughed as no one seemed to be able to remember all of the songs' verses.

A local passenger train was pulling out of the station. A bus arrived with boys who lived further away. On a siding was another passenger train of eight cars. Red and white banners hung from the locomotive and the sides of the cars with black-brushed victory slogans. Obata now saw the soldiers among the recruits.

Father said, "Sergeants and corporals," proud of himself for remembering the illustrations in the pamphlet. The recruits were dressed mostly in black or blue school uniforms, usually old ones, farmers' crude kimonos, and Western-style business suits of simple style.

Before going onto the station platform Obata turned to his father. "Father, I doubt the soldiers will give us time to say goodbye." He looked into his father's face. "I am honored Father to be your son. I will do nothing to dishonor our family."

"I am most proud of you, Yoshiro. I have no doubt that you will bring honor to us, the Empire, and the Emperor." His father threw his arms around his shoulders and squeezed hard. He had not hugged his son in years. "Be brave."

Obata had difficulty looking at his father as they broke apart. They sharply bowed. His father gave a tight smile, but in his eyes Obata saw sadness. "Remember your mother and write when you can. I know it will be hard to sometimes."

The sergeants were shouting the recruits into lines. Blue-uniformed railroad police armed with clubs ringed the broad station platform. Corporals sat at small tables with printed rosters. Obata, caught up in the excitement, lost sight of his departing father.

The sergeants were politer than Obata anticipated. They shouted, but that was to be expected with all the echoing noise and shuffling. The corporals at the tables were gruffer, but they had to check off each man and keep them moving. Obata picked a line at random and fell in behind what smelled like a fisherman.

"Orders," demanded the corporal, holding out a hand. Obata pulled out his papers and the corporal ran a finger down the columns of names and numbers. He read off his name, birth date, and home address, which Obata confirmed. The corporal marked a big 六. "Car 6. Do not forget the number and stay with that group. Board now." He turned to the next man, a bedraggled worker in muddy blue denims.

Obata looked back for his father, but he had disappeared in the crowd. *Will I ever see him again?* He pushed through the throng toward Car 6, boarded, and took a window seat. The car filled quickly. A sergeant and corporal entered from opposite ends. "Sit in your seats and stay there," shouted the sergeant. "No talking." He stomped down the aisle. A boy raised his hand and the

38

sergeant clipped it with a lash from his riding crop. "No talking!" They were beginning to act as Obata had expected now that they were out of sight of families. The boy lowered his head in shame and kept it there for the entire trip. This was not a time to eat his mother's *norimaki*. Obata had heard stories of brutality during training. It was said the daily discipline and punishments once assigned to a unit were no different than in training.

He peered out the window, watching people beginning their day of toil. The train's destination was the Nagoya Barracks. He had been told the barracks had been built on the grounds of the ancient Nagoya Castle and spared from demolition under the Meiji Castle Abolition. It had been spared by none other than a minister in the German Embassy who admired the castle's splendor. They passed the colossal brown and tan stone Nagoya city hall with its mix of Imperial Crown and modern styles.

Slowing, the train was switched to another track, and they found themselves in a vast crowded railroad yard. After an hour a corporal said they would be there awhile, as troop trains and freight trains with military loads had priority. They could get up one at a time to use the latrine in their car. They could talk, but quietly, and they were not to speak to anyone outside their car.

Their train sat for hours and the sun sank in the west. A work detail of recruits delivered three buckets of water and some cups. No one dared ask when they would eat. It was dark when a whistle sounded and the car jerked.

Less than half an hour later they pulled onto a siding outside the Nagoya Depot with jerks and thumps. Someone muttered as they unloaded from the car, "We could have walked here instead of waiting all day."

Street performers on the station's platform acted out "paper plays"—*kamishibai*—where they unrolled picture scrolls—*emakimono*—on the dimly lit title floors. They told stories of martyrdom, self-sacrifice, and heroic deeds supporting the National Policies of the Empire at war. Banners on the walls gave air raid and firefighting instructions. The eight groups formed up with about sixty men each. One of the sergeants was attempting to teach the inharmonious crowd *"Hohei no Honryō"*—"The Skill of the Infantry"—with little success no matter how often he applied his crop. As a public service, a high school marching band at the platform's far end tried desperately to drown out the off-key singers.

A sergeant handed one of Group 6's men the folder with the group's roster. "Stay close to me." Trying to shift his handbag to his other arm to grip the folder, the recruit dropped both. Without hesitation the sergeant lashed him across the face with his riding crop, a forearm-long hardwood handle with a thick leather thong. Someone muttered naming him "Sergeant Whiplash."

Another head hung in shame. *Is it too late to apply for an essential worker's exemption?* Obata wondered. Relegation to the rolling deck of his uncle's saltwater-sprayed fishing boat was suddenly a most appealing option.

Chapter Five

> "This high name of distinction and soldierly repute we who are Marines today have received from those who preceded us in the corps. With it we have also received from them the eternal spirit which has animated our corps from generation to generation…"
> Marine Corps Orders
> No. 47 (1921) HQ, U.S. Marine Corps

The railcar's ceaseless side-to-side sway had run from annoying to tolerable to nearly unnoticeable as day turned into night, the silhouettes of trees, bushes, and telegraph poles speeding past the fogged-up windows. The fifty-passenger Pullman coach was crammed with sixty-five future marines.

Some tried in vain to grab a few hours' sleep on the upright seats, slumped in less than comfortable positions. Another group sat in the front end shooting dice in the aisle. Once the train had started moving, smuggled-aboard liquor bottles emerged. They had to be stepped over to reach the toilet room, attracting shouts of "Ya big lug," "Piss out the window," and "Watch your clodhoppers, hayseed."

City boys and country boys were finding out how different they were. Not only clothes and grammar, but attitudes. "That's a toilet, grit; don't forget to pull that chain," said a white-shirted dandy. "It's not the reading light," advised another city kid.

In the back end was the ladies' salon, which they had at first avoided even though there were no ladies around. As more young men boarded, they were forced to migrate there. They occupied themselves trying to read as others told jokes and stories. It was obvious who was already homesick.

The train had originated in Chicago, and Henrik and some thirty others had boarded in St. Louis.

A Marine sergeant stomped into the coach, making it clear he was in charge. Henrik knew the three-point up chevrons and a horizontal bar identified a staff sergeant according to the pamphlet they had been given. Maybe the sergeant was in charge of the "stinking 'cruits," but their porter said otherwise about the sergeant claiming ownership of the coach. Seeing the immaculately uniformed black porter in action, Henrik agreed the porter was really in charge.

They found out that his forest-green wool service uniform was unofficially called a "pickle suit." Not as fancy as Blues, but a distinguished uniform nonetheless.

Once the coach was filled up, a battle broke out over turning the heat up or down. The porter stepped in and set the thermostat on what was the best compromise for the chill outside and the warm bodies inside, warning them in his deep base voice, "Any of you jarheads tamper with this I will call in your sergeant and you do not want that."

It smelled like a locker room with sweat, hair oil, aftershave, and spilt beer. At a station stop one of the boys got an old codger on the platform to buy him a quarter-gallon, "Victory"-size bottle of Acme brew. Upon discovery of the brown bottles, the staff sergeant immediately threw the ill-gotten beer out a window. Fortunately the sergeant seldom made a pass through their coach. On those rare occasions he did, he seemed to have a hound dog's nose for sniffing out infractions.

Some city boy who'd boarded with them in St. Louis said, "These porters, there's one in every car, work for the Pullman Coach Company, not the railroad. If you're nice to them they'll do chores and help you out. They aren't paid squat. You tip them even a nickel and they'll treat you like a king. Like that porter said, he's the man-in-charge. This is his coach. He can kick you off it."

The staff sergeant told them, "Normally porters shine the passenger's shoes overnight, but there's too many troops on the train and Marines are expected to polish their own boondockers."

He pointed to a St. Louis boy who'd been in ROTC. Henrik didn't know what that was, except some kind of military training in school. "Private Russel."

"Sir."

They'd been sworn in by a Marine officer at the Armed Forces Induction Center in the St. Louis Post Office. Henrik didn't feel like a Marine private regardless of what the sergeant called them. They had no uniforms, other than a black armband with a white "V" for "Volunteer," just a piece of paper saying they had orders to ride a special express from St. Louis to San Diego, California. It was a five-day trip sleeping on bench seats and fed cold sandwiches and weak coffee. Breakfast was oatmeal. Not a single egg to be seen.

"At the next stop, Private Russel, that'll be Oklahoma City, organize a detail of three men. Hop off and buy a dozen cans of black and brown polish, a bottle each of black and brown dye, some shoe brushes, and see if you can scrounge up rags from the depot cafe."

"I'm doing y'all a favor. You'll know how to spit shine boondockers by the time we get to Dago. That's important," he added.

"How do I pay for it?"

"Do I have to tell you everything, Private Russel? I thought you were in 'Rot-See.' Take up a collection and don't be buying no pogey bait." He looked thoughtful. "That means candy for you candy asses. I'll send someone back to show you how to polish those gunboats you're wearing."

A fella from Joliet was all smirky when the sergeant left. Henrik didn't like being around him. He didn't have anything good to say about anything. "I don't see why I should tip for chores those nigger porters should be doing. That's what they're paid for."

"Listen, pal," said a football-player-looking fella. "Porters are barely paid. They have to buy passengers' shoe polish out of their own pockets. We're taking care of the polishing ourselves but we oughta tip them what we can, even if it's just a nickel."

"Bunch of suckers," grumbled the Joliet fella and pushed his way back to playing with marbles—the dice-tossing crowd someone called them—betting on pennies and nickels; street craps they called it. There were shouts of "Snake Eyes," "Hard Four," and "Boxcars!"

Continuous poker games were running in other coaches, players drifting in and out depending on their real or presumed luck.

Henrik needed a break from the coach's close smells. He understood what one of the Navy corpsmen meant in the examination room's alcohol-masked gym locker smell.

"You country boys will be missing the smell of cow shit before this is over."

That was when they learned there were no Marine medics or doctors. They all belonged to the Navy and wore Navy Blues.

He stepped out onto the vestibule. The rush of wind, the clink of the couplers, and clacking of the wheels were noisier than the hubbub inside the coach. The cold blast of air enlivened him. Too bad he couldn't see the land, the farms, or the light-dotted towns slip past.

He leaned out over the side railing. Back down that long winding rail was home. Mama, Papa, Ernst, and Johanna were there, finishing up dinner, he judged. He wondered if they were thinking of him at the same time as he was of them. It has to be the hardest on Mama. Before this war, she had probably never given thought to one of them leaving home. Home.

Home was far behind the caboose. He'd be 2,000 miles from home when he arrived in San Diego. He had wondered why he wasn't sent to Marine Barracks, Parris Island in South Carolina, only 800 miles away. A corporal told him it was because he lived west of the Mississippi. "There's the wrong way, the right way, and the Corps' way, which usually works."

***

Henrik had plenty of time on his 2,000-mile journey to reflect on how he came to be on this train. He had come downstairs after Ernst and Johanna had turned in and sat at the breakfast table with his parents. Mama had poured mugs of hot cocoa. Papa probably knew what he was going to say.

Just blurt it out. "I can take the GED to finish high school and I can join the Marines right away after my birthday."

Henrik tried to make it sound like this wasn't dropping out of school. Papa saw through that even if Mama didn't.

"Vill you be gone a year like those other boys, the ones vint last year?"

"Mama, the Japs did us bad. They hurt the country. We need to pay them back and I need to help do that. It's until the war ends, Mama."

Her face was in anguish, but there was a steeliness beneath the sadness. "It's for sure, under a year…to beat those Japers?"

"No one knows, Mama," said Papa, patting her hand.

"But you'll finish the school, right?"

He could only bring himself to nod. It still felt like a lie, a GED.

He knew she had resigned herself when she said after long moments of thought, "I hope you can scribe a lot of letters. Ve have to know vhere you are and dat you're healthy."

"I'll write whenever I can, Mama."

Her lips quivered. His saying that was a confirmation that he was really going.

Papa gripped both of their hands and Mama prayed for the wellbeing of her first child and "for those Jap hooligans to be finished off quick."

***

Two fellas blundered through the door, crossing the vestibule into the next car.

One was arguing, "That dang Harris was the one saying we signed up for the Merchant Marines."

They vanished into the milling, shouting, laughing mob. Henrik laughed to himself. The two disgruntled Marine recruits really had thought they were joining the Merchant Marine.

Car headlights stopped at a railroad crossing momentarily blinded him. A streetlight changed to red a block away, and the next street was spangled with neon lights before the lonely town evaporated in the blackness.

He and Lewis Harman had hitched a ride to Warrenton and the Army recruiting station. They filled out paperwork, were fingerprinted, and took a written test. Appointments for the Armed Force Induction Center in St. Louis came with bus vouchers. Henrik was almost sent home because he didn't have his high school diploma or GED certificate.

"I've taken the test," he told the grisly Army sergeant; not a Marine. The sergeant had four ribbons on his chest. One looked like a rainbow—the Great War Victory Medal. He'd fought in the "war to end all wars" twenty-four years ago. "I'm just waiting for the GED and paperwork to come back," pled Henrik. "I hope that doesn't take too much time. I'm raring to go."

There was a small green dragon statue on the sergeant's desk with Chinese characters. The sergeant asked him some odd questions: "What year did the Civil War start? What year was the Emancipation Proclamation signed? On whose side did Italy fight in the Great War? What's the planet after Saturn? What's disparage means? You good at math? Be honest."

Nodding when through, the sergeant said, "I'll give you the benefit of the doubt. Sounds like you'll probably pass the GED. We'll forward the paperwork, but it'll be pulled if you don't pass that test."

"Thank you, sir. I'm sure I passed it."

"That's sergeant, you're not in the Marines yet," he said with a smile.

"Can I ask a question, sergeant?"

"Yes?"

"I expected Army recruiters would try and convince fellas going for the Marines to join the Army instead?"

He leaned back in his swivel chair and chuckled. "We thought we could do that too. Trying to convince you boys hooked by that fancy blue uniform is a waste of time. You're determined to be seagoing bellhops."

"That's me I guess, sir…I mean, sergeant."

He was happy climbing onto the blue and white bus at the Union Bus Terminal. An hour to Warrenton, but they had a long hitchhike home.

***

The wind and mist chilled him even through his brown hunting coat. *Time to head inside and put up with the racket.* Stepping inside, he was drowned in the chatter.

An accountant-looking fella was telling yet another joke. It turned out later he was a moving picture projector operator. He'd seen all the newsreels, but he was talking about building a school now.

"This town needed a new school, so they went to this here bricklayer with a reputation of guessing exactly how many bricks were needed for a building. Saved moolah. He made his estimate, bid low, and built the school. Trouble was he's one brick over his estimate."

There were some, "Well I be dog-gones" and "Dangs."

"So you know what he did with that leftover brick?"

"Got no idea." "Don't know."

Looking at them like a bunch of duds, he said, "Why, he throwed it away!"

They were all looking at him like rubes at a traveling carnival waiting for a belly laugh.

"You clowns don't get it?"

Shaking heads.

"Think about it, it'll come to you. Here, try this one."

"I hope it's better than the last one," muttered a fella from Chicago.

"See, this here traveling salesman was in a Pullman coach like this one. He was smoking a real smelly cigar, big black thing. Nobody liked it and this fancy-dancy lady had this lap dog that was whining up a storm. She says, 'Mister, your awful cigar is upsetting my Fifi. Please put it out.' The fat salesman ignores her, blowing a smoke ring, so she complains to the porter.

"The porter asks him to please put out his cigar. He ignores him, so the lady comes over, yanks the cigar out of his pie-hole, and throws it out the window. He, all indignant, grabs the mutt and tosses it out the window."

"That's terrible," shouted one fella. "Sombitch," said another.

"The lady's balling her eyes out. The other passengers want to toss him off the train. The porter's going to throw the salesman off at the next station. They pull into the station, the door opens, and in prances Fifi with guess what in her mouth?"

Everyone chorused, "The cigar!"

"No, you bunch of goofs—the brick!"

That got almost as many blank stares as laughs.

At 1 a.m. the porter dimmed the lights and things quieted down. Mr. Sprick, Henrik's history teacher, had given him a worn leather-bound *Mutiny on the Bounty*. "It takes place in the Pacific and might be of interest to you. Besides, it's an adventure story full of daring and foolishness."

"I'll mail it back," said Henrik. "It looks expensive."

"I hope you'll bring it back in person," said Mr. Sprick.

It took a couple of days for Henrik to realize what he meant.

***

The St. Louis Federal Building had been huge, twenty stories of Art Deco brick and terracotta. That's how one of the St. Louis boys described it.

There were almost a hundred young men filling out forms, mainly medical questionnaires. A couple of boys had been pulled out. The word was that they couldn't read or write.

An Army medic watched over them, giving quiet advice. "Listen up. You'll check 'yes' or 'no' for a lot of medical things on this form. When it says headaches or stomach pains don't check 'yes' just because you've had a headache or a tummy ache once. Check 'yes' only for serious stuff."

Eye, ear, and teeth exams followed. A few were delayed until they got their teeth fixed. Doctors pressed cold stethoscopes to their chests and backs, instructing, "Cough." A medic bellowed to 200 men gathered in a huge examination room, "Strip down to your skivvies. Drop your clothes in a pile." Two doctors strolled past them as they faced inward. The medic shouted, "Hold your arms level out in front and squat. Stand on your right foot, now your left. Rotate your arms." They were checking to see if you had the right number of body parts and that they worked. Three boys were physically disqualified, two with "essential hypertension"—a fancy name for high blood pressure. On seeing their glum faces at being declared 4-F, Henrik felt sorry for them—"Morally, mentally, or physically unfit," as a corpsman said.

There was a draftee trying everything to convince the doctor he wasn't physically qualified. He told the doctor he was short-sighted. The doctor rated him "suited for close combat."

After doing a urine test, the recruits watched as a medic walked through the lines with a rack of filled test tubes. "Okay, who's number seventy-nine?"

An arm reluctantly rose from among the skivvy-clad recruits.

"This yours?" he asked, holding up one of the test tubes notable for its lime-green contents. Everyone backed away.

"Yes, sir."

"Come with me."

The word spread later that "Mr. Green" was on some kind of medication.

"He wasn't communicable, contagious, or infectious," declared the corpsman.

Later the police arrived and picked up two real criminals—one wanted for stealing newspaper bundles left at storefronts and hawking them on the street, the other for taking buckets of whitewash and painting houses with a stolen ladder.

In a waiting room, boys talked about which service they were joining and asked questions.

"What's this 'gyrenes' mean when talkin' 'bout the Marines?" asked a country clod.

"My recruiter says it's how Chinks try and say Marine."

"And what does this 'leathernecks' business mean?"

"In the sword-fighting olden days marines wore leather collars to protect against sword slashes. Made them look stiff-necked."

Three fellas said they were joining the Merchant Marine and wondered whether they'd be going to the Atlantic or the Pacific.

Russel, the ROTC fella, said, "I don't think you sign up for the Merchant Marine here. Are you sure you didn't sign up for the Marine Corps?"

"Nahh, we going to the Merchant Marine to sail freighters."

"Okay then," said Russel.

Later a Marine corporal with a shaved head, khaki shirt, and blue trousers stepped in, "Yous three pukes, come wit' me."

"Or maybe not," said Russel. "At least U-boats won't be shooting torpedoes at them."

***

Sunday, the day before he shipped out, was Henrik's farewell dinner. At church, Pastor Schäfer recognized Henrik and a couple of other boys who had enlisted. At the service's conclusion the congregation spontaneously sang "God Bless America" and "Battle Hymn of the Republic." Henrik about choked on the lump in his throat, trying his best to hide stinging tears. Mama looked like she was about to cry too.

Mama and her sister, Aunt Heloise, and other women of the family outdid themselves with a memorable dinner. Baked chicken with white gravy, peas, corn, mashed potatoes and brown gravy, three casseroles, and about eight assorted pies and cakes. He had to sample each. Mama was fretting there wasn't enough space in the icebox for leftovers, but with over twenty relatives present, there were few leavings, as Papa called them. Mama had skimped somewhat on the Christmas dinner since he was leaving on January 5th, a Monday. They weren't shipping recruits out between Christmas and the New Year.

Here we are at war, Henrik thought, still fearing an invasion, *but we're letting the boys spend the holidays with their families.*

As platters and bowls were passed from table-to-table, family stories were recounted with laugher. Henrik felt a sadness trickle though him. He was going to miss them all, not only family, but the two cranky mules, the half-wild dogs, the docile milk cow, and even the pecking chickens that only Johanna could manage. The school too, he was going to miss that, and the little town that had been his world. He thought about that. Other people, strangers, foreigners, for some unknown reason wanted to take it all away from him or make him do whatever they wanted. They didn't even like his church.

He watched his parents, aunts and uncles, his brother and sister, his cousins. He was going to a war, someone else's war, as he had thought of it until a few weeks ago. He was going to protect these people he loved so. *I better stop this, I'm going to get all teary eyed again. That's no way for a marine to be.*

"Hey, Henrik," his cousin Arthur shouted, jolting him from his thoughts. "I'll be old enough to join next year, if you don't win the war first. How about you telling me what you think about the Marines? Herbert Redding's leaving for the Army next week. He's going to tell me how it goes for him." He gave Henrik a scrap of paper with his address.

"Sure, a couple of other fellas asked me to do that."

"You know you're the first Marthasville Bull Dog to join up."

"I guess I am. I've not thought of that." He realized the Marine mascot was a bulldog, Smedley, in tribute to Major General Smedley Butler, who had fought in every war from the Spanish–American through the Banana Wars and one of the few to win two Medals of Honor.

"Hey, you're famous, the first marine out of 200 local yokels in this Podunkville to join up and actually get to leave."

Arthur didn't think much of small-town Marthasville. His dream was to get a job in St. Louis and go to some trade school to be a welder or machinist.

"You're as famous around here as Daniel Boone's grave."

Henrik laughed at the old story. Although Daniel Boone had been buried in Marthasville in 1840, he was dug up and reburied in Kentucky in 1845, resulting in a long-running feud between the two states. He'd miss that too.

"You're a hero, man!"

He didn't know if Arthur was funning him or not. He was like that. Henrik chuckled. "Right. No, a hero around here is the winner of the school accordion contest or the blue ribbon for best apple butter in town." He was hesitant to admit that he was happy to depart right away. He didn't relish repeated going-away parties.

There was a knock at the door. *Strange. Everyone simply walks through the door that's never locked.*

Aunt Ruth peeked out the window. "You'd better get this, Henrik." She smiled.

Henrik didn't have time to question as he opened the door to find Karen Hathaway standing there in a royal blue dress, glimmering. Blonde barrette-clipped locks spilled over her shoulders in a hundred shades of gold, reflecting the porch light. Her reddish cheeks and bright red lips caused her to glow all the more.

"Hi." *Thata knock her off her feet.*

"Good evening, Henrik," she murmured. Her brother Eric was closing his pickup's door. "May we come in?" She'd always had a breathless tone like she was excited about whatever was happing.

"Oh, sure, sorry, come in." *I hope I'm not looking like a complete knucklehead.*

Henrik's parents, aunts, and uncles greeted Karen with hugs.

"Howdy, Henrik. I didn't know you signed up and all until yesterday," said Eric, firmly shaking his hand. "Got a friend said, 'Don't tell them you speak Kraut. They'll yank you out of the Marines and give you to the Army.'"

"I'll remember that." Henrik did speak a little German.

Mama looked surprised to see Karen; Papa didn't. Henrik hadn't seen her since school started the past fall. The few times he'd gone to Washington across the Missouri during the summer she'd been in nearby Union, housekeeping and babysitting for an aunt.

"Have a seat, you two. I'll clear out a couple for you," said Papa.

"Oh, we can't stay long it being a school night. I just wanted to say goodbye to our Marine here."

Darn, he thought. *I've never seen her so good-looking, except in her yellow swimsuit.* They had never really dated, but they somehow always managed to run into one another at local fairs and festivals. She'd be with her girlfriends, but she'd slip away and they'd explore the handicraft displays, livestock competitions, and food contests.

"Dad helped me come up with something you might need," she said, handing him a white-wrapped box addressed to "My Favorite Marine." He hadn't expected that.

It contained a set of Williams Glider brushless shaving cream in big toothpaste-like tubes, a safety razor and spare blades, and a small metal mirror. "I can't thank you enough, Karen. It's something I needed." All he had packed was a hand-me-down razor and bar of shaving soap.

She visited with a couple of folks until Eric said they needed to be on the road.

Karen and Henrik stood on the front porch and she threw on a red knit shawl. Her blue eyes looked up at him. "I do hope this horrible war is over soon"—she glanced at him shyly—"so you can come home."

A floating feeling rose through him. He'd never thought about anything like that. They were "just' friends, but he did feel attracted to her. She never seemed to have a boyfriend, and he assumed that her parents were strict about that. He'd met them at the fairs a few times. Her dad owned the Cost-Right Pharmacy.

All he could say was, "I'll try as hard as I can to make it back, I promise."

"My address is in the shaving kit. Please write when you can." Taking his hands, she stood on tiptoe and planted a soft peck on his cheek.

He'd never forget the way she waved and her smile as the pickup rolled away. Her address card, written in flowery script, concluded with three red-penciled Xs. In spite of having to rise earlier than usual, sleep was a long time coming.

***

Entrained in St. Louis, they sped on to Kanas City, which was in Missouri; then Wichita, Oklahoma City, and Dallas. There were endless miles of Texas scrub prairie, dry rocky deserts, low mountains, El Paso, and Phoenix, and more endless deserts. At each sprawling city they picked up more young men with strange accents, different clothes, different attitudes; strangers but with a common goal. "I wantta bag me as many Nips as I can." It was like a boy's game, but the urge to inflict revenge for Pearl Harbor was intense. "Slap a Jap."

Chapter Six

> "Superiors should never treat subordinates with contempt or arrogance. Except when official duty requires them to be strict and severe, superiors should treat subordinates with consideration, making kindness their chief aim, so that all ranks may unite in their service to the Emperor."
> *Imperial Rescript to Soldiers and Sailors*
> January 1882

Obata could only see darkness and felt only cold and pain. He did not know what hurt more—the back of his head or behind his knees where the corporal's riding crop had struck. He finally decided the cold was worse. He did not think he could move. It was his hands. He could not move his fingers. He could not move anything. Mud, cold mud, he was lying in slimy mud. It was still night. There were discomforting sounds—groans, moans, and quiet crying, the owners trying to stifle them.

The hard ground was slathered with pasty mud. The drill field had once been gravel-covered, but years of marching boots had pounded the gravel into the rocky soil. Angry commands echoed off the massive barracks' brick walls. The windows were dark, but Obata sensed or guessed they were being watched by eyes in the deep shadows.

A boot slammed into his crotch. "Get up. Get Up! GET UP!" The boot struck harder with each shout. He pushed himself to his feet and the boot slammed into his hip, knocking him onto his side. The boot struck his ribs. He wanted to shout, to beg the unseen assailant to stop so he could get up. "Get up!" It struck again.

As another boy was pummeled, he managed to make it to his hands and knees and then to his feet. He could not stand straight let alone rigidly at attention. Glancing around, he could see boys still sprawled on the wet drill field. One recruit on hands and knees barfed into the mud. A corporal rushed over and gleefully kicked him in the belly. The boy rolled onto his side, barfing on himself until he made gagging noises.

Obata had been told to expect rough harassment. The corporals made light of the brutality, calling it *takoturi*—octopus teasing—reminiscent of children teasing octopuses caught in trapping pits dug in the sand where they would hide at high tide, but trapped when the tide went out. He had not expected anything like this. After marching to the Nagoya Barracks from the railroad station, they had been broken down into sections of twenty-four boys. A great deal of pushing and shoving ensued.

A number of corporals took charge of them and marched them mercilessly around the field for a couple of hours. They were punched and shoved and yelled at. Each section lined up in the order of their height and were repeatedly told how unmilitary and sloppy they looked. One could tell who had undertaken drill in school. Obata had disliked their Captain Yamamura for his strict drill and marching routines…and gasmask drills. Today he appreciated that boring training. He seemed to receive fewer blows.

The corporals, China veterans according to their ribbons, wore dark olive drab wool uniforms with heavy overcoats and perfectly wrapped puttees. Their red-banded service caps sat squarely on their close-shaved heads. Their cap visors, chin straps, gloves, belts, and shoes were of polished brown leather. They carried bayonets hung from the left hip. One corporal was so enraged at his section's poor marching he drew his bayonet, but instead of taking off a head as they feared, he whacked a boy's backside with the flat of the blade. An overseeing sergeant quietly spoke with him, possibly suggesting that bayonets were not to be used, at least for now. He re-sheathed it with a frown.

They had been kept awake all night and had had no lunch or dinner, not even a rice ball. Now they stood at attention, shivering in their soaked and muddy clothes, in three ranks of eight men to await breakfast, they hoped. The wind whipped at them, and rain showers passed. Occasionally a boy crumpled, succumbing to injuries and exhaustion.

When the first fell, two boys nearby stopped to aid him. Three corporals descended on the pair, lashing them with crops and sandals, and shouting, "Get up, Get up!" Others were accused of being weak and worthless for even shifting their feet or collapsing to their knees and then lurching back up.

Obata saw a sandal being carried by their swaggering corporal. It was made from a leather-soled boot with iron hobnails. The upper leather was cut down, and sections of the foot portion were cut out to look like straps. He could only hope he would avoid a sandal's swat to the face. The riding crop was bad enough.

The showers ceased in the afternoon, but the cold wind still blew, drying their muddy clothing and sending a shiver through the hungry, defeated recruits. The coating of hardened mud almost made the clothes windproof.

The sky darkened. The clouds hung low in the sky. Still no meal. Obata tried not to think of home, his mother's cooking. All sense of time and even direction were driven away.

Obata's blurred mind recalled his Uncle Asahi on his fishing boat, an endless night with the sea amusing itself tossing the boat from one wave crest to another. They had to pump out the bilge constantly and take in the sail to save the mast. He did not know the time. His uncle's watch was waterlogged. It must have still been hours to dawn when he asked the time.

"It is of no matter." When he saw the agony of Obata's face, he reassured him, "All bad things come to an end."

Would this ever end?

They huddled in the mud like sheep in a snowstorm. It seemed like forever since the weak Sun had risen from the eastern sea. Now he was waiting for the Sun to set in the storm-cloud-shrouded west. Did the Sun set in the west? He could not understand directions. He was convinced the sunset would bring their dismal state to an end and, more importantly, dinner. He would cherish even cold gummy rice and a half-cup of water.

The wind whipped at them fiercely; the rain fell in sheets. Half of the recruits lay on the ground. A few, with uncharacteristic hardness, would struggle back to their feet. Some managed to stay erect, though wavering. Some never made it back to their feet. Corporals would stroll through the section giving a kick to those prostrate, maybe to see if they were alive.

Obata noticed when he glanced in the direction of sunrise—or was it sunset?—that the corporals were quietly drifting to a position in front of their sections. Across the drill field out of the wet darkness came a brusque, grating "Attention!"

The corporals were suddenly all over the recruits. Even those barely able to stand hurriedly scrambled to their feet, spurred on by the officers' crops, sandals, and leather belts. The recruits were hustled up the barracks' stairs through the double doors into a foyer. Obata noticed that the second- and third-floor lights were on, and men at the windows shouted and hooted at them. The rain and wind rattled at the doors. Their corporal screamed at them to run down the hall and enter the first room on the left. It was hard to see in the inky darkness, and some tripped over cots and crashed into each other. Then, the lights switched on and the glaring brightness dazzled the confused recruits.

"Fall in!" They stumbled around until they formed a line down the aisle with cots on both sides. "Fall in in your number order. You will be punished if you have forgotten your number."

The boys were helping each other find their places. The corporal stuck the slow ones. If someone ducked the corporal's swinging crop, it angered him even more. They stood at attention gasping for breath and shivering. One recruit rested a hand on a rolled mattress and the corporal promptly rapped his knuckles. He whacked one across the back of the head, remarking, "That will help you to remember." He struck another on the side of his head when he was unable to recall the section's number. The corporal whacked him with each number he called out to aid the boy's memory. "…seven"—*whack*—"and eight"—*whack*. "Section Eight, you fool."

The shivering recruits were a mess, dripping muddy water and tracking mud. Blood-traced mud smeared their faces, hair, and hands. Other sections were herded into their rooms, propelled by kicks and shouts. One corporal flung a wooden bucket at his slowest man, sending him sprawling on the tile floor.

Obata tried his best to suppress his shaking. He did not want to appear to be shaking from fear or even the endless cold.

As the recruits stood at attention, the corporal stared at each man in turn, daring them to lift their eyes toward him. To do so was to question his authority. They had agonizingly learned that was never tolerated. At least no one collapsed. "This is your section's home," he smirked. "You will live, study, clean your rifle and equipment, and eat here. You pigs have already fouled your room. In the washroom you will wash your foul clothes and hang them on the drying cords." He looked around. "I know what you are thinking. What will we sleep in? I will tell you. In your breechcloths and the blankets stacked on that table." He walked to the door. You may leave this room only for the washroom and latrine. Only speak to each other when necessary and do not speak to anyone in another section. Once your clothes are washed and hung, you will mop the floor. Cleaning materials are in that cabinet. You will be standing at attention here on a clean floor at 0500 in the morning and wearing your washed clothes." He stepped to the door. "A corporal will look in on you frequently. If you displease him you will displease me, greatly."

Before stepping through the door his eyes swept over the recruits. "I am Corporal Kaneko." He bowed and left them as they returned the bow.

They urgently scrubbed their clothes. Some of the boys had washed clothes before. In pairs they rung them, twisting the water out before hanging them up damp. The floor they scrubbed down and fortunately someone realized they had better clean the sinks and washtubs. A boy stood on duty to mop up dripping water.

The breechcloth was damp and the single blanket thin when they turned in. Obata's last thought was, *This may not be like I supposed.*

***

"Attention!" The recruits scrambled about in panic hearing the riding crop cracking on cot frames and skulls.

"Attention, get up. On your feet! You were supposed to be on your feet at attention at 0500. It is three minutes before five, why are you so late?"

"I am beginning to see how they think," muttered Endo Kiyoshi, a boy from Osaka who had been working at an iron plate and sheet mill. "I was an apprentice roller operator."

"What does that mean?" Obata had asked politely before the lights went off.

"We fed flat steel sheets into rollers and it turned them into corrugated sheet metal. It was not a hard job, but it seemed unending to feed sheets to the machine for ten hours a day with two short meal breaks. The day after the war was announced they cut one meal break."

They fell over one another trying to find their clothes on the washroom cords. The corporal appeared to be trying to keep from laughing. While pulling the cold damp clothes onto their shivering bodies, the corporal returned to the sleeping room and started throwing their shoes and sandals about the room. They scrambled trying to match up their footwear. Some fell in line with one or both wrong shoes. Standing at attention, they stared straight ahead, their eyes unmoving as the corporal threw mattresses and blankets on the floor. "These are improperly rolled…" "Here is a speck of mud on a cot leg…" "Someone vomited on this blanket and failed to adequately clean it…" "There is grit in the floorboard seams…" and on and on.

A boy from another room ran down the hall crying with a gash across his forehead. Two recruits ran after him, having been ordered to retrieve the "weak mother's baby."

"He will not last long," someone whispered.

"Quiet," shouted the corporal. He could hear all.

As the recruits tried to organize the room and correct the deficiencies, Corporal Kaneko suddenly stiffened. Pointing at a boy, he said with apparent sincere concern, "When was the last meal you had?"

He cringed, expecting a beating if he gave the wrong answer. He first mumbled, then spoke up. "Breakfast the day before yesterday, Honorable Corporal."

"The day before yesterday!" he shouted. "I profoundly apologize. Finish organizing and cleaning the room and we will see if we can find a meal."

Obata was frightened of what that might mean. The corporal took four men with him.

When was the last meal? Obata was so disoriented he was not sure what meal they were actually waiting for. Time, it was meaningless.

They pumped ice cold water from an outdoor cistern and washed their faces and hands over a wooden trough. They had to wait in line in the washroom as other sections had beaten them in. Most brushed their teeth; some did not bother, having lost a tooth or two. One boy sat on the floor staring blankly at nothing. There was little speaking. Most held a deep shame being humiliated by their own poor performance, according to the corporal. Having hung the brooms and mops in their rack, the ration detail returned. Corporal Kaneko's eyes swept the room, but he said nothing about it meeting his standards.

The kitchen detail he had taken set insulated metal food pails on a table. A large wooden tray, carried like a stretcher by two men, was stacked with scores of white Bakelite bowls, the Army's black-outlined star in their bottoms. They were told to each take a large and a small bowl and a pair of chopsticks. One of the detail set smaller tea bowls on the table as another poured already cooling tea from an uninsulated metal pitcher. They lined up by the number for their first meal in the Emperor's service. Gummy rice was spooned into the larger bowls with a ladle of soybean sauce. A dry piece of baked fish and a few slices of yellow pickle were placed by tongs in the smaller side dish bowl. Kaneko ordered them to stand at attention on both sides of the table in number order.

"You will sit in number order in these same seats even if a recruit is absent or has been sent home unable to perform his duty here."

They bowed and then shouted *"Tenno heika banzai!"*

They sat on the benches and ate in silence, trying not to greedily gulp it down. The rice was sticky, the fish pasteboard like, the tea weak, no sugar, and everything was already cold.

As if reading their minds, Corporal Kaneko told them that soldiers received better rations than civilian workers to help keep them fit.

One of the section said their meals were an effort to make up for vitamin deficiency. His brother had served in the Army. He said too that sergeants and corporals had their own mess with better food and the officers' mess was still better. "They pay for professional cooks and buy their own food. All officers could pick an orderly and that was often decided by the soldier's cooking skills."

***

The room was cleaned again and the bowls and cups washed. They stood at attention around the table as the bowls were inspected.

Corporal Kaneko told them their group was a *naumu han*—training section, specifically Section Eight. "You live, eat, train, and march together. You will work as one for the same goals as well as national goals. You will help one another, guard your possessions, and are not to trust other sections. The other sections will steal from you to make up for lost or damaged equipment." He hinted they knew what to do about making up their own shortages.

"Everything entrusted to you belongs to the Emperor. Its care and safekeeping is the responsibility of the section and each of you." He slapped the feared riding crop against his leg to make clear the importance of this responsibility and that it would be enforced.

***

All the sections ran outside. By now they had learned how to fall in correctly with a minimum of beatings. Side-by-side they stood in formation, as a sergeant with a limp and more ribbons than other sergeants strolled up in front of them. Obata had heard one's service time referred to in terms of *menko*—"rice bowl." It meant that the number of menkos a soldier consumed was more important than the numbers of stars and stripes on his collar tabs.

The sergeant glared disdainfully at them. "It will dishonor the Emperor if you fail to clean your uniforms properly or wear them incorrectly. You will cherish these uniforms and always wear them correctly. To do otherwise is to dishonor yourselves, your section comrades, the Imperial Army, and the Emperor."

Uniforms!

Even in their beat-down condition, cold, hungry, and demoralized, the sagging recruits wearing still damp everyday clothes perked up. *Uniforms! At least they might be warmer.*

Obata thought the uniforms would make them recognizable as soldiers of the Emperor and they would be treated with respect. After all, how could they be beaten and derided while wearing the Emperor's uniform?

They were ordered to form up with one section behind the other. The column marched, slipping and tripping up a short icy road to a large warehouse. They formed up differently than they had before—two long columns trailing down the road. The first section proudly filed into the big building. The next waited at the bottom of the low steps and entered when called.

Eventually Obata's section passed through the double doors. For once the corporals refrained from harassing the excited recruits.

They were ordered to remove their clothes, stripping down to breechcloths in the cold building. On their feet and holding their clothes in their arms, they shuffled into a large room. Placing their old clothes on the floor, men in white smocks measured them with yellow tapes as they held their arms out. The smocks proved to be civilians and worked quickly, jotting numbers on paper stripes. They moved to a place with painted lines and their feet were measured. Efficient civilians were bringing stacks of folded clothes and confirming the name and number of the man issued them. Moving deeper into the building, the recruits received their boots. They sat on benches, first pulling on socks to be sure they fit. While uniform-issue was rushed, they took time to ensure the boots were well-fitting.

Obata looked over his brown marching boots. Most of the recruits had never worn leather Western-style shoes much less these low-topped, laced boots with thick leather soles studded with hob-nails and a sickle-shaped steel cleat on the heel. They threaded bootlaces and some needed to be shown how. Most had worn only sandals. They were told they could keep their sandals for barracks wear. Farmers and fishermen tended to tie overly secure knots difficult to untie. Even worse were the puttees, wraparound cloth strips that were precisely wound around the legs from boot top to below the knees. It demanded hours of practice to properly secure them. They could keep their belts of a thousand stitches and the small Rising Sun flags. What Obata much preferred over boots were the black canvas, split-toed *tabi* shoes worn off-duty and for certain work details.

They tried on the one wool olive drab uniform, shyly complaining of its ill fit, but were told, "Tailors will take care of that." They were issued the newer Type 98 uniform with a turndown collar on which rank insignia were worn rather than as shoulder tabs, plus it had skirt pockets as well as chest pockets, unlike the Type 90 uniform wore by longer-serving corporals.

A worker said their old clothes would be mailed home. Obata doubted the truth in this.

Then came two sets of white drill uniforms, two pairs of long underdrawers, two undershirts, a wool/cotton blend vest, three pairs of socks, a heavy wool overcoat, and a waterproofed rain cape with a hood. Those they were thankful for. One recruit said, "If they allow us to wear them."

Next they were issued their equipment, a tangle of leather belts, straps, buckles, ammunition pouches, a water bottle, a pack, a tube roll, and other strange items, even a little shovel. The canvas backpack was a nest of web straps called "octopus legs." They hurriedly stuffed the uniforms and equipment into the tube pack, a canvas roll like a "beggar's bag" for extra clothing. Wearing their overcoat and field cap, its yellow star on the pinched front, they marched back to the barracks with equipment dangling and swinging. No one dared drop a single item of the Emperor's property.

The corporal talked a man through how the uniforms and equipment would be folded and stored on shelves over their cots. The room and stowed uniforms were to always be ready for inspection. They would handwash their clothes twice a week. He left four bottles of ink with pens and instructions to pen their unit number and family name on every item of clothing and where the markings would go. He left telling them, "After marking your uniforms and equipment as I showed you, I will return for inspection."

One of the recruits held up a little cloth-wrapped sewing kit they had all received. "I know who will be tailoring our uniforms."

Another said, "I am a tailor by trade and I can fit your uniform and make the Emperor and your father proud, for a modest fee."

Obata had made repairs to sails and even torn clothes at sea. He might be able to manage his own tailoring, perhaps even do some for others. His monthly pay was a mere six yen and he could expect little from home, not that he wanted to ask his father.

The inspection resulted in everything being wiped off the shelves, the cots overturned, and clothes and blankets thrown all about.

For the recruits, now uniformed as soldiers of the Emperor, things had not changed much. For two weeks they mostly marched in lines, files, columns, echelons, multiple columns, changing and reversing directions, and running in formation—and they had better be in step. Understanding who and when to salute was also essential.

They did learn much about their personal equipment. Everything in the tangle of light brown leather had a use. Regardless of one's waist size, all were issued a one-meter-long belt to which the equipment was attached. On the right and left front were two leather cartridge boxes, each holding thirty rounds in five-round clips. The lids opened away from the body to help prevent losing cartridges if a box was left open. In the back center of the belt was a thirty-round reserve ammunition box with straps on one end holding a small oilcan. The bayonet was hung on the left side. A two-and-a-half-pint water bottle hung over the right hip on a shoulder strap.

They marched about with this equipment, but without rifles and helmets. They saw few rifles, even in the hands of training sections which had been there longer. They heard that First and Second Period Examinations normally lasted three and two months, from January to May. Rumors said their training would be shortened, but not by how much. Like much else, that was a military secret. Strict obedience to orders and subservience were expected without question.

At some point they filled out more forms and received a *Soldier's Pay Record*, a small booklet. Someone said it was small since the pay scale was small. They were told that, once discharged, if they lived they would receive a pension—more if they had been wounded, injured, or were severely ill. If they died their families would receive the pension.

They each received a single oval brass identity tag stamped with "Infantry," the regimental number, and their soldier's number within the regiment, which was suspended by a cloth tape. They were never to remove it. If killed they would be cremated, probably with the tag, one veteran reservist said.

There were classes on first aid, physical fitness, *kendo* wooden sword fighting, and bayonet fighting with wooden rifles—the muzzle and butt ends padded—and the enviable reading of the *Imperial Rescript to Soldiers and Sailors*. They were lectured daily on the *Five Principles of Battle Ethics*: loyalty, courtesy, courage, truthfulness, and frugality. As the days wore on the marches became longer, tramping through streets on the edge of town.

Civilians were expected to scurry out of their path or corporals and sergeants would remind them who had the right of way.

They were never told what would happen on the coming day. They were told just enough to ready their uniform and equipment.

"We are marching fifteen kilometers this morning," said Number Twelve.

"How do you know such military secrets?" wryly asked Number Nine.

"My cousin is an officer's orderly."

"Make certain your water bottle is full."

"We can never drink any…" Obata let his words trail off. Such comments would be interpreted as complaining and disrespectful.

By now the section was taking the ten- and fifteen-kilometer marches in stride, even if they were carrying increasingly heavier pack loads. "Still no rifles," most men quietly complained. They hoped that the issue of a rifle would somehow lead to more respectable treatment. Obata awaited a rifle too, but it would add four kilograms.

They marched a different route through rolling hills at faster than usual paces. Returning to the barracks, the corporal ordered, "Open your canteens and empty them." Anyone finishing before his comrades would stand guard at the gate with the regular sentries. The recruits stood only two-hour shifts, but the thirsty recruit would stand all-night guard.

On a dreary Monday morning they were ordered to fall out with full field equipment. They stood at attention with the other sections as wet snow spattered the drill field. The limping sergeant stood at attention before them. Much to their surprise a lieutenant appeared, a personage seldom seen, a pistol holster on his right side and a white cloth-wrapped sword and scabbard.

The section corporals each reported all men present except five in hospital and one confined as quarters guard to scrub the floors and latrines. The sergeant reported to the lieutenant who returned the salute and simply said, "Proceed, Honorable Sergeant."

The sergeant bowed and orders were shouted, and one by one the sections wheeled right and marched across the drill field. The snow floated down denser.

It was soon apparent they were marching toward the armory. A ripple of excitement spread through the recruits. A sentry stood at attention at the iron-reinforced door and saluted the lieutenant, then held the door open so the officer and sergeant could enter. One at a time the sections filed in, reverently, as though entering a temple. In a long hallway they lined up against a wall. The sergeant told them they would be issued a rifle, bayonet, and steel helmet. This was a great honor and privilege. He reminded them that these items were the property of the Emperor. They were to safeguard and maintain them meticulously. A stylized chrysanthemum, the Imperial Seal, was embossed atop the rifle's receiver, signifying it as the Emperor's property.

Rifle racks filled much of the room, with artificers' and leathercraft workshop spaces. Another sentry stood guard inside. They found that whenever there were arms in the hands of troops, handpicked sentries were detailed from the headquarters. The sentries had ammunition, and their bayonets were fixed as they stood at attention and alert.

The lieutenant stood to the side and watched as each man received his rifle, then filed into a large classroom next door and attached the bayonet to their belts and adjusted their helmets. Outdoors the bayonet would be fixed to the muzzle, emphasizing combat readiness.

They were taught how to safely handle the rifle, the name of its many parts, how to fix the bayonet, and the rifle's characteristics. Many recruits at first handled them gingerly; for most it was the first time they had ever handled a firearm.

The sergeant said the Type 30 rifle was invented in 1897 by Colonel Arisaka Nariakira and was a very effective firearm. It would provide the basis for the Type 99 adopted in 1939, the rifle held in their hands. It boasted several refinements over the original 6.5mm Type 30 and 38. The 6.5mm lacked range and penetration. The Arisaka had a stronger bolt lock than the German Mauser and American Springfield.

The sergeant went on, "The 7.7mm Type 99 has a fold-down wire monopod, a leg to help support the heavy rifle when prone. There are little folding arms on both sides of the rear sight that helped lead when shooting at airplanes. A cleaning rod is held in the forearm and there is a sliding metal bolt cover to protect from dust and mud. German, American, and Russian rifles do not possess most of these refinements."

The rifle was as long as some of the men were tall. Many had difficultly handling the Type 99.

"The long barrel is of benefit," the sergeant lectured. "Because of the faster burning powder charge we use and the long barrel, there is very little muzzle flash and less recoil than with our enemies' rifles. This is an advantage as we prefer to fight at night, which our enemies fear."

They learned how to place the rifle on safety and how to make it ready to fire by manipulating the checkered back plate on the end of the bolt. If the notch on the plate's edge was on the left side, it was ready to fire. Pressing the back plate in with the palm of the hand and rotating the notch to the plate's top locked it in the safe position.

The Type 30 bayonet was almost as revered as the rifle. Every man carried a bayonet, even if not armed with a rifle. They found that it was the only arm carried by many heavy weapons crewmen. The long blade was held in a black-painted scabbard soldiers called a burdock sword—*gobo ken*—looking like the burdock's long, dark-colored, spike-like root.

"The rifle and bayonet are long. Jab and slash at the enemy, batter him with the butt stock's steel plate. Force and twist the enemy's rifle down and away from you. Then kick him in the knee, belly, or the balls," he growled.

Some of the boys laughed or giggled. The sergeant scowled and pointed at each boy trying to stifle their smiles and laughs. They were ordered to stand at attention in front of the tables. He told the boys to remove their eyeglasses before lashing their faces. "You are being silly like babies. Now sit!"

The simple dome-shaped Type 92 steel helmet had a small star soldered on the front. The corporals went around the room checking that the helmet suspensions were correctly adjusted and taught the intricacies of the double chin tie-tapes. They learned their field cap could be worn under the helmet for warmth.

Later that day they stowed the rifles in the barracks' arms room. Their helmets and bayonets were placed on their shelves. Finishing up washing their dishes, they found three of the more senior recruits from upstairs in their door.

"It is time for some amusement," snarled a burly Second Period soldier.

***

Even though these men had only been in the Army for a few weeks longer than the arriving recruits, they were permitted control over them when off duty. They often made the recruits polish their boots and leatherwear, clean their barracks area, wash their clothes, run errands, and even serve them their meals.

Obata thought it silly they were forced to play a child's game—*min min semi*. A recruit would be chosen to play the role of the cicada, complaining of the coming summer heat. Summer begins when the first cicadas start their racket and winter begins when they fall silent. Spaced down the room's centerline were ten-inch varnished wooden posts. The designated recruit was ordered to cling to the polished pole with his arms and legs wrapped around it. No matter how firmly he hugged the post crying *min min*, the cicada's annoying chirp, he would slowly slide to the floor and had to leap up and repeat the performance. He would do this until exhausted and sore. Both the senior recruits and the recent arrivals bet on how many times he could repeat this.

It might have sounded silly, even childish, but a crop or a sandal slap reminded them that at least some here took things seriously.

Chapter Seven

"We must not again underestimate the Japanese."
Admiral Chester W. Nimitz, Commander in Chief of the Pacific
Fleet—after the bombing of Pearl Harbor, December 1941

"Stand with your toes on the white line." Men shuffled around, striving to be precise. "Quit movin' around! Drop your bag by your right side. Stand at attention until I'm tired of watchin' you. You! Keep your yap shut! Butthead. Yah, you. You over there, you see somethin' funny? Do you? You ain't got nothin' to be happy 'bout. Ever again!"

Hundreds of recruits in rumpled civvies stood in ranks on a broad parade ground—what they soon learned was the "parade deck." Trucks were still arriving from the train station. As the men disembarked, they were disappointed to be met by Navy Shore Patrolmen instead of Marines. Groups of recruits stood lined up on the white line as names were called—strange names. Henrik wondered if there were enough letters to spell some of the names. Groups were trying the form up and others were running to wherever sergeants were waving. Still others were doing pushups. Some were running around a track carrying their bags. Dust wafted over the open field.

The sign over the gate proclaimed, "Marine Corps Recruit Depot, San Diego."

Henrik looked about his surroundings. A clear morning sky, probably in the mid-sixties. At home it was freezing and icy. Even more alien were the swaying palm and eucalyptus trees, the smell of mint and the ocean just across the bay. Strange too was the stucco-walled and red-tile-roofed Spanish architecture of the headquarters and H-shaped two-story barracks. He hoped he'd be able to see the ocean sometime. The parade deck was huge—more like an airfield. Just then a silver two-engine plane lifted off from behind the big barracks and winged north. Everyone looked up, expecting to see a military aircraft. It was the first airliner Henrik had seen. Someone said the San Diego city airport was between the Marine base and the bay. On the opposite side of the parade deck were dozens of corrugated steel arch Quonset huts. At the far end of the parade deck could be seen masses of marching recruits under a haze of dust. There was a reason the parade deck was called the "grinder," a place where gravel was ground to dust by hundreds of boondockers.

They had formed into a group of fifty-eight when their names were shouted off a roster. Henrik remembered some of them boarding at different stops. It made him recall the "platform girls," one in particular. That's what they called the ladies and girls on station platforms with picnic baskets and pasteboard boxes. They passed ham and cheese, chicken salad, and egg salad sandwiches to boys hanging out the coach windows. Sometimes they had paper coffee cups of potato salad or coleslaw, even donuts and cookies. And hot coffee too. After passing Dallas they'd often gotten tacos wrapped in newspaper. Henrik had never heard of them. It took eating a couple before he learned how to keep the spicy fillings from falling out and decided he liked them.

Sometimes they were allowed to stretch their legs on small town depot platforms. No one was going to change their mind and head for home out in the middle of nowhere. One dusty town they stopped at was Sierra Blanca, Texas, before reaching El Paso. The ladies were organized by church groups and women's clubs. They turned down marine offers to pay for the treats. Among the mothers were teenage girls. Henrik chuckled at some of the fellas flirting with the women.

"I heard some of those gals are hookers," someone sniped.

"Where're you goin' to book a room, wise guy?" said one of the boys stepping off the coach. "We'll only be at this whistle stop for a few minutes."

Henrik said, "I don't think there's any girls like that here."

"Are too," barked a rough-looking lout in over-patched bib coveralls. "I heard 'bout 'em. Call 'em victory girls, khaki-wackies, or patriotutes. They give it away to boys headin' to the front."

"Not likely here," smiled Henrik, looking over the mesquite, cactus, and Sierra Blanca's namesake "White Mountain." A sign said it was the 1881 joining point of the southern line of the nation's second trans-continental railroad. No wonder he'd never heard of it.

"Oh yeah?" Coveralls shouted furiously and swung an unprovoked punch at Henrik. It failed to connect as he ducked. It wasn't Henrik's first kids' fistfight.

The sergeant bounded out of the shadows, grabbed Coveralls' arm, kicked his feet out from under him, and slammed his face onto the platform. "Behave, junior, we're guests here." He shook his head. "Now get up, dummy!"

Coveralls was smart enough to stand at attention and keep his mouth shut.

With a bulldog's grin, the sergeant growled something into his ear.

Coveralls went red with embarrassment, but like a good marine-to-be he stood at attention, loudly spewing as ordered, "I wish to apologize for my shabby behavior to the kind, virtuous ladies of Sierra Blanca, Texas."

"That's real good, boy," hissed the sergeant. "Keep repeating it until we get the 'All aboard'."

That's when Henrik heard from behind him, "*Gracias, señor* for defending our honor. I will never forget."

She was maybe five feet tall, with straight reddish-brown hair in a long ponytail, and a light dusky complexion with a sprinkle of upper cheek freckles. Her oval face, high cheekbones, and wide nose made her different from anyone he'd ever seen. She might be fifteen or twenty. She kind of looked like the Mexicans on the platform, but not quite. Her ankle-length skirt was pale brown, topped by a form-fitting rosy-pink blouse, and a too big beet-red sweater.

He hesitated, not knowing what to say. "Uh, my pleasure, ma'am. It's the least I could do, you folks sharing your food with us. That's awful kindly."

"No one ever call me ma'am." She looked down when she spoke; kind of shy. "It is our church and everyone want to help the boys going to the war." As she looked up, Henrik noticed her striking green eyes. "Do you know where you go?" Her voice jingled like sleigh bells, and she smiled.

He remembered being ordered not to say where they were going or their travel schedule.

Surely this girl's no enemy agent. "We're just going to California, that's all I can say."

"Oh, that is where they all go, San Diego." Her full lips smiled. She glowed. "I hope you have safe trip and to be safe wherever this war take you."

"Thank you." *Why not ask her?* Henrik thought. "Can I...ask your name?"

She blushed slightly as she replied, "Guillermina. That is Wilhelmina in Americano."

"I'm Henrik."

"Alla'board!" demanded the conductor.

"I have to go." His voice's disappointed tone surprised him.

"Here, take the last donuts," she said, passing him a paper sack. She touched his hand. "And this. Is a gift."

"Thank you." She'd handed him a Stars and Stripes flag no bigger than his hand. Desperate to give her something in return, he fished from his pocket a yellow, red, and blue recruiting leaflet and shoved it in her calloused hand. He grabbed the rolling coach's platform railing.

"*Gracias mi amigo*," she said warmly, clutching the leaflet in Marine colors.

"*Gracias*," he shouted from the coach's vestibule platform.

"*¡Éxito!*—Success to you, Henrik!" she called as she trotted after the train.

The Guadalupe Mountains flowed past in the distance as the train picked up speed.

A little disoriented by the hurried encounter, he turned to the porter and asked, "What is she?"

"What is she? Oh, I don't rightly know, they call them round these parts *mestizos* or *cholos*. I guess those are Indian tribes. Texans got a lot of different words for things. Me, I'm just from Ohio."

Henrik took his seat where he'd left his bag. Sharing out the donuts with his seatmates, a burst of regret flooded through him. He shouldn't be thinking about that girl, no matter how cute and…and what, *exotic*? He'd never come this way again. Karen Hathaway, that's who he should be thinking about. She'll be waiting at the home fire.

Karen would be the first he'd write to when he got the chance. He rolled Guillermina's flag around its little stick and shoved it in a coat pocket.

***

"What are you doin' starin' off into heaven?" a grating voice asked. "Lookin' for salvation? There ain't any, Buster."

Henrik was jolted back to his current reality as a sergeant barked at him, mere inches from his face.

The sergeant stepped back. "Listen up. You all got a busy day. Pay attention. Don't be askin' me a lot of questions. If you need to know about something I'll tell you. Stay with this group, always. Pick up your bags. You're now Platoon 276. Two-Seven-Six—say it."

Somewhat reluctantly, the group mumbled, "Two-Seven-Six" as the sergeant scowled at them.

They assembled in four ranks, facing him. The sergeant wore forest-green trousers, brown shoes deeply polished, khaki shirt with a matching necktie, and a tan tropical helmet. "If you're taller than the man in front of you move up. Keep movin' up. Right, face! Your other right!" he directed at the confused ones. He shouted the order to move up again.

When it was over Henrik found himself about halfway up the second line. That line was designated the 2d Squad. There were about fifteen men in each of the four squads. "From now on when you all fall in you'll do so just like this. Remember who's to your right and left."

Everyone glanced around.

"Are you stupid? Do not move when you're at attention!" He glared around at them. "Lord, I'm going to hell. What sin did I commit to deserve this mob of halfwit misfits?" His expression of anguish looked genuine.

"Christ almighty. Any of you morons been in ROTC?"

Henrik had only a foggy idea of what that was and few others appeared to. Two hands went up.

"You, front and center. What's your name?"

"Cadet Bevers, sir."

"You're not a cadet anymore. Private Puke Bag Bevers here will demonstrate the correct manner of executing a Marine pushup…It's the same as an Army pushup just done more rigorously," he stage whispered. "Assume the position."

Bevers dropped to the ground, his arms supporting him and elbows locked. His head, back, hips, and legs were perfectly aligned.

The sergeant started counting, "One and two and three…" With each count Bevers sharply lowered himself. "Arms are locked in the up position and when down your chest touches the ground, but never your knees. When you hear, 'Drop,' you will drop to the up position, arms stiff, and knock out twenty-five proper Marine pushups; no saggin' bellies. No butts pointin' at the sky." He spread out the platoon, teaching them at the same time what "at double arm intervals" means. In all, probably they did a hundred progressively feebler pushups and were increasingly unable to keep that mandatory head-to-heels straight line.

Falling back into formation, he addressed them again. "I am Sergeant Gilroy. I will guide you through the next few days here in the Receiving Barracks. I am not your mommy. I am not your drill instructor. If you survive you'll meet him soon enough and I grieve for you…not really. They haven't eaten 'cause the colonel thought feedin' the guard dogs is more important." He paused. "Actually, I don't feel sorry for you. 'Tough titty, said the kitty.' I don't want to hear your piss poor problems. I will guide you through the physicals, inoculations, tests, and uniform and gear issue. You'll get dog tags, I.D. cards, your service record filled out, and a Marine haircut. I'm goin' to teach you how to stow and display your uniforms and gear for 'coffin inspection,' and how to make your racks. It's called 'coffin inspection' because you're dead if you fail it. "Pla-toon…Ten-Hut!"

He marched, or more accurately, herded them to the mess hall. "Always start on your left foot. Your other left, puke." After the travel days of living mostly on sandwiches and oatmeal, the scrambled eggs, bacon, sausage, cereal, toast, milk, orange juice, and coffee were heaven-sent from the galley. They just weren't given much time to partake.

Run out of the mess hall, they fell in. "Pla-toon…Ten-Hut!" Still carrying their baggage, they lined up outside the barbershop with stools, not real barbers' chairs. Within seconds a dozen white-jacketed barbers had buzz-cut their hair.

"You want to keep your sideburns, son?"

"Yes sir."

"Hold out your hands."

One boy in the same squad as Henrik grumbled in a strange accent, "They 'ad to pay a silver dime outta our owns pocket. That ain't right." Someone said he was a Cajun, whatever that was.

"Pla-toon…Fall in!" As they fell in, they tried to come to terms with the strange feeling of a quarter-inch of top stubble and white sidewalls. Marched to a warehouse that said "Quartermaster," they filed in and were given cardboard cartons for their bags and the "civvies" they wore. Henrik was supposed to send home the shaving kit from Karen, but he kept it as did others and sent home the issue stuff. He threw away the kit's carton but remembered to grab her address card. In freshly issued white "skivvies" they shuffled along counters where civilian fitters eyeballed their correct sizes and presented them each with a stack of items. Two khaki shirts and trousers—with no hip pockets, forest-green—"pickle suit"—winter service coat and trousers, three tan shirts, raincoat and overcoat, more skivvies, web belts, and a cordovan leather belt for the greens—called a "fair weather belt," a "field scarf"—what they called a necktie, and a "battle pin" to secure the field scarf's knot, two pairs of laced low-top dark brown boots—"boondockers"—and canvas leggings. Henrik couldn't decide what good leggings were. They learned caps and hats were called "covers."

They received two envelope-like garrison caps, green and khaki. No big-crowned visored cap. They learned that marines were called "jarheads" after the old cap with a smaller crown and shorter visor than worn by other services, making them look like the plain cap on a ketchup bottle.

"Secure everything in your seabag. Pull on one of your sets of tan winter shirts and green trousers, and sit your sun helmet on your noggin. Your leggings too." Those took time to lace correctly.

"Okay, listen up, pukes. That Globe and Anchor ornament pin on the front of your sun helmet. When you get your rifle record card you'll pin it under the ornament so it doesn't get sweaty in a pocket. With a pencil, write on the underside of the helmet's front brim your service number and name. When you draw your rifle, write its serial number there too so you'll remember it."

"We look like great white hunters in Africa," said one of the boys with a tipped back sun helmet, making like he was aiming an elephant gun. Henrik was disappointed they didn't receive the new steel helmet he'd seen in a newsreel. They were more disappointed that they were not issued the famous Dress Blues that caught the eye of so many young damsels, the Marines' way of dressing to the nines.

The sergeant said, "Only fancy-dancy marines get Blues—marines posted to Washington Navy Yard Barracks, the Marine Band, embassy guards, ship's detachments, and recruiters. You can buy your own for four months' pay."

As they marched across the parade deck Sergeant Gilroy explained, "The bronze Globe and Anchor on your helmet is officially called the Eagle, Globe, and Anchor ornament and represents the Corps being worn on uniform collars, covers, and coat buttons. It's also on our standard—that's a flag to you lugs." Gilroy was right, the insignia was everywhere. They soon discovered it was not a good idea to call it a "bird on a ball."

A building called "Processing and Classification" was filled with tables behind which clerks perched generating a ceaseless typewriter clatter. Progressing through different lines, they were photographed, fingerprinted, filled out forms with personal information, and were assigned a service number—"Memorize it before you leave the buildin'." They gave one form to a man behind an addressograph machine. Typing as if at a typewriter, he stamped out two I.D. tags and tied them to a cord in the prescribed manner. "Never take your dog tags off. When you get your footlocker key, tie it to it as well."

Stamped on Henrik's oval aluminum tags were his name, six-digit service number, "P" for Protestant, blood type, tetanus inoculation date, and "USMCR"—U.S. Marine Corps Reserve.

"Reserves?"

"That means we reserve the right to do whatever we wants to yous, 'cruits. That notch in the tag ain't to jam it 'tween yous teeth when yous checked off dead. It's for the addressograph's positionin' pin."

They were looking over their tags and a fella asked, "What's that?" In parentheses after his name was "N.M.I."

"No Middle Initial."

"But don't that give me three initials?"

"Don't get smart, dumbass."

"You don't have to worry about him gettin' smart," observed the sergeant. "Drop."

***

Marched to the Quonset huts, Platoon 276 was split between two Quonsets. The racks were single stacked with blankets, sheets, pillows, and mattress covers heaped on them. Footlockers and buckets were at the foot of each rack, and on the bulkheads were shelves and clothes hanger rods. They spent the hour learning how to make the racks and that you could indeed make a blanket so tight that a quarter bounced on it. They hung and stowed all their clothing in a uniform manner. Someone mentioned the deck was concrete so they'd not have to wax them like the white linoleum decks in the big H-shaped barracks.

Lunch was a pork chop with a gob of reconstituted smashed potatoes holding a dipper hole of brown gravy. A canned peach slice floated in the gravy.

"Get outta my mess hall," shouted the mess corporal after they'd wolfed down their food.

Marched back to the barracks, they found all their carefully made racks were destroyed, with the bedding and mattresses and uniforms thrown about the room.

"Try again, pukes. Gear issue in an hour," shouted the sergeant. "Bring those buckets," he added, slamming the door on his way out.

An hour later they stood in formation in front of the "Post Exchange"—the "ge-dunk shop."

Some more experienced recruits walked past. With four weeks under their belts, they were actually permitted to walk unattended by a corporal.

"You'll be sorr-eee!" they shouted in unison.

"Ignore them," shouted their corporal. "You pukes drop!" In seconds they were knocking out twenty-five pushups. "Sorr-eee my hinny," the corporal shouted.

"What's wrong with you, the sun gettin' in your squinty little eyes 'cruit?" One of the boys was holding his hand up to block the midday sun's glare.

"Sir, no, sir, my mistake."

"It sure is. What you're tellin' me is that the sun helmet the Corps issued you isn't doin' its job. Ground your helmets and don your buckets, now! All you alls!"

The platoon scrambled to overturn three-gallon galvanized buckets on their heads. They heated up fast, and the NCOs rapped their swagger sticks on them. "Ring that chime!"

Carrying a bucket, they filed through the aisles, picking up the items directed by the sergeant: laundry powder, scrub and shoe brushes, brown leather polish and dye, bath soap, toothpowder and brush, safety razor and blades, shaving soap, Brasso polish, cigarette tobacco and "roll your own" papers, and two white bath towels marked "U.S. Marine Corps" in red. Lastly was the 1940 edition of *The Marine's Handbook*, 242 pages of everything they needed to know—"The Red Book"—which cost a buck. They were flabbergasted to learn their mandatory purchases cost them $15 out of their $31 monthly pay.

"What you mean there's no comb, 'cruit? What do you think you're goin' to be combin', bonehead?"

When they returned to their Quonsets, the racks and footlockers and their contents were again found scattered across the deck. A couple of frustrated boys flung their buckets into the wreckage.

Tempted to do the same, Henrik refrained. *That'll get us nothing good.*

"Fall out, you unkempt scumbags. I'd be embarrassed for my mother to see this mess...if I had one. You're drawing web gear and rifles in an hour. Maybe I'll be lucky and you'll all shoot each other."

Once the mess had been cleared, the sergeant announced, "You're pickin' up your 782 web gear." No one dared ask what "782" meant. "The minimum gear you'll carry when under arms is the cartridge belt, canteen, field dressin' pouch, and bayonet. You'll always don a cover or helmet whether it's a sun helmet or steel pot when armed, indoors and outdoors," he explained.

They lined up alphabetically outside a warehouse and filed down the supply depot's counter, as disinterested supply clerks tossed at them all manner of tan-colored canvas bags, pouches, and tangles of straps and buckles. They tried to keep in step marching back to the barracks, despite dropping things and tripping over dangling straps, with the sergeant chewing on them for their clumsiness. "My baby sister can march in step better than you clods without dropping her baby bottle or bayonet."

Someone stage-whispered in bold defiance, "What's her bottle full of, Dago Red?"

Knowing he'd not catch the culprit and secretly admiring his gonads, Sergeant Gilroy answered, "No—gin, you dunce. All you alls…Drop!"

With weary arms, the men proceeded to sign the receipt form, the mystery of "782" revealed as Marine Corps Form 782—"Quartermaster Receipt for Individual Equipment."

The recruits arranged themselves in a circle outside the barracks, the sergeant in the middle. "I'm goin' to show you what each item's for and how it all fits together," he said, and held up a belt affair with five pockets on each side. There were eyelets in the upper and lower corners of the pockets. "This is a cartridge belt." He called it a "cat-ridge belt." He showed how to adjust it to fit around their waist and rest it on their hips. "These two sections of the three-piece belt have five snap-closed pockets. Two five-round stripper clips fit in each pocket. There's a little strap inside each pocket to keep the clips from fallin' out. We'll show you how that works when we go to the range. In all that gives you 100 rounds of ammo. That's twenty stripper clips."

"What happens we run out of bullets?" asked Willy, an Ozark hillbilly.

"Cat-ridges, not bullets. A bullet is the pointy thing that goes down range. You let the squad leader know you're low, say when you're down to twenty or thirty rounds. The platoon sergeant or platoon guide will send a detail back to the company ammo point for more. They'll send back at least a bandoleer of sixty rounds for each of you all. The bandoleer's cheap cloth, six pockets with two stripper clips per pocket. You can throw away the bandoleers, in a fight, but here you turn them in to reuse. On patrol in Nicaragua we all carried one or two spare bandoleers anyway. We also carried a spare clip in a pocket, just in case." That stuck in Henrik's head.

The sergeant picked up a metal bottle with a metal screw-on cap held on by a little chain. "Here we've got your one-quart canteen. Fill it every chance you get. This is your canteen cup. It holds a pint and a half and fits on the bottom of your canteen." He slid the cup over the canteen's bottom. "Here's the foldin' handle. Make sure it locks before puttin' Joe in it or you'll have a lap full of hot Joe."

"Who's Joe?" asked Willy.

"Somethin' Marines drink without spoilin' it with milk and sugar. Too many questions, Willy. Drop!" The platoon hit the deck in unison.

"See this lip around the cup? You put hot chow or Joe in it and this lip will burn your flappy lips. The canteen and cup go in this cover and it's got these double-hooks on the back. They hook on these eyelets under the last ammo pocket on your right side."

Everyone fumbled around hooking their cover to the belt.

"Everybody know what a bayonet is? It's a long knife, Willy, that fits on the end of your rifle so you can stick Nips in the butt."

"Oh, I seen them before. Like them pig-stickers in the War Between the States."

"Drop!" The platoon responded immediately.

"You'll get bayonets with your rifles. It's a foot and a half long and comes with a scabbard. It's got double-hooks like the canteen cover and fits on the cartridge pocket forward of the canteen. Put your hand on that pocket; remember that's where your frog-sticker goes."

Next is the field dressin' pouch. It holds a Carlisle dressin'. It's a big bandage in a sealed tin box for if ya shot. It's in this pouch with two snaps; looks like a canvas envelop."

"When we going to—"

"You'll see the dressin' bandage when we do first aid trainin', Willy. Don't anybody open it unless you've been shot. It hooks on the cartridge belt under the last cartridge pocket on the left side, Willy."

He had everyone put on the cartridge belts. He held up two long narrow straps with two small straps on one end, making it look like a long "Y." "There is a little snap hook on the end of all the straps. This is your X-back suspenders. Have your buddy hook them on the back top corner of the last pouch on both sides of your cartridge belt, cross the straps behind your back, and then hook the front ends in the top front eyelets over the first and second pockets. It doesn't seem heavy now, but that'll change when the canteen's filled, you have a bayonet, and a hundred rounds of ammo. Those X straps will take the weight off your hips." Everyone was moving around trying to adjust the tangle of straps.

"Tomorrow we'll cover the Marine Corps pack. As you can see, it's really two packs. I'll show you what all goes in them. Fall in! Pla-toon...Ten-Hut!"

The platoon formed up at the armory, where the sergeant gave them the dos and don'ts of drawing weapons. "Treat it reverentially with tender lovin' care or an armorer will brain you with it. The rifle is your most valuable possession and it needs your constant care."

As they stood at attention, he lectured on the "U.S. rifle, caliber .30, Model of 1903," or as he affectionately called it, "the Springfield" or the "Oh-Three." "It's the best rifle in the world today. You'll learn to love it as much as your girlfriend. Wait, I'm sorry, how could any of you scumbags possibly have a girlfriend? I mean, what self-respectin' dame would have one of you dirtballs, not-fit-to-be-a-marine for a BOYfriend?" He glared over the platoon. "Raise your hand if you think you have a girlfriend like that?" Not a hand rose.

As they waited to enter the armory, someone asked, "Anyone here shot a gun?"

Henrik was surprised that only a quarter of the hands went up, boys from farms and small towns. Most of the platoon were from cities.

A guy named Bills said to Henrik, "You said you were rabbit hunting when you heard about Pearl Harbor. You do that much—hunt?"

"I did. We have a 20-gauge shotgun, a .22-caliber rifle, and a .30-30 Winchester for deer."

"You ought to be a good shot then."

"Maybe. All of those are a lot different than the Springfields we're getting."

"Ain't most guns alike, rifles anyways?" asked a fella from Chicago.

"Nope," said Henrik. "I've an uncle who has a Spanish–American War Krag, sorta like the Springfield. They operate a lot different and are a lot more powerful than even our .30-30."

"Only guns we have in Chicago are the ones gangsters own. The Marines got Tommy guns like Al Capone."

"Ain't he in prison?" someone asked, followed by a dramatic "rat-a-tat-tat."

"Nope, he's dying of syphilis of the brain in Florida or someplace."

"At least he had fun catching it."

"More fun than catching a Jap bullet in the noggin."

"Don't talk that way," said Bills.

"You a good shot, Henrik?"

"Kept my family fed. We never had to eat a fried corn and potato dinner."

"I had my share of those depression dinners. Anyway, that ain't the same as shootin' Japs, I wager."

Henrik thought on that. "You're right. They're bigger targets than deer and a lot bigger and slower than scampering squirrels."

"Just show me where to aim, boys," said a wiry fellow from Lubbock.

"Hey, ain't them Nips littler than us?" said the hillbilly.

"They say. I looked up Japan in the encyclopedia, *National Geographic* too. There were pictures of them. Little fellows, mostly wearing bathrobes. Lot of them slopes wear glasses."

"You must be a professor or somethin'."

"Nope, I just like reading."

"Professor."

"Might be harder to hit Nips them being little fellas."

Sergeant Gilroy stepped up. "You all need to know how to do pushups with rifles. In the up position you lay your rifle across the tops of your hands, palms flat on the ground. The rifle doesn't touch the ground. You all're talkin' too much. Pla-toon...Ten-Hut! Drop!"

After they'd finished knocking out pushups, the platoon stood at attention.

"You pukes don't need to be talkin' about Nips. You don't know squat about them. I've seen Nips in Tientsin when I was in the China Legation Guard. A lot of them are short and wear glasses, but there are a lot of tall ones too, taller than most of you. They're tough bastards and they'd march up a volcano and jump in if ordered." With thumbs and forefingers set in circles around his eyes like glasses, he said, "If it's for their emperor, they'll run up that volcano's side screamin', *banzai, banzai!*"

The platoon laughed and he yelled, "Pla-toon! Drop!"

***

They learned it's a rifle, weapon, or piece. Never ever a mere gun.

Sergeant Gilroy showed them how to rig the Marine Corps pack as promised. It consisted of two packs. The one worn on the upper shoulders was a haversack and could be packed with a day's C-rations, blanket or poncho, toilet kit, spare socks, and other items depending where they were. Holding up a little shovel with a T-handle, he went on, "This here is an entrenching tool, or e-tool. I don't wanna hear ya calling it a little shovel, a spade, or a banjo like those doggies do." It was less than two feet long and had a round-nosed blade and a T-shaped handle. "Ya'lls going to become real familiar with it digging lots of holes and filling in those holes. It can go on the back of the haversack or on your cartridge belt. The bayonet can go on the pack's left side or the belt too."

"Why are we—"

"You'll find out later why ya fill them in, Willy. It fits in this canvas carrier and has double-hooks to attach it to your haversack or might be carried on the belt if not carrying a pack, which isn't often."

The smaller second pack was the knapsack and attached under the haversack on the small of the back. It carried spare clothing and was often left at the company supply point. "That's why it's call a 'leave behind pack,' Willy."

The sergeant held up the bayonet in his fist, pointing at the sky. "The Japs got a bayonet just about like ours. Theirs has a fifteen-and-a-half-inch blade. Ours is sixteen inches, but we've got an even better advantage on them Nips in a bayonet fight. Our arms are longer, we've got more reach, and we're Marines!"

Everyone growled. Henrik noticed Willy looking over his arms with some doubt. He was a short fellow after all.

"But there's something you need to know that gives the Nips an advantage, a little one. They got this hook shaped like a 'J' on their bayonet guard. In a fight they'll try and hook your rifle's bayonet blade or your own bayonet's guard, and yank it right outta your hands."

Willy raised his hand. "How come we don't have a hook like that?"

The sergeant thought a moment. "Cause you're goin' to be a better bayonet fighter than those little sumbitches. You don't need a hook."

Henrik was happy he was so sure.

"Now get in there and draw those rifles. Don't fool with the sight, open the bolt, flip the safety, or try and poke your little finger in the muzzle. That's the front end, Willy."

"I know what the muzzle is sergean—"

"Drop!"

They did not make a production of issuing rifles. Each man went to attention while a corporal took a rifle from a rack, clearly read off the serial number to a clerk who wrote it in a logbook and on a "Rifle Card" before firmly slapping the rifle into his hands. "Card goes in your rifle's slot in the barracks' rack when you draw it."

They spent the rest of the day—the barracks weren't wrecked for once—learning the names of the Springfield's eighty-eight parts. The trouble was they were issued packed in a thick viscous grease called Cosmoline and wrapped in paper. It took hours scrubbing and wiping in gasoline-filled troughs. A sign reminded, NO SMOKING!

Henrik hefted the rifle, shouldered it, and quickly aligned the sights on a light-switch plate across the room. *Perfectly balanced, swift to aim.* He was suddenly looking forward to taking it to a range. They disassembled it, an easy undertaking. *Nothing complex*, Henrik thought, handling the bolt, watching how the locking lugs solidly cammed the bolt shut. *It's a rugged rifle, reliable. I can feel it.*

About the first thing they were taught was working the safety. It was a lever atop the knob-like cocking piece projecting from the end of the bolt. With the safety lever to the right the lever read SAFE. Flipped to the left it read READY.

After their third round of disassembly and assembly the sergeant said, "Some of you have eight thumbs and two pinkies. Henrik, you've got this down pat. Give these fumble-bums a hand."

"Lay your small parts out in the order you removed them and then reverse the order when you put them back in," Henrik advised.

Most appreciated his help, some didn't.

"I can handle it on my own," said a belligerent Tom Wesley. *A loner*, thought Henrik.

The sergeant put an end to that. "You haven't showed *me* that you can handle it."

***

The new the platoon fell out ready for uniform and rifle inspection. Sergeant Gilroy wasn't present as expected. Instead there was a sergeant with three chevrons and a rocker. Behind him were two corporals. To describe the sergeant as unhappy was an understatement. His face was leather-like, with eyes long used to staring into the sun.

"You sorry pukes, drop! Look at you," the sergeant groaned. "You think you're ready for inspection? You think your rifles are ready?" He looked skyward in anguish. "What in hell did I do to deserve this worthless uncoordinated mob of misfits and miscreants?"

Grinding his fist into his open hand, he glared at the platoon. "I'm Platoon Sergeant Summons and these hateful individuals are Corporal Beck and Corporal Call. I've not looked to see if they're still behind me. They haven't run away after seeing this crowd of rabble? No? Good. Whatever they say, it's the same as coming from me and whatever I say comes from the Major General Commandant of the Marine Corps himself."

The three noncoms quickly inspected Platoon 276. Every man failed the inspection, at least three times over. No surprise.

"Right now you are nothing more than undisciplined, unfit, unprincipled civilian sewerage. I am here to instill discipline, make you fit, and teach you the principles necessary for you to become the most capable fighting men in the world, or some of us will die, most likely that'll be you sorry asses.

"Raise the roof, you lugs. That means hold your rifle over your head, arms stiff. Now prance around the track until I'm tired of watching you. I'd better not see those arms anything but stiff as tent poles." They ran four quarter-mile laps.

At the command "stack, arms," they propped their rifles in tripod-like sets of three secured together by stacking hooks near the muzzles and lay their fourth rifle against the tripod. Two guards were left in attendance. The rest double-timed to the sand pit. Half the size of a basketball court, it looked like a sandy furrowed cornfield.

The platoon lined up with a squad on each furrow, leaving every other furrow empty. Sergeant Summons stood at the opposite end, and Beck and Call were planted at either side.

"You're lucky today. You're going to practice the low crawl. You will crawl dragging your fat, weak bodies as fast as you can up and down the length of the sandpit until I get tired of watching you all. You'll crawl back in the lane to your left. If you're faster than the weak-kneed softie ahead of you, crawl over him. Low-crawl, not on your hands and knees, but with all you all's face and belly in the sand."

The platoon stood rooted, awaiting orders.

"Well, what are you all waiting for? Start crawling, pukes!"

The lead men gingerly went to all fours, each in alternating furrows.

"Get on down and get dirty, crawl! Don't let anyone get in your way."

They crawled.

"Chin in the dirt, you slugs!"

"At least it ain't rainin'," muttered one boy.

"*Don't let anyone get in your way,*" Summons had ordered. That reminded Henrik of Mr. Bergmann's hogs. He'd dump buckets of slop and they'd run through the one-hog-at-a-time gate. The biggest, meanest ones forced their way through first to hog the slop. *"Don't let anyone get in your way." Like the hogs. The sergeant wants us to summon up our strength and aggressiveness.*

The man in front of him dropped into a low crawl and Henrik followed. He hesitated an instant, feeling bad about what he was going to do. It was Coveralls, the troublemaker he'd crossed with before. He smelled the sea sand, sweat, and possibly blood and tears. He crawled a few feet, reached out and grabbed Coveralls' ankles, tugged back, and crawled right over the fella, trying to keep his elbows and knees from gouging him. There was a momentary regret of humiliating the man.

At least it didn't turn into a fist fight. At the end of the furrow Henrik looked up at Sergeant Summons glaring down at him, arms folded. Apprizing Henrik, he grumbled, "Get up and stand over there at attention. Give me twenty-five while you're at it."

Some caught on; others didn't, and they made four or five repetitions. Those finished stood at attention while Henrik and another fella relieved the rifle stack guards. They tried to shake out the sand that had infiltrated their pockets and shirt fronts.

Marching back to the barracks leaving a trail of sand dust, every man was dropped at least twice for pushups.

"You're moving to brand new barracks tonight, girls. And you get to wash your filthy khakis and polish your scuffed-up boondockers. If you've got time you can wash your grubby bodies." The showers only managed to dribble cold water.

"Sorry about crawling over you," Henrik muttered to Coveralls, feeling he'd treated the fella unfairly.

"It's okay, wish I'd thought of it." He turned to Henrik. "Clovis Griffin," he said, offering a hand.

"Henrik Hahnemann."

"Hahnemann. I'll call you Handyman."

"Well, I'll call you Griff."

> Pvt Henrik C. Hahnemann
> S/N ....
> Platoon 276
> Marine Corps Recruit Depot
> San Diego, Calif.
>
> January 11, 1942
> Miss Karen R. Hathaway
> 830 W. 5th. St.
> Washington, Mo.
>
> Dear Karen,
> I am here in California. My address is on the envelope. They sure give us a lot of food, but not much time to eat it. The first thing we learned was how to make our rack, that's what we call a bed back home, so tight that you can bounce a quarter on it. I'm not sure how that'll help us win the war. The best thing I've seen here are the two pairs of boots they gave us, what we call boondockers. Best boots I've ever had. Hope you can write soon. It's kind of lonely here with no one around from home.
> Your good friend, Henrik.

He started to write some Xs under his name like Karen had, but that embarrassed him. Besides, she wasn't really his sweetheart.

Chapter Eight

"*Messhi hōkō*—Deny the self, serve the people."
Wartime slogan

Obata was painfully aware of the lieutenant, three sergeants, and Corporal Kaneko clustered around him in a prone shooting position. Especially the officer. They were seldom seen, especially on the rifle range. The corporal was as uneasy as Obata.

"What do you estimate the range, recruit?" demanded the firing range sergeant.

Range estimation was a class he had excelled in, much to his surprise. He gripped the release latches and slid the sight aperture up to the "6" on the rear sight tree's right arm. The left arm was marked with odd range numbers from "15" to "1500" meters.

"Six hundred meters, Honorable Sergeant."

The sergeant did not say anything one way or the other, but Obata knew he would be nodding or shaking his head to the spectators whether his estimation agreed with Obata's.

"Fire when ready," whispered the sergeant.

Obata shrugged his shoulders, propping his elbows in a firm position. The 7.7mm rifle's forearm rested atop two sandbags. Pulling the shoulder stock firmly into the hollow formed by his shoulder joint and collarbone, he took a breath and slowly let it partway out. He kept steady, aligning the rear sight's peephole with the front sight's triangular blade centered on the man-sized paper target. The instructor had said they used to call the targets *rosuke*—Russians. Now they called them *amenko*—Americans. Both were disparaging words for the Empire's enemies.

Gently he squeezed the trigger, slowly and evenly, so he would not know when it… *Crack!*

Peering through his binocular, the lieutenant said, "Excellent. Centered on the chest with the first shot." He looked at Obata. "Why do you remove the bolt's dust cover?"

The query from an officer actually speaking to him startled Obata. *Am I in trouble?* No one had said anything of it before. He scrambled to his feet.

Bowing, rifle at his side, he replied, "Honorable Lieutenant, the rifle balances better without the cover and I can reload faster." He expected a slap.

The lieutenant and sergeants stepped away and conversed.

"Clear your rifle, collect the empty cases, and return to the section," said Corporal Kaneko. He did not say anything about the bolt cover. Obata slipped the metal cover back on.

Section Eight sat on benches working oily rags over their Type 99 rifles.

"If you are trying to impress the officer, you are accomplishing it," said Number Six. "What did he say to you?" All eyes were on him.

"He asked me why I removed the dust cover."

"He did not beat you?" said a man winding the cord as he tugged the pull-through with its oily cleaning patch.

"Not this day."

"You must have impressed him with your shooting skills."

"It is only because of Corporal Kaneko's expert instruction." He felt shamed for a moment knowing the corporal was within hearing. Possibly that was not so bad. When it had come to the corporal's notice that Obata was a superior shot, it seemed he felt the riding crop less frequently.

The corporal approached the group and they went to attention. "Recruit Obata, you are attracting notice with your shooting skills. I suggest you make an extra effort to keep your rifle and equipment clean. You may have other visitors. I would be upset if an officer or sergeant expressed their disappointment in your appearance. That would reflect poorly on my supervision of you." He glared around at Section Eight.

Obata was already brushing dust off his rifle's leather sling.

"You all should take that advice whether you are a good shot or not." He caught Number Nine on the nap of his neck with the crop. Nine was likely the worse shot in the section. The first time he'd hit a target at over 200 meters, it was the man's next to him, five meters to the right of his own. He was easily distracted. The section joke was if you were next to Number Nine in battle, then you should dig an extra deep *takotsubo*—octopus trap—meaning you were a doomed soldier trapped in a foxhole like a beach octopus trap. It was unfortunate that he was called Number Nine—*ku*, which means both "nine" and "suffering or torture."

They spent the afternoon learning and practicing breaching barbed wire obstacles using wire cutters and entrenching shovels. Their instruction was rigid. They would stand at attention while the corporal, or sometimes another corporal or sergeant, lectured on the subject. Then a section of recruits in their second quarter of training would demonstrate the skill. They would then be talked through the action themselves and repeat it two or three times, being increasingly hurried. The instructor would point out errors with his crop or boot. After the evening meal they often practiced it again in the dark, rain, or snow.

***

Obata was completely surprised the day he received a letter from his mother. His father had previously sent two brief notes. Obata had thought his mother to be near illiterate. Many women were. Few were taught any *hiragana* or *kanji* with their thousands of characters. Those were unnecessary to make a home and considered by many too difficult for women to learn. He knew it was women of the Court who long ago developed their own means of writing, *onnade*. Over generations it evolved into *katakana* or simply *kana*. It had fifty syllabary characters and was used in official documents, newspapers, books, and so on. He could picture his mother cross-legged on the kitchen floor painstakingly penning this letter under a dim oil lamp.

She wrote of little things, everyday events like the difficulties of the blackout order and funny things like people becoming lost in their own darkened neighborhoods. There was the policeman obsessed with barking dogs and slamming doors, fearing the noise might attract enemy bombers. She wrote too of a neighbor struck by an automobile at night. There were few cars because of the scarcity of petrol. Charcoal-powered cars were being made. Some reasoned that banned car headlights meant fewer pedestrians and bicyclists would be rundown by cars and trucks at night because they were seldom driven in the dark. There were food shortages, with fresh meat almost impossible to find and cooking oil scarce. "Not that it matters," she wrote at one point. He could visualize her smile. "What good is cooking oil if there is no charcoal or kerosene to cook the food?" Eggs were available but tripled in cost. Fortunately, Uncle Asahi always brought them two or three fish when he came in. "One day they reduced the rice and cooking oil allocation without first announcing it," she wrote, "but a week later when the allocation was slightly increased, but to less than when it was originally reduced, the government presented it as a major increase." Rice had been rationed since April 1941. They failed to again increase the allocation of cooking oil. Tofu, fruit, and vegetables were seldom available.

She was disappointed they decided to start the war in the middle of winter, making every kind of fuel scarce, and when her vegetable and spice gardens were dormant. She mentioned little else about the war, a wise thing. The government frowned on talk of the war unless it was good news. There was good news, though, in light of the many Southern Army victories. Nippon had or would soon seize the treasures of the Southern Resource Zone, what they called the American colony in the Philippines, Netherlands East Indies, and the English Straits Settlements and their South Seas colonies.

He thought of his family far longer than usual that night. He had his own difficulties, but their life was not so comfortable either and might become worse. There was nothing he could do for them other than send a few yen home, very few. His mother had ended the letter saying they were all well and would cope with the shortages. They had no other choice.

***

The section made it through their First Period Examination. Most did anyway. There were four who were physically or mentally unable to accomplish all the tasks. A man in another section hung himself. Still in shock, the instructors marched each section into the barracks to view the grisly scene. No one had noticed any signs of distress. The instructors seemed to have expected it. "He will not be the last," said a sergeant bluntly. Sickened, Obata felt that possibly his life meant little. He kept it to himself.

"He was weak and his cowardly passing is no loss to the Imperial Army," screamed Corporal Kaneko, whacking the boy's naked leg with the flat of his sword. He hung from a rafter by two knotted rifle slings. "He could not even tie proper knots."

They had learned much. It was not all marching and senseless punishments. They learned everything about rifle marksmanship, bayonet fighting, and hand-to-hand combat: *judo*, *keno*, and *kendo*. They learned only basic hand-to-hand combat skills viewed more as physical fitness training than a means to defend oneself.

While the long bayonet was a far cry from the traditional samurai sword, they conducted extensive bayonet training and linked it to the Empire's sword-wielding warriors—"fighting with a drawn sword" meaning to "fight the enemy face-to-face." They practiced against each other with sticks padded on both ends and hand-carved mock rifles, then rifles without bayonets, and finally with rifles with fixed bayonets covered by scabbards. They also fought bayonet dummies to learn the vulnerable attack points.

"If your opponent has a rifle and bayonet, he may have a longer reach than you, so slash at his hands."

Several of the recruits struggled with their bayonets, clumsily prodding at the dummies. The corporal shouted in frustration, "You will not be fighting dummies made of boards and horsehair-filled sacks that do not fight back or die because you poked them with a bayonet. In China we practiced on bandit prisoners. It takes many thrusts to kill a *chankoro*"—what they deceitfully called a Chinaman.

Obata had heard rumors of such. The corporal spoke of such practices no further.

Obama disliked bayonets, dreading the thought of a long, cold steel blade slicing through flesh and organs, or repeatedly vicious thrusts until one collapsed, seeping blood or bleeding to death internally. They were taught to twist the imbedded blade, causing more severe hemorrhaging.

They learned about hand grenades, digging fighting positions for one and two men, trenches, first aid, field sanitation, and identifying rank insignia. There were endless readings and discussions of the *Imperial Rescript to Soldiers and Sailors* and the *Five Principles of Battle Ethics*. The way these lessons were couched seemed to suggest they did not necessarily apply leniency to enemies of the Empire.

Much of their day was spent on rifle practice and maintenance. There was not always much ammunition available, so they practiced sight pictures and snapping the trigger, striving to avoid all movement of the rifle's barrel. They were given demonstrations of other infantry weapons, the light and heavy machine guns, grenade dischargers, and rifle grenade launchers. They threw a great many rocks and short pieces of pipe to simulate hand grenades. Instructors told them that Americans and British could throw hand grenades further, so accuracy and speed of throwing copious numbers of grenades were emphasized.

Corporal Kaneko sometimes stood at attention, serving as a grenade target. None dared hit him of course. This only resulted in him throwing the fake grenades back at them. He frequently scored hits as they scrambled for cover while he cursed their clumsy inaccuracy. "A blindfolded *chankoro* is more accurate than you uncoordinated weaklings."

Forty-kilometer marches became common, and eventually the marches were being completed at faster rates with heavier packs. Obata's soles were as tough as his boots'.

Much to the recruits' surprise, small groups of officers often led off the marches. They started ahead of the recruits and quickly outdistanced them. By the time they returned to the barracks the officers were nowhere to be seen. The corporal said, "The officers can outmarch you anytime, night or day. They are hard, toughened men as they should be to serve the Emperor.

The officers led by example. They believed in the Spirit of Yamato to expand the Empire, but it was the strength of individual will that would defeat the enemy. In wartime it included the mobilization of the national will. Every man and woman did their share, for the Emperor. All were expected to lay down their lives for the Empire and the Emperor. It was an inborn feeling. The people based their lives on obedience and if necessary, they wished for the very best place and manner of death. To fail to do so dishonored themselves, the Army, the Empire, and the Emperor.

The worst march was the "snow march." This was a five-day ordeal covering twenty to thirty kilometers a day marching on country roads and hill trails—rain, snow, and ice. They had to carry all their rations and cook them for most meals. Horse-drawn unit kitchen carts and cooks provided some hot meals. It was training for them too. Although the recruits had winter clothing and two blankets, it was nonetheless cold and exhausting. They spent the first night in eight-man tents. At least they were out of the wind, but the tents provided little warmth. The other three nights all they had were canvas shelter-halves—two rectangles of canvas erected as an open-ended tent. They were even colder and suffered until the corporal, who was nowhere to be seen at night, taught them a better way.

They were not permitted to cut or even pick up dead wood. It was the Emperor's property and allowed only to be salvaged by peasants—*heimin*—owning no land or marketable property. They could cut fir and pine limbs with bayonets and collect layers of ground leaves to insulate the frozen or wet ground.

After they had laid a layer of leaves and needles, the corporal directed, "Lay one shelter-half on this. Two of you will wrap up in your blankets with enough to cover your heads and boots. Lying on your sides, front-to-back, spread open one overcoat to cover both your heads and shoulders and the other to cover your lower torso, legs, and boots. Spread the second shelter-half to cover both of you. If one of you turns over, so must the other. You will not be barracks warm, but you will not freeze. Not that I care," he added. Those were long shivering nights with little sleep.

Once when they returned from a march the corporal ordered, "Eyes, left." They turned to see a separate ornate two-story building set a distance from the street.

"That is the *kaikosha*. It is a private club and meeting place for officers. All garrisons have one. It is also where officers purchase their special uniforms and equipment. They have a bar and a library and gaming rooms. If you are ever sent to deliver a message to an officer, never go inside. Tell the door guard which officer you are to see and wait outside at attention until the officer or an orderly comes to you. Always wait to see if he has a response message before you depart."

After passing their First Period Examination, they thought they would see the end of harassment by the senior recruits. They did not, even after they had completed their rifle training. What they learned was that the nail that sticks out gets hammered down.

Obata thought the games which they were involuntarily made part of were childish. A particularly foolish one was the "flight of the warbler across the valley," in which long barracks tables were pushed into a line down the center aisle with a meter-wide gap between them. A single hapless recruit was ordered to "fly," or rather scramble, on all fours under the tables to pop up in the "valley" gaps between the tables. Emerging between the tables the "warbler" would have to sing "*ho go-kekyo*," remaining exposed as men on the cots barraged him with shoes, cups, spoons, manuals, and even rocks. It was in fun, but some saw it as an opportunity to settle scores picked up in the past weeks. Facial cuts, bruises, and knots on the head were common.

***

As they had passed the First Period Examination, called *ikki*, they were allowed off-garrison passes on some Saturday nights and on Sundays. They were not permitted to visit home, even those living nearby. Their families could visit them on Sundays.

They could also visit sake shops and cafes on their own, but there had to be at least three men in the group. The police questioned them, demanding their passes and pay record books. They would always write down their names and unit numbers. The older soldiers said this was for intimidation, that the police never turned in their reports.

Much to his relief, Obata's family visited three times. It was like a dream going back to his past life, one he might never see again. The first time, not knowing what to expect, they met him at the main gate. There was a small park nearby and they visited at one of the wooden benches. He was glad to see Fumiko who marveled at the vastness of Nagoya Castle's ancient walls. One of his mother's sisters had accompanied them.

He told them what his days were like, but without mentioning the frequent harsh treatment and the seemingly endless hours. He did not wish to upset the women and his sister. Father had brought a *shōgi* board and the twenty hand-carved wooden pieces for each side. The pieces were arranged on the board to point in one direction or another, indicating which side they belonged to. The women watched in fascination as the two men played three rounds of the ancient chess-like game. Father won two rounds, but Obata suspected Father allowed him a win the third.

"The Army should make you an officer," remarked his father as he returned the pieces to their leather bags. "You managed to retain both of your silver and both gold generals and even promoted one."

Mother had brought a *hinomaru bento* for each of them, a low-sided aluminum lunchbox filled with rice and a flattened-out pickled red plum, very salty and tart, centered to look like the Japanese Sun flag—*hinomaru*. It is what many civilians now had for lunch.

"It is considered very patriotic," said his aunt.

His family seemed satisfied with the light lunch, but Obata felt empty after the more filling meals he had had over the past weeks. He felt guilty for the meager meals his family endured.

The next visit was special. They went to a small cafe, something they had never done. It was a simple meal, but an exceptional one nonetheless. His father and he walked about the park's gravel paths. Mother, Fumiko, and his aunt explored other paths.

"Yoshiro, I know this is hard for you. I noticed the bruises and cuts on your face and hands. Are they that brutal?"

Obata hesitated a moment. "Father, it is very difficult for all of us. There are times when I regret doing this, but then I remind myself that it is for the Emperor and the people of the Empire. They are hardening us by exposure to the elements and challenging our resolve."

"Has anyone been seriously injured?"

"Yes, we have had a couple with fractures, and one was hurt, a cut forearm, by a bayonet." He did not mention the three suicides, none of which had occurred in his section. "One man almost drowned crossing a rain-swollen stream. The irony was that two days later we started swim training."

"That is horrible. Was there an investigation?"

"There was only an inquiry, and it was ruled as an accident because of an all-night rainstorm. A natural accident."

"You must be careful, Yoshiro."

"I am always cautious, Father. The training is hard, but it is essential that we comply with immediate and unquestioning obedience. As one of the sergeants told us, even monkeys fall from trees."

His father looked at him.

He explained, "We all make mistakes but learn from them."

"You will emerge from this as a man, Yoshiro. You will find all else confronting you in life will not be so difficult. You will make your mother and me proud."

His father told him that business was increasing. There was an order for larger fishing floats; apparently one fishing company was experimenting with larger nets. "The Army has ordered more of those strange, small spheres."

**

On the third visit Father had four good-sized mackerel provided by Uncle Asahi, hidden in newspaper wrapping. Obata gave the gate guard two cigarettes to avert an eye. Upon presenting the fish, Obata was hailed as a hero within Section Six. They filleted and cut the flaky white meat into strips to grill on a small fire behind a coal bunker. The other recruits did not notice

Number Six disappear into the shadows as they cooked over the scraps of a broken-up wooden ammunition box. They warmed saved rice liberally doused with soy sauce and one man donated some miso-glazed eggplants. When the feast was ready, they passed around their mess kit lids as servings were spooned in.

Number Six returned, his shadow dividing and revealing Corporal Kaneko, arms akimbo. "What is going on here?"

The section scrambled to their feet in panic.

"Relax, you fools. Number Six was so bold to invite me to your illicit party. I humbly accept." He bowed and the section hesitantly returned the gesture. "Sit, sit and enjoy this nourishment. You will need it tomorrow." He accepted a lid heaped with rice and fish.

They sat eating in awkward silence, until the corporal produced a bottle of sake. He swallowed a gulp and passed it around. He broke the tension with, "A soldier's life is hard, it must be to honor the Emperor and protect the Empire. But there are rewards. It is the comradeship, no matter how hard and demanding our duty may be, how deadly a battle might be. I do not always recall the endless blood of China, but there were times when we served in unison for not only the Emperor and the Empire, but among ourselves. You fools will experience more moments like this and cherish them."

They took in his words and one boy produced four cigarettes. They were lit and passed around until the corporal said, "These are *Kinshi* brand cigarettes, the favorite of many soldiers. The *Kinshi*, as you have been taught, is a decoration for valor. Before the new war the cigarettes were called in English, 'Golden Kite,' a hawk-like bird, which means the same as *Kinshi*. Rules now order all products with English names are to be renamed with Japanese names."

"The same as with American baseball no longer being permitted," said Number Nine. "I never liked it anyway," he hurriedly added. Others quickly agreed so not to be accused of once liking the decadent American sport, what was called *yakyu* or field ball in Japan.

The corporal suddenly stood. "It is late. Tomorrow is another day to soldier." He bowed and the section quickly stood and returned the honor. He left without further words.

The morning greeted them with another brutal day of marching and senseless punishments.

The section, though, felt for the first time they were soldiers.

***

Their Second Period Examination not only meant advanced skills training, but repetitious training on the earlier learned skills. The staff apparently thought they would forget their earlier training if not frequently repeated. It did include more weapons training.

They learned about the Type 96 and Type 99 light machine guns designed by General Nambu Kijirō himself, what they nicknamed a *rahmabu*. He had also designed the Type 14 and Type 94 pistols and most of the machine guns used by the Imperial Army and Navy.

Light machine guns were allotted three per platoon. The Japanese Army did not call sections, or squads as the Americans called them, "rifle" squads and platoons, but "light machine gun" sections and platoons. Their tactics were built around those guns. Riflemen protected light machine guns, and light machine guns protected heavy machine guns in the battalion machine gun company.

The Types 96 and 99 were similar, the first being the old 6.5mm caliber and the second 7.7mm. They were fitted with bipods and fired using a shoulder stock. They had a thirty-round magazine attached on the top and a carrying handle. The 2.5-power telescopic sight made them more accurate than their American and British counterparts, the Browning automatic rifle and the Bren gun. The telescopic sight permitted them to be used for sniping. The Type 99 had a cone-shaped flash hider lacking on the Type 96. Four men manned a gun. They were taught on both weapons as it depended on where a unit was stationed on whether they had 7.7mm or the older 6.5mm rifles and machine guns. The new 7.7mm weapons went to China and Manchuria and selected units in Nippon.

"Important points," the machine gun instructor told them, "the 6.5mm cartridge is shorter-ranged than the 7.7mm. It has less penetration through bamboo, underbrush, trees, building walls, earth piled around fighting positions, and sandbags. There are no 6.5mm tracers or armor-piercing bullets while there are for 7.7mm."

"The Type 96 cartridges are oiled when loaded into the gun by the magazine loading device. The Type 99 does not need oiled cartridges."

There was another weapon found in the light machine gun platoon. "Few countries have a similar weapon." The instructor set the odd-looking weapon on a table. None of the recruits had seen such a device before. "A light machine gun platoon's 4th Section has three Type 89 grenade dischargers, the platoon commander's own artillery."

The unusual weapon consisted of an almost 300mm-long 5cm-caliber barrel with a smaller diameter tube about the same length. This screwed into the base end of the barrel and had a curved base plate that was wedged into the ground and angled 45 degrees toward the enemy. The kneeling gunner held the small base plate in place with a boot while holding the barrel with his left hand and his right gripping the firing lanyard at the barrel's base. The loader dropped the projectile down the barrel, the gunner yanked the short lanyard while aligning the barrel with the target and, holding it at a 45-degree angle adjusted with a range knob to vent the propellant gas. It could fire fragmentation hand grenades with a small propellant charge screwed into the base or larger round-nosed explosive, incendiary, and smoke rounds. They were positioned to fire barrages from 120 to 670 meters. They were especially effective when the enemy assaulted at close range to be greeted by a barrage of explosives and fragmentation. There were also colored smoke and flare rounds for signaling. "We call these colored signals 'dragons.' The Russians and Chinese fear it greatly. No other army has a weapon like it," the instructor declared.

Obata knew that their training was reaching its end. Now he thought about what would happen when assigned to a unit. Where would that be? Someplace in the Home Islands, Korea, Formosa, Manchukuo, someplace in China or in the Southern Resource Area where fighting was still underway with the Americans, British, and Dutch? They could simply be swallowed up in the vast convoluted wilderness of the Empire.

Chapter Nine

> "To Our Brave Ones
> Long will we remember
> How you fought and died.
> How you suffered and bled.
> You who were our pride."
> Florence Wreford Besteiso
> Mother of a boy on Bataan

The recruits lost all sense of time, surprised by how much they accomplished each day. The farm boys could have told them that; they knew what it was like to be up before dawn and kick mud off your boots as the sun sets. To Henrik it was much like working on a farm, apart from the harassment. Gradually he learned how to ignore most of it and not let it get under his skin.

At some point they marched through San Diego to the former Del Mar Racetrack. It was now called Camp C. J. Miller. Here they learned survival swimming and how to keep a wounded man afloat. Anyone who couldn't swim quickly learned. They learned the difference between Boot Camps in San Diego and Parris Island, South Carolina, in abandon-ship drills. At Dago, boots were taught to pinch their noses shut, while at the much-derided Parris Island they clasped their hands over their balls.

Starting at 4:30 a.m., their days were filled with close order drill, camouflage, manual of arms, first aid, physical fitness, obstacle courses, and bayonet fighting. And there was military law—the Articles of the Government of the Navy, or "Rocks and Shoals," describing the difficulties of staying on the straight and narrow under the Navy's unforgiving ways.

The fifth and sixth weeks were what many recruits looked forward to. They marched thirteen miles to Camp Calvin B. Matthews Rifle Range north of San Diego.

In Henrik's squad was a fella with a most unusual accent. When he had first heard it Henrik thought the boy was a foreigner. Jean Prejean was indeed a foreigner of sorts—a Cajun from southern Louisiana. Henrik learned the Cajuns had been exiled to the state's swamps when the British took control of Canada back before the American Revolution. Prejean spoke English, but with a thick French accent with a lot of strange words mixed in. Henrik had never heard of Cajuns. Most lived in the swamps trapping and hunting, fished, or worked sharecropping farms. They stayed much to themselves and had little use for the *gros bête*, the "big stupids"—non-Cajuns. Too them, everyone was a *yan-kee*.

Prejean experienced difficulties straight off. No example of ineptness was off limits. The massive tome of *The Marine's Handbook* was beyond his grasp with his Fifth Grade education. He was boastful, telling a lot of tall tales, especially his conquests of *shas*—girls—who he declared were eagerly attracted to the less than handsome and not too bright Cajun. Part of his problem was an obvious lack of confidence, dexterity, and coordination.

Sergeant Summons was perpetually on Prejean during dismounted drill. Corporal Call spent much of his time trying simply to get him to march in step and not hit the men next to him with his rifle when snapping to port arms. "Fill your left pocket with sand. Maybe you'll remember it from your right."

"Henrik, you can drill without sticking your rifle in your eye or tripping. After chow, take Prejean behind the Quonsets and teach that clod the manual of arms without hurting himself. We can take care of it or he gets stuck in Company Q for those losers who can't stay in step."

"Yes, sir."

The cooks brought chow out to the range, a ham slice, undercooked white rice, green beans, an apple, and crackers.

It took four frustrating evenings for both of them, but Prejean came around. Henrik praised him when he got a movement right—it happened sometimes. Prejean looked like a puppy used to being kicked finally being given a friendly head scratch. As the two became acquainted, Prejean gradually revealed his home life was less than idyllic. It turned out his *pere*—father—was a drunk and hateful toward Prejean. "I like it here, *poda*—partner. I be treated here more better than *le maison*—home."

That was a chilling thought to Henrik. Thinking back to his own comforting family, he truly felt sorry for the self-proclaimed woman-chasing Cajun.

There was some confusion over the pronunciation of Prejean's name. The sergeant pronounced the Cajun's name as "Jean Pre-Jean," as it was spelled, but it was actually pronounced "John Pre-John." One of the Texas boys got up the nerve to tell this to the sergeant. With a shrug of his shoulders, the sergeant muttered, "Sure."

Prejean had gotten so used to his mispronounced name that at the next morning's rollcall when the sergeant correctly shouted, "Pre-John," there was no response.

"Pre-John! Damnit, I know you're here. Sound off!"

Henrik turned quickly, "That's you buddy."

"Oh, okay, I be here, sarge. All the day long."

"I've been detailed to hell," groaned the sergeant. "Drop, Pre-John or whoever you are."

***

Pvt Henrik C. Hahnemann
S/N ....
Platoon 276
Marine Corps Recruit Depot
San Diego, Calif.

January 18, 1942
Mr. Karl H. Hahnemann
R.F.D. North Rte. 211 4th St.
Marthasville, Mo.

Dear Papa,

I hope all are well at home. I miss all of you every day. The weather there must be better by now. It's clear and fair here. I promised to tell you about our rifle training. At Camp Matthews we live in tents with wooden ~~decks~~ floors and folding ~~cots~~ racks. We only get a shower every three days, and dig startle latrines, but the ~~chow's~~ food's good. The drill instructors are rarely seen and they don't harass us. They want us to concentrate on shooting. We have musketry instructors and that's all they do, teach shooting. Funny name musketry, because the '03 Springfield's certainly no musket. At night we learn the rifle's eighty-eighty parts as we fieldstrip them, often blindfolded, and clean them. We get up at 5:00 a.m. and take our meals in mess tents. We even do Church Call in the field. The minister is a Navy officer. All the Marine chaplains are Navy, all the medical people too. Some nights they bring a movie projector out for training films and newsreels or a regular movie. One night we saw "Foreign Correspondent," a British movie about an American reporter trying to catch German spies in Britain before the war.

We do a lot of shooting and we pair up taking turns firing and coaching during "grass week." Other times we operate the targets on the Known Distance or "K.D." range at 200, 300, and 500 yards. There's a trench, called the butts, with a piled dirt backstop. They say "butts" comes from the ends of logs cut by English longbowmen for targets. We sit in the trench and slide the big bullseye targets up and down in a wooden frame, marking where the bullets hit, and paste patches over the bullet holes. I do pretty good getting close to the top score. Sergeant Summons says I'm the best shot in the platoon and he doesn't very often tell anyone they're good at anything. He sure lets us know when we're doing poorly. To make Expert I'll have to score at least 305 out of 350. I can do that and guess what? I'd get an extra five bucks each payday.

I'll say this about the Springfield. There can't be a better rifle in the world. Once the rifle's zeroed, and we do that each day we shoot, I can put bullets just about where I want. The scoop is that we'll be given new M1 Garand rifles when we graduate and are sent to a Fleet Marine Force unit. That's the Corps' fighting units. The M1's an eight-shot semi-automatic. Many of the instructors aren't too enthused with the M1, saying it's too heavy, too many parts, and too complex for us dumb recruits.

Pa, I have to tell you something funny about Cpl. Call. We wear fiber sun helmets, not those doughboy tin hats. They look like the safari helmets we saw in that Life Magazine article. The old helmets are khaki tan and new ones green. Our platoon was issued a mix of tan and green helmets. Cpl. Call goes crazy about not being uniform and is always trying to get the quartermaster to give him enough of either color just so we'll all be the same. Sgt. Summons just laughs at him and he's taken to wearing a green helmet on odd days and tan on even days just to annoy Cpl. Call.

You asked what we eat. It's not Mama's chow, but it's not bad. Something we can count on is fish on Friday, chicken on Sunday, and chicken leftovers Monday. I'll copy the day's menu they post in the mess tent and send it...

***

For Henrik's efforts with Prejean, Summons slipped him a couple of quarter-gallon "Victory sized" bottles of Acme beer. "Share with your squad mates, they had to put up with Pre-John too."

Besides the harassment, another thing Henrik didn't mention was the razzing he received from a couple of other recruits.

People were tense about German-Americans. German U-boats were sinking scores of American merchant ships off the East Coast.

It started when a fella from Dallas gave him the Nazi salute. Henrik ignored it until in the head one night he screamed into Henrik's ear, "HEIL HITLER, HERR HEINIE HEINRIK!"

"Don't do that again, *Dummkopf*," Henrik said quietly.

"Oh, I'm really scared of 'Heinie the Kraut.' The only reason you're here is they're afraid you'll side with your goose-stepping pals if we go to Europe."

The next night Henrik was ready for Dallas' loudmouth when he entered the shower room. He'd lye-soaped a hand towel. The instant Dallas opened his mouth to "Heil Hitler" and throw a stiff-armed salute, Henrik lobbed the balled soap-saturated towel straight into his gapping mouth. A scuffle commenced and several others sprang into the fray, but it broke up quickly when they realized everyone was naked and an avalanche of embarrassment crashed on them.

The other fella, Knolls, was from St. Louis, practically a neighbor. There were a great many German emigrants in southeast Missouri, so many it was called *Kleines Deutschland*. The pro-Nazi German-American Bund or Federation was active there, but few German descendants joined. From 1939 and the war in Europe, the Bund's popularity plunged and there were fewer rallies, demonstrations, and parades. It was considered a serious insult to be accused of supporting the Bund. Bund leaders were often arrested for tax evasion and embezzlement. There were still people who felt most German descendants supported the Nazis, especially if they had even a faint accent.

On a night that Henrik didn't have a two-hour fire guard shift he had the fire guard wake him at 0300 hours. In the head he and Griff mixed a packet of cocoa powder with a dash of water in a C-ration can. With the fire guard's aid they cautiously lifted Knolls' blanket and sheet and smeared the thick mixture on the sheet's bottom side at butt level. They gently laid the covers back on and enjoyed the barracks' commotion when Knolls discovered his "accident" at First Call. He was henceforth dubbed "Asswipe."

Chow was one of the most prevalent subject of barracks banter. "What's the most beloved gyrene chow?" someone asked as the barracks' inhabitants discussed the situation.

"German."

"What, kraut chow? No way."

"Frankfurters and hamburgers, they're German inventions, right?"

"*Jawohl*."

"Hotdogs and burgers are from Frankfurt and Hamburg, Germany. They're as kraut as sauerkraut and schnitzel."

"What's that?"

"Then there's *Muckefuck*. That means substitute coffee, like chicory. Bad bitter stuff."

***

They began to be granted liberty on Friday nights and Saturdays, sometimes even Sunday after Church Call. Summons advised them to go into Dago, in groups. "Never go alone."

The drill instructors bemoaned past peacetime rules allowing them to visit Tijuana across the Mexican border, reminiscing about the anything-goes Maria girls and great *cerveza*—beer.

Two liberty marines came toward Henrik and Griff after rounding a building corner near Cannery Row in Dago. "SPs comin' round the corner, brothers," one warned. They straightened their garrison caps and field scarfs. They didn't need a gig report because of some minor infraction on their greens. It might cost them next weekend's liberty.

The marine and sailor bore "SP" armbands and billy clubs. The marine was wearing a green "pickle suit" and the swabby a black Cracker Jack sailor boy uniform. It was necessary to pair marines and sailors because no self-respecting marine would take orders from a lone or even paired squids, "SP" or not.

"Evening brothers," said the marine. The sailor knew to keep his mouth shut, being among three jarheads. "Liberty cards?"

"Right here, pal," said Henrik, producing his white card.

"Let's see your ID tags, marines," said the sailor.

"That's not necessary, Charlie," said the marine. "They're wearing field scarfs. No need to dig them out. Not as easy like with that girly looking scarf you wear like a hangman's noose."

"How'd you end up here street-walking with an anchor-clanker?" Griff asked the marine.

"Ahhh, you know how it is, fellas, I barely made Marksman and couldn't get infantry so they stuck me in the MPs."

"Survey that," said Henrik. "Maybe you can re-qualify sometime."

"I can only hope. Don't like the idea of gumshoeing Dago sidewalks and hassling swabbies for the duration. Looks in order to me," he said, handing back their cards. "Stay out of trouble brothers and be home by midnight."

"Yes, mom. You too, squid." They laughed.

"Yeah, yeah, you jarheads can get away calling me a squid, just don't call me a gob."

"Gob of what?" asked Henrik.

"Get outta here, wise guy."

***

Not surprisingly, Jean Prejean experienced difficulties qualifying with the Springfield rifle. He claimed to be a *première* duck hunter, telling exaggerated "on-my-own stories usin' a twice barrel shoot-gun."

Camp Calvin B. Matthews meant two weeks of rifle firing. From the beginning of Boot Camp everyone was endlessly asking what they were doing next or where were they going. They'd learned by now that it made little difference. Wherever they were sent, the instructors had things lined up. What was up next was no longer a topic as they marched or trucked to some range, desolate training area, or hot stuffy classroom.

Between live fire and dry firing and different firing positions they were taught more hand-to-hand combat and bayonet drill. The road marches to ranges were short. It was all about shooting and chasing the ultimate goal, a Marine Expert Rifleman. A Marksman was the lowest rating and one to be avoided. Sharpshooter was an average shooter and the most common rating achieved. Expert was the top rating with less than fifteen percent reaching that exalted rating.

They also fired the .45-caliber M1911A1 pistol mostly carried by machine gunners, mortar men, antitank gunners, and officers. The seven-shot semi-automatic pistol was called the .45 Colt, but they were surprised to learn it was developed by the machine gun designer John Browning. He'd also designed the .30- and .50-caliber air- and water-cooled machine guns as well as the BAR. They learned that meant Browning Automatic Rifle, spoken as "B-A-R" and never called the "Bar."

Henrik had seen pictures of the BAR before, but that was all. His Uncle Werner had a Remington .32-caliber Model 8 semi-automatic rifle—same kind the FBI used to shut down Bonnie and Clyde. It had a five-round magazine and he used it for deer. Henrik had fired it a few times. It wasn't anything like the BAR. There was much more to the BAR with over 130 parts. Many were so small and fragile that timed field stripping and reassembly weren't permitted. They had to spread out a blanket or poncho so dropped parts could be found.

Henrik was again called upon to get Prejean going in the right direction.

"Handyman," said Summons after the first couple of live fire days. It had become apparent the Cajun was as incompetent with rifle firing as he was with dismounted drill, his conquest of the fairer sex, and potato peeling. "I want you take Prejean to Firing Point One and keep Points Two and Three empty so he won't be distracted. You teach him to at least to hit the bull's eye close enough to make Marksman."

Fearing this could be a lengthy ordeal for both of them, he asked, "How long do I have, sir?"

"All day, until it's too dark to see the targets. If he's not made it, you can start over tomorrow after breakfast."

Henrik stifled a groan. "Yes, sir."

"I've got faith in you, Handyman."

That doesn't add up to two of us.

Turning back to Henrik, Summons added, "And keep your patience, Handyman. You're not a drill instructor, no screaming or threats. Ask him what his most comfortable shooting position is and take it from there. Say something to make me happy."

"I'm glad for the opportunity, Sarge."

"Sometimes, Handyman…I just don't know."

There were four required firing positions. The sergeant had just told him to let Prejean qualify from the easiest position for him and scratch the rest.

Prejean wasn't happy, Henrik wasn't happy, Summons was never happy.

"We'll make the best of this," he told Prejean, but you have to pay attention, listen to me, concentrate, and don't give me any crap. Can do?"

"But I—"

"No buts. I'm going to get you qualified no matter what. Maybe you'll be able to hit a duck. You hear me?"

"*Allons!*"—Let's go!

Placing Prejean in a sitting position, Henrik had him fire off a five-round clip. "Aim as best you can."

From the 300-yard butts Henrik faintly heard, "Hey, Handyman. Can you get him to at least hit the target sheet somewhere so we can mark the misses?" They waved "Maggie's drawers" erratically, the little red flag signaling a miss.

Henrik waved his arm dismissingly.

The next shot drew further advice from the butts. "He missed the barn, Handyman. Put him inside the barn and lock the door."

In his notepad Henrik drew a sketch of what the sight picture should look like with the rear sight notch, the front sight's blade, and the target's ten-ring lined up with the fist-sized black center spot with an "X"—the X-ring, the "magpie." He coached Prejean through breath control—taking a breath, exhaling a little, and gently squeezing the trigger.

"Handyman!" from downrange. "He can't hit a whole flock of barns."

Prejean gave the pit crew a one-finger wave and stuck his tongue out.

"Okay, Prejean, I see what's happening here. You're closing your eyes when you squeeze the trigger. Try keeping them open no matter what. You're anticipating the recoil. The recoil doesn't really hurt, does it?"

Prejean nodded. "Cept when I squeezes the trigger too hard." He cracked off another shot.

"We've not used any paper patches yet," the target marker shouted from the butts. Bullet holes were covered by pasted paper patches, but one first had to make a hole. "You want me to make some holes with my M1903 pencil?"

"Not yet, pal."

Henrik had Prejean extend an arm, holding up his trigger finger aligned with a distant telephone pole. He told him to close his right eye and then his left.

"Did your finger look like it moved away from the pole?"

"Yeah, *pods*," he said, surprised. "Did you see dat finger jump ala way cross, *homme*?"

"Then you're right-eye dominant. When you aim keep your right eye open and close your left. Can you do that? We can put tape over your left eye if you can't keep it closed."

It took almost twenty rounds before he was hitting the target sheet consistently and even achieved some "magpies"—hits within the "3 ring" of the black bullseye. Another twenty and he barely scored Marksman.

"*Poo-yi*, my shoulder hurts now, *homme*."

The next day they fired for record and Prejean squeaked through with a score of 260, just ten points over the minimum for Marksman. Summons gave Henrik half a dozen new cans of 3.2 percent Buds.

"You feel good about that, don't you, Jean?" Henrik asked, church-keying open a can and passing it to the Cajun.

"I got bumps of the goose all 'round about me, *homme*."

***

Before their final week of Boot they performed a week's Mess Duty. Reporting at 0400 hours, they worked into the night helping the cookies, serving chow, washing dishes, bubble dancing pots and pans, unloading rations from delivery trucks, spit-shining garbage cans, swabbing and cleaning up after every meal, and serving officers' meals. The sergeants and corporals ate after the recruits were fed. The noncoms though were always awaiting them when they fell into formation.

Prejean caught an inch-long scorpion, cut its stinger off, tied it to a short length of white thread from his sewing kit, and knotted it to his undershirt. The scorpion, like a small dog, ran back and forth across his belly tethered on its thread leash.

"Watch this." He winked and walked through the mess hall's screen door.

"Scorpion!" shouted the headcount PFC and slammed a stainless steel mess tray into Prejean's belly.

He stumbled out the door clutching his belly to cover the brown splotch sprouting legs. "Sorry, sorry," he gasped and ran to the head followed by howls of laugher.

"What the hell was that?" asked the confused headcount. "I heard them coonasses'll eat anything."

"Wash that tray," shouted a cook.

Today was another "picnic day," eating on the range—cubed Spam, apple sauce, baked beans (cold), a slice of galley-baked bread…from last week.

After testing to demonstrate their Marine skills, they'd made it through the seven weeks of Boot and finally could proudly be called Marines. Sergeant Summons and Corporals Beck and Call celebrated with Platoon 276 at the slop chute trying to see who could guzzle the most beer, even if it was just

3.2. As a special treat, the NCOs had snuck in a couple of six packs of civilian 7 percent beer. Prejean shouted, "*Laissez les bon temps rouler!*"—Let the good times roll! They aptly listened to the NCOs beating their gums about service in foreign places, none good, but all memorable. There were more funny sea stories than gloomy ones. They felt like they'd been knighted with the NCOs' unspoken acceptance of them.

Summons had done duty across the sea as a gunner aboard a Special Service Squadron gunboat. "We called it the 'Banana Squadron.' We sailed in both the Atlantic and Pacific sides of South America and all over the Caribbean showing the Flag. We were the Department of State's and the United Fruit Company's strike-breakers…I mean army."

"So you were aboard in a ship's Marine detachment?"

"No, those Banana Squadron gunboats were smaller than destroyers even if they had four 6-inch guns. We marines were aboard for landing and boarding parties, but we had to take a swabbies' berth, so we got our sailor ratings in gunnery, signals, or boatswain's mates doing double-duty, battle damage drills too. Nothing to brag about. Those swabbies," he said, shaking his head. "At least we got good galley chow, slept in dry racks, drew sea pay, and rated free laundry." Summons hoisted a toast "to the ol' USS *Erie* and *Charleston*," adding, "I don't recall how many passages of the Panama Canal I made."

Summons was one of the Old Breed, the heart of the Corps—hard marching, hard charging, hard drinking, and a wealth of essential knowledge, like knowing where to get V.D. treatment in Havana, Cuba. "It was available at the *Servicio de Profilaxis Venérea, Compostela 178, teléfono M-3346*. It's open all day and night," Summons recalled.

Henrik now understood why the NCOs' little green Memorandum notepads were so important to them.

The platoon found out their two heartless corporals had been Fleet Reservists recalled to active duty in 1940 when Roosevelt declared the "limited emergency" with the war in Europe. As civilians, Corporal Beck had assembled hot water heaters, and Call was a delivery truck driver for Sears, Roebuck. He knew he'd be reassigned to a Fleet Marine Force unit someday and hoped to avoid "Motor T"—Motor Transport. "I'm not interested in driving a ton-and-a-halfer."

The men's training was far from over. On a Friday afternoon they received orders for specialty training. Platoon 276 was surprised they were totally broken up. It was a sad thing for most as they had formed a bond. They knew the strengths and weaknesses of each man, good, bad, or indifferent, who could be counted on and who might not be so reliable.

Now, 276 was dissolved, never to serve as a body again. They parted with wishes of good luck, exchanges of home addresses, and the hope that "Maybe we'll cross wakes somewhere 'round the world, brother."

Some received orders for the sprawling Camp Pendleton, over thirty miles north of San Diego, for training as artillerymen, engineers, motor transport, signals, and amphibian tractors. Most of the platoon went to the Infantry Training Battalion at Camp Elliott's 19,000 acres of rolling hills, ravines, and scrub brush. It would seem they ran and crawled up and down every one of those rocky hills. Camp Elliot was twelve miles northeast of Dago on dry, windy Kearney Mesa. Most troops were quartered in tent cities scattered about the unfinished training center. Besides infantry training, much of the 2d Marine Division was based there. The H-shaped wooden barracks were still being raised. They laid out their own weapon ranges as contractors worked on permanent facilities. Every day, bulldozers and road-graders changed the landscape.

Henrik discovered his future during the evening formation. He was to be a Rifleman, Specification Code Number 745.

One thing Sergeant Summons reminded those selected for infantry, "You're what the Marine Corps is about, the entire Corps is there to support you. Everything else is secondary."

Henrik was satisfied with that, until the sergeant said, "That doesn't mean you're not going to be shot to pieces on some bloody beach. But you've got enough sense that you might make it." He slapped him on the back with a laugh.

Great.

The unexpected part of infantry training was that they could mark their first and second choices for training: rifleman, BAR man, machine gunner, mortarman, or antitank gunner. All hands fired the different battalion weapons for familiarization and could disassemble and clean them. All of the riflemen and machine gunners learned the BAR.

Henrik wasn't given a choice. The classification officer matching up marines' qualifications for the needed positions told him that he would no doubt be assigned as a sniper once reaching his new unit. There were no telescoped rifles available for training. The few the Corps possessed were assigned to deploying units, mainly the 1st Marine Division at New River, North Carolina. "You'll probably be given one once you've shipped out. In the meantime, concentrate on your regular rifle marksmanship."

"Yes, sir."

He was assigned to a training company along with a half-dozen of Platoon 276 boys. He'd learned that it was a good thing to have a few familiar faces around. He was glad to see Griff on the roster.

On 9 April the Infantry Training Battalion's CO announced at the evening formation that 12,000 American and 63,000 Philippine armed forces had surrendered on Bataan Peninsula. Maybe a hundred marines were suspected to have remained on Bataan. The Philippines might have been American territory, but they were to be given their independence in 1946. Corregidor still held out with the 4th Marines defending the beaches.

They'd found out too that First Lady Eleanor Roosevelt's popular weekly radio show, *Over Our Coffee Cups*, was cancelled and that civilian coffee rationing had been cut in half.

A grim resolve hung over the classrooms, lecture areas, and training grounds. Few spoke of it except maybe two or three buddies walking down the company street or sitting on their footlockers spit-shining boondockers. Beneath the hushed tones lay a seething anger.

On the machine gun ranges the new gunners were taught to fire repeated ten-round bursts by shouting "Fire a ten-round burst" and rattled off the requisite ten rounds. Some imaginative gunner came up with the alternate, "Shoot down ten Nips."

The gloom lifted somewhat, even if temporarily, when on 18 April B-25 bombers led by Jimmy Doolittle raided Tokyo. President Roosevelt commented they had launched from Shangri-La, but that was a mystical Himalayan kingdom in some novel. No one cared to speculate that it was not exactly a massive air raid and didn't inflict much damage. Regardless, it was a morale boost for the US and a humiliation for Nippon and a Jap concern from where the bombers came.

Henrik's papa sent a birthday gift. Unpacking the oiled skin wrapping, he found a Marble's MR443 sheath knife, brown leather stacked grip, six-inch satin-finished tool steel blade, and a brass blade guard complete with a sharpening stone. One of the best reasonably priced knives made, it would go on his belt once they sailed into the Pacific.

The BAR was the squad's machine gun and intended to provide the squad's base of fire for the maneuvering riflemen. The almost four-foot long M1918A1 was eighteen and a half pounds, twice the weight of the Springfield. There was a folding bipod on the front end of the forearm. It could be fired semi-automatic or full-automatic in short bursts. One complaint was that the twenty-round magazine made it heavier and had to be changed too often to lay down steady covering fire. Plus, the Jap equivalent had a thirty-round magazine. The instructor said there was an improved M1918A2 version, but they hadn't reached the Fleet Marine Force yet, with them going to the Army.

Henrik and other prospective snipers spent most of their time on the KD range firing at ranges of up to 800 yards. They even fired at 1,200-yard targets, but it was rare to hit a man-sized silhouette without a telescope. The Springfield's regular sight was graduated to 2,750 yards. It wasn't possible to hit a man-sized target at that range other than by a freak of nature. That extreme range was a holdover from when massed formations fired long-range rifle barrages at the enemy. Machine guns made that concept outdated.

One of the BAR instructors wanted Henrik reassigned as a BAR man. Firing a BAR in short full-automatic bursts, Henrik, could knock down one- and two-man targets at a thousand yards. He had a recommendation from the company commander assigning him as a sniper to some future unit and avoid carrying a heavy BAR.

Camp Elliott was south of Camp Pendleton where construction was just gearing up. The nearest liberty town was Oceanside, which offered few amenities. There was the Ocean View House, a rather rowdy roadhouse, which Henrik avoided. He and others found the 101 Cafe on the Coastal Highway more to their liking. Not everyone was on skirt patrol. It didn't take long for landowners to bring in small house trailers and rent them to marines and their wives with deployed husbands at a less than reasonable price. More beer slops opened up with their endless open crap games.

To Henrik the 101 was an ideal place to chow down on a greasy burger—when gristly ground meat was available. The preferred brew was the Famous A.B.C. Beer brewed by Aztec Brewery down the street. Henrik had discovered hamburgers on his train trip to California. He agreed that it was the perfect American food, especially with fries and ketchup. If not, a hot dog filled the bill. One end of the cafe had extra chairs for relaxing marines. Most just wanted a break from Marine routine and wrote letters home, against the backdrop of the breathless surf surge from across the highway.

A couple of marines Henrik didn't know were talking about the port of San Diego having so many sailors' wives, and other services' wives, there were few places for them to live. Their husbands might not return for two or more years. In spite of the aircraft factories and other war-based industries and business, there weren't enough women's jobs. The lucky ones got jobs as "blue moons"—dime-a-dance girls. In spite of the winds of patriotism, the outsider women were often ignored and even hassled by locals. Rental apartments and trailers were scarce and exorbitantly expensive. Women were sleeping in hotel and movie theater lobbies, unlocked cars, and even huddled in phone booths. Service stations locked their restrooms overnight to keep out women in search of a place to sleep or to sell themselves. The two marines' nookie patrol plan was to cruise movie theater lobbies and accost streetwalkers in need of a bed. These two already had a motel room booked. He felt like mentioning this in the letter home he was penning. He decided not to. His parents could not even comprehend treating people that way.

***

Henrik had an urge for a long-lost taste of independence. Ever since donning Marine green he'd been in the company of other fellas in pickle suits, twenty-four hours a day. Ill-advised, he decided to strike out on his own. He figured a short foray out Gate 2 wouldn't hurt. Said gate was defined by a pair of black-and-white-striped guard huts.

"You going out solo, Mac?" questioned the MP.

Henrik handed over his liberty card. "Just a leg-stretcher. Down the road for a brew. I'll stay in sight of the gate, if that's okay, Mommy?"

"Smart ass." The MP gave his uniform a cursory look-over and returned the card. "Stay outta trouble, Mac."

"WILCO."

State Highway 305 was an asphalted, sand-covered road promenaded by a few pairs of gyrenes, likely with no more than two dimes between them. They too just needed to get out of the barracks. In the final weekend before the end-of-month payday, most marines were penny poor.

The road looked more like one of the shantytowns they passed coming to California. The shop fronts were plank-faced or tar-papered tin roofs. The most prosperous shops boasted boardwalks. Barbers, photographers, bakers, seamstresses, laundries, watch shops, pawn shops, payday loans, tobacco, and notions. Food and drink were the main draw—beer, cold sodas, burgers, sandwiches, soup, and chili. All were hole-in-the-wall establishments with a dusty, rundown, worn-out look. The eldest sagging shacks were just months old. A few old jalopies were parked on the rutted street and others in back. Marines passed the word on which were fair and who were crooks, their statuses changing with owners. Those labeled "honest" were not above gouging prices when they spied a sucker. Then there were the conmen, flimflam men. Henrik hadn't dealt with any but figured he knew enough to peg them. The "twenty percent men" worked the street, and you never went to the back with one of the hustlers where "payday loan deals" were concocted.

There were few such thugs hanging around now. The MPs ran them off and marine buddies, when one of their number was bilked, would hunt down the fraud and plant some warning knots on his head. They'd just turn up working the gates at other camps. The San Diego County Sheriff's Department seldom bothered with the unlicensed shops or the cons. Occasionally, they'd crack down on the pro-gamblers, loan sharks, bamboozlers, and hookers unless they got a piece of the action.

Buck's Burger Bar was reputed to be a decent joint.

"Ya out alone tonight, son?" asked the gray-bearded seemingly cheerful proprietor who may or may not have been "Buck."

"Yes sir, just grabbing some air outside a tent." He pulled a rickety stool to the open-air countertop.

"Missouri?"

"Sir?"

"Ya from Missouri, ain't ya?"

"I am. I guess you are too."

"Nope, I jus' got an ear for…dialects, I guess."

"Can you tell what part of a state someone hails from?"

"I ain't that well tuned, but I can tell ya ain't from St. Louie."

"You're right, sir. How about a cheeseburger, chips, and a brew?"

"I'm sad to report I can't help ya with a burger. The beef rationin' and all."

"It's that bad now?"

"Shore is. I could give ya a B.L.T. without the 'B'." He chuckled. "The bestest I can do is a Polish pork sausage on regular sliced bread. Got no cheese either unless ya like Mex goat cheese."

"That sounds real good. Beats chowhall grub. I need a change."

"We all do, son, we all do." Cackling, he opened a red eight-gallon Coca-Cola cooler, tonged out a sausage, slit it open, and heated it on a hotplate while smearing mustard and relish on slices of Wonder Bread. He set an A.B.C. Beer bottle on the counter extracted from the same cooler.

"Coolish tonight, ain't it?" Buck set a basket with a steaming Polish before him.

"It is, sir."

"Don't give me that 'sir' business, I was a petty officer." Henrik noticed he was wearing a black peacoat and watch cap.

"How come navy blue is really black on squid, I mean Navy, uniforms?"

"Oh, that's an easy one. 'Cause different blue-colored cloth fades unevenly."

The old codger was medically retired from the Navy. "I was a PO 2nd class, a special optical artificer."

"Wow, what kind of job is that?"

He laughed. "Nothin' fancy. I repaired telescopes, binos, rangefinders, compasses. The USS *Texas* was my home for eight years. The 'Mighty-T's' 'bout the oldest battlewagon in the Fleet now." He told some funny sea stories, one about how he reinserted the reversed lens in an ensign's bino. "I can still hear him sayin', 'that destroyer is as big as a battleship'." Buck slapped his thigh with a hacking laugh.

"I guess there were times you wanted out of that crowded tub to get some air."

"Ya wouldn't think a gent would get lonely in a crew of 1,200 souls." He paused, deep in thought. "But ya do." He winked. "Looks like somebody's lonely now."

"Not me," said Henrik, popping in a potato chip from the offered basket.

"Not ya. Her. How ya doin' tonight, Jo?"

"Oh, just lonely and a little cold is all."

Henrik turned on the stool to see a thin girl, her brunette hair victory-rolled, wearing a knee-length plaid skirt, pale red blouse, maroon sleeveless pullover sweater, and scuffed black and white saddle shoes with droopy yellow knee socks.

His first thought was, *She's kind of pretty, but sad, and she looks bushed.* "Hello," was all he could manage.

"Hello yourself, fella." She glanced anxiously from Henrik to Buck and back. "This here's Joanne."

"Friends call me Jo. What's your name?" she asked, almost shyly.

"Henrik."

"Have a sit, Jo," said Buck. "Ya looks cold-like, hon."

"I am cold, tired too." She wore a pair of old-style round eyeglasses. Dark circles underlined her brown eyes.

"I was goin' to say ya looks plume tuckered out, hon. Ya want a cup of java?"

"Thanks, Buck, I surely do." She laid a nickel on the counter.

"Let me get that for you," said Henrik. He'd finished the Polish—*Bratwurst,* Mama would have called it.

Buck poured a mug, spooned in a lot of rationed sugar, and slid the nickel back to her. "Us folks on the road here give Jo a hand here and there. She turns down handouts. Okay if I tell your story, Jo?"

"You always do, Buck." She sighed, propping her head on her arm.

"Jo's mom passed from this life three months 'fore Pearl Harbor. Died from consumption, what they call T.B. now. The other bad part is that Jo's dad is a petty officer 1st class assigned to the Asiatic Fleet in the Netherlands East Indies. He was aboard the cruiser *Houston* when she sunk on the 1st of March. They have no idea of what became of any survivors except that most, over a thousand souls, were lost in the…what is it, Jo?"

"Battle of Sunda Strait."

"I'm really sorry to hear that," Henrik whispered. "That's got to be hard to deal with. Your mom too." He'd never heard about the *Houston*'s loss. There was so much going on the war was like watching a three-ring circus, not that he'd even seen one.

Buck said, "I have to ice more beer for the crowd comin' through ahead of quarters-report time." He turned on a Sonora table model radio rendering Vera Lynn's "Yours."

She wrapped her chilled hands around the coffee mug. "It…it is hard, the not knowing part and the way they talk to me, the people at the base casualty office."

"How's that?" He noticed her eyeglasses' left lens was missing.

"Oh," she peered into her mug, "they say it might be months before they know anything. One clerk even told me they may never know with them sunk in the deep sea and the two ships with her sunk too. They don't know if the Japs picked up any survivors, slant-eyed bastards."

"That is sad," he said. "Where do you stay?"

"The shops here, they take turns putting me up. But I'm no parasite, I pay my way," she added, almost crossly. "Those clerks don't know what to do. Sent my 'Captured by the Enemy' Claim to the Navy Department, but not a peep."

"I didn't mean to say—"

"I know you didn't mean anything. It's okay. It's just not easy making a living this way. Everyone wants so much."

Henrik was confused and must have shown it. "What kind of living? People want what?"

"You are a country hick, Henrik, aren't you?" she said with a strained grin, cutting her eyes at him.

"Most likely," he admitted. She was kind of cute, even with her tired, tired eyes.

"You want to help? Let me show you something." She intertwined their fingers and led him around to the back. He was too confused to even question what was going on.

She yanked open the rear door of a gray 1935 Ford sedan. She fell onto the towel-covered backseat, hoisting up her skirt. "I may have my troubles, but I get by." She held up three fingers. "Don't you say anything and don't ask to write me. We'll both sleep better."

He noticed bruising next to her left ear.

***

Henrik wandered back to Gate 2 befuddled and bemused. Sad-happy was what they called such a conflicted state. *Or was it happy-sad?* Fog had moved in and they'd lit smudge pots to mark the gate. Presenting his liberty card, the bored MP said, "They're cracking down; make sure you visit the pro-station inside the guardhouse head. Sign for and use the pro-kit whether you need it or not. And don't piss on the deck; we gotta swab the head 'fore going off duty."

Henrik nodded, feeling peculiarly guilty, and headed to the "clap trap"— prophylactic station—for a prophylactic kit, a santitube of sanitizing cleanser, and a soap-impregnated towelette.

During Boot, a Navy medical officer had scared the bejeebers out of them with an explicit lecture and a graphic black-and-white film highlighting the horrors of V.D. infection. Some fellas swore they'd avoid all women, regardless of how "respectable" they appeared. Some even feared their saintly mothers and sisters now.

He realized that Buck's car was an arranged deal and in passing he wondered to what extent Buck was involved. That passing the nickel back and forth may have been a code. What the heck. It was hard times. Sure he was involved. What should he expect?

That's when the guilt hit him. He felt he'd somehow breached his parents' trust. It was just something he'd have to keep to himself. *Can I even be honest to myself?* he wondered. He simply couldn't bring himself to think of Jo, if that was her name, as a "victory girl." And then he remembered Karen. He felt like a total crudball. *I can never mention this to her.*

"Hey, Mac," said the MP, "they're showing us a mandatory movie tomorrow called *Reefer Madness*, ought to be a good one."

A movie about mad or maybe rabid refrigerators? What are they shoving on us next?

***

Henrik saw Jo on the street another evening. She was crossing the road, and although she squinted in his direction, she either didn't recognize him or she chose not to. Maybe the former; from a hundred feet he looked like any other pickle-suited marine. It didn't matter, he told himself. She was like so many other girls, on her own, no place to go. He realized that unknowingly he always had his family if he was ever in difficulty. He could count on them. He wondered if Jo had any family remaining. Were they far away? He knew nothing about her of course, but still felt sorry for her. He'd mentioned her to Griff.

"Don't get mixed up with a gal like that, pal. She's just another pick-up girl," he advised and probably wisely so.

On the seedier side, maybe that's what Jo wanted to do. He hoped not. Was she disowned by her family? Was she "owned" by a pimp? He'd never heard of that before—men selling girls and keeping most of the money for themselves. That seemed about as low and sleazy as one could go. Was Buck her pimp? He hoped not; he liked the old seadog. But it was hard times, he reminded himself again. He even found out that there were women pimping too.

"Three bucks a pop, Mac," an informed SP had advised, "Don't give a cuddle bunny two Tom-notes—two-dollar bills—and expect to get a buck back in change."

There was a bespectacled, straw hat-wearing flimflammer in a black suit with a clerical collar. Henrik knew he wasn't a Lutheran minister or a Catholic priest. Such crusaders were often street-corner preaching about sin and screaming that vice was destroying the town. Few cared; they weren't from Dago, just passing through and passing the hat.

A swabby met Jo at the crosswalk and they ambled up the boardwalk holding hands. She had a bandage on her chin. *They're probably headed for that old Ford.*

***

During a weekend pass a beat-up 1930 blue Chevrolet Club Sedan pulled into the 101 Cafe's trifling parking lot. Dark shapes emerged and stalked toward the door. Late-working businessmen were about the only automobile travelers in the evening hours. Military vehicles weren't permitted to stop at civilian businesses.

The door opened with a bell's jingle and in stepped three, well, at first Henrik didn't know what to make of them. Then he realized he was getting an introductory look at zoot-suiters. So they were for real. He'd thought the fellas telling him about them were just pulling this farm boy's leg. Henrik had heard of zoot-suiters, but he secretly thought that they were a gag, like snipe hunting.

The three Mexican boys were indeed bizarre, even more so than he'd been told. Everything was exaggerated. The dark coats reached almost to their knees, with broad flared lapels and over-padded shoulders. Their pants were voluminous but pegged tightly at the ankles, sprouting patent leather pointed-toe shoes. Long watch chains drooped to their knees. They were crowned by silly, exceptionally broad-brimmed felt fedoras set on thick slicked-back hair. Henrik barely kept from bursting out laughing as he imagined Corporals Beck and Call inspecting the zooters. *"Straighten that gig line, Poncho. Lock your heels, puke. Take up the slack in that watch chain. Ain't you got any pride?"*

Henrik could see the three boys were as surprised to see Marine uniforms as the gyrenes were to see the outlandish zooters. Henrik didn't understand what they were about other than that the trend started in New York and had taken hold in Los Angeles. Many dodged the draft and there was a petty criminal element. A complaint was that their excessive clothing wasted certain fabrics, which was being rationed.

"What brings you *pachocos* to these parts?" said a brawny marine heaving to his feet and slamming down his brown bottle.

"We don want no troubles, *señor*...sir. We jus' lookin' for open petro station."

Henrik knew that "I don't want any trouble" was the worst thing to say to a sozzled drunk looking for trouble. You'd surely serve it to him.

"Well, you're lookin' in the wrong place, greaser."

"That's okay," spoke up the elderly cafe owner doubling as waiter, it being a weeknight. Pointing, he said, "There's a Union Oil station two miles up the road, boys. If you hurry it'll still be open."

"Yeah, hit the road, spic-boy. We don't need your kind joyridin' and partyin' while we work our butts off defendin' the country. You punks shove off before you get de-zooted." He laughed at his own attempted joke. No one else got it.

The apparent leader turned to the marine. "Hey, *vato*! We takin' my cuz to San Diego for a job he got at Republic Aviation."

"Why ain't the rest of ya'll dirt bags workin' or in the Army or somethin'?" He'd said "Army" deliberately, implying they weren't fit for the Marines.

Henrik knew this was getting out of hand. Glancing at the increasingly nervous owner, Mr. Feldman, he could see that the man had no idea how to stop what was coming—the resultant flying fists and furniture, property damage, Shore Patrol, and the Oceanside Police.

The zooters were balling up angry fists and the marines rose from their chairs. The zooters were outnumbered and out-brawned. Zooters were known to carry switchblades or straight razors and most marines had pocketknives.

Suddenly Henrik felt impelled to act. This was so pointless and would lead only to trouble and expenses for one and all. The local hoosegow too, until the duty NCO sprung them from jail and tossed them straight into the brig resplendent with punk and piss. Keeping his voice even but firm like Sergeant Summons, he said, "I'm sure Mr. Feldman would appreciate if we were to take this outside."

With a look of relief the proprietor exclaimed, "I'd appreciate that boys. Just had the place fixed up after last weekend's scuffles."

Henrik stepped over to open the door, sweeping his arm toward it. "Beauty before age," he said, flashing a smile.

The three zooters glared, tried to look tough, and filed out the door. The mouthy marine and his buddies headed for the door after them. Henrik shoved it shut and threw the bolt.

"Hey, what's this, pogue?"

"Let it go, Mac," said Henrik, looking him in the eye, "or would you rather do a week in the brig on punk and piss?"

"He's right boys," said Feldman. "Don't make any trouble for yourselves and end up on bread and water."

Obviously embarrassed, the flustered gyrenes reclaimed their chairs, grumbling. "We coulda kicked those greasers' asses."

They heard the car start up in the lot and gun south on the highway.

They left early, allowing time to walk back to Camp Elliott in case they couldn't hitch a friendly ride. Mr. Feldman clasped Henrik's hand. "That was a mighty smart move, son."

Henrik shrugged. "I just didn't want to put up with SPs tonight."

"Your coffee's on the house from now on."

***

> Miss Karen R. Hathaway
> 830 W. 5th. St.
> Washington, Mo.
>
> February 18, 1942
> Pvt Henrik C. Hahnemann
> S/N …………..

Platoon 276
Marine Corps Recruit Depot
San Diego, Calif.

Dear Henrik,

I so hope this finds you well and in good spirits. I have wanted to tell you about how things are going here with the war. It's affected everyone and everything. We're supposed to report people taking pictures. We do air raid drills at school and they put a siren on the water tower that's tested every Friday at noon, so frightening. People run out when they hear an airplane now. They're going to start rationing gasoline and we're supposed to drive no faster than 35 m.p.h., the Victory Speed they call it.

But that's not what I need to talk to you about. Henrik, I'm scared and I don't know what's going to happen. I'm sorry; we're not supposed to talk like that. We're supposed to tell our servicemen that everything's fine at home. Henrik, things aren't fine. They say this war will be long and we all have to make sacrifices. There's so much uncertainly. It makes me ill to say this, but I'm so afraid you may not come home. I know that's a terrible thing to say and I pray every night that you will make it home. I'm just so afraid of not knowing, not knowing where you are, what may be happening to you, and if you're safe.

We've been good friends and I enjoyed running into you at all those fairs we went to. That was always a surprise. The fairs were great fun, but they're cancelled now. Henrik, I have a new friend who takes me to the movies. More people are going now for the newsreels. I think you know Clarence Baily. He says he will not be drafted because he's in some special category called 4-F. We're just friends like you and I used to be and I hope we can still be friends.

I hope you'll still write if you want.

Your friend with best wishes,
Karen

P.S. Mom says hi and the Washington Blue Jays beat the Marthasville Bull Dogs last Friday.

Three times Henrik started to reply. He never finished one. He appeased himself when he recognized the striking blonde was just another pogue.

***

There was too much to do. He had to put Karen out of his mind, but no matter how hard he tried to forget her, she still popped up.

Some of the boots tacked their Dear John letters on the company bulletin board and the drill instructors voted for the best one. They bought the winner a consoling six-pack. Henrik couldn't do that. Replaced by a "4-F," how mortifying. *Yep, she's a pogue.*

Besides weapons training there were squad tactics in the defense and offense, plus patrolling. Of course, forced marches on the beaches and hills could be counted on. They'd be sucking air through every orifice.

"I thought I'd spend more time on ships than on my boots," groused one boot. The platoon was fast marching down the beach.

"Quit your beefing, brother. Lucky you ain't a squid. You can walk further than you can swim," observed a foot-lagging boot. Regardless of sore feet, they all kept up.

"I never got blisters swimming."

"No, just shark bites."

"Do sharks have a favorite 'tween swabbies and gyrenes?"

"Gyrenes, we're saltier."

"Quit your yapping, you meathead clods," bellowed the sergeant. "Or would you like for me to march you through a foot of surf instead of this nice soft sand?" The damp sand was like packed asphalt.

"The surf might cool our boondockers, sarge."

"Shut up clowns or we'll all be—" started someone in the rear ranks.

"Pla-toon, halt. Left, face. Port, arms."

They faced the Pacific Ocean from the surf's strand, rifles held before them.

"Double arm interval. Dress right, dress. Six paces forward. Forward, march. Pla-toon, halt."

With the platoon standing in a foot of surf, he shouted, "Drop and give me twenty-five."

***

When not on the ranges they breached tangled barbed wire, dug foxholes, and ran obstacle courses. They broke windows in nearby homes while setting off demolition charges, improvised rope bridges and swayed across them, camouflaged anything and everything, bruised their shoulders with more rifle firing, and learned the difference between cover and concealment, and always the police calls. Protection from gas warfare was taught and how to use and care for silly looking Navy gasmasks—"torture hats"—bag on their left side now.

They practiced first aid and black-eyed one another in hand-to-hand fighting. The sergeant cautioned, "You've learned just enough hand-to-hand to go to an Oceanside slop joint and get the crap beat out of you by some solider boy Coast Artillery shell-shoveler."

They looked forward to landing training. "Debarkation Drill," they called it. A real boat ride followed by charging across a beach pretend-shooting Japs. They just didn't know they would do it half a dozen times before breakfast. A cargo pier rose twenty feet above the water. Hanging off the high pier were rope cargo nets reaching water level. They marched up the pier and watched over the side as two corporals nimbly scampered down the net into a ship's thirty-six-foot longboat.

"Those new Higgins boats with bow ramps you see in newsreels are going to troop transports. They're not available for our training."

The sergeant narrated as the corporals surefootedly descended the net. "When you go over the side make sure you're keeping yourself balanced with the weight of your pack and weapon. You'll go over four men at a time. It's not a race. Stay even with each other and don't stop because the cuss above can't see you. Grip only the vertical ropes so the man above you won't step on your paws. There are two men at the net's bottom controlling it and pulling it away from the boat's side. The boat's going to be bobbing like a cork, not just up and down, but sideways and stem-to-stern. The net handlers will tell you when to dismount the net. Listen to them. At sea a boat can bob six to eight feet and the ship too is bobbing on its own."

The first couple of times they went over the side was without packs and rifles. Then they climbed back aboard another net. It wasn't any easier climbing up. Next they donned packs and slung rifles.

"If you drop a rifle you'll be diving for it until you bring it up dead or alive," said the sergeant.

"Me or the rifle?" quipped a boot.

"Makes no difference to me. Drop."

Like most of the others, Henrik had his hands stepped on. Eight men fell, resulting in a broken ankle, a fractured collarbone, and numerous bumps and bruises. Three went into the drink. No one drowned, and they would have died before letting go of their rifles. "Your parents would have to pay for that rifle even if your funeral's courtesy of Uncle Sugar."

Later, the tangled boatload of troops long-boated to a beach and piled over the sides for a cold Pacific waters soaking. Then they got to run across the beach with fixed bayonets, yelling, "Bang, bang," "Ratta-tat-tat," and "Take that ya Nip bastards." They flung rocks for grenades, invariably deteriorating into rock fights. The battle ended when the signs identifying "Pillboxes" were stormed, followed by a forced march back to the pier to do it again.

That didn't keep a boastful marine from observing, "Damn, a Girl Scout troop could've made the landing we just did!"

***

Graduation day finally arrived. They were Marines and received their billet assignments. The word was that most would be going to the 2d Marine Division, the "Silent Second," or as other marines called them, the "Hollywood Marines."

"Ignore that jab," said one of the noncoms. "They're jealous. It was actually the old 20th Marine Reserve Battalion in Los Angeles which posed as war movie extras before they were called up in '39. No, they didn't wear sunglasses like those pussies at Parris Island think. Besides, Hollywood's over a hundred miles from Dago."

Henrik learned his fate, finding his name on a mimeographed roster with a couple of hundred names. He was surprised by the alternate specialty code.

Hahnemann, Henrik C.   S/N ...   Pvt Grade 7   Spec 745 Rifleman
                                  Alternate   Spec 761 Scout-Sniper

Henrik was assigned to the 2d Marines, the Corps' oldest regiment, itself part of the 2d Marine Division now residing at Camp Elliott, California, just up the road.

A lieutenant lecturing on the regiment's history said, "It was raised in 1913 as the 1st Advance Base Regiment but was renamed the 2d Regiment in 1916. Don't ask me why, that's the Corps for you. But it's still the oldest regiment."

The scoop was that the regiment had orders for "duty beyond the seas." They were going somewhere and it likely wasn't Hollywood.

In the base God box the Navy lieutenant commander chaplain after Mass advised, "You boys scheduled for deployment, I strongly urge you find a different entertainment than pursuing our chaste and not so chaste maidens."

This drew some chuckles.

"Yes, I see some guilty faces out there. I'm available for Holy Absolution the rest of the afternoon. Seriously, I do urge you to refrain. You do not wish to find yourself aboard a troop ship enroute to a war inflected with that revolting Russian disease, *rot-yer-crotch-off*."

Chapter Ten

Hakko Ichiu
Putting all the eight corners of the world under one roof.
(The "one roof" being Nippon.)
Tanaka Chigaku (ultra nationalist)
1940, but the concept evolved earlier

After graduating the Second Period Examination and demonstrating their advanced skills, the troops were confined to barracks. They worked to clean anything and everything, even cleaning bits of grit in floor corners. This was followed by spotlessly cleaning the latrines and washrooms. There were occasional details outside the barracks to clean outbuildings and stables, groom the packhorses, plus clean their pack saddles and leather equipment. They even cleaned the coal bins and stacked the coal chunks according to size.

Meals were minimal—rice and some fish. No other meat, few vegetables. The *Imperial Rescript to Soldiers and Sailors* was read daily.

One line in particular gripped Obata: "*Whether We are able to guard the Empire, and so prove Ourself worthy of Heaven's blessings and repay the benevolence of Our Ancestors, depends upon the faithful discharge of your duties as soldiers and sailors.*"

One day they drew their rifles and meticulously cleaned them. Obata's rifle was inspected three times before the armorer accepted it. The next day a dozen civilian artificers arrived and went to work in the armory with tools and gauges. Soldiers detailed to help them reported they disassembled each rifle, quickly inspected each part, and reassembled them after replacing worn parts.

One soldier detailed to help the artificers said, "I have never seen anyone disassemble a rifle as quickly as those old men."

"They were riflemen before your mother met your father. They probably fought Russians at the siege of Port Arthur."

"You are a mere child. Your parents met ten years ago."

"Port Arthur was in 1904," reminded Number Six.

"We taught the Russians to respect the Empire, the first Asian empire to defeat a European army and navy, the Russo-Japanese War."

"To help secure our domination of Manchuria and Korea," parroted Number Nine.

"It makes no difference," said Number Three. "The artificers refurbishing our rifles can only mean we are being sent to war, somewhere."

"That is no surprise. It is our duty. We are surrounded by enemies."

"My cousin in the 2nd Company says he heard Malaya."

"It could be anyplace in this war. It might be someplace we have never heard of."

"We are not to speak of unit deployments. They are a military secret and we could be punished for talking about it."

"What difference does it make? We are only speculating and do not really know."

"It makes no difference," said Number Six. "If someone hears us talking about deploying, reports us, and one of the places we talked about is actually where we are going, we could be arrested and interrogated by the *Kenpeitai*—Military Police."

***

After two more days of make-work jobs, almost 200 soldiers from a different garrison arrived in the late morning. The unit's packhorses were turned out on the parade ground. Veterinary officers inspected each and every animal. A few were quarantined to one side.

"They will be shot on the rifle range and sold to butchers in town," remarked Number Nine. "With the scarcity of meat, the townspeople will be appreciative."

"You should not talk like that," muttered Number Six.

One of the corporals ordered them to again clean out the stalls. "Make them fit for your grandmother to sleep in."

"Which grandmother?"

"The one who looks like a horse."

No one was sad to see the horses go. They required a great deal of work—grooming and feeding them, caring for their tack, shoeing them, exercising them, and mucking out their stables.

They worked at it most of the night. The corporal finally gave his approval, mostly as he was ready for some sleep. As he departed, he ordered them to, "Wash your uniforms and clean the washtubs and troughs."

"When we deploy, I wonder if they will keep us together?" said Number Six.

"I hope so," said Obata. "We work well as a group."

The section all agreed. "We serve the Emperor."

"We are most certainly deploying. It is not China or Manchuria," Number Six speculated. "I do not know if all those strange lands in the Southern Resource Zone are good for packhorses. It is terribly hot and often wet in the south and they have poor roads, I understand."

"It is winter."

"Not below the Equator."

***

Passes were allowed in the evenings and sometimes on weekends. Movies and newsreels were popular, but there were no new movies of any kind. Most were recent war movies or films glorifying ancient battles and heroes. They learned only one studio was allowed to produce movies and was closely supervised by the Ministry of Education. The rumor was that they were now producing movies reflecting the new war, but it would be some time before they were released.

That weekend the troops were granted a pass into town to include overnight. This led to further rumors that they were indeed soon deploying.

This was the first time Obata was able to visit home.

It was a pleasant visit and especially meant much to his mother. He thought she felt uncomfortable seeing him in uniform. Unfortunately, he was not permitted to wear any civilian clothes. When indoors he removed his tunic and wore only his white undershirt, soothing his mother. He did not mention the possibility of overseas deployment. Once he mentioned that he had a good rifle shooting score. Both his mother's and father's sadness caused him to change the subject. Instead, he talked about silly things some of his comrades did when washing clothes and trying to cook in the field, which always resulted in burnt, gooey rice balls. His mother laughed at the antics, covering her mouth. The next day she taught him the proper way to cook rice with soybean oil in a small pot similar to the one in his mess kit.

"Always use brown unpolished rice if you can. It is more nutritious than polished white rice. They use the white because it can be preserved longer. The Navy eats barley instead of the Army's less nutritious white rice."

On barracks kitchen duty he had managed to sneak out a couple tins of pickled plums and a package of dried seaweed and red beans, which he presented to his mother. She treasured them. She proudly showed him her tiny spice and vegetable gardens. She had prepared for the winter planting field peas and clover to protect the vulnerable seeds and bulbs.

Mother said, "Many people remain at home at night now. That means there are fewer people hit by cars. Just last week though one of the air raid wardens on a bicycle street patrol was run over by a policeman on horseback."

Father added with quiet laughter, "They got in a fight and caused more injuries to themselves than their collision. The horse was not injured." He winked playfully.

Uncle Asahi visited and brought a five-kilogram bonito for dinner. "Is training as difficult as they say, Yoshiro?"

"It is not easy, and they are very hard on us for all mistakes, even small things. The most difficult part is not knowing what we will be doing next, the constant cleaning, and the forced marches, every other day."

He laughed. "I always told you that your life at sea would toughen you. You are not one of those weak schoolboys."

Bowing, Obata replied, "I appreciate what you taught me, Uncle. It did make my way less difficult. Even though I am a soldier hoping never to be out of sight of land, I learned much aboard your boat that has helped me."

"Such as?"

"I learned that hard work toughens your spirit and resolve and that exposure to brutal weather hardens you physically and spiritually." He glanced at his uncle. "The knots and rope rigging you taught me are extremely valuable."

"Do not be embarrassed, but you are the hardest working of my nephews."

"Did you find a replacement for Isamu?"

"Yes, I found a boy, but he is Class B-3 physically unfit for military duty, which means he is barely useful as a deckhand. He is all I could find. The big fishing companies can pay good men better than I."

His father could feel that Obata would soon be departing. "You are wise not to have mentioned to your mother that you are leaving. It will be hard on her when she finds out."

"It worries me too, Father. I do not know of an easy way to tell her."

"Do you know when this will be?"

"I do not, but soon."

"Let me know if you can."

"I will, Father. I heard that once we are ordered to deploy, we will be confined to the barracks and not permitted to tell anyone, including our families."

"Will you be able to write?"

"Yes, even our sergeants who fought in China said they could write home and receive mail and even food parcels."

"I will certainly tell your mother to send such parcels."

He did not say anything, but he would not ask that, knowing there were food shortages and rising prices.

They spoke of the increase in business with the war. Father's firm was making more fishing floats and certain rope items, especially heavy-duty cargo nets.

"You may come home to a wealthy family, Yoshiro," he laughed. "So long as the Empire continues to face enemies who run when victorious Japanese soldiers boldly approach."

"I will pray for our prosperity at the first Shinto shrine I can find."

"Speaking of the factory, I have had to go to the prefecture military affairs clerk and ask for work exemptions. Even though I have hired six more men, they are not experienced. I have lost two experienced workers who cannot be replaced. The Imperial Army had greater need."

"Father, those small special glass spheres; are you still producing them?"

"Yes, we are. In fact, we received another order from the Army for…well, a great many."

"You still do not know what they are for?"

"I have no idea. The more I think about my idea that they are grenades to blast glass shards at the enemy, the more I agree with you that such an idea is not very practical."

***

Obata also spent time with his sister, Fumiko, when on pass. Being ten years old she could not understand why he had to live away from home. "Do you have new friends?"

They played some card rounds of Trump—*baba-nuki*. He was surprised he could remember the rules as it had been so long since he had played it.

Fumiko proudly showed Obata her rectangular *hagoita* paddle used in *hanetsuki*. Girls would pair up and each had a "bird" made of soapberry seeds and bird feathers. They would both chant a song as they bounced the bird straight up to swat it again and again. The first one to miss the bouncing bird lost and they started over. The game was traditionally played during New Year, but they continued to play it for weeks afterwards. The paddles were works of art, being painted with colorful birds, women in kimonos, *kabuki* actors, and flowers. Hers displayed a noble black, brown, gray, and orange whistling tree duck. Father must have paid handsomely for it. Mother quietly hinted that Father spoiled Fumiko when he could afford to. Girls of wealthy families collected the hagoita paddles and displayed them on their rooms' walls.

Holding her hands, Fumiko became teary-eyed. "I am so afraid of what will happen to all of us," she said, her eyes pleading for him to encourage her that they would all be safe. "I do not know what they are, but I hear people say the bombers will come and kill us."

He smiled, trying to lighten the mood. "Our soldiers and sailors will protect you. Our airplanes will keep the enemy at bay." He wanted to tell her they were winning the war and had won many victories. He could not think of a way to better reassure her. He had saved the rice paper wrapped caramels for her that came in some of their field rations.

Before he left, Obata's mother gave him a small Rising Sun flag—*hinomaru yosegaki*—on which their relatives, friends, and co-workers had inked their names, wishing him victory, safety, and good fortune. It reminded him they were thinking of him. He would cherish it dearly. He would wear it around his waist with the belt of a thousand stitches.

Father walked with Obata to the railroad station. Turning to his son, he said, "You look fine in the uniform. We will pray for you daily. We hope that your coming travels will be safe and hope what we have taught you at home will make you a strong and honest soldier."

They bowed and gripped hands before Obata boarded the train. "Be safe and strong."

***

The lieutenant standing on a small platform addressed the companies formed up on the parade ground. The Sun had not yet rose over the barracks.

"Attention to orders. All soldiers assigned to the II Battalion of Deployment Draft 4421 are to pack all clothing and equipment followed by an additional uniform issue." He snapped his leather folder shut and began shouting orders to the different section leaders.

There was barely enough space in the backpack, tube pack, haversack, and all the items attached to the belt. They had to lash their two blankets onto their backpacks.

The section formed up outside without knowing if they would ever see these barracks again. They marched to the quartermaster warehouse and filed inside with their equipment and rifles. They were issued two sets of dark green cotton uniforms. Word spread they were tropical uniforms. They were lighter weight than the olive drab summer uniform. There were buttoned slit openings on the sides behind the arms and the loose sleeves were three-quarter length. They also received green field caps with yellow five-pointed stars on the front as their other cap, and two paper-wrapped packages that fitted into a left inside tunic pocket. These were a gauze compress bandage with tie-tapes and a triangular bandage.

An officer appeared and inspected them in formation, interested in only three items: their identity tags, pay record book, and in ensuring their rifles were unloaded. An accompanying corporal tore off a piece of paper tape with "4421" inked on it and said, "Write your regimental number above the draft number and stick it above your left chest pocket."

Eventually they were told to stand-down and were permitted to sit on the parade ground. New recruits came around bearing large food serving trays with cold rice balls, cold tea, and colder soy sauce. Each man was given a *Morinaga* milk caramel candy.

There was little talk. Besides corporals walking about ordering men to be silent, they were still in a state of surprised muteness. All the past speculation seemed hollow.

After noon they were ordered to their feet. An exalted seldom seen captain marched to the platform. In a deep, serious voice he read the regulations related to desertion. Punishment was six months to seven years, and in wartime a deserter was certain to be sentenced with the longest confinement and in a labor unit. Laborers were needed for Manchurian coalmines.

They soon formed into a column of platoons and marched to the barracks' main gate, where a line of brown Nagoya Motorbus Company sightseeing buses awaited. Loaded on the Chevrolet buses, they were driven to the railroad station and embarked quickly onto a passenger train, the officers ordering them not to speak to anyone not in uniform. Once aboard, they found the window shutters and curtains closed, and were firmly told not to open them. After they had accounted for their rifles, checking serial numbers, they sat for a couple of hours. Regardless of their being confused and not knowing their destination, card games broke out and the rattle of dice in *chō-han bakuchi* bamboo cups was heard. Quiet talk and speculation was renewed. More cold rice balls were served in the late afternoon—no soy sauce. Just some sea salt.

As darkness draped over the city there was clanging and thumping as the train started up, their journey punctuated by stops and starts until speed gradually increased. Men peeked through the curtains, but there was little to see as they passed blacked out cities and towns.

Corporals periodically walked through the cars. "Do not open the curtains," they warned. "American planes can see the specks of light and attack our moving train. Do not use the water closets when we pass through towns."

It was an eerie feeling, the rushing clicking sounds as they sped through the darkened somber land. All that was known was they were heading east.

Obata realized he was further from home than ever before. Even aboard the fishing boat he had been closer to home. He regretted he being unable to see the countryside. At dawn the faint light revealed forested hills to the west. They passed through more towns, their name signs covered with woven mats or pasted with newspapers. Someone mentioned this was to confuse invaders. That led to anxious discussion about whether the country was in danger of invasion. They could not be, according to the endless reports of victories in the Southern Resource Zone.

They rolled into a busy city, which was soon identified as Hiroshima. It was 400 kilometers back to Nagoya. Obata wondered when he would be able to write his family or even if they would allow them to tell their families where they were. They were shuttled through railyards full of complete trains and scattered rolling stock on sidings. They soon found themselves on such a siding. The water closets were quite smelly by this time and many of the men were grouchy. Ten men at a time were allowed out of each car for ten minutes to stretch and run in-place in military formation. More cold rice balls were passed out. This time the tea was hot and even accompanied by some sugar. There were even peas in the rice balls, leading the men to think it must be a special occasion.

Noticing the absence of sergeants and corporals, some bold soldiers climbed atop a passenger car to get a better view of the surroundings. They shouted down that there was a great harbor filled with ships, mostly cargo ships, and a few warships.

"Are they ours?" one man shouted back with a laugh.

"You are foolish for saying that. Quiet, for your own good."

***

In the afternoon they were ordered back into the coaches, where every man was checked off on the rosters and rifles again were counted. The train backed down a track, passing through a pitiable workers' neighborhood. Weary laborers on the street filthy with coal dust or oil stains mostly ignored the soldiers. So did dirty children who had probably never worn a school uniform. They rolled into a sprawling area of great brick warehouses before stopping with brake wheels squealing, the clatter of couplings, and a screaming whistle.

Everyone knew to ready their equipment and prepare to disembark. None had much desire to remain aboard any longer. Some were even excited by the prospect of boarding a ship. "It could be no worse than on this endless noisy train ride," declared a young soldier.

A corporal entered the coach and all heads turned toward him, expecting an order to disembark.

Instead, swatting his crop against his leg, he shouted, "You will be disembarking, but it may be a long wait. Be patient. Keep your equipment ready and do not remove the paper tag on your chest. Raise your hand if yours is missing."

No hands rose.

"You will be fed a good meal after disembarking. Tonight, you may sleep on a warehouse deck or you may sleep aboard your ship. There will always be delays."

One man said he knew Hiroshima was the headquarters and departure port for the Army's Shipping Engineer Service. Few knew that the Army operated troop transports and cargo ships, usually contracted merchant ships. Navy officers sometimes commanded the ships.

Much to their surprise, in half an hour a sergeant entered. "Load your equipment. Make certain you leave nothing behind. Check your paper tags. You will march into a nearby warehouse for a meal. Eat fast. You will immediately embark a ship. Do not ask where this ship is bound. Do not speak to workers, other soldiers, or sailors—especially sailors, they are liars and untrustworthy. They do not even know to where or when their ship is sailing."

The dim warehouse was dusty; rice dust it appeared, with heaps of torn and mostly empty burlap rice sacks.

"Maybe they will tell us our destination after we depart," reasoned one man. "There is no one for us to tell since we will be far from land."

Said another, "My cousin was in the Imperial Navy, and he said they were never told their destination until they arrived. He said they were afraid that if a submarine sank them, survivors might be picked up and forced to reveal their convoy's destination."

A horse cart arrived with an old man and three girls. Two corporals shouted the men into a file and kept them moving past the cart. From its open back the unsmiling girls passed out paper sacks of rice, dried crab and seaweed, and miso sauce. While the cold meal was barely palatable, the miso—fermented soybean paste—was quite good. The bottles of cider were a pleasant surprise too. They were warned to turn in the bottles and not break any.

Several men managed to obtain a second food sack, and Obata thought that might be a good idea. One thing he had learned was that meals could not be counted on, nor much of anything else. He fell into the line and was given a second sack and cider bottle. Several of the boys jokingly accused him of stealing from the Emperor.

"I am only ensuring that I can maintain my energy to serve the Emperor."

They were soon marching up a cobblestone street, anticipating the sight of their ship. It was true what the man had reported when he climbed to the warehouse roof. The harbor was full of blue-gray ships moored in the bay or docked alongside wharves. Black smoke wafted from stacks, meaning they were raising steam for departure. The only warships Obata could see were some destroyers further toward the harbor's mouth. An occasional airplane passed over the harbor.

The activity was intense, with launches and barges shuttling between ships and shore. Some of the ships were repositioning as troops and cargo embarked. Troop formations marched up the wharves to ascend gangways. Pallets of crates and nets holding sacks and crates of supplies were hoisted by the ships' derricks and cranes ashore. Some artillery pieces were being slung aboard. Swarms of coolies, mostly Formosans and Koreans, stripped down to breechcloths or trousers carried bags and cartons up gangways.

As they marched onto the wharf a 7.5cm antiaircraft gun was seen in a sandbagged emplacement. Its navy-uniformed crew was tracking a distant patrol airplane for practice.

One man said of the gun, "That is the first thing I have seen that says we are at war."

"Except for the blackouts, the increased cost of whores, and shortages of everything else," another man quipped to draw laughs.

A man shouted at the gunners, "Take care to not shoot down our airplanes, sailor boys."

"We have yet to hit one," replied a gunner. "They sent us the wrong ammunition."

"It is a good thing," said another. "We fear we might hit the whorehouse."

"Which one?"

"To war we go, comrade sailors," said one of their recalled reservists.

"Without gasmasks, *Rikusan*?" said a sailor.

Everyone looked at each other. They quickly made it clear that they did not like to be called that by sailors, *Rikusan*—Mr. Soldier.

"He is right," said the man behind Obata. He remembered the hated gasmask drills in school; they had received none in the Army. He remembered seeing soldiers carrying gasmasks in the movies and newsreels.

The men gawked at the size of the transport ship. Even though most of the troops were from the Nagoya area, few had actually been close to a large ship, due to restrictions on entering the port.

Obata was surprised at how many troops marched onto the wharf—maybe 800. Four gangways led up the doorway-sized hatches with a number over each one. Crewmen in white working outfits or dark blue uniforms lined the deck, looking back at the soldiers. On the stern was painted *PERTH MARU*.

"Is Perth not an Australian city?" asked a soldier recovering from seasickness.

"Yes, on the southwest Australian coast."

"All Australian cities are on the coast," said a former fisherman. Sailors were readying to lower themselves over the stern to paint over the name.

"Why then?"

"Many Japanese cargo-passenger ships are named after foreign countries and seaports as a sign of goodwill since the Empire has or had trade agreements with them."

"*Maru* means what?"

Many Japanese did not understand its meaning, Obata thought. "*Hakudo Maru* was a celestial being who came to Earth and taught humans to build ships. Maru is another name for a circle, something strong and perfect, to protect sailors."

"Does that perfection safeguard the soldiers on board with the sailors?"

"Probably not. The Navy is selfish."

"Warships are not called Maru," said another man.

A Navy and an Army officer approached their group, some 200 men at Gangway One. The Navy officer's rank was unknown, as the insignia on his shoulders was much different than the Army lieutenant's. They did not announce themselves as was common.

He read off a clipboard an endless list of regulations: No lights or smoking on deck day or night, throw nothing overboard, which hatches to keep open and closed, no talking to working sailors, prohibited deck areas and compartments, when meals were served, and on and on. When general quarters sounded or the air raid or submarine-sighting siren blared, they would go to their bunks and remain until the all clear sounded or the order was given to abandon ship. There were uncomfortable covert glances among them, especially from those quartered deep in the hull. Life vests were worn when on deck but not below.

The Army lieutenant ordered, "Ensure your weapon is unloaded, your shipping tag is on your left chest, and remember your regimental number. You will pick up a five-kilogram bag of rice at the bottom of the gangway." He pointed at a pallet piled with rice straw bags. "Drop it off where a sailor tells you. Another sailor will lead you to your company's berthing compartment."

As they trudged up the gangway there was whispering.

"Why can we not wear life vests below deck?"

"It is too crowed in the narrow companionways."

"If the ship is sinking, you will not have time to reach the main deck anyway."

"Did anyone notice there are only two lifeboats?"

"For the officers. They must survive to report their victory."

The rice bag was an annoyance with all the equipment and baggage they carried. After entering the hatch, they dropped the bags, and their boarding number was checked off. Their forward compartment was one level below the weather deck—the main deck exposed to the outside. The berths were two levels of wooden shelves; one on the deck, and just over a meter above it was the second set of shelves with its own meter of clearance below the overhead weather deck. There was space for three men on each platform. They would sleep on woven mats plus their blankets. These berthing compartments were built around the holds filled with cargo that had just completed loading. Gangs of sailors were laying planks over the holds, tarring the seams, and battening them down by stretching canvas tarpaulins. Hot tar dripped through the plank seams, making a mess on their equipment. In the cramped quarters they had to find space to stow their weapons and equipment. They waited in the partial darkness, listening to the sounds of the other companies boarding, the shouted orders, the vibrations of auxiliary motors, and the hiss of boilers. Darkness fell. Some men talked and others tried to read.

A sailor came through with a flashlight. "We will sail in an hour with the tide."

"What does that mean?"

The talkative sailor said, "As the high tide goes out, its current will carry the ship into the bay. It uses less fuel."

"Is it safe in the dark to sail out with all these ships around to run into?"

"The ships will depart in a certain order, and once in the bay they will form into a convoy with each ship in its assigned place. They have running lights so they can avoid one another. Also at night it is impossible for enemy submarines to count the ships against the land's backdrop."

That sounded ominous. "Are there American and British submarines near?"

"Probably not. Most are sunk or on the run. We have antisubmarine patrol boats in the bay."

Someone grew bold and asked the question they all wanted to know: "Where are we going?"

"Cam Ranh Bay, a French port in Indochina that we took over in 1940." He glanced furtively around. "You did not hear that from me. I have not been told where we are bound." As he turned, he added, "The girls there are exotic…they say."

Chapter Eleven

> "Never fear your enemy, but always respect them."
> Technical Sergeant John Basilone
> Machine Gun Platoon,
> Company C, 27th Marines

The name "slop chute" attested to the beer garden's smell and appearance. The patchy weeds had been worn down to gravel by thousands of boondockers. "Coffin nails" and "dead soldiers"—cig butts and beer bottles—littered the ground. Most bottles tossed at 55-gallon trash drums missed. Some lucky unit would be policing up this sloppy mess in the morning, thought Henrik.

"Ain't that right, Handyman," said Griff.

"What's right?"

"What I said."

"What did you say?" Henrik took a sip of lukewarm Pearl.

"Where you at, Handyman? Thinkin' 'bout that frowsy blonde farm girl back home?"

"She's not a farm girl and she's not frowsy, whatever that is, and no, I wasn't thinking about her." *Trying not to.*

"I bet."

"Can't bet on what isn't."

"Never mind that. What I said was 'bout this article 'bout those sailors who got Medals of Honor at Pearl Harbor. The dead ones."

"What about them?"

"You are out of it, pal. It says"—he gave the newspaper a shake—"'they willingly sacrificed their lives to defend their country'."

"Yes, I heard you say that. What about it? How many were there again?"

"Fifteen got medals, ten of 'em dead. Got pos-tu-mos..."

"Posthumous," whispered The Professor, nursing his Dr Pepper. He'd picked up the "Professor" handle after claiming he was his class's Valedictorian.

"There was a marine too that day, died on Midway when the passing Japs shelled it," said Mother O'Leary, who always seemed to be pestering all hands to finish their chores and not forget something important like dry socks.

"First marine to get the Medal in this war was an officer of course," complained an unseen voice.

"What do you think of it, Handyman? Would you willingly give up your farm boy life for your country like these heroes did?"

Henrik straightened up from his half-lean on the beer-stained picnic table. "You think they ever considered giving up their lives? Maybe they didn't think it wasn't too good of a deal after all?"

"Probably didn't have the time or the inclination to think about it," said The Professor.

"I don't plan on givin' up my butt for anythin'," slurred Griff, "but I'd rightfully drill any Nip pointin' a gun…I mean rifle, at me and send him to his an…sisters…cestors," he beer-slurred.

"I don't know," said The Professor, pulling a frown.

"You don't know what?" asked Griff. "I thought you knew everythin'."

"I don't know…I mean, who'd have time to think about it? Handyman's right. Right then, right there on some island, you and a Nip squaring off with cold steel."

Someone shouted, "Long thrust, move!" Griff instinctively leapt to his feet, thrusting his imaginary bayonet into an invisible enemy's guts, yelling, "Aaaah!"

"Gosh, he'd make Sergeant Summons proud."

Grinning sheepishly, Griff said, "Gettin' the Medal of Honor, I don't think those swabbies were thinkin' about any medals for sacrificing their bluejacket behinds. They got caught with their skivvies down on a Sunday morning. All they were thinkin' 'bout was Zeros comin' at them. Rat-a-tat-tat." He gestured as if blasting an invisible machine gun skyward.

"Did ya git 'em?" asked Mother O'Leary anxiously.

"Nah, I couldn't tracer-aim. Nimble little bastards," grumbled Griff. "I'm serious guys."

"Yeah, you're acting as serious as a dud grenade."

"It's serious times, fellas," agreed The Professor. "So get serious."

"I am bein' serious," said Griff.

"The only thing you're serious about is wine, women, and shootin' craps, not necessarily in that order."

"Make that brews instead of wine. That Dago Red rotgut is crap and gives me the shits."

"Look, who knows when a bullet's got your name?" said someone down the table. "You'll fight like you were trained like Sergeant Summons always said."

"By the numbers, line 'em up, knock 'em down," grinned Griff.

"Who has time to think about anything except maybe at night in your rack?"

"Or on guard duty. Or washin' mess trays."

"Is it somethin' ya even want to think about?" said Griff. "Look, we're volunteers, every mother lovin' one of us. Maybe we didn't know what we were gettin' into"—he rolled his eyes—"but even the most naive fellas knew it wasn't goin' to be no picnic."

"Back then all we wanted was to have a go at those sneaky Jap bastards," said someone in the shadows. Bottles clinked in agreement around the table.

"Anyone here don't wantta do that no more?"

It was quiet.

"What else was it Summons said?"

"You're a sorry ass low-life bastard?"

"No, 'bout volunteerin'?"

"You're a sorry ass low-life volunteer?"

"You wantta lay down and drain some blood back into your head?"

"Your mommy wears boondockers."

"Yeah, someone said since we were all volunteers we didn't expect to be treated like crap on a toilet seat."

Someone came back in snappy wit. "Since you're all volunteers, the Corps can do to you whatever it wishes."

"The Corps does do that, no argument there."

"That means, I believe," said The Professor, "that we concentrate on our job, and if we should take a bullet while we're doing that job, then we accept, and even expect, sacrifice."

"Cheery, ain't he?"

"A bunch of highbrow mumbo-jumbo," muttered Griff.

The Professor ignored his critics. "The serious question, the real question…" he lectured without looking up from his crossword puzzle, "is more difficult to answer. What's a five-letter word for 'demise'?"

"Death," said Griff.

"That's it?" said another man, "Death?"

"Don't change the subject now…"

The Professor looked up from his *Maine Corps Chevron Newspaper* and swept a gaze over his squad mates. "The question is, can you take a life and not regret it?" He paused. "And then do it again and again?"

Silence. Then a sudden babble of protests.

"I ain't having any regrets 'bout nailing a Jap."

"After them blindsiding us at Pearl…"

"And taking us by surprise in the PI."

"Wake and Guam too."

"Remember Wake Island!"

"Praise the Lord and pass the ammunition!"

"And God bless every marine, dog face, flyboy, and swabby who gave those dirty Nips everything they had to give."

The anger was vehement and ran deep.

"You don't think you'll ever regret taking a life?"

"You mean regret for killin' a Jap tryin' to kill me or one of my buddies? Not on your sweet life," growled Griff.

Holding up a hand, The Professor said, "Don't smash a beer bottle over my head. I'm going to play the devil's advocate."

"Shoot then," said Griff. "Nobody clout The Professor on the head until I say it's okay."

Quiet mutterings.

"Look," The Professor went on, "yes, we're all pissed about those sneak attacks. It's not the American way. Heck, you can see that in Western movies. You're a skunk if you back-shoot even an outlaw or some sneaky Indians about to ambush pioneers. I never saw a pioneer ambush Indians. So yes, Americans disdain sneak attacks. But most of all, Americans don't like to lose."

"You got that right, the sneaky Nip bastards. I don't think anyone's goin' to regret pot shootin' them monkeys."

"Regardless of what we call them, they're still human beings."

"Barely human."

"You're sure of that?"

"After seein' that newsreel from Nanking of Japs buryin' Chinks alive, it don't make 'em look very human."

That moving picture image stuck in Henrik's mind like barbed wire ingrown round an oak tree. Squatty Jap soldiers dragging Chinese men, women, old people, and even kids, into shallow pits and shoveling dirt onto them. The film jumped to a later clip, same angle, and the Japs were tramping down the dirt with their boots. Henrik had nightmares of suffocating Chinamen trying to squirm in the packed mud.

"Remember what Summons said about the time he saw his first dead marine machete-killed by Nicaraguan Sandinista bandits? 'When you see that butchered marine, you'll know what to do.'"

"You fellas aren't going to like this either," said Mother O'Leary.

"Probably not," said Griff with an exaggerated snarl.

"Anyone ever think that Japs have moms and dads too, even little sisters?"

There was a moment of silent contemplation.

"Swell, so what? You think any of those Jap flyboys thought on that for half a second when they put armor-piercing bombs into the *Arizona* and killed over a thousand swabbies?"

"I don't expect to see any Nip surrender flags. If I do, it'll make no difference. Only good Jap's a dead Jap.

"I hear ya, brother."

"It'll put ya a step and a half from Hell."
"We're bound for Hell anyway 'cordin' to that Holy Joe chaplain."

***

Henrik never was issued a telescoped Springfield. The 1st Marine Division had most of them and they were in North Carolina and as far away as Western Samoa. It was of little bother as he'd never used one. However, he and some other snipers were issued National Match M1903 rifles that had been "star-gauged" at Springfield Armory. These were rifles with specially selected barrels with consistently gauged rifling grooves. Selected new parts were particularly fitted, such as the trigger sear and rear sight. A little star-burst imprint was stamped on the muzzle face. That was fine for precision long-range target shooting when misses were measured in fractions of an inch. All he had to do was hit a man-sized target seldom more than 300 or 400 yards. He'd still like to have had a scope.

Like many fledging marines, Henrik was confused over what unit he was in. His orders merely stated the "2d Marines, 2d Marine Division, Camp Elliott, California."

"What's that mean?" he asked a corporal.

"Fool," the corporal snapped, spraying spittle on him, "the 2d Div's one of two Marine divisions with rumors of a third being raised. The 2d Marines means you're assigned to an infantry regiment, but we never call it an 'infantry regiment.' The 2d Mar Div has the 2d, 6th, 8th, and 10th Marines. The 10th is artillery, but we don't call it an artillery regiment either. We're only about 8,000 troops. We're supposed to have 20,000. The 6th Marines had been sent to Iceland for nine months and when they came back it was split to raise the 2d Marines. Our 8th Marines have been in American Samoa since January. After Pearl Harbor the 2d Marine Division defended the California coast from the Mexico border to Oceanside."

A sergeant told them how new regiments were raised by splitting an existing regiment. They'd prepare two rosters each with half the regiment. The original commander and the new one would flip a coin to see who got which half. That way they didn't stack the deck with all the best NCOs and men in either of the now two regiments. Many of the original hands would be promoted a grade or two as leaders, and the vacant enlisted slots filled with non-rated men out of Boot and specialty training. Often many of the replacements had only Boot. Officers mostly came from Marine Barracks, New River, North Carolina (what would become Camp Lejeune), Platoon Leader Course, Officer Candidate School, ROTC, and commanders and staff from the Field Officers School and even other regiments.

They started gasoline rationing in May on the East Coast. Everyone was certain rationing would soon affect everybody. Papa managed to get a treasured

"C" sticker for the third-hand, sometimes-it'll-run Model T Ford because he ran a farm. One of the fellas whose dad was in the gasoline business said the real reason was to preserve tires. The Japs had cut off rubber production to America. It was said that synthetic rubber was under rush development.

That same month a Marine detachment arrived in Northern Ireland. Scuttlebutt was rift with the news of Marines in New Zealand, Samoa, Ireland, the Caribbean, and Alaska. A frequent question was, "Where the hell are they going to set us down?"

May was important too because a U.S. and Australian fleet turned back a Jap offensive attempting to land in New Guinea—the Battle of the Coral Sea. Both sides lost a carrier, a destroyer, and the same number of aircraft, but the Navy had tuned back the Japs for the first time. Something else happened in May that delivered a blow to the Corps. The 4th Marines and other U.S. and Filipino troops on Corregidor surrendered. Some of the noncoms had buddies there. And a bunch of Nips had kicked American ass. The anger level was deadly.

Some of Platoon 276 had stayed together and were assigned to 3d Battalion, 2d Marines—3/2—and were assigned to squads alongside Icelandic vets. Besides the three battalions commanded by lieutenant colonels or majors, there was a regimental weapons company with 37mm antitank guns, .50-cal AA machine guns, and two 75mm antitank guns on half-tracks.

"There are four companies in 3d Battalion: I, K, L, and M—ITEM, KING, LOVE, and MIKE. MIKE's the weapons company, with three platoons of four water-cooled machine guns, twelve guns total, and an 81mm mortar platoon with four tubes," said the company XO, 1st Lieutenant Charger, second-in-command of their company. "Yes, private," he said in response to a raised hand.

"Where's Company J?"

"There is none, private. Fellas, you'll hear stories about how a Company J lost its guidon flag in some unspecified battle in an unknown war so there's no JIG Company in any regiment now. Others will tell you a dog-face soldier didn't know the alphabet when detailed to write up his regiment's roster. Neither's true. They skipped JIG because back in the 1800s they wrote capital 'I' and 'J' the same in cursive.

"Our company has a thirty-man HQ with cooks, supply, and support. We're about half full right now. The company weapons platoon has two .30-caliber air-cooled light machine guns—Browning guns—and two 60mm mortars."

The lieutenant continued. "You new men have been assigned to squads. There are four in the rifle platoons. The 1st, 2d, and 3d rifle squads have nine men, the sergeant squad leader, a corporal assistant squad leader, six riflemen, and a two-man BAR team. The 4th Squad is the automatic rifle squad; the squad leader and seven men in two two-man BAR teams plus three riflemen.

"The platoon headquarters is seven men: a lieutenant platoon leader, a platoon sergeant who really runs the platoon—don't tell this to any of these new lieutenants we're drawing." That drew some chuckles. "There's a buck sergeant platoon guide who takes care of ammo and ration resupply, a demolition corporal, and three messengers."

There'd been no mention of snipers. "Sir, where are the snipers assigned?" asked Henrik.

"We've been assigned one or two per platoon. They'll take the place of BAR squad riflemen. You a sniper, marine?"

"Yes, sir."

"Make sure your platoon sergeant knows."

"Deadeye Handyman," muttered Griff.

It was just one of many briefings on who did what and how. The men found it a little discouraging, as this was a new unit organization with new tactics that had not been tried out in combat. They were assured that battle-experienced marines with years under their belts had put it all together.

A great deal of time was spent on these small unit tactics, patrolling, renewed amphibious landing exercises, and more forced marches. Directives also came down from the top that the Japs preferred to conduct night operations. They might attack after dark or before sunrise and anytime in between. The British relayed those lessons learned in the Netherlands East Indies, Malaya, and Burma. The platoon was soon conducting night marches and attacks—hard to do in dense vegetation. They learned it was easy for two units to shoot each other up while converging on an objective. It was just as easy to become lost in the hills, gullies, and brush.

The night problems were invaluable, even if the troops would rather have been chasing beer, skirts, and shaking dice. The noncoms taught a great many skills not found in manuals. The BAR squad leader, Sergeant Clyde Stickler, told them about right-hand angled flashlights.

"Cut out the red disc from a Lucky Strike package. Unscrew the lens retaining ring, lay the red disc on the lens, and screw the retaining ring back on. When you turn it on to read a map there's less glow for the enemy to see, but mainly, it won't destroy your night vision. Just don't mark your map with a red China marker because it disappears under red light." The "stinky flashlights" were made of a plastic that gave off the smell of formaldehyde.

One problem they ran over and over saw one of the platoon's four squads positioned in a defense as the "enemy." The other squads knew the "enemy's" general area. Scouts located the "enemy" while avoiding detection. Once located, the platoon maneuvered to hit the "enemy's" flanks, or better, their rear.

The XO giving the class said, "Frontal attacks are avoided." He glared around. "That said, whether you like it or not, when you engage the enemy, more often you end up making a frontal attack. The terrain does not always cooperate, and you just don't have time to work out a plan and maneuver to the flanks. Nature and the enemy don't always let you have your way."

Another problem was ambushes on trails, roads, streams, or any route the enemy might follow. Sometimes they quietly closed in on a hut or some stacked ammo crates as the "objective," lying in wait for hours without taking a sip or a pee. Patience and silence were invaluable, they were repeatedly lectured.

They ran these and other problems day and night…as noiselessly as possible. The sergeants and corporals made them unlearn all the shouting and yelling they'd been encouraged to do in Boot. Arm and hand signals, and close whispering were now the rule. There were some squads which seemed to not be able to keep the clamor down.

After running the problems dozens of times, they went on to company problems with one platoon, or sometimes the weapons platoon, playing the "enemy." They also did a few live fire exercises with the two machine guns and two mortars actually firing, although the rounds were fired at distant targets to the flanks. It was enough to let them hear the crackle of overhead machine gun fire through the tree limbs and the thump of mortars.

The company would quietly move into an area and send patrols out to locate enemy outposts and then launch an attack. Other times they'd send squads to clear out enemy outposts and hopefully drive the rest of them away. While they did set up defensive positions at night, they concentrated on the offense; to attack was the preferred tactic. No one wanted to see the nightmare Great War trenches.

One day in a newly built classroom a major gave them a presentation on the June 1918 Battle of Belleau Wood in France. The troops were surprised to learn the 5th and 6th Marine Regiments and the Marine 6th Machine Gun Battalion made up the 4th Infantry Brigade of the Army's 2d Division. The German objective was to push toward Paris. The Marine brigade was instrumental in halting the Krauts and suffered huge losses. The Krauts went into the defense along a ridge with much of the French army in the sector retreating toward Paris. They urged the Marines marching forward to turn back. A Marine captain retorted to the French, "Retreat? Hell, we just got here." The Marines fought their way through the defenses, suffering appalling casualties, but in the month-long battle the Krauts were forced out, calling the Marines "Devil Dogs" or *Teufelshunde*. The 5th and 6th Marines and the machine gun battalion were bestowed the French Cross of War, a green and red cord or *fourrragère* that hangs from their left shoulder.

The major said, "I strongly recommend you don't call it a 'pogey rope' or 'noose' and do not call them 'pogey bait.' They take a dim view of that, pogey being candy and ice cream sold at the ship's geedunk bar."

So much for the Great War history. It sounded like there was an expectation for marines to diligently serve as bullet-stoppers.

"Gee, pal, ya don't get a BAR, ya only get a candy bar, ya pogue," a corporal taunted.

They practiced map reading and compass navigation. "Hey, Heinsworth, go to supply and get ten compass batteries."

Heinsworth, a gangly boy from Nacogdoches, Texas, returned two hours later empty handed. "Shucks, Sarge, I went to every dang supply room 'tween here and the Field Music School and there ain't a compass battery one in this dad-blasted place. At least not for a 360-degree compass." A corporal explained to him that compasses were magnetic and not battery powered.

Sergeant Stickler was a practical sort of leader. He'd joined up before the war and had a "hash mark"—"bean stripe," on his coat cuff—four years' honorable service; had a Good Conduct Medal too. That meant more than being a goody-goody avoiding trouble, but rated his efficiency and exemplary behavior—"I didn't catch the clap," he said.

There were always landing exercises and forced marches. "War's hell. Splash through the cold water to get good and wet and then walk 'em dry to harden those blisters on top of blisters."

"Stop your bitchin', Heinsworth. Once your boondockers are broken in they'll feel better than your fuzzy slippers at home."

"Ahhhh, sarge, a marine's gotta right to bitch."

"Only when I can't hear you and you ain't no marine anyway. Drop, Heinsworth!"

They heard of another battle after the beginning of June. There was lots of scuttlebutt, but the word was the Japs lost four carriers and two other ships trying to take Midway, which was mostly defended by Marines. The U.S. lost only two ships. The loss of Jap carriers was said to be a serious blow. They had a dozen, while America had only five with one in the Atlantic. It was important that the odds be evened.

The lieutenants loved to set up compass courses. They'd borrow aiming circles—like surveyor transits—from the artillery—and precisely measure azimuths and distances to points where they'd drive in two-inch-diameter stakes.

Stickler grumbled, "I never had to look for a two-inch stake in the jungle; we looked for bandit gang camps or hideout shacks up on ridge sides. The mistake everyone makes is to try and follow a beeline from Point A to Point B no matter how thick the brush and mangled the terrain is. There's no way anyone can follow a straight line up and down ridges, crossing streams and gorges, wading swamps, and winding around tree clumps and too thick brush. They expect you to manage all that and walk right up to that little stake…at night."

"What do we do 'bout that, sarge?"

Looking up from the stick lines he'd drawn in the dirt, he said, "You don't try and follow that impossible route. Look here. You pick a linear feature like a stream or trail that you can find at night that's maybe 200 yards or so from the stake, your objective. You need some other terrain feature, like a road crossing a stream or a distinct bend in a stream. Now what you do is purposely aim to the right or the left of the terrain feature and take the easiest route to it."

"You miss on purpose?"

"You do. That way when you hit the stream, trail, or whatever, you know that you're to the right or left of the objective and you follow the stream or trail in that direction rather than guessing which way you missed it. When you find the feature it's only a short distance to the objective stake. We'll practice it with you fellas taking turns."

It worked out pretty good.

Stickle told them not to wear canvas leggings. "They cut off your circulation, keep you from easily removing your boondockers to dry them, and leggings take forever to dry. They chaff your calves too. They do help keep out leeches."

The men broke into a chorus of "Gross…Nasty…Disgusting…UUUGGGG."

"They're not that bad. Touch a coffin nail butt to them and they fall off."

He also taught them to double-knot their boondocker laces, making it less likely for them to come undone.

"Heinsworth," shouted Stickler, "run to supply and get me a hundred yards of contour line."

"On the way, sarge."

"While you're at it, get me a mouth full of water and don't put your nasty ol' tongue in it, 'cruit."

Heinsworth returned with a supply request form and a quarter-canteen cup of water.

"Now here's a man who can effectively follow orders," Stickler said. "Drop."

***

In the midst of the confusion and rush they were issued new uniforms to replace the khaki "suntans" which had been their work uniforms. They had saved one set for off duty and inspections. The others were becoming stained and worn. Officers at battalion and higher level tended to retain khakis.

The new utility uniforms, or simply "utilities," looked like workers' outfits. They called them olive drab, but they were a gray-green which faded with every washing. They were loose fitting and worn without the shirt, or officially a "coat," being tucked in. The sleeves were allowed to be rolled up. A pair of pockets were on the coat's front waist and a smaller one on the left chest;

no flaps. "USMC" and the "Globe and Anchor" were printed in black on the chest pocket.

Mother O'Leary noted, "The Corps' keeping up with modern clothing styles; these trousers have hip pockets."

The drawback was they were supposed to be issued two pairs, but they were short and only one set per man was issued. It was not long aboard ship that men wore either utilities or khakis or even blue denim dungarees that some old salts had. They let uniformity slide.

***

There were no M1928A1 Thompsons or M1 carbines available—they'd been issued to the Army, plus Tommy guns to the Brits. They did receive a substitute weapon. At least the platoon leader, platoon sergeant, and the BAR squad leader did, and signalers. The Marines bought Reising .45-cal M50 submachine guns as substitutes. The twenty-round magazine weapon soon picked up the name "Buck Rogers gun" because of its kind of futuristic look. Performance was another matter. The issue of Reisings was another sign they were soon deploying "beyond the seas."

Chapter Twelve

Our Planes Fly South
A 1943 film demonstrating
the innocence of a naïve Japanese pilot.
Many Japanese soldiers suffered the same.

With whistles blowing and engines churning, the *Perth Maru* rocked side to side. They had finally cast off and were slowly gliding out of the Hiroshima Port and into Hiroshima Bay. The men could tell when they reached the ocean with its slow swells. Seasickness was immediate and created an unremitting misery, with lines forming at the latrines and along the deck railing. Below decks men puked in buckets, helmets, and mess kits. In the berthing compartments the stench was insufferable. Mopping parties were on continuous duty. For most men the agony subsided within three days. Others suffered for longer.

Shipboard life proved tedious, repetitive, the work unrelenting. On top of that it was hot. Everything was done rigidly according to the clock. The convoy crept slowly and was much more widely spread than Obata had expected. The nearest ships appeared to be just kilometers away. Once in a while a destroyer cruised past at what appeared to be a startling speed. Their talkative sailor reported their transport was making eight knots—barely over nine kilometers per hour. A soldier could march five to six kilometers per hour.

While ship life was boring, there was much to keep soldiers occupied. They swabbed their compartment once a day and had to clean their rifles regularly because of the salt air. The weather decks were scrubbed each morning. Soldiers took their turn at galley duty, helping cooks, serving, and washing dishes.

The latrines and sinks in the lowest deck level were cleaned daily. It was horribly smelly and humid, even with long canvas tubes rigged with the air-catcher canvas hoods hoisted into the rigging. Like fat snakes, these tubes ran down gangways into the lower decks for scanty ventilation.

At dawn they fell into crowded formations on the weather deck. No land was in sight and patrol planes were infrequent. The troops would stand to at sunrise and sunset, a favorite time for submarine attacks as the ships were silhouetted on the horizon. They learned where life vests were stowed and could find them in the dark. They each removed a bulky kapok-filled life vest from the weather deck cabinets and practiced donning them and securing the tie-cords. They were to carry their gasmasks at all times once issued. They found these had been stowed aboard before they embarked. It was said they protected against burning fuel and smoke. A sailor who had been a firefighter before conscription mentioned, "Masks would not protect from smoke. Smoke displaces oxygen, and if your mask fills with smoke you cannot get enough air to breath." They of course practiced donning them anyway.

Larger-caliber antiaircraft guns had yet to be mounted on the *Perth Maru*, but pedestal mounts had been fitted with 7.7mm Type 92 Navy machine guns. It was confusing because the Army also used a 7.7mm Type 92 heavy machine gun, but the cartridges were not interchangeable and the guns were of entirely different designs. The Army's was copied from a French Hotchkiss design. The Navy Type 92 was copied from the British Lewis gun—called the *Ru-Shiki* meaning "Lewis Type." Sailors taught the Army machine gunners how to operate them. They had to become familiar with the pan magazines much different from their own gun's curved top-mounted magazine. The guns were manned day and night.

They also undertook firefighting training. Fire crews were organized and they learned how to use the big firehoses, the few fire extinguishers, and sand buckets—those that had not been emptied to puke in. Part of their training was to hose-out the reeking latrines. The fire crews would also saltwater-hose the soldiers stripped to their breechcloths twice a week; cold water of course.

The section cornered their sailor. "How come there are only two lifeboats?'

Hemmed in, he revealed, "The *Perth Maru* is a passenger-cargo ship and not meant for hundreds of soldiers. If the ship has to be abandoned, then everyone dons life vests and leaps into the water. Destroyers will rush to them and pull them aboard."

"Do you really believe that?" asked Number Nine.

"No," said the seaman sadly. "That would attract submarines or airplanes to the targets, even if only damaged transports. The rest of the convoy would speed onward and the escorts would look for the enemy submarine."

No one said anything further about it. It was war, and although they had been prepared to expect anguish, they at least wanted to have some chance of surviving.

Their amenable sailor relayed that they were no longer bound for Indochina, but Java south of mysterious Borneo. There were rumors of vicious headhunters the British and Dutch were unable to subdue.

A surprise, which at first sounded exciting, but proved to be boring like much else, was torpedo watch. Everyone participated. There were two twenty-man watches, one for each side. Men lined the railings equipped with every available binocular. They were told to look for periscopes and faint torpedo wakes. Everyone expected to see torpedo wakes on the surface like in movies. Then they were told the torpedo might be three to six meters deep and seldom seen from a ship's deck. Even the Army officers' binoculars were collected and used by the torpedo lookouts much to their owners' chagrin. They were tagged with the officers' names and the owners checked on who was using them when they had nothing better to do. Many officers had bought their own quality binoculars. The fear of torpedo attack was a quietly held concern, more frightening than air attack.

There was training, with classes on first aid which attracted the soldiers' attention. They learned that there would be entry and exit wounds, the latter causing the larger wounds. The compress they had was for the exit wound—or the entry wound if there was no exit. The triangular bandage could bind a wound or be used as a tourniquet or sling.

The worst part of the voyage was sleeping below decks. During the day the steel ship absorbed the glaring Sun's heat, making the insides an airless oven. That and there was little shade. Every two hours the watch changed, with men coming and going. After a few days the ship's captain allowed men to sleep on the weather deck using their life vests for pillows. The officers were quartered in the former airy passenger cabins aft of the bridge. They could occasionally be seen up there strutting around with their swords. *Do they need swords on a ship?* Obata wondered. The Army officers were seldom seen. They saw more of the white-uniformed Navy officers.

They appeared to now be heading in a southerly direction through the East China Sea. They were told that one night they passed unseen Taiwan, a Japanese colony from which the invasion of the Philippines was launched. Rather than entering the South China Sea, the convoy turned east toward the rising Sun. There were rumors about landing in New Guinea, but they continued east. For days they crossed a vast emptiness devoid of islands. Finally, they found themselves several kilometers off a large island. For days they sat offshore. The island proved to be Saipan. Nippon had seized the Mariana Islands, except for Guam, in the Great War from Germany and ruled it under a League of Nations mandate. The Americans had taken Guam from Spain in 1898 for themselves on the south end of the Marianas. One of the first victories over the Americans in the Pacific War was to seize Guam, now called *Omiya Jima*—Great Shrine Island. Formed up on the deck, a Navy officer described the humiliating American defeat. A Japanese Special Naval Landing Force and an Army regiment landed on the island. In less than two hours the Americans surrendered, suffering only twenty-four dead out of

750 defenders. The Japanese lost one man. The Navy officer emphasized it was the Special Naval Landing Force troops who did the fighting, not the Army. The American marines were held in spite.

An Army officer took the Navy officer's place in the lecture. He proved to be a major and in command of all Army troops aboard the *Perth Maru*. He emphasized the Americans, including the supposedly formidable Marines, had no stomach or spirit to fight for their President Roosevelt, their nation, or their own honor. He went on to berate the Americans and British who often surrendered with minimal intimidation or shamelessly fled—the Americans especially. They were a new country with no rich traditions, politics borrowed from European convolutions, all lacking a sense of honor, having taken the land from the native peoples. They were a confused people having to make choices on who ruled over them. They had no sense of unity or harmony. The British, even though an old kingdom with strong imperial traditions, were little better than the Americans. The British were having difficulties with their many colonies scattered around the world. He doubted the two countries could unify to fight a war with Nippon as they lack the necessary cooperation and spirit. "How could they trust each other since the Americans had rebelled against their mother country only 165 years ago?"

He finished with, "The French buckled two years ago when their homeland succumbed to the Germans as did the Dutch. We may soon test the spirit of the British."

Where is the Emperor sending us now? Obata was left wondering.

***

The convoy grew in size as they sailed south through the South China Sea. Then a southeast heading was taken that led them past the Philippines. They listened to more lectures on the overwhelming American defeat in their Philippines colony from when Imperial forces invaded on 10 December 1941 through the disgraceful surrender of Corregidor Island on 6 May 1942. They did not bear toward Borneo, which would have taken them eventually to Java.

They seemed to sail on forever. It was said that they were no longer needed in Java. The Netherlands East Indies, rich with oil and valuable minerals, had been secured in January through March. The anti-submarine zig-zagging must be using more fuel than a straight course, they speculated. Fuel always seemed to be a concern.

Instead, they emerged from the East Indies and sailed westward, skirting the north coast of New Guinea and then through the Admiralties. New rumors switched their destination between New Ireland and New Britain. These British-administered islands had been quickly subdued by the Japanese, in January 1942. They had virtually no defenses, the British relying on their remoteness. What army would squander troops to secure such remote places, their main value being coconuts? The British administrative center for the Solomon Islands soon began to be developed as a massive Japanese naval and air stronghold at Rabaul on the north end of New Britain. The convoy changed its composition, adding and shedding ships as they passed developing Japanese bases. Seldom did they learn the islands' names.

The fear of submarines diminished, although the threat remained to some degree. Patrol-bombers—four-engine amphibious reconnaissance airplanes armed with torpedoes—prowled throughout the region. For the *Perth Maru* the fear was American and Australian Catalina PBYs flying out of French New Caledonia and Port Moresby in New Guinea. Japanese ships had to be alert for the Japanese patrol-bombers as well. It was essential they send the recognition signals as soon as possible when they were sighted high in the sky. Sometimes at night they flew much lower, searching for surfaced enemy submarines and the wakes of surface ships.

It was Obata's turn at manning a deck machine gun, in this instance on the port quarter fantail. The Sun was an hour below the horizon, dark enough to make it difficult to differentiate between the sky and sea. A thin mist blotted out the sea, but the sky was dotted with stars. One tended to ignore the stars, as any perception of depth was erased at night. The gentle roll of the ship merged with the swaying stars. The other ships had disappeared in the mist.

Looking sternward, Obata saw the wake's greenish tint trailing behind them. The plankton photosynthesis caused the green glow effect. The soldiers on torpedo lookout and manning guns had asked if the green glow would highlight a streaking torpedo or cause enough glare that airplanes could detect the ship's wake and follow it to them. "Sometimes," was the answer.

The lieutenant they asked berated them, calling them "uneducated dupes." He never gave them what might be a clear answer. Obata was familiar with the green tint, although it was not as apparent around the Home Islands with their rougher seas.

The rocking of the sea, the moving ship, the hiss of the water rushing down the hull's sides, the rumble of engines lulled Obata into a sort of trance. Most nights they would talk of home, family, friends, and school or work. He became friends with Takeo Matsui, a store clerk from Gifu, north of Nagoya. Tonight they were talked out. They listened to the sea and the ship. They peered through binoculars, gazing at the moonless sky and sweeping over the surging surface.

Obata jerked awake from mere seconds' slumber resting on the machine gun's stock. A pair of close-spaced lights slipped low across the sky and seemed to turn slowly toward him.

"Airplane port astern!" He cocked the gun, which meant he did not have to release the safety while trying to track the plane. Spent cartridges spewed out the right side and yellow tracers streaked at the plane. More tracers streamed from the *Perth Maru*. Lines of tracers sprang from other ships in other directions. The tracers arched downward far, far short of the plane turning toward him. And then he saw stars and the airplane lights vanished.

Orders were being shouted: "Ceasefire, ceasefire!"

Someone was clambering up the ladder. An officer emerged. "Who gave the order to fire!"

Obata went to attention and saluted. "2nd Class Private Obata, Honorable Lieutenant."

The slap stung, making more stars, and tore through his sense or honor.

"I thought I saw an attacking airplane. I opened fire to protect the ship, but was mistaken, Honorable Lieutenant."

Another slap struck. "I did not ask for excuses. Sergeant, relieve this soldier and confine him to quarters."

All on the port quarter fantail saluted the lieutenant as he slid down the ladder, pitching a final scowl at Obata.

"What did you do?"

"I thought some of the stars were airplane lights, Honorable Sergeant. They looked like they were moving."

"You are foolish. Go to your quarters and remain there until we investigate this blunder."

He remained in his quarters for four days. His comrades brought him meals and he was allowed to the latrine and wash racks. He was the brunt of jokes as the "antiaircraft sniper," but his only work duties were to keep his section's quarters clean. It was easy duty even if humiliating and boring as he sat below day and night. He expected to be ordered to report for punishment. One of the sailors said he might be thrown overboard with water-filled kerosene tins lashed to him like they did with dead sailors.

It was rumored that the ship's captain had once inflicted that punishment on a sailor for failing to polish one of the five brass buttons on his dress uniform coat front opening. The one he missed was the one situated over his navel. He attended a social function to be horribly humiliated.

The seaman's actual punishment was to polish all the ship's officers' brass for a week.

Chapter Thirteen

> "I wish to have no connection with any ship
> that does not sail FAST;
> for I intend to go in harm's way."
> Captain John Paul Jones, 1778

"Duty Beyond the Seas." That's what the orders posted on the company bulletin board said. To some it sounded swashbuckling. To others it was ominous. The Professor said it sounded "quaint." No one admitted any apprehension.

They were expecting deployment. Now it was here and they had no idea where they were bound or when. It was said that before an overseas deployment at least part of the unit would often be granted a week or two's furlough home. There wasn't time. The money was on them going somewhere in the Pacific. Things seemed out of kilter. Here they were, thousands of miles from whatever was happening, but endlessly urged they had to hurry up and wait and get to wherever they were going.

There was a strong sense of urgency to load-out and embark. Even liberty was suspended, much to the frustration of the men with girlfriends in town. Of course there were some who had hitched up with Allotment Annies who relished their "husband's" imminent deployment. The "cuddle bunnies" would soon be rid of the marine they'd "married" using a fake identity to receive an allotment check—twenty dollars a week plus 10,000 bucks if her marine died, combat or not. Now with their marines shipping out and the latest batch of boots arriving, the "chippies" snatched up another husband for more easy money, or they simply continued hooking, or both. All they had to do was change their last name on their fake birth certificate. Trailer parks were opening and some women bought worn-out trailers to call home—"shacks on wheels" or "chippie wagons." Some didn't bother. As long as there were sidewalks, they'd have a job.

"My uncle says romances blossom in wartime; he was in the Great War. So many G.I.s ended up married and made a little money," declared one recruit.

"And a little you'll make in the Marines," elaborated another recruit.

The unit was ordered not to talk to troops outside the 2d Marines. They worked fourteen to sixteen hours a day packing unit equipment and loading cargo, mainly the regiment's rations, ammunition, and medical supplies—beans, bullets, and bandages. Jeeps and 1-ton trucks were loaded, but few 2½-ton cargo trucks or trailers. Scuttlebutt said where they were going there was little room to drive vehicles, there being jungles, swamps, and mountains.

Officers complained they were short of all sorts of equipment and supplies. The marines on loading details couldn't believe the amount of ammunition they hoisted aboard. Every type imaginable and some they've never seen. There were mountains of C-ration cases, which they'd not been issued before. Curious, they pilfered some cases to see what they were like. No one was impressed.

Other details crated unit equipment: office supplies, records, typewriters, radios, telephones and wire, and tool kits. The officers were concerned that all the cargo was stowed in a certain order, what they called "combat loading." It demanded 300 men per ship. Scuttlebutt said this was the order in which gear and supplies were loaded, allowing it to be unloaded with the essential gear on top. Ammo, rations, and medical supplies were on top. Barbed wire, sandbags, camouflage nets, and spare clothing were loaded in the lower holds.

They were issued the new M1 steel helmet with a dark olive drab steel shell and a resin-impregnated cotton duck liner with the suspension system and chin straps. "So we don't look like Brits any more and more like Germans," quipped one man.

"Ain't no Krauts where we're goin'," said a corporal.

***

At the morning formation, work assignments were made and an order read reminding the men that missing a troop movement, that is, failure to board a troop transport by cast-off time, was a court-martial offense, the same as desertion in time of war, up to a life sentence.

That night scores of men went over the fence, sneaking through Camp Elliott's maze of gullies and trails. They knew this was their last chance to say goodbye to girlfriends and wives, real or pretend. Most of those fellas were down in the mouth when they returned. Others were happy to be shipping out and leaving behind a tramp or floozy.

It crawled around in most everyone's head—they were leaving, leaving America for they knew not where. Some no doubt weren't coming home. They had signed up for it, but that didn't make it any easier. Yes, there was some excitement, a sense of adventure, to see foreign places and people. They just knew it wasn't going to be easy, more likely the hardest thing they'd ever do. Most felt they were ready, others not so much. Some even had second thoughts, even dread. But they were marines and this is what they'd signed up for.

The USS *President Adams* was docked at a Naval Operating Base, San Diego pier, along with three other haze gray-painted troop transports—"cattle boats," marines called them. They were only months' old ships built in Virginia, armed, provisioned, and dispatched to Dago. They undertook their shakedown cruise during their voyage, which took them through the Panama Canal. At Dago they ran landing exercises with the 2d Marine Division at Catalina Island and on California beaches. They had been ordered to report in Dago fully loaded with troops and crew rations and full ammo loads. They expected to be carrying the units they trained to their first amphibious assault. The swabbies were as inexperienced with their ship as their cargo of marines were as infantrymen.

Henrik and all hands were impressed with the ships when they conducted their first landing exercise. The briefings they'd received told them the transports were 500 feet long and could carry 1,400 troops and 3,300 tons of supplies and equipment with a crew of 600. They sprouted two dozen 3-inch, 40mm, and 20mm antiaircraft guns. To land the troops they carried thirty-five landing craft, three of them big "Mike boats," able to land a light tank.

They'd been through the boarding routine with the landing exercises, except this time they carried aboard everything they owned in their seabag and transport pack. It included both the haversack on the upper back, the knapsack on the small of the back, and a horseshoe roll with blanket, poncho, and shelter half with its tent poles and pegs plus three C-rat meals.

This time there was a different sensation. After all their training, scuttlebutt, daydreams and nightmares, countless magazines and newspapers, all fueled by the whoopla of newsreels and movies, they really were sailing off to "somewhere in the Pacific." Their confidence varied from "Lookout Tōjō, we're coming to kick your ass," to a silent, *I've no idea what I'm doing here.*

Bayonet sheathed and rifle slung, they shuffled to the gangways, their seabags already loaded in the holds. They'd not see them until the operation was over, however long that took. They might never see them, or their bags may never see them again.

They each saluted the ship's National Ensign and then the deck officer. "Sir, I request permission to come aboard."

A blue-clad Navy band on the pier played "The Marine Corps Hymn" and "Anchors Away," having led off with the lively "Little Brown Jug" when boarding began.

"Climb the gangway, shout your name, and last four to the officer with a clipboard." He had a holstered pistol. They'd heard it before as a swabby automatically barked, "Grab a lifebelt from the stack, wear it only on deck.

Inflate by squeezing the two red arrows together with a hard quick grip and release. CO_2 cartridges will inflate it. There are backup oral inflation tubes. Never inflate below deck."

They followed a swabby down ladders and through constricted companionways, "The Battle Hymn of the Republic" playing faintly in the background. Someone ahead quietly sang, "Mine eyes have seen the glory..."

"Can it, Gorski."

"Up yours."

Cramped, stuffy, hot, and humid, and above all, smelly, even if the ship was less than a year old. The too narrow racks provided only a couple of feet of head clearance and a thin mattress. There might be four to six stacked racks. Web gear and packs were shoved under the bottom racks, hung on the end frames, or suspended from overhead waterlines and other piping along with rifles. Stowing machine guns and mortars was a problem. Weapon crews were told to take their weapons if abandoning ship.

"Right," said more than one mortarman, "I'm going overboard with a forty-pound 60mm in my paws as the ammo goes down with the ship. Who thinks of this boloney?"

The troops and sailors free of duties lined the shore-side rails as they cast off. The sailors too were sailing into harm's way. Wives and girlfriends waved from a pier. Henrik wondered if Jo was on that pier. Most likely not, unless she was waving to another marine or even a swabby, some non-rated apprentice seaman on permanent sea and anchor guard useful for little else. They faintly heard the strains of "Auld Lang Syne" as they churned into the bay. It was 1 July 1942.

Dago may have not been home for most of the men at the railing, but they knew it might be the last American town they'd see for a long time... or forever. Silently, they took in the sight of The Red, White, and Blue Stars and Stripes ensign snapping on the fantail against the low San Diego skyline, their eyes drawn to the tallest building, El Cortez Hotel, with its fifteen floors crowned with AA guns.

Homesickness was one thing, but seasickness struck before the convoy cleared the bay. It went on for days, with earnest discussions about why some were afflicted and others weren't. Then there were the tough guys who thought they could beat seasickness. The unaffected didn't feel so fortunate, having to endlessly swab latrines and companionways and help the ill up and down to decks and berthing compartments. Chow lines were shorter though. The Navy didn't provide any seasickness treatment, but officers had the foresight to buy Scopolamine out of pocket before boarding.

In spite of seasickness, when the squawk box announced beer was prohibited aboard ships, it was greeted by boos and hissing. It didn't help when it was learned that officers were permitted hard liquor.

As they sailed into the "passive sea," as the name means in Spanish, they were heading toward the setting red sun—which seemed daunting.

"The sun shorely looks big way out here," said a "hay seed" marine.

"Low on the horizon, the sun appears larger," explained a swabby. "Its apparent proximity to the earth's horizon makes it appear larger in its perceived size."

Henrik had to admit that sounded pretty smart coming from a swabby, what the bluejackets call ratings. *Must be a navigator or something.*

Later Henrik heard a Navy lieutenant counsel an ensign. "Ratings are dumb but crafty and bear watching." The two officers chuckled. Any marine could tell them that.

It seemed the ships meandered, but they followed a set zig-zag course making 20- or 40-degree turns every 10 to 15 minutes, and the entire zig-zag pattern changed every 40 to 80 minutes. Each ship had a special zig-zag clock set to the same schedule.

Files of men snaked through companionways and up and down ladders. They stood in line two to three hours for all three meals—those who could eat. Sometimes after an hour in line the men found there was no lunch, what they called the "lunchless hour." When there was lunch, often it was sandwiches or soup and, if fortunate, crackers. Metal tables and benches fixed to the deck were for meals. Some slept under the tables to stretch out better, but they'd better be cleared out by breakfast. Breakfast might be oatmeal or "collision mats"—pancakes, or powdered eggs. Hash-slingers might toss in bits of eggshell to give the impression that real eggs were used. Officers usually got real eggs, much to the men's frustration and confusion. "Where'd they come from?" they asked. Seagulls was one theory.

After three or four days most jarheads had overcome seasickness. There were lines for sick call and dental call; for shaving, brushing teeth, saltwater showers—which didn't make them feel clean—crapping, drawing water, and reviewing records. It occupied the time. There were fire drills, air raid drills, and lifeboat drills. "Lifeboat" was an understatement for the dozens of oval life rafts—Carley floats—clinging on the ship's sides. Yanking a quick-release strap they'd fall into the water. No matter which side landed upright, the rafts could be boarded. The landing craft took too long to lower if sinking, especially if the ship was listing.

The rocking and jostling didn't help when writing letters, and the mess tables were crowded. It quickly became obvious that it would be some time before letters found their way home. There was no telling when they might expect a mail call.

Lights were few and they were directed not to use flashlights, as batteries were in short supply. Officers had to threaten three days in the brig on bread and water for using the rechargeable battle lanterns fitted throughout the ship.

It was a surprise to many that the Navy really did punish infractions with bread and water rations—"piss and punk" or "angel cake and white wine." They could be locked in a brig for three days, or longer. Scuttlebutt said the confined could have all the bread and water they wanted. Not exactly true. "Meals" were served three times a day, and the inmate was asked how many bread slices and cups of water he wanted for the next meal. Then he'd be served that amount and had better eat it all. If the turnkey didn't like the jailbird, the bread was stale.

"What if you're stuck in the brig and we're torpedoed?"

"Cheery thought," muttered a corporal. "Why don't you think about something pleasant like jumping off this sinking bucket into burning oil?"

Henrik found himself in a bad mood that day.

"If you wind up in the brig there's a turnkey who'll let you out. He's not somebody you want to piss-off and bitch at."

They had no idea of the convoy's size. Around the *Adams*, marines detailed to lookout identified the USS *President Hayes*, USS *Crescent City*, and USS *Alhena*. Destroyers swept past and PBY Catalina patrol-bombers with depth bombs made big sweeping turns. Other transports and warships could be made out on the horizon, sometimes clearly silhouetted and other times fading into the mist or sun glare. The carrier USS *Wasp* accompanied them, seldom seen other than one of its occasional scout planes. The entire 2d Marines, reinforced with artillery, tanks, engineers, and other support troops, were loaded aboard what they called Transport Division DOG of Transport Group X-RAY. That didn't tell them anything. These were just names the Navy gave to task groups of ships. They did find out they were now attached to the 1st Marine Division, which was in New Zealand. The scuttlebutt quickly spread that they were on their way to New Zealand, as one of the 1st Marine Division's regiments was on Samoa. Morale skyrocketed with visions of lonely New Zealander girls, their husbands and boyfriends serving in North Africa.

One evening before sunset and the "darken ship" order, there was a commotion starboard with men rushing to the rails. Henrik followed the pointing fingers to see a silver-gray blimp just a few hundred feet above the waves.

"It's a Navy antisubmarine blimp," reported an anchor-clanker. "The damn thing's 250 feet long and can make sixty miles per hour, lots faster than a sub running on the surface. It can fly 2,200 miles."

"That big thing?"

"How do Zeppelins take on subs?"

"They're not called Zeppelins anymore," said the sailor. "B-class non-rigid airships. They put together B-class and limp to make Blimp. They carry four depth charges, ten-man crew. They can spot submerged subs real easy like."

"There are Nip subs out here?"

"We act like they are just to be safe."

Once at sea they tried to conduct classes. Little was accomplished owing to the lack of deck space. They tried double-timing around the deck, but there were too many marines and sailors doing their own jobs. Units were allotted short periods to take calisthenics to keep active. Classes with the men sitting on the sun-heated weather deck couldn't hear the instructors with the rush of wake, wind, engine hum, and PA speakers always squawking. The heat below was stifling, but the deck was so sun-heated that they had to sleep on blankets. There wasn't enough space for everyone above. Below deck, condensation trickled down bulkheads. It was rumored Navy and Marine officers had fans in their cabins up in "officer country." A cornered Filipino mess steward admitted that was true.

They test fired their weapons and cleaned them. Owing to the salt air, cleaning was an everyday chore. Live fire shooting at bobbing oil cans from aboard even slightly rolling ships was basically a waste of ammunition.

One day they were issued full ammo loads. Most of it was dated in the 1920s, but there was nothing wrong with it, being in airtight crates. They opened the tin-lined wooden crates and after filling their cartridge belts, they slung two bandoleers—210 rounds total. The squad helped fill their BAR's twenty-one twenty-round magazines. A squad leader told them to load only eighteen rounds so as not to strain the magazine spring. "When the shooting gets hot, load twenty rounds since you'll burn it up fast."

There were suddenly not enough whetstones to sharpen bayonets, machetes, hatchets, sheath knives, pocketknives, and e-tool blade edges.

"You keep sliding that sharpening stone on your bayonet and it's going to look like a darning needle."

They weren't told when they crossed the Equator. There were no traditional silly Shellback ceremony antics and hazing from King Neptune as Pollywogs crossed the Equator. Most had never heard of the sailor's traditional initiation ceremony.

***

0300 hours. The squawk box screeched, "General Quarters, General Quarters! All hands man your battle stations! Material Condition ZEBRA."

The claxon sent a collective jolt though the mostly sleeping marines.

ZEBRA condition meant to expect ship-wide casualties or the ship was in danger of fire, flooding, and other damage—in other words, prepare for the worst case. Companionway hatches became "shin-busters" as the men stumbled through the tight darkened companionways.

It was a mad scramble for the sailor boys, and the marines asleep on deck were ordered below. They stayed by their bunks half-lacing on boots and donning lifebelts. Designated marines stood by at all berthing compartment hatches. Others manned battle lantern stations and firehoses. Handpicked squads quietly stood-to in tweendeck companionways exiting onto the weather deck. They lacked packs but carried web gear and rifles with bayonets fixed. Their duty was to maintain order if the abandon ship order was given. Sailors stood by to release the Carley floats or "doughnuts," and gun crews scrambled to break open ready-service lockers.

The marines took unauthorized peeks out portholes and hatches. Instead of gun flashes, burning ships, AA bursts, and tracer streams, they saw only quiet blackness on a swelling sea.

0350 hours. On the PA the Boatswain's Mate of the Watch announced orders of the day. "Breakfast call at 0400 hours. All personnel to man debarkation stations at 0700 hours. The smoking lamp is still out."

"What's going on, Jack?" they asked every hurried swabby. They seldom got an answer unless a wisecrack—"The skipper's goldfish is drowning!" Just another drill, but this one would be a routine rehearsal, or so they thought.

The landing craft davits and derricks could be heard. More questions were asked. "Are we preparing for a landing?" It wasn't the same as the exercises off California.

Even the noncoms were in the dark. "We wouldn't be landing without a briefing on what we're doing or what we might be facing on an unknown shore."

Barely an officer was seen, not that they felt they needed them. The noncoms always quickly got things rolling in the right direction.

Breakfast was sausage, runny reconstituted powdered eggs, underdone toast—or burnt—and canned pears. Fruit was always welcome. The heavy, greasy sausage wasn't so much admired with the prospect of bobbing landing craft.

"Why's the eggs green?" someone finally asked a chow-slinger.

"Cause the aluminum cookin' pans react with the sulfur in the eggs," declared a cookie. "It's harmless. If ya don't want it the man behind ya does."

Sunrise was 0630 hours. The company manned debarkation stations as practiced off of California and enroute here, wherever "here" was. As the troops filed onto deck they were greeted by a sight to behold. Everyone was heading to port rather than starboard. An island sat a mile away. It was like nothing most of the young marines had ever seen. The hilly island was crowned with coconut palms, and even darker green pines, Indian beech, and high brush reached almost to the water's rippling edge—so green it hurt one's eyes. The narrow beaches were bronze edged by glass-clear water turning into aqua, azure, teal, sapphire, and turquoise. A comfortable light breeze was in the 80s.

"Is this New Zealand?"

"Nah. Its heaven or paradise or some shithole."
"Seen it before," muttered a Floridian.
"I'd rather be in California."
"Make it Oregon for me, brother."
"I need to talk to the skipper."
"Why for?"
"So we can stick a flag on the beach claiming it for the US of A and sit out the war. Someone's gotta defend the place."
"What's wit ya, Frankie, outta the mood to knock off Nips?"
"They can wait."
"You expecting to find Dorothy Lamour in a red sarong like in her *Aloma of the South Seas* movie?"
"I'm keepin' my eyeballs peeled."
"I bet there ain't no women here."
"If there are they'll probably look like something out of *National Geographic*."
"I could go for that."
"Those skanks? Not me."
"Speak for yourself, Butler."
"I've seen you with worse, bud."
"Yeah, that was your mother."

Chapter Fourteen

"Do not adhere to any set principles, but adapt to each situation."
Musashi Miyamoto
Go Rin Sho—The Five Wheels, c. 1641

Battle alarm, 0400! The alarm pierced through the *Perth Maru*, crackling with static. This was the first action alarm since Obata set off his own erroneous emergency alert.

His section leader ordered, "You must help man the guns. No excuses for remaining below decks while under attack."

He had no desire to be caught inside the ship, doomed to drown, suffocate, or incinerate.

As before there was no gunfire, screaming airplanes, or flares.

The guns were manned. Petty officers were ensuring lights were extinguished, ports and hatches dogged, that all on deck donned life vests, and fire crews were readied. Crews stood by the longboats. One petty officer ordered the spare men at the guns to check the cartridge seating in all their forty-seven-round pan magazines.

***

Islands dotted the water all around them, great cone-like peaks and steep ridges of green floating on a crystal blue sea. The skies were as fair as *Takamagahara*—the High Plain of Heaven, but the scent of sulfur fouled the enlightened breeze.

"*Nyūburiten*"—New Britain—said a sailor.

From behind a jungle-covered ridge rose a plume of white smoke.

"That is the South Daughter," said the sailor. "There is also a North Daughter and Vulcan is across the bay."

"The daughter of what?" Obata asked.

"Of the Mother, the biggest of the four volcanos," the sailor replied, peering at Obata like he was an ignorant country boy.

"Why are we here then?" Obata countered, peering at the sailor like he was a fool.

He did not answer.

"New Britain, are there *Igirisu* here?"

"There were. This was the capital of the British-administered Solomon Islands, which they took over from the Germans in 1920. They fled, 8,000 *Igirisu* civilians when we landed here in January. Some *Igirisu* were left behind and were caught and executed as punishment."

"You sound like you have been here before."

"Yes, many times before this war. I was a deckhand aboard a coastal merchantman."

The convoy rounded a peninsula dominated by three volcanos. The smallest, the South Daughter, boiled smoke. Its lava-creased slopes were black while the others were green forested.

"This is Blanche Bay," said the sailor. "It separates New Britain and New Ireland to the west. We seized New Ireland too."

"This is not the French Indonesia then?"

"No, does the exalted Imperial Army teach you nothing?"

Apparently not.

Rounding the Gazelle Peninsula and its volcanos, they entered Simpson Harbour, crowded with transports, cargo ships, oilers, and smaller coastal freighters, even sail-rigged schooners once used to speed fresh fruit to markets. There were only a few destroyers for protection. A surprisingly large town edged the bay's north shore, backed by a forested ridge twice as tall as the volcanos.

"There was an eruption in 1937 on the south side of the harbor, Tavurvur and Vulcan. Thousands were evacuated to New Guinea. The British were going to move the capital, but the war stopped those plans," lectured the sailor.

"What is going on here now?" Obata asked. A scout plane circled over the arriving convoy.

"The rumors say we are building a large base for the Navy and the Army. There is only one airfield now, but they are clearing land for several more. They say there are plans to take the lower Solomons and then to take over French New Caledonia, British Fiji, and American Samoa. Some say by taking those colonies we can cut Australia off from America." He knew a lot, but said, "Do not tell anyone you heard that from me."

The troops aboard the *Perth Maru* were ordered to spotlessly clean their quarters and the latrines when entering Simpson Harbour. The galleys too. They docked at a pier at Rabaul Port. The town had white-painted wooden buildings, mostly single-story with corrugated steel roofs. Streets near the waterfront were oiled, but others were packed reddish-brown volcanic dirt or crushed coral. The coral caused dust and led to rutting. The derricks were soon at work unloading cargo. Only a few sailors were unloading, but hundreds of the black-skinned natives labored. Most of the soldiers had never seen Melanesian natives, and there were so many. The Japanese felt uncomfortable near the natives with their wild looks and frizzy hair. They were taller and more muscular than the Japanese. Obata and others felt intimidated.

"They are so large and savage looking," said one of the meeker soldiers.

"We are their conquerors."

"They say Americans are large too," said a sailor.

No one commented.

Navy petty officers and other sailors in green army-style uniforms were ordering the native stevedores around and directing the cargo's debarkation. Meter-long bamboo canes cleared up any misunderstandings, urged haste, and added emphasis to shouted instructions in incomprehensible tongues. The Japanese berated the natives for speaking an incomprehensible Pidgin-English, not that the soldiers and sailors could speak a second language themselves.

Heavier cargo was loaded in the few trucks, both Japanese and British-made. Most cargo was borne by strong backs and horse carts to nearby warehouses and sheds. Some sheds were guarded by Navy Guard Force troops, some wearing white sailor uniforms, with helmets, belt equipment, putties, and bayoneted rifles. The Navy 8th Base Force and Guard Force sailors operating the new Japanese base lived in the abandoned houses. Officers shared European managers' cottages. The much-looted Church of England parish church now served as a barracks for native laborers. "Stay away from it," they were advised by a dockman. A rumor said British priests and teachers had been murdered by the Japanese.

It was a strange feeling for the 800 troops so long confined aboard the *Perth Maru*. There would be no missing the ship's discipline and slavish attention to the clock, not that the Imperial Army's discipline was a lighter burden.

Standing at rest in formation with all their equipment, the men felt uncomfortable sensations, as if they were moving, even faintly rolling with the no longer present ship. One man standing at rest suddenly stepped forward and stumbled for no apparent reason.

"I thought the deck was moving," he said. Others laughed and a couple of other men stumbled, with one even plopping down on the ground. Corporals barked at their men to display sturdiness, even after one of them fell to his hands and knees.

Once order was attained and a sense of balance achieved, the replacement draft commenced to march through the bustling town. Though still shaky, they made their best effort to display military prowess. Antiaircraft guns were everywhere. Turning a corner onto a crushed coral side street, they encountered a marching section of Special Naval Landing Force troops, the Imperial Navy's own soldiers. Their mission was to seize and defend distant navy bases, allowing the fleet to operate at longer ranges. They were often used in China when shock troops were needed. There were chilling stories of their brutality and ferociousness.

The two bodies of troops regarded each other, the Landing Force soldiers wearing dark green tropical uniforms, caps with their star and anchor badge, light packs, and their rifles were slung with the relaxed air of veterans. Their most striking feature was that they were taller and tougher appearing than many of the soldiers.

There were no catcalls as Obata expected. The Landing Force soldiers did not ignore them either, but simply gave them a curious glance and lost interest.

On the town's edge they were directed to a large field with scattered coconut palms and large pole sheds with corrugated or palm frond roofs and lacking walls. Around the camp's edges were meter-deep slit-trench bomb shelters. There were four kitchen sheds with fire pits, work tables, and pots and cut-down drums for rice cooking. Outside the encampment were latrine pits and drums for catching rainwater.

They spent the rest of the day cleaning and setting up the camp. The officers were quartered in cottages in the town and runners assigned to deliver messages. They were not quartered segregated from their troops; one duty officer was always present with each company.

In a field on the encampment's west side the battalion fell in for rollcall before the evening meal was served, eaten on rice stalk mats. A major stepped out of a tent accompanied by a lieutenant aide and a captain. He stepped onto a low plank platform in a pressed uniform, his white shirt's collars overlapping his green tunic's lapels. He carried both an 8mm Nambu pistol and a sword with its grip wrapped in white cloth—likely an heirloom, which he ceaselessly hand-gripped.

He scanned his battalion standing at attention, motionless. "I am Major Ichiro. I welcome you to Rabaul, New Britain, seized by our victorious forces. We may have to move at any time." It was the first time most had seen him. "As long as we are here, we will work to reconnect our feet to the Earth. We will undertake marches and tactical training to recondition us." He told the battalion that they "are all to work together and cooperate to ready themselves for the coming battle."

No one understood that. Was the enemy coming here or were they going elsewhere to meet the enemy? The major probably did not know himself. He stepped down and turned the battalion over to the captain who read off a lengthy list of encampment rules. No fires or lights at night, no going into town without permission and only in groups of at least three. "There will be no contact with the natives." It was confusing because natives ran the tea rooms, cafes, tailors, barber shops, and brothels inhabited by soldiers and sailors.

They were quietly told not to ask or talk about what happened at the Tol and Waitavalo Plantations the past February. It was whispered, "Almost 200 surrendered Australian soldiers were massacred."

***

Takeo Matsui, the shop boy from Gifu, north of Nagoya, had befriended Obata, bonded by their partiality for seafaring stories. Takeo had been given as a farewell gift a popular British book translated into Japanese, *Robinson Crusoe*. They also spoke of a favorite of both, *Gyosen-dan—The Fishing Fleet*. Takeo loaned the book to Obata, and he entertained Takeo with his own stories of fishing and fighting the sea and weather aboard his uncle's boat. Takeo thought it was all very exciting while Obata attempted to explain that dragging nets aboard filled with hundreds of kilograms of struggling fish, sorting and gutting them, and stowing them on ice held little appeal. His hands were net-cut and freezing enough as it was. Then there was the abysmal food, long hours, little sleep, and constant cold-wet feeling. One of his worse chores was to make minor repairs on the Ford motor in a pitching boat bathed in chilling spray.

Takeo came up with the idea of fishing expeditions. The New Britain native fishermen worked for the Japanese occupiers, but there was not enough fish, much less meat, available, especially since more and more Japanese troops were arriving by ship. Their forced marches over the inland hill trails crossed numerous streams plunging down the hillsides and into the sea. The troops preferred the hill marches. While hot and strenuous, the trails were not overly steep and it was less humid than the shoreline trails and roads. They saw some reasonably good-sized fish in pools along the streams.

Buying a few hooks from native fishermen, they found cartridges for a British revolver at the old police station, which was being used by their Military Police—the mysterious *Kenpeitai*. They pulled the bullets out with pliers, to use as fishing weights. They promised a signalman—called an *imozuru* or "sweet-potato-vine" because of the vine-like wires of a switchboard—they would gift him a fish for which they bartered five meters of twine.

***

At a morning formation Obata's name was called along with a dozen other men. Some he recognized as previously designated snipers from the Nagoya rifle range. A sergeant marched them to a warehouse with them carrying their rifles.

They quickly turned in their Type 99s and signed a statement. They were each issued a new Type 97 sniper rifle along with a heavy-duty leather carrying case for the 2.5×10 telescope.

The sergeant had them compare the scope's five-digit serial number with the rifle's number. "The two serial numbers must be identical. The telescopes are not interchangeable between rifles. They cannot be adjusted for elevation and windage or focused. That is set at the factory. You must not drop or jolt them or the rifle's zero will be knocked out of alignment. You cannot readjust it."

The telescope was slightly offset to the left so that the bolt handle could open, the five-round magazine loaded with a charger clip, and the iron sights used if the scope was damaged.

There was a problem with ammunition, however. The Type 97 rifle was a telescoped version of the older 6.5mm Type 38 rifle. Their unit though was armed with newer 7.7mm Type 99 rifles. The 6.5mm was more accurate, put the 7.7mm was more deadly. A sniper version of the Type 99 had been adopted, but they were not yet fielded. This was obviously a problem. They replaced their 120 rounds of 7.7mm ammunition in their belt pouches with 6.5mm. They were also each given a heavy wooden box with 360 rounds of 6.5mm in twenty-four fifteen-round cardboard packets and stuffed those into a haversack. No one was happy with the arrangement or the extra weight. Once in the field though there would be no 6.5mm resupply through the company.

"That is almost 500 rounds," sagely prophesied one soldier. "That should last you for what life you still have in you."

Issued another sixty rounds, they spent the afternoon practice firing at ranges from 100 to 800 meters. Obata made fifty-two hits out of the sixty rounds, one of the highest scores among the snipers. A lieutenant said, speaking through the sergeant, that he would be submitted for the 1st Class Marksman Award, a gold cherry blossom badge with crossed rifles and silver trim.

While Obata would have preferred a longer ranged 7.7mm rifle, he did admit the 6.5mm caused much less recoil. He could re-aim quicker. The 6.5mm had longer barrels than the 7.7mm and a very fast burning high-quality propellant. The propellant burned up in the bore, eliminating muzzle flash and smoke. This made it difficult for the enemy to locate snipers. Two other things Obata did not like were the trigger's hard pull and that he had to give the bolt handle a hard pull to fully eject the spent cartridge.

"Take care of your telescope," admonished the sergeant. "Treat it gentler than your girlfriend."

"What if we do not have a girlfriend?" asked one of the snipers.

"Ask any of the sailors here," he suggested as they marched back to the encampment.

***

It did not take long to learn there were sanctioned brothels in town with at least 2,000 comfort women. They were operated by Japanese contractors, often retired sergeants. The contracted women were mostly Chinese, some Koreans and Taiwanese, and local black girls plus a few *hafu*—half breed—mixed black-and-white girls. Most of the girls had been tricked, being told they would be stage performers, singers, and musicians. They were commonly called by their Pidgin-English nickname, Mary. It originally meant any European woman but came to mean "prostitutes," as there were no refined women left.

Many of the men were initially reluctant to have even paid relations with the *gaijin*—foreigners. They considered Chinese, Koreans, Taiwanese, and native girls to be especially inferior and a danger to Japanese racial purity. The *hafu* mixed or half-casts as the British called them were especially shunned, by some at least. That soon changed.

A sailor they met on the street told them about the brothels. Laughing, he said, "Any reluctance will disappear in a few weeks and you will all soon be visiting a *piya*—a comfort house, or more formally a military brothel—*jugun ianjo*. The officers have their own brothel said to provide a variety of exotic girls. It is next door to the *Kaikosha*, the officers' private club."

"Officers have their privileges," said another II Battalion sniper.

"If you desire something even more exotic, there are unique samplings found at the few illegal brothels on the back streets. I have even heard that at the House of the Seven Seas there is a...." the licentious sailor whispered into Obata's ear.

"Oh no, I am not having any of that!"

"We will see," Takeo smirked.

They had not known they would receive a twelve-yen overseas pay allowance. Soldiers joked it was meant as "prostitute benefit pay."

***

It was 0930 hours. Clean up and other work details were well underway. The encampment was appearing more ordered, and improvements appeared daily. As the five notes of the assembly bugle call pierced the air, the soldiers rushed to secure their equipment. Trotting to the parade ground, Obata saw several fighters winged over and make a circuit of the harbor. At least they bore the Sun's red discs on their wing tips. Other droning planes could be heard. Ship horns were drifting from the harbor as they got underway. A corporal said they would sortie into the open water where they could maneuver instead of being trapped in the harbor's confines.

The battalion fell in with all the officers present. Some Obata did not recognize.

Major Ichiro fast stepped onto the platform. "This is an emergency alert," he began without preamble. "This morning before dawn, American aggressors invaded Guadalcanal Island in the lower Solomons and are attacking our airbases in the area. The battalion will prepare to embark on order."

The cooks were ordered to make up all the double-cupped hand-sized rice balls they could and wrap them in palm leaves. They were emergency rations or could be consumed on marches or when embarked. "Once prepared for embarkation, all air raid trenches will be dug a half-meter deeper. Trenches for unit commanders will be logged and earthed over. The heavy machine guns will be set up on their antiaircraft mounts in the best available aerial fields of fire."

With all assignments accomplished the next day, they waited.

***

There was a sudden buzzing in the direction of Simpson Harbour. Fighters were launching; Zeros and other fighters were roaring over and steeply climbing. Some, including two-engine bombers, had been launched from other airfields in the area. Sirens sounded and those able to see the harbor saw ships getting underway. Most had kept up steam so they could immediately maneuver into open water and begin evasive maneuvers. At 0950 and 1045 hours the two waves of B-17 bombers passed high over, almost too small to be seen. *Why did they not drop their bombs?* Obata wondered. They droned on, disappearing into the haze. Abruptly, huge geysers spouted out of the harbor's waters—black with volcanic silt covering the harbor's bottom. Other blasts struck in the town with clouds of brown and gray smoke and dust. Then some bombs hit in the airfield area. *Were they even aiming for the ships?* After a surprising delay the thump of the explosions reached them, followed by a jolt of concussion. The second wave of six four-engine bombers experienced its own wait, and all eyes were turned to the swerving ships. Two almost collided. Instead of the harbor, fountains of brown earth and smoke burst around the airfield. Ships were still heading for the open sea and scattering, leaving snaking wakes.

"That was of little concern," Takeo muttered at their machine gun post. The machine guns were worthless with the bombers so high they could barely be seen.

Obata nodded slowly. "I expected to see falling bombs and earthquake-like explosions. Maybe the feared American bombers are not so fearsome." He admitted though that the bombs impacted two or three and more kilometers away. It would be no doubt that bombs falling in their immediate location would create a different sensation and fears of its own. The strangest part was that this battle was mostly silent. They heard no drone of bombers and fighters, no rata-a-rat-tat of machine guns, nor even the thump of bombs. A few hit the water, throwing up spray spouts. The AA guns had not even fired.

For the rest of the day the troops were excited. They gradually settled down and began to feel like bloodied veterans. With no more attacks and fighter patrols circling the area, their confidence levels rose and they took the day's events in stride. There were rumors though the Americans might drop bombs on the volcanos, causing them to erupt. By nightfall they were bored manning the AA machine guns.

A question was making the rounds: Why had there been no antiaircraft fire from the 7.5cm guns deployed throughout the area? Some suggested that maybe the bombers were flying too high, higher than the obsolescent guns' best vertical slant range. Others thought they endangered fighters attacking the bombers. As it was, word spread that 12 fighters had suffered minor damage from the bombers' machine gun fire. There was easily repaired damage to the runway. Engineers had organized native crews who quickly backfilled craters and carted off debris.

"The odds look mostly even," whispered Takeo. "Neither side lost any airplanes or ships. The bombs just made holes in the ground and the water."

"You must not talk like that," cautioned Obata.

Chapter Fifteen

> WANT ACTION?
> join
> U.S. Marine Corps!
> Wartime recruiting slogan

The rising sun revealed more ships to Henrik, standing as an air observer lookout. Forty and more were reported. They soon stood down, but the AA guns remained partly manned at Condition Two. Other ships appeared to be more active in the distance. Packs and rifles were returned to the berthing compartments. Each company of 3d Battalion, 2d Marines, received a briefing from the Bn-2—the battalion intelligence officer—1st Lieutenant Scholar. He had covered Operation *Dovetail*, in which they were now undertaking. The task force dropped anchor off the small island. Part of the task force, the carriers, battlewagons, and cruisers, were over the horizon. It was a morale hike to catch sight of the big warships. It was 25 July.

The paradise where they were anchored was five-by-ten-mile Koro Island in the British-administered Fiji Islands. The lieutenant informed them they were now sixty miles northeast of Fiji itself. These islands were defended by U.S. Army and New Zealand troops. "Sorry, fellows, they don't need our help defending the place. Their commander sends his regrets, but there are barely enough women to go around for them."

Once the catcalls died, he said, "The reason we're here is to conduct a rehearsal for a planned landing on a Jap-held island far to the northwest." This generated a new round of shouting and hisses.

"Knock it off, fellas," the lieutenant mockingly pled as the troops shouted, "What island?" "When we going?" "Let me at 'em." "We're ready to get off this tub and kick Jap butt."

Settling the men down, Scholar explained they had rendezvoused with the 1st Marine Division from New Zealand and other units from Hawaii and

Samoa. Operation *Dovetail* was a rehearsal for the 1st Marine Division's 5th and 1st Marines leading the landing. The 2d Marines now attached to the 1st Marine Division would not initially take part, as they were the division's reserve to be deployed when and where needed. There was a lack of time and a sense of urgency. All the troops did was check their gear, clean their weapons again, and watch the few Higgins boats and two of the big Mike boats their crews launched for practice. They were surprised to find there were two M3 Stuart light tanks in another troop ship's hold. In the distance they watched other Higgins boats motor back and forth for two days. The 2d Marines were ordered to "debark stations" a few times and then stood down again.

Trying to find something to kill time, Henrik and a couple of buddies looked over the Carley floats and were curious about the various containers lashed to the floats with stenciled warnings, "Do Not Open." It was too much for marines to ignore.

"Say, Jack," Henrik asked a passing swabby—he was certain most sailors were named "Jack." "I've got a question."

"Okay, shoot, Mac." He was certain most jarheads were named "Mac."

"What's in all these big cans in the floats?"

"About everything you'd need if lost at sea." Patting one of the five-gallon-sized airtight cylindrical cans, he added, "It's got first aid and fishing kits, distress signals, flashlight, rope, paddles, and lifeboat rations."

"There's chow in those big cans?" asked Griff slyly.

"Not anything you'd want to feast on. Brick-hard crackers, pemmican, chocolate, and malted milk tablets, and lots of cans of water."

"Thanks, Jack."

"It's Benjamin."

"Good to know what all's in those cans."

"It'll keep you alive for a spell, if anyone bothers to come looking for you out there in the big drink."

On the night of 31 July they departed Koro without fanfare, bearing northwest. The 2d Marines watched the island quickly fade into the gloom sadly not having set foot on dry land for a month.

"The ocean's clean," observed Mother O'Leary. "Not like the mud and dirt and insects on these paradise islands."

Only a few units had actually landed and pretended to storm the narrow beaches. Koro had been poorly reconnoitered and unknown coral reefs forced many 5th Marines to wade 200 yards to shore. Poor coordination with naval gunfire and air support, weak ship-to-shore communications, and little regard given to landing supplies further fouled the exercise. Despite all the practice back in Dago, troop over-the-side debarkation was too slow. The top brass were said to be concerned about departing for a major action without the problem areas being resolved. There wasn't time. Wherever they were going, they had to get there fast.

"Hey, Jack," said Henrik, meeting a swabby in the tweendeck companionway. "You look in the know. Where are we going?"

"I couldn't tell you if I knew."

"Come on, pal. Dugout Doug knows you know."

"You mean General MacArthur?"

"Oh, you know him too. See, I knew you'd have the scoop."

The swab glanced furtively down the companionway. "Guadalcanal."

"What's a Guadalcanal, Jack?"

"We looked it up in the *World Gazetteer* on the navigation bridge. It's either an island in the South Pacific or a landlocked town in Spain."

"Now I know why General Mac trusts you. Thanks, Jack."

"Sure thing, Mac. It's 1,400 miles nor'-west for six days."

***

Two days passed. The task force was steaming comparatively fast to lessen the chance of discovery by Jap reconnaissance flights. Zig-zags were less frequent.

Staffs were frantically working on operation orders which had to be worked out as they sailed on to this Guadalcanal place. There were no maps other than pre-war navigation charts and marginally accurate sketch maps and aerial photographs, which mostly showed palms, brush, trees, and occasional cleanings. The other information was written reports rendered by Aussie and Brit government officials, planters, and missionaries. It was a case of little time, even less information, and they had never planned an operation of this scope and complexity. To make it worse, logistics were inadequate and there were shortages in most key areas. To top it off, the 1st Marine Division's cargo was not combat loaded. Gear they might need right away had often been loaded in the bottom of the holds.

The 2d Marines' regimental intel officer was Major Van Ness, the R-2. He kicked off with a briefing on the Solomon Islands and the tactical situation.

"The Solomons are a double chain of seven large islands and almost a thousand small islands and islets. They run from the southeast 700 miles to the northwest end of Bougainville. Beyond Bougainville, where the Japs have a big naval base, there's an even larger Jap base. It's on the north end of New Britain, a place called Rabaul." He snapped his pointer on the map.

"We knew we were going to have to stop the Japs somewhere in the Solomons and we were getting ready for it. We didn't expect the Japs to begin to move so soon."

There were men thinking that the Japs had gotten the jump on them again. Henrik was one of them. *The Japs move and we react.*

"The Japs occupied the northernmost of the Solomons in March. Like us they were marshalling forces. They attacked the British administration on Tulagi at the beginning of May. They occupied it to establish a seaplane base to attack Port Moresby in New Guinea and keep an eye on Allied forces in New Caledonia, Fiji, and Samoa. We think they plan to take those islands so they can cut off the sea lanes between Hawaii and America to Australia and New Zealand."

Now they understood why there were so many Allied troops at all those places.

"On 4 May the Jap Navy seized Tulagi and Gavutu and set up a seaplane base at Tulagi. These are small islands on the south coast of the Florida Islands, a group of islands twenty miles north of Guadalcanal separated by Sealark Channel. We discovered they were building an airfield on Guadalcanal on 4 July. We bombed it at the end of July, hoping to delay its completion.

"I'm not going to sugarcoat it, marines. The Navy's estimated there are 5,000 Jap construction and service troops plus a reinforced 2,100-man infantry regiment on Guadalcanal and the Florida Islands."

Among the whistles and discouraging comments could be heard "Let's go get 'em" and "What are we waitin' for?"

"The airfield's 3,700 yards inland from the mouth of the Lunga River on Guadalcanal's north-central coast. That's where most of the Japs are. There are about 300 at their HQ on Tulagi and 500 on nearby Gavutu. There are no Jap aircraft at the airfield, yet. The seaplane patrol-bombers and float fighters moored at Tulagi will be hit by the Navy on D-Day morning."

The R-2 went into a lot of detail on Guadalcanal itself. It was ninety miles long and thirty or so miles wide. The island was densely forested with mountains over 7,000 feet above sea level. Those mountains had actually never been explored. The marines were caught off guard by its size, thinking most Pacific islands to be sandbars with a few palms as seen in cartoons. There were coconut palm plantations in the area of operations, and the rest of the island was densely forested with hard and softwood trees, brush, and coastal mangrove swamps. There were some open areas covered by kunai grass several feet high. They even raised cattle there.

The temperature ranged from the low 70s to the high 80s. While this was the dry season, rain showers blew in from the northwest, affecting the north coast the most, where they were headed. Humidity was in the high 90s.

"I need to let you know that these islands are going to be hell. They're populated by a venomous coral snake—it's rare—as well as crocodiles, bats, rats, leeches, spiders, scorpions, centipedes, sand fleas, mosquitos, and pigs."

"Pork for supper," shouted a machine gunner.

"Except they're wild and will try and kill you," responded the R-2. "Diseases are nasty and include malaria, dysentery, elephantiasis, dengue and blackwater fevers, leprosy, smallpox, tuberculosis, plague, and other nasties."

A ripple ran through the troops. Nobody felt good about this, and there was little boasting about toughing it out and kicking Jap butt. A BAR man did vent his opinion: "A field dressing, sulfa powder, and a handful of aspirin and I'll be fine."

"I'll have to keep an eye on you, gyrene," said a Corpsman.

"Now, for our mission. The 2d Marines is the 1st Marine Division's reserve regiment."

There were boos and hisses. "The pogues are going in ahead of us?" "Those candy asses will run like Army dogfaces."

"Settle down, marines. There will be no shortage of jobs for the 2d Marines. The 5th Marines will land on Beach Red on Guadalcanal. They're going to follow the coastline west to Lunga Point where the Japs are bivouacked. The 1st Marines will follow them ashore and they will thrust..."

"Make it hurt!" someone shouted. "Run them sombitches back to Tokyo."

"Settle down, marines. The 1st Marines will follow the 5th Marines ashore and push inland a mile and then head west to seize the airfield. We'll expand the area and dig in around that airfield and our engineers and the Seabees will finish it in short order. When ready, our own fighters will arrive and help defend the field along with the aircraft carriers supporting us." He looked around the intent faces. "The Japs aren't going to give up that piece of property at a bargain price. We estimate they'll come at us hard. They're going to throw everything in their shop window at us. They already have established almost a dozen airfields several hundred miles to the northwest on New Georgia and Bougainville and they have an advanced navy base at Shortland Island. That's at the south end of Bougainville. I can tell you that they're going to throw fighters and bombers at us day and night, and at night we're expecting destroyers and cruisers and even battleships to make a lot of holes in that newly acquired runway of ours." He paused for a moment to let his words sink in.

"So much for what the 1st Marine Division will be up to. I'll tell you what us 2d Marines are going to do."

"Kick some Jap butt. Make 'em pay for Wake," a marine shouted. "And Corregidor too," another added. "Jus' let me at 'em."

Henrik felt that old thirst for revenge during the days after Pearl Harbor and the other defeats. The intensity of training had refocused his mind, but that burn was coming back.

Waving a hand to quiet the boastful men, the R-2 continued, "We were projected to take the Santa Cruz Islands on 1 August. That's an island group a couple of hundreds of miles east of here. Then we would roll through the Solomons, but because of the Jap airfield under construction, it would place Jap bombers in range of our most forward airfields. Instead, we're going for the gold and heading straight for Guadalcanal. We needed more planning time to land on Guadalcanal so the operation was delayed until the 7th, that's Friday.

"As I said, we're the division reserve. We still might be sent to take Santa Cruz. The Navy wants us to do that, but the problem is there are no Japs there and it would be difficult now for them to reach Santa Cruz as our task force is in the way. Instead, we have other tasks of more immediate need and to be conducted just hours prior to the main landing on Guadalcanal."

Two staff rat marines taped up a sheet of butcher paper with the outlines of the five-by-twenty-five-mile Florida Islands marked in black grease pencil. On the south-central coast of the Floridas was a much inleted bay. With his pointer he tapped on the largest islet. "Tulagi with the Jap HQ and seaplane base, and two miles to its east are the smaller Gavutu-Tanambogo islands connected by a 250-yard concrete causeway."

"Where's Guadalcanal, sir?"

"About twenty miles south. On the deck below us."

He was answered with chuckles and nodding heads. It gave them a sense of scale.

"There'll be six battalions involved in this phase of the operation, kicking off before the main landing at Lunga Point on Guadalcanal. The Navy will attack the 15 seaplane patrol-bombers and seven float fighters moored at Tulagi at sunrise.

"In sequence, the 1st Battalion, 2d Marines, will land at 0740 and 0845 hours at two sites on Florida flanking Tulagi and search for possible Jap presence. At 0800 hours the 1st Raider Battalion will land on Tulagi to clear the island and later 1/5 will join them. The 1st Parachute Battalion will land on Gavutu at 1200 hours and also take the connected Tanambogo Island."

This was the first time it was known that raiders and paratroopers were even present.

"They jumping with parachutes?" someone asked.

"They're only jumping out of landing boats. The 3/2 Marines will be on standby to reinforce the seizure of any of the islands. After that it's anyone's guess where and how the two reserve battalions will deploy. It all depends on what the Japs do. Be ready for anything, boys."

The troops spent the afternoon studying mimeographed sketch maps of the different islands. They learned that islets throughout the Solomons had very narrow coral sand beaches or low limestone cliffs with seldom any beaches. The thick vegetation grew right to the edges of the cliffs and the narrow beaches.

They knew things were getting serious when more ammo was broken out. They had their basic loads of rifle, BAR, and machine gun ammo plus spare rifle bandoleers, but now they drew hand grenades and 60mm mortar rounds.

Henrik carried a hundred rounds of Springfield ammo in his cartridge belt plus two sixty-round bandoleers, and four Mk II fragmentation grenades hung on suspender rings. Two twenty-round magazines were in his haversack for Griff's BAR. Recalling the advice given by a Banana War marine at Dago, Henrik slipped a five-round charging clip into a pocket. Grenades made the swabbies nervous. Noncoms were nervous about accidental rifle discharges, constantly reminding them, "Lock your piece on safe and if I catch you with a round in the chamber you'll be shittin' it tomorrow."

Going into action, Henrik reflected on how he felt about facing the enemy. He couldn't shake the grainy newsreel scene of grubby Jap soldiers tramping down the mud they'd shoveled over old people and kids. He thought about Johanna, his little sister; white-haired Grandma and Grandpa, two of the kindest people ever. He even thought of Karen, whom he'd pretty much stopped thinking about, and the peculiar striking girl on the Texas train platform, and Jo too. The Japs killed folks because they were different or they had no use for them.

The 3d Battalion, 2d Marines, was the last battalion in the division reserve. There was a fact few understood. Infantry units have three sub-units; the battalion three companies, a company three platoons. Two are attacking or defending the frontline, and the third is that unit's reserve. Being in reserve could mean being left out of the initial fight, but as the battle evolved, the reserve gets committed where the most desperate fighting takes place. There was a "rule": don't reinforce defeat. The reserve would be committed where the most serious and successful fighting occurred. They had to finish the job.

More dismal than going into action was a medical issue. They were started on quinine and atabrine to help prevent malaria. Medics were at the end of chow lines to make sure they took the tablets. Quinine was a bitter horse pill, hard to choke down, while the little atabrine pills turned their eyes and skin yellow.

"You look like a Nip, Handyman," Griff announced with a chuckle.

"Look in a mirror, smart aleck."

PART TWO
Guadalcanal
Gadarukanaru

Guadalcanal Island in the southern Solomon Islands is the largest island group in the South Pacific. The Allied operation to seize the Solomon Islands, ARTHRITIS, was WATCHTOWER. To Americans it was known simply as "The Canal" or "Guadal." It was codenamed BEAVY, but was also known simply as "Cactus." CACTUS was actually the Guadalcanal–Tulagi objective area. Tulagi, codenamed RINGBOLT, was a small island group north of Guadalcanal across "Skylark Channel," aka "The Slot," adjacent to the Florida Islands—RUNABOUT.

The Japanese called the Solomons the *Soromon Shoto* and Guadalcanal was known as *Gadarukanaru*. Both the Marines and the Japanese knew the island as "Starvation Island," the Japanese by the contraction of starvation…*Ga-To*.

Chapter Sixteen

Obata was not speaking to Takeo Matsui, his so-called comrade in battle and fishing companion. The reprobate had betrayed him to Corporal Kaneko.

During a morning formation the regimental engineer officer announced a call for soldiers with experience on fishing boats, barges, ferries, work boats, and anyone who could repair Ford and General Motors or Chevrolet motors. "We have Ford trucks that are still being built in Nippon," he explained. There were also Australian-made Ford and Chevrolet cars and trucks left in Rabaul when the British and Australians evacuated. "They are invaluable for transportation."

Obata failed to raise his hand. He did not wish to find himself on a landing barge or even a battleship.

Takeo asked, "Why did you not respond, Obata? You are an experienced boatman, fisherman, and you know Ford motors."

"Our fishing in the mountain streams is enough, Takeo. I have spent enough time on transport ships too. The only ocean voyage I look forward to it the journey home."

"Obata, your enthusiasm for the war effort appears to be waning."

He did not answer, other than a shrug.

Two hours later he found himself ordered to the company headquarters with two other men. The company commander mentioned that this detail was temporary. The three of them were taken to the regimental headquarters with two other men. They reported to the engineer officer, a 1st lieutenant trained at the prestigious Tokyo University of Science.

Standing beside a large tent with a couple draftsmen and a clerk, the lieutenant greeted them. "You men volunteered to help us operate and maintain vehicle motors. We have much to do. We are forming additional landing barge shipping companies to supply our island positions in the lower

Solomons." Looking serious, he added, "The Americans are already attacking our bases there and we must respond immediately. What are your specialties?"

A nervous soldier said, "Honorable Lieutenant, I was a mere river fisherman with a two-meter boat."

"Did it possess a motor?"

"It was powered only by my paddle, Honorable Lieutenant." He was sent back.

The next man reported, "I am from Otsu, Honorable Lieutenant. I worked aboard a ten-meter fishing boat on Lake Biwa. It was powered by a Chevrolet motor."

"How long were you been employed in that work?"

"Four years, Honorable Lieutenant."

"I recall Biwa is a large lake. I have ridden the train that follows its western shore."

"It is 55 kilometers long, Honorable Lieutenant."

"It is a beautiful otherworldly place. You will do, Honorable Private."

Turning to Obata, he asked, "Your qualifications?"

Obata fleetingly considered lying, but his structured values did not allow that.

"Honorable Lieutenant, I only worked part time on my uncle's twelve-meter motor-sailer outside of Nagoya Bay. I can only do minor work on boat motors, changing sparkplugs, adjusting carburetors and the choke, and similar work. I apologize for my limited skills."

"You will do. What is your infantry specialty?"

"I am a sniper, Honorable Lieutenant."

He hesitated a moment, obviously glancing at Obata's rifle. "This is only temporary duty. You will soon have the opportunity to put your marksmanship skills to use."

Obata had thought it was the end of his fishing enterprise, but because of Takeo he was forced to continue it grudgingly.

***

Obata of course had seen numerous *Daihatsu* "large powered boats" in Nagoya tied to piers, motoring across harbors, and carried by some of the troop transports. Sailors liked to boast they were such good boats that the American Navy was trying to develop similar landing craft. The Imperial Army's Shipping Engineer Service and the Imperial Navy had been sailing them since 1930.

There were six of the 14-meter-long, three-meter-wide, nine-ton vessels tied up to the pier in side-by-side pairs. They were rectangular open-topped boxes with a high upswept bow holding a drop ramp. A truck or even a light tank could be carried in it or twelve tons of cargo, or sixty to seventy men. The coxswain's station was in the stern protected by a bulletproof shield. The 60-horsepower gasoline motor was in the fantail compartment, giving it a speed of nine knots. They had a reputation for robust construction.

The Daihatsus were meant for amphibious assault landings, but they were widely used as supply barges and as local ship-to-ship and ship-to-shore lighters. Obata found out that even though it was over 1,000 kilometers to Guadalcanal, the Daihatsus would be employed to transport troops and supplies southeast to that mysterious island.

Of course there was talk they might not have to do this. Rumors suggested troops had already been sent to attack the American foothold before they could dig in. It appeared the Americans had taken over an uncompleted airfield on Guadalcanal. No one knew for certain what the situation was, but seemed to think they exclusively knew what was going on.

More Daihatsus came in through that day and the next, tying up to piers and jetties all around the harbor. Larger barges arrived too, seventeen-meter Toku Daihatsus. Dozens of the barges were painted in olive drab, greens, and grays. The hope was that they would all be repainted green to blend with the vegetation growing to the water's edge on these islands. AA machine guns were being mounted.

A barge crewman mentioned they had only a 180-kilometer cruising range. On hearing that, Obata decided there was only a slim chance he would even depart for Guadalcanal.

His work was simple, making minor motor repairs and adjustments. Obata oversaw a three-man detail cleaning and resetting sparkplug gaps. Most also needed a tune-up and some wanted for coolant hoses. This proved a challenge as there was a shortage of the proper size hoses. Overseeing the work, a 2nd lieutenant travelled from pier to pier inspecting, directing, and solving problems. He was a graduate of the Army's Mechanized Equipment Maintenance School in Tokyo and often came up with workable solutions.

The lieutenant spoke with Obata as he adjusted a motor's choke. After asking him questions about the motors, he said he needed an assistant. Equipped with bicycles, they rode about the harbor area in search of abandoned automobiles and trucks. The next day the lieutenant gave Obata an authorization letter allowing him freedom of movement throughout the port area to recover abandoned vehicle parts. It was signed by a lieutenant colonel of a service command whose military title Obata could not decipher.

He was issued a blue-painted Australian Comet bicycle with a wire basket on the handlebars and a fruit crate wired to the rear rack. Armed with tinsnips, pliers, a scarce adjustable wrench, hacksaw, and screwdrivers he explored Rabaul's backstreets, junk piles, and scrapyards. He even found three serviceable truck motors which they recovered from Honest Maccas' Garage. He had been told to be on the lookout for goats and pigs left by the Australians. Most had apparently been collected by sailors and natives. Dogs too were sought.

He had to be on alert for teenaged natives bent on ambush, intent on heisting his found parts. Since a *"Japman,"* as the boys called him, was collecting automobile parts they must be valuable and worth stealing, even if they had no idea whom to sell them to. Having found a thick-bladed wooden cricket bat in a garage, Obata would brandish the bat shouting, *"Ron bo. Blong mi fela!"*—Run boy. Belong to me fella!—essentially exhausting his Pidgin-English. Other, more obliging, boys led him to abandoned vehicles. He awarded them with a jar of stale Australian butterscotch rock candies he had found in a glove compartment.

One boy was so bold as to steal his bike. As the boy could barely reach the pedals, Obata managed to chase him down. Dragging the thief off, he gave him several swats with the flat of his bayonet, shouting, *"Ravis bo!"*—Bad boy!

More difficult was the occasional *Kenpeitai* patrol. Rarely did he encounter the Imperial Navy equivalent, the *Tokkeitai*—Special Police Corps. The Kenpeitai were identified by black double-chevron insignia on their chests and red-on-white armbands. The military police were arrogate and smug. Pistols and hand-carved judicial whipping canes backed their authority with on-the-spot street punishment for thieving and idle natives. Some conceitedly carried British Webley revolvers.

Revolvers menacingly drawn, the Kenpeitai would wave him to halt. After searching his salvaged goods, they would gleefully declare he was pillaging with intent to peddle the items on the black market. Obata would flourish his signed pass which they would earnestly read. They would reluctantly dismiss him, but still admonished him as though he had been caught plundering for personal profit. Simply a face-saving gesture on their part.

Still, they made it known that they had shot natives for pilferage, theft of Imperial food and medical supplies, and failing to show respect.

***

Simple cafes, restaurants, and bordellos—*piya*—catering to the Japanese sprang up as flowers throughout Rabaul—what was called the "water trade." Former British and native clubs, cafes, and houses were taken over and prospered or died depending on the quality of management, food and drink, and amenable accommodations, especially those of the more tender kind provided by the girls. Not only did the Army and the Navy have their own establishments, but even units had specific businesses they accommodated—for example, the infantry, artillery, antiaircraft, engineers, and most other branches.

While most soldiers thought the girls—comfort women or *pi*—worked for specific whorehouses, and some did depending on contract arrangements, others worked two or three clubs on different nights. Some men followed their favorites from club to club. Other soldiers, either too shy or too poor, merely gathered as street-corner sightseers, wishing only for the pleasures of the make-believe geishas. Even country boys were familiar with the dream world of the geishas formally trained in the arts of entertaining men with conversation, dance, and song. This was for men of wealth and power of course—businessmen, officers, and government officials. True geishas were far beyond the reach of mere soldiers. The girls were but only shadows of genuine geishas. Even their scant poorly copied makeup and cheap worn-out kimonos were make-believe.

Obata would pedal past the clubs and stop for a rest and chat with soldiers who may have noticed abandoned vehicles and appliances he could reclaim. Mainly though, the rest stops were simply to catch glimpses of the exotic girls drifting through the lounges.

***

One day, while Obata explored a backstreet, a native teenage boy motioned for him to follow, leading him through a backdoor of the *Girasole*—Sunflower—one of many "hostess clubs" that used native boys to lure in customers. Instead, the fat middle-aged Japanese manager said he had heard Obata was a motor repairman. They had a small petrol motor in need of mending, an Australian-made Briggs & Stratton 5-horsepower. It powered some lights and an old refrigerator; an appliance Obata rarely saw. Looking over the motor, Obata thought he could receive a nice payment, as he could easily report the motor and refrigerator and confiscate them. The manager informed him that in lieu of monetary recompense he could have twenty minutes with one of his "sunflowers." Obata reasoned this would be more beneficial than reporting the manager and confiscating the motor and appliance. It was such a surprise that at first he respectably declined, but he changed his mind when a girl drifted past clad in a thin red robe. "I will examine the motor and see if it can be repaired," he announced.

Encouraged by inexplicable urges, he made quick work of the repairs. He had only to clean and re-gap the sparkplug, blow out the fouled fuel line, clean the gunk out of the carburetor, and give it a good overall cleaning. With the manager and several of the girls looking anxiously over his shoulder, he gave three strong yanks on the starter cord. It kicked over and the 1930s-built Westinghouse refrigerator hummed sweetly. They gave him a round of cheers, pleased that they would be able to enhance the club's reputation with ice and cold drinks.

Wiping his hands with a rag, he was directed to a room in a corrugated tin house behind the Sunflower. There were three or four rooms. Through a draped open door he saw they were curtain-divided into two roomlets, each with a cot and washstand. Soft throaty sounds emerged from a backroom. There was only an illusion of privacy for intimacies.

This was new ground for Obata and he became increasingly nervous, a nagging reluctance tugging at him. The idea of slipping out the backdoor and pedaling away was tempting. But he was a soldier of the Emperor and required to demonstrate valor and fortitude. Bravery in these circumstances was no doubt required. Would the Emperor approve? He must; the clubs were operated by civilian vendors contracted by the Imperial Army in the Emperor's name, discreetly.

She passed through the curtained door, blowing out the candle on the shelf. There was still enough light to make out her threadbare pink housecoat. Thoughts of fleeing on a pair of wheels evaporated. She had an agreeable face of desirable pale tone. She was not thin, but was not plump either. She moved slowly but purposely without seeming to hurry. "Your first time, is it not?"

How does she know? Denial formed on his lips, but why lie about this? Certainly she would know. "Yes."

Her accent differed from his. "Where are you from?" he asked.

"Where are *you* from?" she asked softly like he had not first asked her.

"Nagoya."

"A large city on Honshu. I am from Naha on Okinawa."

That explained why her Japanese was different. "I have never met anyone from the Ryukyu Islands."

"I have met many brave soldiers from Nagoya," she whispered, unbuttoning his shirt.

"Your accent is very similar to Japanese but some syllables sound different." He was rambling in his shy reluctance.

She unbuttoned his shorts and let them fall and pressed her softness against him. "Lie back on the cot. You have to do nothing." She withdrew the long thin wooden pins from her hair, letting it descend softly over her shoulders. The housecoat slid to the floor.

Sparrows chirped in the rafters.

***

The next B-17 bomber attack was even less spectacular than the 7 August bombardment. There were always a few fighters on aerial alert high over Rabaul town, harbor, and the airfields. More Japanese fighters, single- and double-engine, and bigger two-engine bombers arrived almost daily as parking ramps were completed. They had ample warning of the bombers' approach. It was rumored that the Japanese had established lookout posts on small islands further southeast in the Solomons. It was just one of many rumors.

As the bombers rumbled over, Obata was in no hurry to shelter. This part of town held native-dug air raid trenches near most intersections. There were only six B-17s in this raid's single wave. A few bombs landed in the harbor. Passing over, one of the bombers curved away from the formation, angling slightly downward and leaving irregular puffs of black smoke that changed into a solid thickening trail. Many of the fighters broke off and followed in hopes of an easy kill.

He had heard stories of fighter pilots going after damaged airplanes—glory hunting—and machine-gunning airmen as their parachutes lowered them to Earth's salvation. Did Japanese pilots undertake such malicious tactics? Pilots were said to be honorable, educated, handpicked men. It was later reported that two of the American bandit bombers had been shot down.

Obata felt they must have flown a great distance to reach here. No one even guessed where they were coming from. Rabaul was a long way from this Guadalcanal. *Were the ineffective American raids doing any good? This Guadalcanal must be important.*

The lieutenant called Obata to walk with him. "You have done very good work, Honorable Private. There is another assignment that the regimental operations officer wishes to speak to you of."

***

In fine-tuning the motors Obata realized that the motor he had repaired at the Sunflower might need its governor adjusted. He returned with a tool bag and offered to adjust the governor to prevent its damage and ensure it would run more effectively. Using a crescent wrench and screwdriver, he full-opened the throttle and adjusted the locking nuts on the governor arm. It did not take long, but he informed the manager that he had to check his adjustments frequently to ensure proper operation.

The manager was ever grateful for his efforts to maintain the little motor's efficiency.

Mornings were slow and the girl from Okinawa was without companionship. She called it "sharing a cigarette."

Chapter Seventeen

The USS *President Adams* accompanying Transport Group YOKE was west of Guadalcanal. At 0310 hours, 7 August—eight months to the day from the Pearl Harbor attack—it passed Savo Island in the middle of Sealark Channel. Reveille and Breakfast Call sounded. The men were groggy from a short night and what restless sleep could be grabbed—and, well, look at where they were. They were fed beefsteak, baked beans, real eggs, biscuits and jam, coffee, and orange juice. "Chocolate cake tonight in celebration of a successful landing," promised a cook.

Regardless, they had lucked out. They suspected the Japs were not aware of their approach. Jap patrol-bombers at Rabaul were weather-grounded on 5 and 6 August. Henrik wondered how long that little surprise would last, with some sixty ships of an invasion fleet cruising down Sealark Channel at twelve knots.

Orders ensured each man had a full ammo load, one day of C-rations in haversacks, and canteens topped off. The stay-behind knapsack wasn't needed. They'd been told to shave, brush their teeth, and take a piss as they readied. The CO had ordered squad leaders to ensure grenades were secured and not hanging on gear by their pull-rings. That had been brought up at a final officers' call. Apparently there had been some accidents.

The platoon sat in the tweendeck companionway waiting. Most dozed or tried to. A few read with hands shrouded over their flashlight lens. Someone played a harmonica—a cowboy song meant to quiet cattle.

"That'll wear out your batteries," someone advised to no avail.

Some penned yet another final letter. They'd ask a swabby to drop them in the mail room slot. Squids and jarheads picked on one another, but at these times their outlook changed. The squids knew the Marines were heading into hell.

Diamond, the BAR squad leader, tossed Sugar Babies candy into his mouth. Snacks repeatedly popped bubble gum balloons. Griff worried a gob of chewing tobacco around in his mouth, shared with him by a swabby. At least he had a condensed milk can to spit into. McKern snored.

They wore utilities, by now faded to a lighter sage green, more gray than green.

This is it, the real thing, thought Henrik. *It's not training, it's not an exercise. It's not a rehearsal.* He demanded of himself not to dwell on the bad things that could happen. *What is the opposite of this place and this time, this hotbox still sunbaked from yesterday? The dead stale clamminess soured by sweat and humidity?* He sat on a steel deck among men he knew well or not so well. *What is the opposite of this cramped, blistering little world?* he wondered, wishing he could take himself there.

Sitting cross-legged, Henrik felt a drifting change. He mentally sat on an old burlap game bag through which he could not yet feel the snow's cold. His back rested against an ancient oak. It wasn't actually cold, but he could no longer feel the sweat trickling down his sides. A pure chilled breeze drifted toward him from the deer trail. Clean, chilled, and dry. No odors, just pure country air and the freshest scent of the cold sleeping forest. A scene from *The Call of the Wild.*

"All hands," bellowed the PA. "It's 0600 hours. Man your embarkation stations."

"Wake up, Sleeping Beauty." Griff nudged him.

"I wasn't sleeping," mumbled Henrik, rubbing his burning eyes.

"So what? I wish I was," muttered Gentry, a BAR man.

"Let's move it, kids," said Diamond.

On deck they couldn't make out anything, not even the hulking shapes of the Florida Islands close to port. By now Henrik was more or less thinking in nautical port and starboard references.

"Unbuckle your chin straps and cartridge belts. Be ready to ditch them if you're sinking." Henrik shuddered at the thought of his water-filled boondockers dragging him to the bottom.

The two transport groups, YOKE for Florida and X-RAY for Guadalcanal, with eight and fifteen transports, respectively, crossed wakes before reaching Savo Island. At 0614 hours the fire support group opened up on probable targets on Guadalcanal. No response. The Japs had no coast defense guns. Navy fighters hit the Jap seaplane base at Tulagi at 0630 hours, destroying all the amphibian planes. Not one made it aloft. They could see high-octane fireballs plunge skyward. They were strafed until the riddled hulls and floats sank.

Memories of that day were confusing and perplexing. So much happened so quickly. Most everything went as planned, sort of. There were problems of course, the unexpected, and some changes had to be made immediately; other things that should have been changed weren't. The Japs were more stubborn and tenacious than expected, at least on the small islands off of Florida.

It was a different matter on Guadalcanal; rumors reported some 3,000 Jap construction laborers had fled into the brush with barely a shot.

The first offensive landing made by the Marines in this war saw Company B, 1/2 Marines searching Florida Island at 0740 hours west of Tulagi. The rest of the battalion followed an hour later. Meeting no resistance, they returned to their transport and stayed cocked on standby. From one of the islets they saw a green flare. "First wave's landing," a shadow glumly remarked.

The 1st Raider Battalion soon landed on Tulagi, blocked by coral and heavy fire. They had a rough fight against Special Naval Landing Force troops in the extensive fortifications and natural caves piercing the rugged limestone hills. Reinforced by 2/5 Marines, they fought all night, and the island didn't fall until the next evening. The 200 Japs fought to the bitter end. The marines had expected them to be resolute, but to fight to the last man, literally? It took 1,500 marines to finish them. "imperial marines," someone muttered. "Don't call 'em marines," groused an NCO.

Marines of the 1st Parachute Battalion amphibiously assaulted Gavutu–Tanambogo at 1800 hours after blasting by naval gunfire and carrier air support. The two small islands were connected by a 250-yard-long, six-foot-wide concrete causeway. While the paratroopers took most of Tanambogo, the fight lasted all night and the battered paratroopers had been hit hard. The 3/2 Marines had to reinforce the paratroopers and complete taking the two islets. They would land directly onto Gavutu in the late morning and finish securing it. With suppressing fire from Tanambogo, they would assault across the causeway and clear connected Tanambogo. Henrik considered that, running fully exposed across a causeway two and a half football fields long. Obviously a bad deal.

**

"All hands. Man your embarkation stations."

"On your feet, off your butts, outta the shade, and into the sun, kids," shouted Sergeant Diamond.

They had watched Jap torpedo-bombers make runs at them. The torps missed and one had streaked under them, scaring the daylights out of those seeing the faint white streak out of the blue.

Four men at a time climbed over the gunwale. A seaman on either side of the net helped the loaded men over the rolling ship's side. The first LCPs had been hung on davits, allowing the troops to first climb aboard the boats before being lowered. No need for the clumsy landing nets. They circled off to port, awaiting the slower loading boats that had to be lowered by derricks, and the troops climbing down the nets. The sea was rough enough to make net climbing hazardous. The two gunners of the landing craft crew clung to the net's bottom end, trying to hold it away from the landing craft's gunwale and the ship's lunging side. Henrik's haversack and ammo load felt like they were trying to pull him off the heaving net.

Across the channel could be seen the hilly, tree-covered islets of Gavutu–Tanambogo. Oil tanks on Gavutu burned, sending thick columns of black smoke high into the sky. Gavutu was a 148-foot hill. Curious heads popped up to quickly eyeball the islands. An Avenger scout-bomber from the *Wasp* shrieked over, causing the passengers to first think it might have misidentified them as Nips.

"That had to be a 500-pounder blockbuster," someone shouted, as debris rained down around them, chunks of limestone landing in and beside the boat with a spray of water. Distant booms and rumblings filled the air. Aircraft drifted over them, too high to identify. One black speck began to tumble erratically earthward, with pieces flying off and flaring into a fiery column that soon burned itself out. Crossing white contrails could be seen even higher. *What is it like to be strapped in a cramped cockpit with spraying oil and flames billowing into the compartment? Think of something different, stupid. How would it feel to be machine-gunned in the water and attacked by sharks? This line of reasoning isn't working…*

Henrik looked southward, barely making out the veiling clouds and the high ridgelines of Guadalcanal. Being twenty miles away, there was no smoke or aircraft to be seen. *I need to be thinking about our objective island and pay no attention to Guadalcanal.*

The LCPs wallowed about as the deckhands shoved off. Engines gunned and they gathered-way, circling and then forming a column. They bucked through the surf toward the small islands at eight knots. Spray showered the thirty men in the 36-foot plywood boats. "AP26-18" was painted on the bows, translating to Troop Transport 26, Landing Craft 18. The two machine gunners—deckhands—manned their .30-caliber Lewis guns in the forward cockpits. They lacked bow ramps with the troops debarking over the sides and off the bow. The coxswain was in the aft portion near the motor.

"Keep your stupid heads down, ya bunch of dumbass jarheads!" the coxswain ordered. He meant well.

Another shower of debris splashed about them. The sharp smell and taste of burning fuel saturated the air.

"They dropped that last bomb right on Gavutu," Henrik shouted. "I thought the paratroopers held Gavutu?"

"They do, but the Japs still hold maybe a fifth of that shit pile."

"Great."

Something heavy splashed into the waves. The briefing had said they'd first finish clearing Gavutu and then clear the causeway to the smaller Tanambogo. An entire parachute battalion had fought all day and through the night and they only held a piece of Gavutu. The islet was only 500 yards long and 250 yards wide. Tanambogo was about two-thirds smaller. The word was that the paratroopers' casualties were high.

The crack of bullets passed over them. They could hear ripping fire from the islets now, as the paratroopers were laying down suppressive fire to cover their approach. The Japs realized where the boats were heading as they changed their bearing directly for Gavutu. Oily smoke stung their eyes and throats, prompting a chorus of hacking coughs. *Wish I had time to open my canteen for a gulp.*

Henrik could see details of the islets now—rugged limestone, blasted wooden buildings, fire-boiling black smoke, and wreckage scattered everywhere. The column of boats broke up when the control boat hoisted a red BAKER flag, "Land the Landing Force." They spread into a line formation and made the landing run.

A peek at the shoreline revealed lush green brush and palms hanging on the water's edge. Bullets smacked into the water. It wasn't like the pipsqueak splashes of water in war movies. Six-foot gouts of water sprayed.

The three boats suddenly slowed. The bow gunners gripped the obsolescent Lewis guns' butt stocks. They weren't firing. They and the passengers had been told not to fire during the approach unless they saw live Japs. There were friendlies already ashore.

Approaching the islet's south end, they could see half of it was a rugged, blasted hill sloping down to the water's edge. The blunt bow jammed into the shore. One of the bow gunners clambered out of the cockpit and dropped into the troop compartment to give the troops a boost. "Get the hell outta here, jarheads. Kill them Nips!"

Doing our best!

The troops scrambled over the bow, with bullets cracking even more insistently. Some men went over the sides. Grounded ten yards from shore, the men were in hip-deep water. Looking back, more three-boat waves ran toward them. The beach was too narrow, and Eureka boats were jammed side by side and the following men had trouble getting ashore. Boats were trying to back out. Machine-gun spray snapped among and on the boats, sending wood splinters flying. Concussion-killed fish drifted in the surf. One was a glittering royal blue, so out of place.

Henrik splashed through the water and went prone on wet sand with his legs washed by waves. His eyes were wide, trying to take in everything. Gentry was beside him. He turned to Henrik with a confused look. "Oh no." He gagged and his mouth gaped impossibly wide as blood gushed out. His face dropped into the water, tendrils of red swirling around him. Henrik grabbed a shoulder strap and on hands and knees dragged Gentry a few feet to clear the water. He convulsed and went still. "Diamond!" Henrik shouted.

The BAR squad leader turned back and scooped up the BAR. "Get his belt, Handyman."

He slung his rifle and struggled to get the belt harness and pack off Gentry. "Geez, heavy damn thing." Eight magazines, canteen, first aid pouch, cleaning gear and spare parts, and a couple of grenades, plus the heavy C-rat filled haversack, poncho, and e-tool.

The platoon leader was yelling, "Get up the hill." There were caves, gullies, and outcroppings everywhere. Loose gravel crumbled under Henrik's boots and he kept sliding back.

"Get up to the top of the hill with the mortar OP," the LT ordered Henrik. "Get that MG squad up there."

The weapons platoon LT and mortar section leader were already at the crest. *How'd they get up here so quick? They landed behind us.* They were in a rusted, broken-down corrugated steel shack with Japanese-dug fighting holes in the dirt floor. Gravel sprayed from Jap machine guns' hammering bursts. Yellow tracers bounded in all directions. More holes than Swiss cheese. The paratroopers might have a foothold on the island, but it was a tiny shoe.

As soon as the gunner flung the low tripod down, the assistant gunner slapped the Browning gun onto it. In one swift movement the gunner rolled behind the gun, cocked it, and the assistant fed in the web belt, sending a spray of old-issue green tracers into the islet's flat area toward the causeway. There were numerous burnt and burning buildings. The two 60mm mortars' rounds started bursting about that area too. The noise intensified as more of the battalion came ashore, adding their firepower. Other troops were crowding the rear side of the hill. There were wounded, stragglers, and some reluctant to charge into the fray. Camouflage-suited paratroopers were scattered among them, many with field dressings, handkerchiefs, and even empty bandoleers as tourniquets.

"You're a sniper, aren't you?" It took a moment for Henrik to recognize his sand- and mud-covered platoon leader.

"Yes, sir."

"Then start sniping!"

He considered putting rounds into bodies, just to make sure, but he couldn't tell Japs from Americans and wouldn't take that chance. Anyone down there was trying to hide. He decided to shoot into the wrecked corrugated buildings, firing a five-round clip through each. He aimed low, as any occupants would be hugging the deck. It did some good. A man darted from the back of one and rolled into a ditch. A barrage of marine rifle and BAR fire fell on the ditch.

Return fire intensified, with more automatic weapons joining in with rifles and mortars. A roaring noise increased, and Henrik looked up to see a blue and white Avenger pulling out of a dive. His eyes fixed on the bomb, he felt a hollow sensation. Nothing made sense.

"Down!"

Almost simultaneously with the bomb's impact, he saw the bent water pipe with a white Jap flag bearing a red "meatball" fluttering over their position.

He came to in stages. *Am I dead?* There was only a yellow glare and a rushing sound. He decided the black specks drifting on the breeze were high-flying aircraft. The rushing grew steadily louder. He could hear muffled gunfire. *Maybe I'm alive.*

His legs hurt, arms too. His left arm was numb and blood-splattered. He still wasn't convinced he was alive. Must be, however. He'd just wait until some feeling came back. His head ached and felt like it was full of wet cotton balls. He was lying on his back, head down the slope. The Jap flag was gone. A ripping barrage of shells crumped among the wreckage on the island's level half. Bits of debris peppered the ground. He remembered the USS *San Juan* was providing fire support with its sixteen 5-inch guns. The antiaircraft cruiser could fire 240 rounds in two minutes, shrouding the islets in explosions. Scout/observer floatplanes from cruisers orbited the area.

"Hey, Mac, you still in one piece? Ah, hell, I guess not." The corpsman crouched and felt Henrik's arms and legs, his torso too. "Let's get you to your feet." More explosions and debris.

"All that blood must be theirs." Henrik nodded at the mangled machine-gun crew and some other marines; three dead and nine wounded by the bomb. *These are fellas I knew.*

Still feeling wobbly, Henrik and a couple of others followed the corpsman down the hill, where they were turned over to the battalion aid station in the old British Lever Brothers office. Eventually he was checked over and a few small fragments were picked out of his arms. He was lucky with the largest fragment. It was hot enough to cauterize the wound and he'd not bled. The surgeon, Doctor Eisenberg, told him to rest for a time and drink some grape juice before returning to his company. After leaving, he found an ammo supply point and replenished his ammo and picked up a half-dozen bandoleers, figuring they might be needed.

Henrik found his platoon near the small boat basin and the Tanambogo causeway. By now Gavutu was cleared except for the occasional stragglers hiding somewhere and usually weaponless. Gavutu was now being called "U2" and Tanambogo was "Bogo."

He was brought up to date. At 1620 hours Company I would land by Higgins on Bogo's northwest end. Two 45-foot Landing Craft, Mechanized, or LCM Mk IIs, would each land an M3 Stuart light tank from Company C, 2d Tank Battalion, on the east shore. They were armed with a 37mm gun and five .30-cal machine guns. Henrik's company would rush the causeway from U2.

There was a ragged exchange of rifle and machine-gun bursts, either to harass or provoke the others to reveal their positions. Most tried futilely to sleep, the air too thick with tension to allow them to rest. Some men filtered back to the rear to treat minor wounds and returned with ammo.

Henrik had fired off some 50 rounds at anything that might hide Japs. He refilled his cartridge belt pockets. There was little water and what was available was brackish. No one even thought about eating.

He considered they would be completely exposed for the 250-yard sprint—two and a half football fields. He thought about the hundred-yard sprints he'd done in school. *No way. But I have to.* There wasn't much of a plan.

Platoon Sergeant Krass relayed, "Cross single file in at least ten-foot intervals, bayonets fixed, don't stop even for your wounded best buddy. You'll just become a target. If hit and you can move, try to go over the side and hide under the deck." The causeway was only two feet above water. "Once on the far side start clearing out the buildings, caves, ditches, wreckage, dugouts, and fortifications."

Shy of 1600 hours, the word spread to standby. Squad leaders checked ammo and did a quick grenade reallocation. The battalion aid station set up a forward collection point near the foot of the causeway. Company K's 4th Platoon, with four water-cooled Brownings, covered Henrik's company, sending streams of new-issue red tracers into buildings, pillboxes, rubble piles, and other likely targets. They talked about screening the causeway dash with smoke grenades, but there weren't any.

"Pass out those 60 Mike-Mike rounds to 3d Platoon and have them drop them off at the mortars."

The new destroyers USS *Buchanan* and *Monssen* softened up Bogo and again regrettably caused marine casualties. It was impossible to determine precise marine positions. At 1615 hours the heavy machine gun platoon started hammering rounds, sweeping the blackened wreckage heap of Bogo. 60mm and 81mm mortars began dropping rounds on the already battered corrugated and wood plank buildings.

The idea of marines running zig-zag, hitting the deck frequently, rolling, and bounding to the next bit of cover was impossible on the bare-backed causeway. At 1620 hours the first squad started over, ten to twenty feet between men. No one fired; they just ran in a beeline as fast as boondockers could carry them and wishing themselves as small as possible. Most made it. Few were hit. Jap machine guns on Bogo were partly screened by buildings and vegetation.

Henrik glared up the causeway. At the far end was a pile of broken concrete. That was his goal. There were bodies on the causeway. *Ignore them*, he told himself, then pushed up and with his rifle at port arms, took off like he was running a sprint. He tripped on broken chunks of limestone, went down, and was up and running. Bullets cracked past him. Lungs burning, face on fire, he dived behind the broken concrete, banging his knee. There was a surreal sensation of passing and ignoring dead bodies. His lungs begged for air.

Gaomi Island was a tiny palm tree-studded sandbar 250 yards northeast of Bogo and now called "Palm." Jap riflemen and a machine gun were hidden there and firing on the causeway with effect. A squad leader spotted the MG's flash and was directing riflemen reaching Bogo to fire on it. Henrik and others reached the far side, taking cover in craters scattered through the overgrown golf links.

He found a big enough bomb crater and crawled into it. With his e-tool he cut a slot through the blasted heaped earth rimming the crater. He laid some brush limbs and palm fronds over the front. When he could make out movement, he took an occasional shot at little Gaomi Island. Sometimes it was mere vegetation fluttering in the breeze. Nightfall was 1820 hours.

Two LCM lighters emerged from U2's shadows where they had first landed to pick up troops to cover the tanks. They signaled they were landing on Bogo's east side in support of the nearby Company I landing. Beaching a couple of hundred yards from Henrik, they ran into shore. The Japs let loose with a barrage of fire, having no effect on the tanks. They opened up with their 37mm and machine guns, which were joined by the LCMs' .50-cals. Without warning, dozens of Japs lurched out of the wreckage and brush as the M3 Stuart tanks rumbled down the bow ramps. Marines who could bear on the action all along the shore opened fire on the swarming Japs as they threw grenades and Molotov cocktails at pointblank range and even jammed a wrecking bar into the lead tank's treads. Having left its few accompanying marines behind as it charged ashore, the tank had stalled and was overwhelmed. The platoon leader and a crewman were killed, but forty-two dead Nips lie clustered around the burned-out tank. The second tank came ashore and its accompanying riflemen stayed with it.

Company I landed just to the north of the tanks and surged up the hill firing, bayoneting, and grenading their way over the top. They mostly cleared the two islands by 2200 hours.

Henrik and others in their company were left behind at Bogo's causeway, keeping Jap stragglers from slipping past. They placed fire on little Gaomi 250 yards away. It was still occupied by a few Japs who sniped at passing LCPs delivering supplies and evacuating wounded.

***

It was an hour past sunset. A wooden jetty poked out from the shore to Henrik's left. Three floating bodies bobbed under the broken pier, along with wooden debris. He had buddied up with Griff to share the bomb crater. It still held the burnt TNT smell. Henrik noticed the blasted soil was devoid of moisture—dry and crumbly. The LT had given Henrik the job of giving the Japs on Gaomi a bad night. He couldn't see a thing, just a low black blob against a black sky and water. Navy star shells occasionally burst over the channel but were no help, only hampering his night vision. The flares caused drifting, crisscrossing palm shadows, hiding enemy movement. The artillery finally secured firing the yellow-tinted parachute flares as they were revealing where the ships were moored to the occasional Jap bombers.

Surprisingly, there were no star shells over Guadalcanal.

Dawn was far off, and neither Griff nor Henrik had a watch. They guessed at their two-hour shift changes, but they were probably much shorter than they thought. The urge was to habitually clean their rifles, but no one dared for fear of Japs plunging out of the darkness. The order was to fix bayonets to meet a Nip charge. Henrik didn't like that. It had been drilled into him that a bayonet on his rifle would affect its accuracy, owing to the added weight at the muzzle and vibrations or harmonics as the instructor taught. He realized it made no difference when shooting at short-range dodging and ducking forms.

He set frag grenades on the edge of his hole and tried to remain as alert as an exhausting day allowed. He tried not to think of the charred bodies, the bloated and afloat bodies, the sprawling bodies peppered with bullet holes and shot so many times to make sure they were dead, and the mangled bodies torn open by explosions. His canteen was almost empty.

On the hill a dead marine his age had been caught by death so swiftly he didn't know he'd died. *That could be me in the next thirty seconds.* He had found himself counting down to thirty as he clawed his way up. He ordered himself to stop. To stall, he bent over "examining" a Jap's corpse and busted off the rifle's stock. He'd never get used to mangled dismembered bodies.

Now from his hole at the water's edge, Henrik counted the three floating bodies under the jetty. He thought maybe the tide would carry them out. How many times had he counted them? Now there were four. How could one have drifted in and the others remain there? Unless they were tangled in nets or debris. He started to wake Griff. *No, let him sleep.*

He couldn't determine which floater the new arrival was, until the third from the left started to drift ever so slowly. It stopped. Had the breeze shifted? Had debris hung up the drifter? It was moving again, steady. The others were stalled. It was moving toward him, or appeared to. Henrik took careful aim. Maybe fifty feet away. Let it drift. It passed in front of him and drifted more to his right. It "ran aground" beside a pile of broken-up crates at the water's edge. Twenty feet away, it moved, barely noticeable. Henrik had quietly shifted to aim over the heaped sand around the crater. A distorted shape slithered silently out of the water. Blending into the broken wood, it rose to all fours. He couldn't make out a weapon. The thumb safety lever on the end of the bolt had already been turned to the left. A distant star shell cast enough light to outline the figure, now rock still. If he'd not known it was there he'd not have discerned it from the piled wood. He locked his arms in a supported position and aligned the rear sight's notch with the front sight's blade. This alignment led to the center of the head that Henrik viewed as a disc, a bullseye.

Another star shell glistened, backlighting the Jap with swaying shadows. He inhaled softly, let out a breath, and smoothly squeezed the trigger. A crack and a fountain of water sprayed.

"What?" muttered Griff.

"Nothin'. Go back to sleep."

Within seconds Griff had drifted off.

Henrik wondered what that floating Nip had intended to do.

Sometime after 0100 in the early morning hours, the marines noted distant flashes to the west. It went on for the rest of the night, flickering flashes, wavering glows that died and recurred, and lots of star shells. Sweeping spotlights silhouetted ghostly ship superstructures through the smoky haze. Deep rumbles washed over the intervening waters. Dawn washed out the flashes and flickering afterglows. They were replaced by smudges of black and gray smoke on the western horizon.

"Had to be a big naval action," muttered Griff, rubbing his grit-filled eyes.

They expected increased air activity, but there was none to be seen; no white stars with red centers or any solid red "meatballs."

They had been distracted by a few assorted landing craft making runs to the small islands around Tulagi. Marines were being ferried to even the smallest islets to mop up Jap stragglers. Shots and machine-gun bursts were faintly heard. Occasional grenade thumps shook the air.

Henrik realized he'd not eaten, but he'd had no appetite since that exceptional shipboard breakfast two days earlier. The flies grew worse as it warmed up.

Platoon Sergeant Krass came down U2's scorched hillside carrying some dog tags. He'd let them look through them to see who bought the farm. "You clowns notice anything?"

"We need to run a police call to tidy up the place?" asked Griff, shifting his BAR.

"No? You couldn't pour soup from your boondockers with the instructions on the sole." Sweeping his eyes around, he said, "There's not a ship or aircraft to be seen anywhere."

Chapter Eighteen

Obata's unit was merely a deployment draft. The officers called it a regiment, but it was a temporary unit serving only to move a couple of thousand soldiers to the battle area and replace casualties. They were of less strength than regular regiments and while they possessed a full complement of most weapons, they had no motor vehicles, radios, telephones, engineer tools, and other essential equipment. They did have minimal cooking gear. The medical unit barely had adequate supplies and materials. They would never fight as a unit.

A messenger arrived after first formation and was led to Obata by his section leader. The message ordered 2nd Class Private Obata to immediately report to the regimental operations officer. The section leader quickly checked his uniform and his fingernails too, cautioning him, "The captain is fastidious about hand cleanliness."

The headquarters personnel looked at Obata as if he was in trouble. Maybe he was suspected of theft and pillaging. The section leader accompanied Obata and the messenger to the regimental headquarters in a small cluster of white wood-frame Australian houses. Obata was directed to a flimsy folding chair facing a small rattan table and chair. A guard stood at attention at the door. Upon entering they removed their caps.

The messenger carried in an ornate Western-style dining room chair, setting it against the wall opposite Obata. A lieutenant suddenly stepped in, followed by a captain.

"*Keirei*"—salute—shouted the lieutenant.

The captain, who looked older than most other officers of that rank, was no doubt a reservist but had seen active duty. He abruptly sat in the ornate chair. His expression stern, he sat stiff-backed and stiff-armed with his legs spread open and white-gloved hands clamped on his knees, his sword set across his thighs—a classic pose favored by samurai. He glared at Obata, who assumed the scowling unintroduced captain was the operations officer.

The lieutenant seated himself at the rattan table with a notebook and binder. He made a production of uncapping and readying his German Soennecken fountainpen. He concentrated on scratching on the notepad, then opened the binder. "Be seated," he said, glancing at Obata.

Obata bowed to the captain, then the lieutenant, and sat.

Unlike the captain, whose eyes never left Obata's face, the lieutenant barely glanced at him. Clearing his throat, he said in a squeaky voice, "You are 2nd Class Private Obata Yoshiro, Deployment Draft 4421, Nagoya City, Nagoya Military Affairs District?"

"Yes, Honorable Lieutenant."

"You are qualified as a rifleman and sniper?"

"Yes, Honorable Lieutenant."

"You have successfully assisted in the recovery and salvage of automotive parts?"

"Yes, Honorable Lieutenant."

"You have aided with repairs on large powered boats?"

"Yes, Honorable Lieutenant."

"You have worked on a fishing boat?"

"Yes, Honorable Lieutenant."

He went on with more questions, all resulting in the same response.

Finally, "Congratulations, you are promoted to Private 1st Class."

Obata quickly stood, bowed to both officers, and sat down. Was this about a promotion? He had seen it undertaken much differently in company formations.

"You have furthermore been assigned to a special detachment to travel by large power boat to a designated island. The detachment will serve as coastal observers to record and notify higher headquarters as to enemy ship movements and airplane flights in the vicinity of the island. You will provide protection for the observers and the radio section. You will also be called upon to make boat motor repairs."

Obata came to his feet again, bowing to the officers. "I am most honored."

"You will return to your quarters with the messenger and report back here immediately with your field equipment and rifle. You are not to mention where you are bound, what your duties are, and anything about this important mission."

Bowing, he left with the messenger.

"Do not ask me what this is about," said the messenger. "But you are not in trouble…yet."

"I do not know, but it may be better to be in trouble, in this case."

"My father said, 'a wise man never finds a body'."

"Maybe I am the body," Obata muttered.

Obata signed out with the company sergeant major. He looked putout, not having been informed.

"I was told that this assignment is temporary, Honorable Sergeant Major."

"No matter to me," he muttered.

That is not true, Obata thought. He does not like being left out on the assignment of *his* soldiers.

"They did not tell me you were promoted. I have a say in that." He made a notation of the change in the company roster and noted his rank change in Obata's pay record book.

***

Obata lugged his equipment, including the box of 6.5mm ammunition, the messenger helping by carrying his tube pack. It suddenly occurred to him: *I have been promoted! Now I am paid a whole nine yen instead of six, plus 12 yen overseas allowance. Where am I going to find new collar tabs?* He would now wear red tabs with two gold stars. Since he was on temporary duty it was doubtful the stingy company supply sergeant would issue him any.

Arriving at a large, but low-in-the-water pier, Obata was reminded of the piers where his uncle docked to offload fish. A Navy Daihatsu landing barge was tied to the pier with its ungainly ramp lowered to the pier's deck level. One of the three sailors tinkered with the motor, and the coxswain and deckhand were directing where ammunition and ration crates were to be stowed in the fourteen-meter-long boat.

Some 20 soldiers milled around, loading ammunition and ration crates and water cans. Most wore dark green tropical uniforms and a couple had tan summer uniforms. All had Type 99 rifles but for a single Type 99 light machine gun and a Type 89 grenade discharger. The three-man crews were armed with two Type 94 pistols and a rifle. The pistols came with a poor reputation of being crudely designed, easy to fire accidently, and had only a six-round magazine for its weak 8mm cartridge.

A sergeant was speaking to a 1st lieutenant peering over a clipboard. They both looked experienced with field-worn uniforms. The sergeant motioned Obata to approach him.

"I am Sergeant Toshio, your platoon sergeant. Your papers?" He logged Obata on his roster. "You are the sniper?"

"Yes, Honorable Sergeant."

The lieutenant asked, "How much 6.5mm ammunition do you have, Obata? That concerns me."

"I have 480 rounds, Honorable Lieutenant. I carry it all myself."

He glanced at the sergeant. "That should be sufficient. Do not accidently lose any. Does the telescope serial number match the rifle's?"

"Yes, Honorable Lieutenant."

"Show me."

He opened the telescope's case, showing the rifle's and the telescope's numbers.

"Very well." Turning to the sergeant, he said, "Fall in the platoon."

Reporting how much ammunition he carried, Obata wondered, *How many rounds may I actually fire in this war?*

They formed up in two ranks on the pier with their equipment belts and weapons. One of the two corporals headed each rank. The lieutenant walked down the ranks checking over and asking how many rounds of ammunition they carried. He asked other questions about their skills. It was apparent that most professed to be good shots. One was a professional boar hunter, some were fishermen, farmers, there was a butcher, and two were familiar with boat motors. Few were city dwellers.

Both the machine gun and the grenade discharger crews comprised three men. The lieutenant quizzed them on their proficiency and amount of ammunition, which he declared adequate. He compared the machine gun and its telescope's serial numbers—they matched.

"How good of a grenade discharger operator are you, Honorable Superior Private Kazuo?"

Bowing, he replied, "I can hit a man-sized target at 300 meters with the second or third round, Honorable Lieutenant."

"Of course you do not have to directly hit a man with a grenade," reminded the lieutenant.

The three-man radio section was led by Superior Private Isamu. They had spoken little to the rest of the platoon, seeming to be somewhat aloof. They were specialists with lengthy training in radio operation, electronics repair, radio and antenna theory, encryption, and Morse code.

"Do you have sufficient padding materials for your equipment?"

"We do, Honorable Lieutenant."

They had three stout-looking crates carried by shoulder straps. They seldom saw, much less spoke to, radiomen, specialists who received bonus pay.

"Excellent." Turning to the platoon, he said, "I am 1st Lieutenant Kiyoshi, 20th Infantry Regiment. This is Sergeant Toshio, my liaison sergeant." The platoon bowed. "This group has been formed for an important mission requiring special dedication with superior individual skills. You will speak to no one outside this group about the mission or our destination. If anyone asks questions, tell them to speak to me or Sergeant Toshio, no exceptions. At a given time and place you will be fully briefed on the mission." He turned the platoon over to Sergeant Toshio and went to speak to the coxswain.

At one point the lieutenant was concerned there were only four flashlights—his, the sergeant's and the corporals'. They were fortunate to have that many. They were carried in a small canvas case. On the case's front was a small crank handle. The little flashlight was connected to the case by a short cable and stowed inside. When used the light was aimed and the handle cranked to make a thin winding sound. At least they needed no spare batteries.

With everything loaded the platoon again fell in, this time with the crewmen. Toshio marched them to the pier's land end and to the water's edge, where they stood at attention on the seastrand. They knew what was next.

"Attention. March in place."

In unison they marched, tromping their boots into the centimeters of water lapping the shore, churning up the coral sand. They sang the *Umi Yukaba*—"If I Go Away to the Sea."

> *Across the sea,*
> *Corpses in the water,*
> *Across the mountains,*
> *Corpses heaped upon the field.*
> *I shall die by the side of the Emperor.*
> *I will never look back.*

Written by Ōtomo no Yakamochi in AD 749, the song spoke of the dedication and sacrifices they would make for the Emperor.

They loaded into the barge and shoved off from the pier as the ramp was raised. At first Obata was concerned about motoring out into the bay in daylight, with the many transports and merchant ships serving as tempting targets for the Americans. He was not the only one.

The coxswain shouted over the throbbing motor, "Be not concerned my land-bound comrades-in-arms. The few air attacks have yet to hit a ship and those high-flying bombers have no interest in battleships as small as ours."

"That is what worries me," laughed the machine gunner, Superior Private Koji. "It is the bombs that miss the big ships that I am concerned with."

The reluctant soldiers-turned-temporary-seamen laughed. Even the lieutenant did not appear to be agitated with the hilarity. The barge chugged across the bay with the coxswain standing proudly beside his armored shield, waving at larger ships' deckhands. A couple of the men found they had not outgrown their propensity for seasickness.

They made their way across Simpson Harbour to shore-side Lakunai Airfield. Two men argued which was bluer, the cloudless sky or the glimmering bay. As they neared shore, they made out the largest aircraft any had seen. A four-engine H8K1 Type 2 patrol-bomber was moored next to a floating pier, its blue hull and wings and the gigantic red Sun on the sides contrasting with the jungle-green backdrop. The wings' leading edges were yellow for further identification means. They pulled up to its side. Rope fenders were hung over the barge's side. The crates, cans, and boxes were laboriously loaded onto the pier, and a line of sailors passed them through a small passenger door in the side aft of the wings. More sailors loaded and secured the cargo. The soldiers were not allowed to help, as it was part of the sailors' required singular experience. A petty officer told them the huge airplane—they called it a *Seikū*, meaning "Clear Sky"—had a great deal of space for their cargo and the troops as they normally carried bombs and torpedoes. "It has a 38-meter wingspan. Its ten-man crew is necessary for all the machine guns and 2cm automatic cannons spouting from its hull." They were given kapok life vests and told not to don them if a forced landing was necessary. They would not fit through the side hatches wearing the vests. "Don them once in the water."

Most of the troops were noticeably nervous. It turned out not a single man had flown before, even the lieutenant. Obata was just as nervous as anyone but wondered if he could write his family about it. They sat on the aluminum deck without seats or safety belts. "Jam together so you will not be thrown around as much when we crash," laughed the Navy loadmaster.

"Might there be American fighters during daylight?" asked the lieutenant.

"Not this far north. We will be escorted by two Zero fighters for the 750-kilometer flight," he added. They could easily fly that roundtrip range.

That is a great distance, thought Obata.

After much rumbling, revving, and ceaseless vibrations, the monster airplane crept into the bay and turned into the wind. More urgent revving and finally, like an iceberg getting underway, they quickly picked up speed, bouncing on the wavelets and then with hard jolts as they slowly rose from the bay's grip. The engines howled and they were jolted around by the choppy air. Glittering sunlight reflected off the wavelets. They could see New Ireland to the left as they turned south. They passed sprawling islands of lush green. The loadmaster pointed out Bougainville with its attendant fleet of dozens of Imperial warships moored off Shortland Island. It looked like an inviting target, but the massed antiaircraft guns and fighter cover made it dangerous. The Americans lacked sufficient aircraft to launch such an attack. Choiseul passed and finally Santa Isabel where they descended toward an indentation in the island's northeast coast.

"That is Rekata Bay, your destination. There are 3,000 troops protecting the temporary air- and seaplane bases. It is from here that we send night bombers to annoy the Americans on Guadalcanal."

The daylight flight found them looking down on emerald-green jungles and variegated aquamarine, sapphire, topaz, and turquoise of the so-inviting sea. Obata marveled at such a startling contrast in a war zone. *If fishing off Nippon's coast looked like this from Uncle Asahi's boat, it would have been a more enticing job.*

He wondered what the girl's name in the Sunflower was. She had never revealed it in subsequent visits. He had asked her once. Her eyes seemed focused on the wall or nothing at all.

***

There was little to recommend Rekata Bay, a low coastal strip dense with coconut palms, brush, and mosquitos. Light breezes and virtually no waves lapped the narrow fringing beaches. There were numerous fighting positions behind the dune line along the dagger-shaped peninsula. Most troops were at inland encampments to deploy wherever the Americans landed. They were more concerned about raids than large invasions, with the Americans tied down on Guadalcanal.

The local native plantation workers and fishermen were kept employed with logging and harvesting from the jungle and the sea to feed the soldiers and sailors. After transferring their supplies into another Daihatsu, they motored to a pier further up the beach. This was an Army supply point with a fuel barge. They were told where they could bivouac and organized the site. The lieutenant made arrangements to mess with the rifle company securing this sector. They were tired of cold rice balls and miso. Some men traded the natives' cigarettes for limes to improve the miso and even fresh fish. It was a welcome meal of tinned crab, sweet potatoes, wheat cakes, plum cakes, and rice. With little to do, many of the men were removing their scratchy collar linings and replacing them with softer cloth cut from triangular bandages.

Falling in the platoon, the lieutenant warned again not to say a word to any soldiers or sailors of their mission, not that they knew any more than before. "Tonight we rest. We will be doing more loading in the morning and will depart for our mission as soon as possible. We have 250 kilometers to cover, to be conveyed by this barge. Do not go alone into the jungle or the village. There are headhunters here and they do not take sides."

Chapter Nineteen

The Jap lay sprawled where Henrik had shot it beside the piled wood—facedown, feet still in the water, the body naked except for the oil-stained breechcloth and socks. The Jap had smeared grease over his body. Maybe it helped in the cool water after nightfall plus it camouflaged him. Maybe it discouraged sharks. There was no rifle or pistol, not even a knife. There was a dog tag. He'd not thought about that, Japs having dog tags, or rather just one. For a moment he considered taking it, but it just didn't seem right. He didn't relish it, but he stole a quick look at the Jap's head. He'd hit him smack in the right temple, face bloated, misshapen, and a gaping pit in the other side. The Jap hadn't felt a thing. Henrik found pinned under the body a two-inch-diameter, maybe six-foot-long spear and with a hand-sharpened, char-hardened point. *That's it? That was his plan? Pretend he was dead, make himself drift around, get close to a gyrene, and go at him with a pointed stick?*

He hoped he could do better than that if push came to shove. *Would I ever be that desperate?* He'd not thought much about it. Did the Japs think about it? Here they were in the middle of a war, a whole world at war. It covered the globe and they had to do whatever they were told or were expected to do it on their own. Did someone tell that meathead to do this—waste his life for some king or emperor thousands of miles away? He didn't want to think about it anymore. *It'll only make you crazy or make you do something you don't want or shouldn't do.*

He made his way solemnly back to the bomb crater.

"Damn, I'm finally hungry," Henrik grumbled.

"Saved you half a can of bean bombers," said Griff, shoving a can of Boston baked beans at him with a spoon stuck in it. Even the Aussies called them Boston baked beans.

As O'Malley liked to point out, "They ain't baked, they're steam-cooked in cans. I can't eat anymore. Gol-darn place smells worse than a Dago whorehouse."

"You'd know."

"Damn straight, Handyman. Wonder if I'll ever see that place again. The Cosmopolitan Saloon and Miss Silvia," he muttered longingly. "Or was it Miss Sharon? No matter. I liked her blonde curls."

Griff wasn't as deep a thinker as Henrik, or so he hopefully thought. He'd thought about Jo for some moments. Just something, someone, he'd crossed paths with. He should have been stronger. Every time thoughts of her crossed his mind, he sincerely wished her a better life. He hoped she was actually a good girl. Could she be if she'd had a better shot at things?

"Wait until the sun's full up," said a voice from a neighboring crater. "This shit hole'll stink to high heaven."

"Shut up, O'Malley."

"You know what we're doing today, don't you?" asked Griff.

"Fightin' a war?"

"Let me check my program guide. Yep, it says here today's 'World War Twice, Scene Six'."

"That's all? What scene is the grand finale in?" asked O'Malley. "About Scene One Thousand?"

"Time just skates by, huh?"

"They ain't full turned us on to the Nips yet, lads."

"So today we'll be planting Nips again," said Griff.

"Hell, I didn't expect we'd be diggin' more graves than foxholes."

Sergeant Lockler appeared behind them carrying a pasteboard carton. "Anyone want a can of lima beans?"

"For breakfast?"

"You can wait until dinner if you wish and have them with steak and mushrooms," he retorted, chucking a can at O'Malley.

"Ouch! Easy, Sarge."

"Here, have another. I can't give them away."

"I don't think I'll ever be able to look a lima bean in the face."

"Mash them up and salt and pepper them," said Griff.

"That makes 'em more eatable?"

"Not a smidgen."

"Almos' as bad as navy beans."

"Navy beans'll make ya seasick. Swabbies don't even eat 'em."

Krass shouted, "Diamond, bring your squad down here."

Diamond left a lookout topside on the gully's lip. There were five men left in the BAR Squad having lost one dead—Gentry—and three wounded.

"We got a job for you fellas," said Krass. "Diamond, you're going to take over 3d Squad, yeah, Monegan bought it. Stiver, you and Peaches are going to 1st Squad. There's no more BAR Squad."

Henrik pondered how fast they'd regressed to blunt truths. There wasn't any time for grief or even breaking a loss easily.

That left Henrik and Griff. "Where we going, sarge?"

He turned to them. "You two are going with Sergeant Lockler, for some kind of detached special duty."

"Like what?" Anything "special" seldom was.

"I got no idea. General Vandegrift might be able to fill you in."

"Where's he at?" asked Griff. "Its 'bout time I had a face-to-face with ol' Archie."

"Oh, I suspect he's at that airfield the Nips keep bombing."

"Or maybe I'll talk to Colonel Arthur on Tulagi. You can see it from here."

"Well, maybe some other time," mumbled Griff.

"Where we going then?"

"Tulagi…"

"There it is. You think I can get an appointment to see our dear Colonel Arthur then?"

"Not likely. Grab your gear, all that you can round up, and find Lockler. A boat's picking you up with some others from Company ITEM at the Lever Brothers' wharf at 1000 hours."

They found Sergeant Lockler at the wharf with a dozen other men. Most they recognized being from 3d Battalion, 2d Marines.

Lockler was Henrik and Griff's platoon guide—sort of an assistant platoon sergeant mostly responsible for issuing ammo, water, and rations. Platoon guides habitually took over a squad when the leader was lost. His beard looked a week old.

No one said much on the two-mile trip over to Tulagi, four times larger than Gavutu–Tanambogo. There had been 900 Japs on the small islands. One marine in the group said they were mostly killed except for 23 prisoners and maybe seventy escaped to the nearby bigger Florida Islands. Solomon Islanders were hunting them down with machetes and shotguns. They were said to be headhunters and cannibals. Tulagi had been the main Australian administrative center for the lower Solomons; it was more recently the Jap HQ.

What would it be like to meet one of those captured Nips? thought Henrik. No point thinking about it. He couldn't begin to understand their gibberish he'd heard in movies. *Headhunters? Looks like we picked the right side to be on.*

***

On Tulagi, now the 2d Marines' CP, they met in the damaged Tulagi Club and tennis courts. *Those Aussies and Brits lived out here better than us gyrenes*, Henrik mused. Blankets and ponchos covered the windows, making the dead air hotter and stuffier. A grease-penciled Florida Islands map hung on a wall beside a Guadalcanal map. The briefer was the same R-2 Captain Bear who'd briefed them on the operation just days ago. It seemed like a month and the R-2 looked two years older.

Henrik looked around at the other men. Most were staff types, but a lot of the filthy unshaved men obviously had had a more personal tour of the Florida Islands. There were no boastful "Let me at 'ems" this time.

Breakfast was two hard boiled eggs, an apple, and a couple of slices of barely scorched toast.

Most were surprised when Lieutenant Colonel Frank Goettge, the division D-2, stepped forward in sweat-stained khakis. His magnitude left little doubt he'd been a footballer for U of Ohio and on semi-pro teams.

"Morning Leathernecks. Are we up for a rough and tumble game today?"

"We're ready for a touchdown, sir," shouted one of the staff LTs. The rest weren't so enthusiastic. Too many bloated bodies on too little breakfast. The colonel made a wave-off gesture.

"Not this time, LT. We're playing defense on this one. We're going for interceptions and make the Nips fumble the ball." He paused with a serious look. "Who's heard of Coastwatchers? Show of hands." Fewer than half the hands went up.

The intelligence officer said, "Coastwatchers are Brits and Aussies who live in the islands. They're plantation mangers, government administrators, Lever Brothers staff, even missionaries. They've been commissioned as Royal Australian Navy Reserve officers even though most have no military experience. They know the Solomon Islands and the people and they're hidden all through the islands. They have long-range shortwave radios and there are natives who work for them. They have to be mobile to survive, always on the move. The natives scout for them and tote their radios and supplies. The Japs know about them and try and hunt them down. Some have been captured, and they're tortured and murdered. The Japs have even bayoneted to death some missionaries and nuns." That led to grumbling.

"What's Lever Brothers?" a sergeant asked.

"A British company which harvests coconuts to make copra—that's dried coconut meat—for making soap and shampoo. When your mom shampooed your noggin with Lux, this is where it came from."

Henrik thought to himself, *We're doing all this so Brits can shampoo their hair? We never had shampoo, just homemade lye soap scented with castor oil.*

"The Coastwatchers are spotted up and down the Solomons and are even near the Japs' forward naval and airbase at Shortland Island up by Bougainville. They give us early warning of Jap ships slipping down the Sealark Channel to attack our ships and land reinforcements on Guadalcanal. They report approaching air raids too. The Japs are already hitting Henderson Field." He took in the men's blank expressions. "That's what we named the Jap airfield we took from them and we're rebuilding it. Named after a Marine major, a squadron commander killed at Midway. They've been bombing the Canal night and day."

He paused, eyeballing the room. "What I'm telling you next is highly classified. It doesn't leave our huddle here."

Goettge had the room's attention. "Coastwatchers are invaluable to us, to say the least. We need more and that's where you men come in. The Aussies are stretched thin and can't provide anymore Coastwatchers and certainly not on a timely basis, like now," he said, stamping a boot. "There are also coordination issues with the Aussies if they operate directly with us."

Men appeared to be getting the idea that they were going someplace besides Guadalcanal—the big island.

"We've picked a small island for our own coast-watcher detail. We're putting sixteen men on this island. That may seem large for an observation post. It needs to be mobile, but by foot, and the Japs may reconnoiter the island. They also have barge traffic passing through there."

A sergeant raised a hand. "Are there other groups doing this?"

"Let's not talk about that. I'm going to turn you over to Maj Van Ness, regimental R-2. Your designation is Detachment 4, 3d Battalion, 2d Marines or call sign KZT—KING-ZEBRA-TARE. Let's win this one for our team, men."

His face grew solemn. "One last thing. Last night Admiral Turner ordered Task Force 61 to withdraw all its carriers, battlewagons, and cruisers. The Navy was caught with their dungarees down. We lost five heavy cruisers, including an Aussie, and another cruiser was damaged off Savo Island. That and the Navy lost so many fighters that they can't protect the fleet and Henderson much less provide us air support. Early this morning the troop and cargo transports also withdrew. They took part of the 2d Marines with them to Espírtu Santo 600 miles to the southeast. What's left is mainly securing the small islands around Tulagi, plus it's the 1st Marine Division's reserve on the big island, which has only two of its regiments."

Someone said there were so many dead sailors from all the sunken ships that they're attracting sharks. That was unsettling.

"Men, you're going to hear rumors, so hear it from me now. They left us with thirty-seven days' rations instead of sixty and only half the ammunition we need. The good news is that we captured fourteen days of Jap rations and lots of rice. Even with that we're limited to two meals a day. Tighten your belts."

"I hate rice," stage whispered someone in the back.

"We all will be before this is over," said a staff NCO.

"Longer if we're POWs."

"That'll never happen."

They had heard the scuttlebutt that a Swedish cruise liner taken over by the US Navy as a troop ship, MS *John Ericsson*, lost much of its refrigeration and most of the chow spoiled. One or two daily soup and bread meals and diarrhea saw an average loss of twenty pounds.

Ignoring the quips, Goettge pointed to Sergeant Lockler's raised hand and said, "No, we don't know when the fleet will return, but it will," he said positively. "Captain Bear, the stage is yours."

A slight, studious-looking man, Bear did not seem particularly fierce, but he sounded like he knew what he was talking about.

Everyone was still digesting the fact that the Navy had left 16,000 marines and sailors on Guadalcanal with limited supplies, rations, ammunition, and vehicles and no naval gunfire or air support. The major Jap bases were much closer to the stranded marines than they were to any Allied bases. They weren't even told what those island bases were named.

Captain Bear introduced himself as the 2d Marines' R-2. "Gentlemen, I realize this is unusual, including all members of the mission in the briefing. We're pressed for time and the mission is somewhat complex. The detachment's personnel will be better served by taking part to gain a full understanding of the requirements. This is especially true since you men volunteered for a dangerous mission."

Henrik looked at Griff, who bore a somewhat astonished expression, then at Lockler. The sergeant gave a "What, who, me?" look. A ripple ran through the other men perched on benches and chairs, standing, or sitting on the deck.

The captain went on. "Most of the Jap ships come down The Slot—that's what they're calling the Skylark Channel now—but they might run other routes winding through the smaller islands. They can't do this with battleships and cruisers, but their destroyers, patrol boats, and landing barges have little difficulty. Now I know some of you are thinking, why should we be concerned about these small craft? Two reasons. They use them to bring troops down to land east and west of Henderson Field, trying to isolate our lodgment. They are also a danger to our destroyers and transports when they return here." He was trying to sound as positive of this as he could. "You'll provide weather reports too."

The mission's starting to sound complex like the R-2 promised, thought Henrik.

Pointing to the Florida Islands map, Bear continued, "We have little information on Pombuana—pronounced 'Pome-boo-anah'," he wrote on a chalkboard. "We think it's the native name for North Island. It's codenamed BEARPAW. We spoke to a former Aussie Lever Brothers administrator. He'd been to the island a few times. We only have minimal info though as at the time we had no idea we might go there. No maps and the only aerial photos are from weeks ago. Navigation charts are incomplete and outdated in this part of the islands. It's almost impossible to see anything on the ground as the island's virtually covered with coconut palms, hardwoods, and brush. There are a few small clearings, but they're covered with two- to three-foot kunai grass or low brush. It's rolling ground with a thirty-six-foot hill on the eastern half and a narrower ridge-like spine on the western half. It's shaped like a pork chop.

"What we can see on the western portion of the south coast is the Lever station for the plantation administration and workers' quarters. Our Aussie source, who we visited in Brisbane, could only give a best guess of dimensions. BEARPAW is some 1,700 yards long east to west—that's just shy of a mile. It's about 1,000 yards wide north to south on its predominant northeast lobe, and about 400 to 500 yards across the narrower western portion. It's completely surrounded by 50- to 200-yard-wide coral reefs. At high tide they can be crossed by our landing craft, as far as we know. The beaches are tan-colored sand ten to fifty yards wide at low tide. They average ten to twenty yards wide around most of the island. The beaches on the southwest side are the wider ones; not a good place to land. There's no pier or dock. They simply landed on the Lever station beach. There's little wave action unless it's stormy weather, which we're not expecting.

"The Lever station is only six or seven wood-frame or thatch houses, a few sheds and outbuildings, plus a workshop. They have tin roofs, some with thatch. No Europeans lived there and the Chinese and natives were evacuated before the Japs arrived in the Solomons. There are no Japs on BEARPAW as far as we know. We recommend though that you treat the station as enemy-occupied just to be safe.

"Now, the mission. We're going to land the detachment tonight. I know that's short notice, but we have no choice. We'll help you out with loadout and try and get anything you need. I do need to say we're short of just about everything, but we'll do our best."

"That means, 'it's all yours if we don't need it'," groused Griff.

"Jap ships may come down from the north around the east end of Santa Isabel through the Indispensable Strait or from the west around San Jorge. The Japs have a seaplane base on Santa Isabel at Rekata Bay, but it shouldn't be a problem. Remember too that while they make their runs from the northwest from Shortland, they also have to return, and they may take this route home even if they made for Guadalcanal by another route. We'll pass to you the going and coming routes they're using if our picket ships and patrol-bombers spot them." He used a pointer to show the islands and routes. "I'll get with the detachment commander one-on-one when we're through here for the details. He'll also get a map.

"You're going to have a radio team and the radio needs to be monitored day and night, not only to be alerted on the Jap approach going or coming.

It's necessary for re-supply coordination and any intel and weather reports we can give you.

"I recommend you check out the island's northeast lobe as an observation post with the radio nearby. We're not telling you where to site your OP, but I want to emphasize you need to reconnoiter any other suitable sites. We can't tell by merely looking over a black-and-white aerial photograph. Just remember, every six feet of elevation extends the horizon about three miles.

"You'll be delivered by an LCV with two weeks of supplies, plus plenty of ammo."

That seems to be mentioned as encouragement, thought Henrik.

"We're going to assign a corpsman too."

That is encouragement.

"How about a cook?" said a freckled redhead. That drew a laugh.

"Besides hunting, can you fish?" Griff asked Henrik.

He nodded. "But I don't recommend it, even at night."

"Are you sure there are no natives on pom-bo-whaty whaty?" a corporal asked.

"Pombuana. Not that we know of. Most have moved to other islands away from the action."

"Smart move," a rifleman said. "It's unhealthy to argue about land ownership on an island owned by marines."

There were laughs, but Henrik thought that had not been entirely true on Wake, Guam, and Corregidor. He remembered Uncle Werner advising, "Never get too cocky."

"The detachment will consist of sixteen men led by Sergeant Lockler. Sergeant, stand up. The sergeant's well qualified for the mission—eight years in the Corps, including a two-year stint in China. He's set to be the next platoon sergeant in his company. He was a hunting guide and river guide in Colorado and Oregon, and was an Eagle Scout."

That last seemed to embarrass Lockler. It impressed Henrik. A couple of friends back home were Eagle Scouts. Thinking about them, he wished they were here, not that he wanted to wish that on anyone. Their camping or woodsman skills would sure be of use.

Captain Bear called off names from a clipboard. He spoke to a corporal who was going to take charge of collecting supplies and whatever else they needed. Lockler would shortly give him a list of needs.

"Handyman, take charge of the ammo."

"What do I draw, Sarge?"

"Find out what weapons we have and draw what you think best. Don't skimp. We're only moving short distances."

Henrik took this as giving him the say on what to carry. He made the rounds, finding each man. If they had a Springfield, he said, "a hundred rounds in your cartridge belt and three sixty-round bandoleers for 280 rounds plus four frag grenades—a 'double dose'."

"Damn, Handyman, that's a lot of ammo."

"You heard the man, this isn't an overnight campout. What do you want, too much ammo or too many Japs?"

He knew Griff was good on BAR ammo. Between him and his assistant gunner, McKern, they had twenty-one BAR magazines. Most of the platoon had one or two spare mags. Ammo from the rifle bandoleers could be loaded into BAR magazines.

Henrik spotted the commo men in their relatively cleaner utilities. The three of them each had six twenty-round mags for their .45-cal M50 Reising submachine guns. Each man also carried two fifty-round cartons for five magazine reloads. Their radio gear was heavy, but they had two or three grenades. They each carried an M14 thermite grenade that looked like a red beer can, something Henrik had never seen. They said it burned like a cutting torch and would totally melt their radio and generator to prevent capture. They were serious when they said the radio could not be captured under any circumstances. Same for the codebook.

He found the corpsman, Pharmacist's Mate 2nd Class Camphor. "Are you packing?" He knew corpsmen were officially unarmed, but many found a .45-cal pistol or an M1903, which while bulky, was better than nothing. It would not be long before they "lost" their red cross armbands. The Japs used them as aiming points. He wore very non-Marine looking patches on his left sleeve, a Navy spread-winged black eagle, a little red cross, and two point-down chevrons proclaiming his rating and specialty.

"I got hold of a .38 Smith & Wesson Victory Model revolver a wounded Navy flyboy gave me for pulling him out of a burning Grumman Wildcat," the corpsman said.

"How much ammo you have?"

"For my job, plenty—a fifty-round carton of .38 Special."

Reporting to Lockler on what he had assigned, the sergeant said, "More."

With help he rounded up a 1500-round crate containing twenty-five bandoleers. He needed help as it weighed 112 pounds. He also got two cases of twenty-four Mk II frag grenades. The yellow-painted grenades' serrated bodies did look like pineapples, leading to their nickname.

When he reported back, Lockler said, "That'll do. Now find some engineers and beg some Mk III demolition grenades. They look like yellow beer cans." Another one he'd not heard of. He traded an engineer sergeant four grenades for three cans of Jap plum cakes.

"Sarge, what do we do with these demolition grenades?"

"Half a pound of TNT, we blow shit up."

Chapter Twenty

The morning's air was thick and dripping with humidity. There was no breeze to carry away the mosquitos which had droned about them in seemingly increasing masses. Obata could flat-hand his forehead and find his palm specked with blood and wrecked buzzing black pests.

"*Bazu, bazu* all night long," groaned Koji, the machine gunner, referring to their insistent buzzing.

The Army Daihatsu was aground on the narrow Rekata Bay beach, a fishing net draped loosely over the barge, held aloft by bamboo poles. The netting was garnished with leafy vines and palm fronds. How well the green-painted barge blended into the adjoining vegetation was questionable. The barge was manned by Army Shipping Engineers, the Army's own "fleet," it was joked.

Takeo and his rifle were missing when the men were awakened by their host battalion's bugler playing reveille. The last Takeo had been seen was by Obata when they turned in that night to sleep just outside of the palm tree line on the beach. After rollcall the immediate area and the latrines were searched. The lieutenant did not wish to report him missing to the port captain. He had enough on his mind. Obata was concerned. His request to search for the deserter was rejected.

"If he is not found I will report him. If he is found, I will personally punish him. I cannot be delayed in this mission." Looking at the platoon, the lieutenant menacingly swept over the assembled men. "If you see him you must detain or report him immediately. Failure to do so will result in your punishment."

The *teicho* or captain of the ship, a bargeman in civilian life, was a fussy, wind-worn sergeant. He directed where each crate and drum was to be placed, how knots were tied, and the load balanced. A balanced load ensured the barge's peak operation in a war zone at sea in the darkest of nights.

Everybody worked. Lieutenant Kiyoshi tried hard not to interfere, but he watched everything like a sea eagle. Sergeant Toshio kept up with the barge captain under the guise of learning what he could, but he too wanted to see the cargo correctly secured. Both the lieutenant and sergeant were veterans for certain. They had learned to let soldiers do their job but unobtrusively oversee their work. They did not lash out with punishment at every minor infraction and error. It was a graduated punishment from quietly pointing out a problem to a shin kick or a thump on the head. The men worked faster and more effectively rather than cringing in fear of a beating.

Two riflemen, bayonets fixed, were posted some fifty meters up and down the beach to warn away other soldiers and sailors and native workers. The lieutenant rejected the use of hired native stevedores. "Secret mission," he earnestly stated.

The barge's bow ramp was lowered, but its bow threshold was too high off the beach and it could not be tied to the few small piers for loading. At low tide it was too shallow for the boat to float beside the hastily built piers. A ramp of local-cut planks was set up. It was steep but made loading easier than over the sides.

They loaded water, rations, and fuel drums. Much had been stocked there prior to the platoon's arrival. The stockpile appeared to be for common use for any Army barges passing through. A truck arrived with more rations and they were quickly loaded.

The lieutenant turned other preparations over to the sergeant. The three "sweet potato vines"—alluding to the tangle of telephone wires—radiomen spent some time looking over their radio set, removing its separate components from the carrying boxes. These were designed for carriage on packhorses and were awkward to man-pack. It consisted of a transmitter and receiver, a remote unit, a one-hand-cranked generator that was strapped to the operator's chest, and wire antenna spools.

"Where have you been?" shouted the sergeant. Takeo trudged out of the palms, looking crestfallen and weary; no rifle. The lieutenant and the sergeant converged on him, yelling profanities. After slapping Takeo, the lieutenant started to draw his sword, but it was wrapped in white cloth for protection from the sea air. Takeo was actually allowed to defend himself and offered an explanation. Just before dawn he had gone into the palms in search of a latrine without notifying the guard. He was disoriented and became more so stumbling through the jungle-covered peninsula. With wave sounds coming from both sides he lost direction. He saw native huts and fearing headhunters he became even more lost. He had only just now found his way.

"I refuse to believe this fable," shouted the lieutenant. "I do not know if I want you here any longer. Your foolishness could endanger this mission."

Poor Takeo spent the next hour running up and down the beach with his pack and his rifle lifted above his head—this without breakfast. He spent another hour standing at attention in knee-deep water with his rifle held in salute to greet the Rising Sun.

After the midday snack, loading was taking longer than planned, Lieutenant Kiyoshi fell in the platoon and for the first time they were organized for the special mission. The Command Section consisted of Lieutenant Kiyoshi, Sergeant Toshio, Superior Private Saburo—the lieutenant's pampered orderly who was less than well liked; Superior Private Hajime—the instrument man whose job no one quite understood; and the three radiomen under Superior Private Isamu. They kept much to themselves.

Saburo was pushy, considering himself with at least the authority of a corporal. The others referred to him as *Aijin*.

"You know what that means?"

"Lover?" He seldom heard the little spoken word.

"No, it means an illicit love affair with either sex."

Nodding, Obata asked, "Why do the others dislike Saburo? He is only doing his assignment."

"He thinks too highly of himself and that he is above all other privates in the platoon," said Takeo."

The Battle Section was under Corporal Masaichi. His tactics were simple. "When I march, you march, when I shoot, you shoot at what I am, and when I run, you run, forward that is, for the glory of the Emperor. The three men in the light machine gun crew were under Superior Private Koji while Superior Private Kazuo had the three-man grenade discharger crew. The riflemen were Obata, Takeo still saluting the Sun, and Ikuo, who was not sniper-trained, but an excellent shot. He had lived with an uncle on Hokkaido, the northernmost of the Home Islands, and hunted sea lions with an old Russian rifle.

It turned out that Lieutenant Kiyoshi was an artillery officer as was Sergeant Toshio and Superior Private Hajime. The lieutenant never fired guns but operated instruments. No one knew what that meant until they opened up a special packing case. Inside was a strange-looking Nikko 8× double-periscope with adjusting knobs. It was fitted on a long-legged tripod that could be set up for a standing man or set less than a meter in height beside a one-man hole. Hajime explained that there were colored lens filters for use in bright and cloud-muted days, moonlight, fog, mist, and rain. They each had a big pair of 8×30 binoculars. The observers never explained how they worked to determine the speed and range of passing ships and airplanes. The bargemen had less powerful 6×24 binoculars.

Obata offered to help with checking the chugging Ford motor, but the bargemen rejected his help. Soldiers were conscious of their assignment, and asking someone else for assistance indicated a lack of proficiency and skill.

As for rations, there were wooden crates packed in paper bags holding four days' worth. Three were A-rations with rice and tinned meat or fish. A B-ration was provided on the fourth day with somewhat less rice, much less tinned meat or fish, but with hardtack biscuits and hard candy. There were a number of crates with tinned soybean paste—*miso*, soybean sauce—*shoyu*, pickled plums and radishes, mandarin oranges, tangerines, peaches, pears, bamboo shoots, plum cakes, seaweed and red beans, plus tins of various dehydrated vegetables. Powdered tea and sugar were in kegs, and bottles of cider and *sake*—rice wine—and some beer packed in straw-padded crates. For backup there was a crate of forty emergency ration packets: polished rice, dehydrated miso, vitamin A and D tablets, vitamin B paste, powdered tea, and tins of heating alcohol. The lieutenant counted on fishing if necessary. The sergeant ensured they took vitamin tablets at every meal.

While loading, someone asked, "What will we do for water?" Many of the small islands were merely sandbars with palm trees. Lieutenant Kiyoshi explained, when a cartload of unusual items arrived, that it rained almost every day plus there might be small springs and catchment basins. They also had four backpacked 25-liter water containers. They thought there was waterwell at the British settlement. That's what they viewed the Lever Brothers station as. They would have to conserve water and build a stockpile. Sergeant Toshio would oversee water rationing if it came to that.

With cargo space still unfilled, a final cart arrived, dragged and pushed by natives. It contained ammunition. Sergeant Toshio did not want the natives handling ammunition, and he knew they were constantly stealing food. Their job done, they squatted to the side awaiting their payment in stale rice and Chinese Golden Bat cigarettes.

Ammunition, supplies, and other items for the platoon were loaded separately and marked. Their items were stowed in the barge's forward portion of the cargo compartment and the rest in the aft. Two small wooden crates were left in the cart.

"What are these?" Obata asked the sergeant. "Should we take them?"

Toshio knelt and looked over the boxes. There were white markings and a brown band. "This says 'Type 1 hand-thrown spherical grenades.' This brown band I think means poison gas."

Some of the men gathered around the cart. Others kept their distance.

"Let us see." He looked at the men. "Anyone wish to don their gasmask?" They looked at one another, but no one did. He broke the lead seal and gingerly opened the top. It was full of sawdust. He brushed off the top layer to find the lids of four cans. Working one out, the sergeant saw it was over a hand high and a hand in diameter with a pry-off lid. It was olive drab with another brown band. A label was pasted to the lid. Toshio studied the label. "I know what this is. I did not think they made them. The lieutenant studied the information too and had to determine the characters for certain technical terms.

"This is a hydrocyanic acid grenade," said Toshio, "a poison gas derived from hydrogen cyanide. There are twelve to a box. In 1939, Russian tanks overran some of our units in Manchuria. These were designed to be thrown at tanks and pillboxes to blind and poison the crews. It is a terribly painful death." He carefully opened the lid and found a glass sphere filled with yellowish liquid sealed by a beer bottle cap. "The cans are double-walled and filled with sawdust-soaked neutralizing agent."

On the label was printed: *Nikkō Tokushu Garasu Kōjō*.

"Honorable Lieutenant," Obata said. "May I humbly say that Nikko Special Glass Works is my honorable father's factory?"

The lieutenant's eyes widened. "This is a spiritual coincidence. Did you know what the glass spheres were for?"

"I did not, Honorable Lieutenant. The factory mostly made larger fishing floats." Obata peered at the glass grenade, remembering his father proposing that maybe they would be filled with gunpowder and a fuse.

The lieutenant looked thoughtful. "Perhaps we should take these since no one else wants them. A victorious warrior seeks advantages and the unexpected to defeat the enemy. Your father is a patriot."

Obata bowed. He was touched by the boxes, like a letter from home... which he had not seen since departing Nippon.

"Will the Americans have tanks?" someone asked.

"Most likely not, but perhaps we can use them for other purposes—if the enemy is inside a cave or building, for example, or we can leave them as booby-traps when we depart. To use one it is simply thrown and it shatters to spread the gas. Tanks are not airtight."

Sergeant Toshio ensured all the men knew what the boxes were and to treat them gently. The barge captain looked like he would prefer to toss them overboard.

Obata recalled reading a newspaper article about the debate in Europe of the legality of war gases. Its horrible effects in the Great War were discussed. It must have been terrifying and most were opposed to the use of war gases, but he was reminded that all armies still had gasmasks.

***

"Takeo, what did you do out there? It is not like you to lose your way."

He gave Obata an innocent look. "I became confused trying to find a latrine. It is so dark among the trees." With a sly look, he added, "A native girl was there and asked for five yen."

"A girl, at a latrine? Wanting money? You do not have that kind of money."

"Yes, I could not help myself. She wore one of those rag skirts and nothing on top but all those bead necklaces."

"I thought you said it was dark?"

"Sometimes the swaying palms let in a Moonbeam."

"Was it worth the punishment?"

"Yes," he replied without hesitation. He broke out laughing. "All it cost me was a rice ration sack."

"You pilfered our rations? You are shameful, Takeo."

"No, I am happy, because we may be going to our deaths."

He has a point.

Barge loading was completed and the netting taken down. The tide's inflow refloated the barge. They backed off the beach gunning the motor and gathered way. A raggedy group of teenage natives meandered down the beach chattering and laughing, a few younger children trailing behind them. He thought those natives had probably had a good life here, until outsiders started a war.

Obata noticed one girl wave and point at the barge. He realized she was waving to Takeo.

"Is that her?"

"Yes." He laughed.

"How do you know? They all look alike and it was dark."

"I recognize her beads," he said, still laughing.

Then they noticed the barge captain was waving at the same immodest girl and Takeo lost his mirth.

"You all are on air watch," shouted Corporal Masaichi. "Not watching for lustful beach invaders." He too waved, cap in hand.

***

All eyes were raised to the skies. It was still daylight. Were they taking a chance? Their single light machine gun on a temporary AA mount seemed terribly impotent. Only an occasional Japanese patrol plane passed over. The barge captain assured them there was little threat from the Americans. If they did appear, they seldom wasted effort attacking lone barges. Infrequent barges were seen in the distance. They gradually picked up speed, but they could barely reach eight knots and only because of the calm sea. Over 250 kilometers. At this rate it will take some time. The low waves soon became choppy. Emerging into the open sea, they paralleled Santa Isabel off to starboard as they headed southeast.

A deckhand erected a bamboo pole with the Rising Sun flag and another with a single black and two red streamers—recognition flags. A squall blew in behind them, graying out the horizon.

An aft lookout shouted, "Vessel approaching from astern."

A destroyer bristling with guns sliced through the squall haze like a knife blade.

Chapter Twenty-One

"I can't wait to leave this stinking place," groaned Griff, laying another coat of oil on his BAR magazines.

"Nothing like rotting bodies, open latrines, burnt copra, burning fuel oil, and Kadota figs. Tulagi's no tropical paradise."

"Give me a break, Handyman. You don't have to describe it, you're making me sicker."

"I'm gagging here," said Corporal Rankin. "You two meatheads just shut the hell up already."

"Yes, daddy," said Griff. "You want some of my sardines?"

"Let me puke in peace, would you?"

"Let the man alone, Griff, he's in anguish," said Henrik. "He's yearning for American food like rye bread soaked in cocoa buttermilk with a dollop of grape jelly."

"Fer Christ's sake, Handyman…"

"My kid brother's friends trying to gag each other," explained Henrik.

"It works."

What Sergeant Lockler preferred to call a "section" was forming on Tulagi. Two landing craft were tied up to the Government Wharf; a rampless blunt-nosed Landing Craft, Personnel (Large)—LCP(L) and a larger ramped Landing Craft, Vehicle—LCV. Both held up to thirty-six troops with room for cargo.

The section was loosely organized with a headquarters consisting of Sergeant Lockler, the corpsman, Pharmacist's Mate 2nd Class Camphor, plus the commo team with Corporal "Sparks" and Privates First Class Katcher and Julien Fletcher. The BAR "Squad" consisted of Griff, the BARman, and McKern, his assistant. Henrik attached himself to the two-man squad, even if Lockler considered him part of the headquarters.

The 1st Squad was Corporal Rankin and Privates "Lefty" Hearn," "Snacks," and "Spud" Hoskins. The 2d Squad was run by Corporal Discoll and Privates "Patches" (describing his utilities), Andreas Dimitrios or "the Greek," and "Mother O'Leary."

Except the three commo men and the corpsman, all were from 3d Battalion, 2d Marines.

"I'm ready to get off this one-horse island," said Snacks.

"I don't think there are that many horses here," muttered Lefty. His constant complaint was that he was a southpaw, but the Corps forced him to learn to shoot right-handed.

"Reminds me of a fella passing through my hometown, Clute, Texas, mosquito capital of the world...well, of Texas anyway."

A chorus of groans as yet another Lefty joke was on the way.

"Mosquito capital? I think we found it here."

"They're worser on Guadalcanal itself, they say," said the Greek.

Lefty moved on undaunted. "This stranger was tooling 'round town in his coupe. 'Say fella,' he says to Bo, my ex-wife's sister's brother-in-law, 'I'm good and lost in this one-horse town. How do I get out of here?'

"'I don't rightly know, sir,' says Bo.

"'Well, how do I get out to the main highway?'

"'No idea.' Bo ain't too bright.

"'There a back road out of here?'

"'Could be, I don't know for sure.'

"'Is there a railroad track I can follow out?'

"'Yep, trains come through once in a while. I hear the whistle of the 3:05 a.m., but I don't know where the station is. I don't think they ever stop other than tossing off a mailbag.'

"'Hell's fire then, you're more lost than I am.'

"'Not really, I just ain't never wanted to leave is all.'"

A long silence followed, with Lefty glancing around for the expected belly laugh.

"Lefty," said Corporal Rankin, "just shut up."

The Greek busted out laughing. "I think's it's funny but I don't get it all."

"You too, just shut up."

"I thought it was funny too..." started Spud.

Lockler ordered, "I want the cargo loads split between the boats. Move that case of grenades to the 'Eureka.'" He pointed at the LCP(L).

Lockler climbed about the two boats with the coxswains and a Navy ensign; like a second lieutenant, but more "know-it-all" because he knew all about ships. He wore bunk-pressed khakis, his face clean shaven, and his scalp close-clipped. When the transports pulled out, they left behind about thirty landing craft to serve as ship-to-shore lighters and utility boats. With them were a handful of junior officers. They were organized into a boat pool on Tulagi. The miniature fleet supported the Marines spotted on the small islands off of Florida and Guadalcanal.

The coxswains and the ensign ensured the cargo was properly tied down. Fuel tanks were full and the machine guns checked. The two deckhands aboard each boat performed a dozen jobs to make the plywood craft work. They wore blue jeans and light cranberry blue shirts—"dungarees"—with white cracker jack caps and helmets at action stations. The LCs had no radios.

Lockler wanted the section to split between the boats. That included the commo team. Instead of splitting the radio pack-loads, though, Sparks argued that if they were separated or a boat lost only part of the radio gear would be available, making it useless. It was all loaded in the LCV, but Katcher, the second most qualified signalman, went in the LCP(L).

"Okay," said Lockler, "the heaviest loads are in the LCV, which goes in first, so we can debark fast over the ramp. That ramp'll drop and I want every man carrying a crate or something to unass the boat as fast as your boondockers can carry you. Drop your load inside the tree line and double-ass-time back for anything that's still aboard. Don't bother looking to see what you're picking up, grab and go.

"Stay close and just inside the tree line. Don't worry about tactical interval. Stay close so we don't get separated. It'll be as black as a well-digger's ass at midnight under the trees. And no talking above a whisper.

"Ensign, sir, tell your men not to fire in the direction we go, straight ahead, even if we receive fire. We'll be firing if we run into anyone so don't think the muzzle flashes you see in front of you might be only Nips. When you shove off, do it slow and no engine gunning. Turn away slow and leave quietly. We don't want any attention-getting noise. Got it, sir?"

"Got it, sergeant."

"I'll take a man with me and we'll give you three flashlight blinks if all's clear."

"Okay, we're ahead of schedule," said the ensign. "We've over an hour before leaving. Captain Bear's arranged for us to mess with Battery H, 10th Marines, emplaced with its four pack howitzers on Tulagi." Supper was rice and beans with tuna fish and stale crackers, about half a mess kit load.

They talked about water supply. The Aussie said there was a waterwell at the Lever Brothers' station, but it could have been purposely disabled when they evacuated, inoperative owing to disuse, or the Japs could have wrecked it if they visited the BEARPAW. The Aussie thought there was likely a rain catchment plus rain barrels. Patches, a farm boy, rounded up a long-handled shovel in case they needed to dig out the well. They had a half-dozen five-gallon jerry cans plus two empty three-gallon fire buckets snatched from the government boatshed.

"There's one other possible source of water on the islands," said Captain Bear. "I don't exactly know how to describe it. He said natives dig taro pits in places where fresh ground water's found. They dig rectangular pits, different sizes, maybe a foot and a half deep. The fresh water fills it several inches deep and taros and sweet potatoes are planted to grow in the pit's bottom. They're simply pulled out of the bottom by their elephant leaves."

"What's a taro?" asked Patches.

"Sort of like a potato, but more fibrous. They can be cooked, boiled, or fried. The locals quite like them."

"That may be a backup chow supply," said Lockler. "Is the water drinkable?"

"It is. But treat it."

There's fresh water on these little islands?" asked the corpsman.

"There's a layer, what they call a 'lens,' of rainwater above the seawater level. Rainwater's lighter than seawater."

The corpsman was adequately stocked with medical supplies and had some extra field dressings and sulfa powder and tablets. He had a week's supply of anti-malaria tablets plus halazone water purification tablets. He advised they boil surface water if possible.

Griff said to the corpsman, "I'm putting my ass in your paws. I hope you have soft hands."

"I rub my paws with Campana hand lotion every night."

They were good on rations. Both boats held a stack of pasteboard C-ration cases, twenty-four two-can meals. The meat unit or M-unit was a small can of meat and beans, meat and potato hash, or meat and vegetable stew. The meat might be beef or pork. Henrik disliked the hash, what they called "dog food." Opening the can with a tiny P-38 can opener—no one knew what "P-38" meant—one found a coagulated layer of reddish-brown grease. If one could heat them, they were okay, but cold C-rats took a real man to poke down his throat. The second can was the bread and dessert unit or B-unit. This held several hard crackers, sugar tablets, dextrose energy tablets, bouillon powder, soluble coffee, and universally hated lemonade powder—"battery acid." The paper accessory packet held three cigarettes, a book of matches, chewing gum, toilet paper, and the P-38 opener.

Repeated requests for mosquito repellent were answered with status slips inscribed "N/A"—Not Available.

No one had taken a count of the cases of canned chow they'd loaded. It included Aussie mutton and lamb, bully beef, corned beef hash—"corn willy"—string beans, peas, baked beans, wax beans, stewed tomatoes, and even dreaded Kadota figs.

With the section and the boat crewmen gathered, Lockler scratched lines on the cleared dirt patch showing the boats' movements and who went where when hitting the beach. He covered light signals, and the challenge is "Lucky" and the password is "Lollypop."

"Griff, follow me and head straight out the ramp 'til I say to halt. 1st Squad goes left and 2d Squad right. The commo team stays behind me. I'll have them fill out the perimeter if we have gaps." He sketched the small perimeter's horseshoe arch, the open heel ends anchored on the beach. "The main thing for the flanking squads is to have someone cover the beach flank and inside the tree line. Once we're sure we're not disturbing someone's beauty rest we'll start toting the cargo into the trees. We'll form a bucket brigade. We should be able to reach from the boats into the trees. Don't worry about how you stack it, just don't make any noise. We'll unload the ramped Higgins first."

"How about my men, Sergeant?" asked the ensign.

"They need to man the boat MGs to cover the flanking beaches and maybe one gun covering your rear."

"Seaward, you mean. I've got three MGs mounted, so that leaves me with three deckhands. They can throw in to help you with the bucket brigade."

"That would help, sir, but maybe not."

It was clear that the ensign was going along to oversee the debarkation. That surprised everyone, even though he had only a pistol on his side. The other crewmen also only had pistols.

Lockler suggested, "It'll be best for them to remain aboard so they don't get stranded with only pistols and no field gear. We'd have to watch out for them ashore. Follow me, sir?"

"I agree, sergeant."

They talked out the further details and went over the plan again. They would receive a resupply in five nights. The ensign said, "We'll fire a green flare about a quarter-mile out then look for your blinker light flashes. If the resupply boat doesn't contact you they'll try to send a boat each night after that." Captain Bear checked in with them. The section was ready to go. Lifebelts were passed out and a final check of the secured cargo made.

They waited for an hour after sunset. Henrik secretly hoped the Japs would launch an air raid to distract lookouts scanning The Slot's surface.

***

"Sarge, I got me this," said Snacks. "A Tommy gun."

"Where in hell did you get that?" Lockler checked it over. "An M1928A1 Thompson. I've not seen one since China."

"Traded it for an electric grinding machine I found in the Aussie boathouse workshop."

"To who?"

"Those pioneer battalion scabs."

"How many magazines they give you?"
"Five, ammo too."
"That'll do. You still have your rifle?"
"Yep."
"Keep it with you," ordered Lockler, "along with its ammo. Lose that rifle and you'll be filling out a QM 782c Rifle Replacement Form, no excuses."
"Okay," Snacks replied disappointedly. "The Tommy gun weighs a ton and I gotta carry the rifle and ammo too. Maybe I can beg the dit-da-dits for a carton of .45."

Snacks huddled with the commo team and soon exclaimed, "Damn."
"What now?"
"Both Thompsons and Reisings use twenty-round magazines, same ammo, but the mags ain't interchangeable," he said, flabbergasted.
"Anybody seen an extra lifebelt?" shouted Spud.
"You lost yours already, Spud?" accused Corporal Rankin.
"It was right here on the gunwale."
"Check over the side. Did it fall in the drink?"
"Nothin' this side."
"They don't float long if they're not inflated," advised a deckhand.
"This is not the right time to find out lifebelts sink."

**

The sun was a burning half disc melting into the sea. *Sunset must be a good sign for the Japs*, thought Henrik, *sunrise too. A twice daily salute to their rag of a meatball flag.*

A yard patrol boat heaved abaft the Government Wharf. The ensign in the LCP(L) cast loose and eased over to the "yippee boat" to coordinate with their escort. The hundred-plus foot YP, looked more like a fishing trawler without hanging nets, would navigate for the following landing boats. It was a thirty-mile trip. The YP's skipper too was a know-it-all ensign.

"All right, 1918 hours. Sun's been down for an hour. Let's get this show on the road. Are you ready, sir?" asked Lockler.
"The Navy's always ready, sergeant."
"Then let's get this fleet underway."

The boat coxswains kicked their engines over, doing some test gunning. They clicked on dim running lights.
"How about them lights, Sarge?" asked Corporal Rankin.
"They're dim enough," said the ensign. "You have to be within about fifty feet to see them. We'll douse them when we start the run to shore."
"I can't ever remember which is port and which is starboard," said Griff to a deckhand.

"Port and left both have four letters."

"Trouble remembering the light colors too."

"Starboard's green and port's red. Just remember, red wine's called port."

Maybe swabbies aren't so dumb after all, thought Henrik.

Gathering way, they slowly followed the yippee boat running west out of Tulagi Harbour and turned northwest. They paralleled Florida Island's coast to starboard and passed the smaller Olevuga Island. They weren't being towed, but the YP boat had its dim white stern light on under the yellow towing light so they could follow the YP and judge their distance separation. They were about at the halfway point and would soon turn northeast to transit the passage between Olevuga and the scattered islets comprising the northwest end of the Florida Islands.

Patches made himself comfortable against coiled rope and played "I'll Be Seeing You" on his fist-organ.

Lights began sharply flashing aboard the yippee. *Blinker light signals?* wondered Henrik. "That can attract unwanted attention," said Rankin. The two swabby bow machine gunners swung their Lewis guns ahead. More lights blinked on the YP's pilothouse as yellow tracers suddenly streaked over; wood splinters flew. A black shape roared over, disappearing in the dark clouded sky. One gunner spun his gun around and let loose a hopeless burst of green tracers. The two landing boats turned to starboard toward Olevuga while the YP swung to port toward invisible Savo Island.

"What the hell!" yelled Henrik. "Was that a fighter?" Then it came to him—*ours or theirs?*

Shouts and cries. Someone was hit. Men scrambled, screaming. Spray washed over the cargo compartment as they made jolting turns. Henrik crouched beside the secured cargo as the boat gradually slowed. They pulled up abaft each other, shouting back and forth if there were casualties. Men were looking skyward, thankful there was no re-approaching roar drowning out the idling boat engines.

"Anyone see our escort?"

"Sarge, Julien's dead."

"Everyone else okay?"

"Corpsman! Lefty's hit," bellowed Sparks.

"On the way," shouted Doc.

The ensign shouted for his boat crewmen to sound off. All answered up. Lockler climbed over the stacked cargo. "Henrik, help Doc."

He scrambled over to Doc and Lefty. "You need me to do anything?"

"Cut open his left pants leg, crotch to cuff. I'll check out this arm. It's not bad. Not much more than a bad nick." He tied on a field dressing. "You won't have to salute anyone for a spell." Next he checked the thigh wound, which turned out to be more serious than it looked. Doc gave the wound a sulfa powder dusting, packed it with gauze pads, and tied on tight a large dressing, not the regular size. He filled out an Emergency Medical Tag.

"Anyone see the escort?" shouted the ensign.

"I ain't looking for it, I'm looking for that Zero. Is that what it was?"

Machine guns and binoculars pointed skyward in anticipation of its return.

"I believe it was a Zero," said the ensign. "The Jap Navy uses yellow tracers. It was a small plane and Zeros are what we've mostly seen."

"I thought the yippee boat was flashing signal lights," said Henrik.

"Those were Japanese 20mm hits and the YP's own 20mm returning fire. Zeros have two 20mm guns and two machine guns."

"Sure made a racket. Scared the piss outta me," a voice said in the darkness.

"Wasn't like practice snapping at our own fighters back as Camp Edwards."

"You and the rest of us are sittin' ducks, brother," said Lockler.

They could hear the drone of a plane off to the west, maybe hunting for them. It faded away. A Zero's fuel radius was short.

The ensign was scanning with binoculars to the east. "Sergeant, we need to cancel this mission and get the wounded man back."

"Why, sir? We've got but one wounded and one dead. We've not lost any mission gear. Doesn't change a thing."

"We also lost our escort and guide boat, sergeant," the ensign added, trying to sound authoritative.

"We have a chart and the boats have compasses. Can't you navigate, sir? Anyway, why did the escort turn west and run the opposite direction of us heading east?"

"That was their evasion plan for air attack. The boats would head to the nearest shore so that if they're sinking they could run aground or the crew could abandon ship and swim for the nearest shore. The escort would run for open water in the opposite direction of the boats. The attacker might chase the escort then. Maybe it actually worked."

"Maybe so, maybe not," said Lockler.

"Besides, you've lost a signalman."

Without turning, Lockler said, "Sparks, can you operate that glorified Motorola with two men?"

"ROGER that."

"One of my LCV deckhands took some wood splinters," said the ensign.

"Can he still man his gun?"

"He can."

Lockler hesitated a moment. "Sir, it's my mission and the brass says it's critical. I recommend we continue. Drop us off as planned and you can evacuate the wounded."

Henrik didn't think Lockler was trying to pull rank, especially with an officer and a Navy ensign at that. Ensigns and 2nd lieutenants tended to be boneheaded about their presumed authority. Lockler was right—the mission was the reason we're here, not to give meaning to a water-taxi service. He was in charge of the mission, once ashore, but that was the real mission. The ensign's job was simply to get them there, one way or the other, and bring the boats back, if possible.

Henrik and the others within hearing expected the ensign to countermand the order.

"Very well, sergeant. After due consideration, I agree with your assessment. We'll continue the mission as tactical necessity dictates."

Lockler snapped a salute—something they weren't supposed to do in a combat zone.

Since they had run toward shore and had been near the Olevuga passage, it did not take long to locate the passage and plot a course from which to make enroute adjustments when they spotted Pombuana.

Lockler suddenly said, "Who the hell are you?"

"PFC Ernesto Molina, Sarge," a shadow snapped back.

"Where in hell did you come from, meathead?"

"DOG Company, 2d Pioneer Battalion. I was on the detail to clear debris at the wharf and helped load your ammo and stuff. I overheard you're going on a special mission or some such. I got on the boat in the dark to help out. I didn't expect all this excitement."

"Neither did we," Lockler said dryly, and turned to the still surprised ensign. "Sir, does the Navy still make stowaways walk the plank?"

"My experience is with marines attempting to jump ship, not stowaways seeking passage to a battle. Walking the plank seems rash—keelhauling perhaps?"

"Up to you, sir. But we could just pressgang the pogue and take him along as a replacement."

"Sounds good to me," said the ensign without hesitation, indicating he didn't wish to deal with the stowaway after returning.

"Mercy on me, sir, I just thought since the boats are coming back I'd take the boat ride, help you unload, maybe see a little excitement, and take the boat home." He sounded pretty anxious about the return trip now. A strafing Zero had undoubtedly provoked enough excitement.

"Well, okay then," said Lockler. "We've lost two men and you have experience loading our cargo. I mean pioneers are stevedores with infantry and demolitions training, right?"

"Well, I guess so," was the reply, in a destined-for-doom tone.

"You put yourself in harm's way, we can use you. Are you wearing my man's lifebelt?"

"Thought I might need it and no one was wearing it."

"Fine then. Rankin, this is PFC Ernesto Molina—"

"You can call me 'Nesto.'"

"Nesto here can fill you in on his immediate transfer to the 2d Marines. Rankin, give him Julien's pack, web gear, and Reising and fill Nesto in on the mission. Can you handle a Reising?"

"We fired them for familiarization in the pioneers."

"You may become even more familiar with the Buck Rogers gun."

"Thanks, sarge," Nesto said. "I guess."

"Beats keelhauling. We'll see if you'll still be thanking me for long."

***

Binoculars raised, Lockler and the ensign scanned the inky blackness. The engines throbbed at the lowest idle setting.

"That should be it," breathed the ensign. "Let's ease over to starboard to check it out closer before picking a landing beach."

They had approached the island's northern portion after swinging around the northeast end.

"Looks all the same to me," whispered Lockler.

"It does. Look, at 2 o'clock. Looks like fewer whitecaps."

"Looks fine to me," said Lockler. "It's your battlewagon."

"We'll move in as slow as we can and still keep steerage-way."

"I'm going aft, give the men a heads up," said Lockler.

He met Henrik. "Sarge, I have to ask you, did you really think the ensign would go along with you and not cancel?"

"No doubt in my mind he'd go along with me. Would you want to be the junior butter bar officer who'd have to go back to the brass and tell them you didn't accomplish their cherished mission, a critical mission directed by Division?"

"I guess not."

"You'll go far, Handyman. Just don't get yourself killed."

"Working on it, sarge."

Lockler slapped him on the shoulder. "Does that lump look like a BEARPAW to you?"

At first Henrik could only make out billowing fog, but it turned into a hill or humped-back rising out of the water with the glimmer of what would be trifling white tops in daylight.

Henrik was kneeling beside the wounded Lefty. "You doing okay, buddy?" He held a canteen to Lefty's lips to wash down sulfa tablets. He had to take six of the dozen sulfanilamide tablets in a carton. "Instructions say for you to drink plenty of water after taking these tablets."

"Says here I can drink wine if there's no water."

"Sorry, fresh out."

"I'm okay. The shoulder hit's just an in and an out. The bullet came out three inches past where it hit. A real flesh wound. Not too bad." They'd heard that in western, cop, gangster, and war movies. His right thigh was bulkily bandaged. "Whatever hit, it went deep. Won't be hittin' the beach with you jarheads for a while."

"You take care of yourself, Lefty. Save us some chow for when we get back."

As they eased toward the strand of light-colored beach, Doc whispered in Henrik's ear, "Lefty's in a lot of pain, his leg. He wouldn't let me give him a morphine syrette. He said to save it; we might need it. They only gave me six syrettes."

"Yeah, he's a jarhead alright."

Henrik tried not to think of Julien wrapped up in a poncho, dead from a 20mm high-explosive incendiary round hitting the side of his torn helmet. Sticky blood had seeped onto the deck. Henrik didn't know him, but hell, he was a marine too.

Concentrate on what's about to happen.

"Land the landing force," the ensign cynically muttered.

No blaze of gunfire so far. A bump and a little jolt. Their forward movement had been at a crawl to keep down engine noise to prevent a hard-beaching. The engine dropped to idle. Instead of dropping the LCV's ramp with a bang as in exercises, it was slowly lowered by winch. Stage-whispered voices, a side-to-side rocking, the smell of seawater, the rustle of surf. The breeze had kicked up. Engine exhaust and the smell of damp greenness.

Henrik grabbed the case of grenades and crossed the ramp to lose his footing as he stepped off into two feet of water. The grenade case slammed into the water, taking him with it. His rifle's sling slipped to hang in the crook of his arm. He fell a second time. Stumbling across the beach, he dashed into the trees' darkness. Their creeping speed hadn't driven the boats very far up the shallow beach gradient. It reduced noise and kept the boats from grounding. In the coalmine blackness, he set down the case. He didn't know where he was but sensed other men halting too.

"Site the BAR over there." *Where is "there?"*

He met another anonymous shape with a C-rat case under each arm.

Ragged clouds hung in the sky, making the jungle all the darker. He stumbled his way through blindly. He made four or five trips. Every time he was inside the trees he had no reference of where he had dropped crates.

Someone on the beach said, "That's it. Get everything inside the tree line."

Unseen and barely heard, the boats backed off the beach and faded into the blackness, their wakes swallowed by swells. A faint "Best of luck, gyrenes" drifted back with the breeze.

"Henrik, come with me." It was Lockler. "Make sure nothing's left on the beach." All he found was a canteen and a can of Kadota figs. Spud claimed the canteen. No one wanted the figs.

Only the wavelets hissed over the sand. With high tide the boondocker prints on the beach would disappear. The breeze rustled through the trees. No other sounds broke the stillness.

***

Henrik awakened in a tropical paradise, to the buzz of mosquitos and other flying pests, brash bird chirps, a blustery morning breeze, sticky humidity, and already scorching heat. *Who left the furnace door open?*

Quiet voices.

He blinked grit out of his eyes, took a swallow of trepid water. He saw only a couple of men moving in the dreary dawn light. Sitting up, he brushed off sand and coconut fibers stuck to his face. Ants were exploring his legs, demanding a brushoff. He wiped down his Springfield with his oily rag. Standing, he could see assorted crates, cases, and water cans shoved under bushes or covered with palm fronds.

"Handyman, over here," a voice said.

"You okay, Handyman?" asked Corporal Rankin.

"Devildogs," Henrik growled, slapping at some never before seen flying bug. He didn't feel like a Devildog, but it seemed the thing to say.

"Lockler says not to eat anything today except for the fudge bars and Kadota figs he's passing around. We can go a day without chow. Gives us an extra day's chow if we're forgotten."

I knew I should have left that fig can on the beach.

"We landed close enough to where we wanted to be that we can stay put. We're on the north side of that lobe they talked about. They're digging in the OP further up the hillside, just over 200 yards south-southwest. We're sending out a patrol. You're going with us, Handyman."

"Figured. I'm ready to stretch my legs."

"Be ready in five."

Chapter Twenty-Two

The Daihatsu's machine gunner frantically swung his impotent weapon toward the destroyer knifing at them across Rekata Bay. The ship's bow wave died and it turned to parallel them. They were close enough to see the frowning antiaircraft gunners behind their mounts. The barge's crewmen cheered and waved caps. The Imperial Navy's rayed Rising Sun National Ensign fluttered in the stiff breeze.

"It is a Mutsuki Class destroyer, our escort," said the barge sergeant to Lieutenant Kiyoshi. We are going to be towed partway to your island much faster than our eight knots. Mutsukis are old torpedo attack boats with a speed of thirty-seven knots. The hundred-meter ship will be able to tow us at up to twenty knots. Later we will pick up another barge for part of the trip.

"How come the gunners look so unhappy?"

"They do not like being out in the open waters in daylight with a tow. It hampers their speed and maneuverability." He paused a moment. "If they are attacked by airplanes they will cut us loose."

"Then we would be on our own," observed the lieutenant.

"Yes, the destroyer would hope we were attracting the airplane from itself. I doubt that though."

The destroyer pulled ahead and they slowed further. The destroyer's name on the stern was painted over to hide its identification. Sailors on its fantail milled about and one fired a line-throwing gun at the barge. The cord arched into the sky, and the weighted projectile landed in the cargo compartment with crewmen and soldiers ducking and laughing. Bargemen scrambled to grab it and several men, including soldiers, hand-over-handed the cord to which a heavier rope, with two coiled and bundled ropes, was lashed on. Unwrapping the bundles, they secured a tow rope with chaff chains to cleats on either side of the bow. The two ropes ran to a bridle connector to which the destroyer's tow rope was secured. Lunging in the increasing waves, the destroyer gradually moved ahead, taking up the slack to jerk the barge. Its high-reaching bow countered the tow rope's tendency to pull the bow downward. The tow rope would momentarily go slack and then taut over and over. It made for a mildly jerking ride, but tolerable. The crews shouted *"Tenno heika banzai!"*

It was over one hundred kilometers from Rekata Bay to a lagoon called Maringe and its Buala village, both also on Santa Isabel. Hidden back in the lagoon was a barge-staging base. The lagoon was large enough, with trees lining the water's edge, helping to shield numerous barges moored along the shore from Skylark Channel. Here barges were repaired and refueled and the crews rested and fed.

The destroyer cast them off some kilometers short of the lagoon, then darted off to patrol the area's approaches. The destroyer would rendezvous with them after dark and they would be accompanied by a second barge.

The barge was nuzzled next to shore with leafy overhanging tree limbs and the fishing net camouflaging the barge's exposed side. Across the lagoon was Buala village, pressed against a high, dominating forested ridge. The other barge, said to be loaded with ammunition, soon arrived, and the two crews rigged the towing gear after turning the barges in the lagoon to ease their exit. It would be towed astern of their barge, dropped off at a waypoint, and follow its own route of which they did not speak.

The platoon had debarked and set up a palm-shrouded camp for their dinner and a little rest. Obata offered to help the crew check over the motor, but they declined. They seemed to think only they had the knowledge to care for their precious motor.

They were too soon ordered to re-embark and, with lookouts posted, the two barges lumbered out of the lagoon under their own power. In the channel the destroyer slipped up even faster than at their first rendezvous. Even though it was dark, they rigged the two barges quicker than before and were soon making twenty knots along the northeast coast of Santa Isabel, heading southeast. They experienced a slightly smoother ride. After making about fifty-five kilometers near the southeast end of Santa Isabel, both barges were cast off and turned their separate ways into the darkness. Blinker lights flashed from the three vessels, wishing each other a safe passage and victory for the Emperor. The three craft took their own routes. With their speed cut by over half under their own power, the barge seemed to wallow helplessly in the Skylark Channel surges.

The word was passed to the platoon that they were heading due south for forty-five kilometers. For the first time they found out their destination—a small island called *Kombuana Jima*. Apparently the British called it Pombuana. They were given a simple description of the island, a mere one and a half kilometers long and just under one kilometer wide at its broadest breadth.

Hilly and thickly forested, there was a small British settlement on the south shore thought certain to have been evacuated.

For the first time the lieutenant addressed the platoon as a group. His attitude and vocabulary was off-putting to the soldiers, most of whom had never experienced members of the educated political and military classes which spawned officers. Some of his vocabulary was simply not understood.

"You were sent here by the Emperor to halt enemy aggression and die to attain His honorable goals."

A couple of the more naive soldiers thought the Emperor was directly in control of their mission.

He gathered the men together at the bow ramp. "Our honorable mission is to establish a plotting control post and operate a weather station. This will be invaluable to our ships and airplanes, especially to let them know when there is fog or clouds or rainstorms for them to hide in before they attack the Americans. That same fog or clouds will allow the enemy to hide. We will report sightings of enemy ships and airplanes heading to Guadalcanal.

"We will soon land on Kombuana Island. This will demand a significant unified effort to unload the cargo that will sustain us through the coming days. You will have to move the cargo off the beach and hide it in the jungle. You will need to be vigilant at all times as we do not know when the Americans may appear."

He glared at the men. "Ensure all of your equipment is properly packed and secured. Leave nothing behind when you debark. Leave only footprints on the beach. You will have to move all of our supplies to other hiding places, and this must be accomplished before you can eat or rest. You must not leave anything in the open that says the Japanese are here or make any noises. You must not shout or make loud working noises. No work songs."

He ended with, "Diligently perform your duties. *Tenno heika banzai! Banzai! Banzai!*" That was shouted quietly.

The lieutenant turned and went back to the coxswain's cockpit followed by his orderly, Superior Private Saburo.

Sergeant Toshio took charge of the men in the bow. "You are going to be in the water to unload. It will be very wet on the island. Wear your tabis. If you do not have tabis, wear your boots without puttees, or you may wear other sandals. Keep your bayonets sheathed so you do not stab each other, and do not fix bayonets ashore unless ordered. They are too cumbersome in the jungle. Wear your life jackets until we are beached and then leave them in the barge. Drink up and refill your water bottles from the barge's water tank. You may eat one rice ball. Private Ikuo will bring around a bottle of miso." He glared at them, his meaning lost in the darkness. "Do not be caught in the open if an airplane flies over, whether Japanese or enemy. Do not fire on airplanes. Work hard and be diligent. No rest until our duties are accomplished."

One of their big patrol-bombers from Rekata Bay flew past, heading south. In Obata's mind there was no doubt that the aircraft's crew was waving at the immodest girl on that Rekata Bay beach.

***

Obata crouched near the raised bow ramp. He had no idea of the time but knew it must be the early morning hours. The sea mist blurred the stars. Everyone was lined up in two files and had a crate or other container on the deck before them. Waves would bounce or jerk the barge and they would grab one another or a rib brace for balance. The motor chugged at a low rate. The waves seemed to build somewhat as the offshore water became shallower. Their speed slowed.

One of the signalmen was perched behind the ramp on the starboard side just an arm's length from Obata. The lieutenant and the barge captain were with him, scanning the approaching island's dark shape. Sergeant Toshio whispered, "Cover your eyes."

Obata knew what was happening. They were flashing random blinker light signals at the beach. If there were enemy ashore, perhaps they would signal back, thinking the formless vessel approaching them was one of their own. If they received an answering signal they would quickly back off and find another landing site. The blinker threw a narrow beam, so they flashed the signals on several different bearings. After waiting a couple of minutes, the lieutenant ordered, "Land here."

The sergeant went back to the coxswain's cockpit, telling him to land straight ahead. Sergeant Toshio would bring up the rear, following the last man out. He would even carry a ration case himself.

Private Ikuo stayed with the coxswain on Toshio's orders. He told Ikuo, "If there is shooting and the coxswain starts to pull out, you are to shoot him." In turn, Toshio told the coxswain to shoot Ikuo if he did not rush out of the bow to the beach and tried to remain aboard.

The coxswain laughed. "To please your sergeant, perhaps we should shoot one another now."

"I will accept the sacrifice and shoot first," said Ikuo with a quiet laugh.

The Daihatsu's motor could barely be heard over the light surf and breeze. The motor gunned once and then again. Everyone was jarred forward as the barge butted onto the sand. The ramp dropped slowly. Two figures darted across the beach. Obata assumed one was the lieutenant. There was more gunning and a few shouts. The figurers returned. Others filed off the ramp lugging the cargo and tossing off life vests. With the last man out, Ikuo bounded over the raising ramp lugging an ammunition crate. The men splashed through inches of water, across firm and then looser dry sand. They were well inside the trees. Low shouted orders were heard directing men into position.

Obata heard the lieutenant talking to Toshio. "The Daihatsu was grounded by that foolish captain. The high tide will float it, but it will be approaching dawn. The tide is already starting to flood. So far there have been no American dawn fighter patrols. It will be a close thing."

"Should we move away from this area?" asked Toshio.

"Yes, we must. This is not the best position, unfortunately. We landed on the south side of the narrow western portion of the island. I will take a patrol to the left and locate a suitable plotting control post. It would be better on the island's west point. The British settlement is not very far to our right. We should be further from it. If the Americans come here—if they have not already—they will certainly visit the settlement."

An hour later the lieutenant's patrol returned. Regardless of some tentative motor gunning, the barge was still grounded.

"I have found a suitable position on the north side around the west point. There is a small knoll for our base close to where we can situate the plotting station itself. It provides a view from due north around to the west and covers the channel well. It is about 600 meters from here following the tree line. Do not let anyone walk on the beach at any time. Only walk inside the tree line. There appears to be a trail just inside the tree line that possibly extends all the way around the island. The men will be organized into teams of four and must stay together so no one becomes lost. We must make haste. For the Emperor."

The teams made two round trips each in soft sand, rock outcroppings, brush, vines, and insects. They carried their equipment, weapons, and twenty to thirty kilograms of supplies to a small knoll about 100 meters inland where the plotting station was being set up. Obata had expected there were few rations left to be unloaded. Most of the men were extremely uncomfortable in the wild jungle night—a totally alien environment.

Just before dawn the Daihatsu finally refloated. Most of the men were again able to refill their water bottles aboard the barge and were even given some tins of rice beer by the crewmen. Obata saw a couple of sailors give a quick bow to the soldiers before boarding the barge. Within minutes of the final items being carried ashore, the barge departed without fanfare, motoring north at maximum speed and without the benefit of even the platoon's light machine gun for protection. The barge disappeared into the darkness, seeking a day hiding place within the labyrinth of inlets and isles making up the Florida Islands.

Only the rolling growl of the surf could be heard.

Lieutenant Kiyoshi summoned Sergeant Toshio and Corporal Masaichi. The instrument man and three other soldiers worked on the plotting station. Another three men, the grenade discharger crew, were clearing a short path between the plotting station and the base encampment on the knoll. There was not much to the knoll, it being maybe three or four meters higher than the plotting station. The path's purpose was to prevent anyone becoming lost traveling between the two sites in the dark and to let them move quietly. The radio crew was setting up the Type 95 Model 3 radio and the Model F hand-cranked generator.

"Corporal Masaichi will lead a four-man patrol to the British settlement following the tree line around the west end and along the south shore. Do not take the machine gun but take Obata. I do not want you to enter the settlement or allow anyone to see you lurking around if it is occupied. I only want to know if there are any soldiers, civilians, or natives there. Stay only long enough to confirm if it is occupied or not and then quickly return. Let me know the general condition of the buildings and if you see anything that might be a waterwell."

The settlement was only 300 meters southeast of the plotting station through the jungle, but the shore trail had to be scouted. That made the trip 900 meters.

"Be careful; do not shoot at anyone simply because you see them. It is important that we not alert the enemy or even any natives of our presence." The lieutenant was familiar with the soldiers' habit of customarily shooting down natives, deeming them inconvenient unless willing to work. He had seen it in China. Officers would post themselves at remote crossroads and await a Chinaman to pass. They took turns lopping off heads. The old Samurai practiced it on insignificant peasants and called it "crossroad-cutting," a test of their blade's keenness and their own skill.

Masaichi took Obata and Takeo. "Absolute silence," the corporal ordered. It was unnecessary, as Obata was among the quietest of his men in both voice and movement. Takeo seemed to mimic the sniper...in some ways.

They followed the edge of the tree line with little in the way of a path to follow. This portion of the beach was the widest on the island. Even with the dense vegetation backdrop Obata felt exposed. There was no sign of footprints. Masaichi, in the lead, was exceedingly cautious: two or three steps, listen, then carefully move ahead. The path led into the trees. Just meters past that was a path-side clearing with a junk pile of mattress springs, bits of scrap metal, and rotted boards. A rusted-out kerosene refrigerator with the door busted off lay on its side. Anything like tin cans and pipes had probably been salvaged. Masaichi waved them to halt and then gestured to move off the path to the left. On hands and knees they crept through the ferns, saplings, and big-leafed plants. The clearing around the settlement was irregular and the cleared ground was really not so clear, being overgrown owing to disuse.

They lay in meter-high ferns with a liberal share of red ants and gnats. The wooden buildings were similar to those in Rabaul, but smaller, simpler, and more weatherworn.

Obata, propped on his elbows, slowly panned his rifle about the settlement, peering into the shadows under the buildings. There were six plus outbuildings. The overgrown grounds revealed little. There, that building—was it a house, an office? In the lightening sky he could make out several steel drums under the building with unfathomable white markings. The morning breeze freshened. Among the big-leaved plants like elephant ears were some curved, silver-painted pipes. "Over there," he said to Masaichi, "it looks like a water pump. I cannot be certain."

"I see it."

"There are some 200-liter drums under the building. Maybe for water."

Bang!

The three men ducked, pressing themselves into the rotting jungle floor.

Bang!

"That was a door," said a startled Masaichi. "Go and look, Obata. Carefully."

He eased up, peering through the telescope behind a screen of leaves. His heart racing, he looked at each building's doors, the ones he could see, expecting British or American soldiers to advance on them.

A puff of breeze moved the door on the building with the pump. A stiffer gust banged the door again. "It is a door."

"I want to get closer, to see if there is an operational waterwell."

Obata knew the lieutenant had said not to enter the settlement. He could say nothing to a superior. It was Masaichi's decision.

Cautiously, they moved further inland and closer to the building.

"Takeo, very carefully; go to the waterwell and see if it appears operational."

He moved slowly through the low vegetation, right up to the well. Obata watched as he ducked below the plants, then suddenly emerged in front of the steps, glanced about, and tiptoed quickly up the porch.

"No, no," whispered Masaichi.

Takeo entered slowly and, seconds later, emerged, darting down the steps. On all fours he returned to their hiding place.

"Why did you do that, you foolish boy? You were to stay out of there." He slapped Takeo in the face before he could answer.

Chastised, he whispered with downcast eyes, "The water pump is an old one. It is not connected to anything. I went inside to see if there was a new pump there. There was not. There was no replacement pump underneath the building either, but at least some of the drums hold water. There was a woman's makeup box."

"Excellent, we could not have gone on without knowing that." Masaichi did not say anything more, and they followed the beach path back to the plotting station.

***

Reporting to the lieutenant, Masaichi avoided mentioning that Takeo had entered the settlement's grounds, much less the building. That may have been his silent apology to Takeo. Once Masaichi had completed his report and bowed to the officer, the lieutenant gave Masaichi his orders on what needed to be completed at the plotting station. This including moving everything to their new site, hiding the buckets and other water-related equipment, and posting two sentries each on the beach paths above and below the site.

The lieutenant decided to reconnoiter the settlement himself. He was especially anxious to find a water source. Leaving Sergeant Toshio in charge, he selected five men including Obata and Takeo since they had already been there. There was sufficient light left when they departed following the same route back to the settlement.

Chapter Twenty-Three

Under the overhanging breadfruit trees around the observation post Sergeant Lockler had everyone dab their green steel helmets with splotches of brown mud to distort their silhouette.

"Don't rub mud on your utilities. Good way to get bug bites infected," said the corpsman, Moscato. Someone had found a can of DDT powder and they dusted around their ankles, wrists, and waist. They'd also dusted the slit trenches they were digging. Bugs moved in before the marines.

"I don't like the color of our OD uniforms either, but they'll become camouflaged enough with dirt, sweat, and gyrene-grubbiness." The common complaint was that utilities were too light colored in the lush jungle green.

The OP was on a ridge finger stretching from the island's thirty-six-foot main hill on its northeast side. They had initially found a possible site lower down on the end of the finger. It lacked sufficient elevation for a longer-range field of vision. Higher up the finger, though, they found a thinly vegetated patch allowing for longer-range observation of the broad Indispensable Strait separating the Florida Islands and larger Malaita to the east; almost as big as Guadalcanal. They had to clear-cut higher limbs and vines to get an open field of vision. The base camp was about three-quarters of the way between the landing beach and the OP. Men in the OP and the base camp could cover the other site with fire. They would cut a trail between the two sites for quiet movement.

"How come we're not putting the OP on top of this thirty-six-foot hill, sarge?" asked Patches.

Lockler said, "I went up there. The hilltop and most of the side slopes are thickly forested. You might be standing on the island's highest point, but it's covered with fifteen- to twenty-foot trees and you can't even see the ocean."

Lockler laid out the grainy aerial photograph and drew a sketch map of the porkchop-shaped island in the sand. Corporal Rankin, Snacks, Spud, and Henrik looked on.

"Here's your job," said Lockler. "You're running a patrol west down the north-side beach to this point about 700 yards west of here. In this area look for a trail on the left that might run due south." He stabbed a pointed stick into the trail junction. "Can't really make out a trail in the photo. Just keep a good pace count and keep your eyes peeled. That trail, if it's there, might take you to the Aussie station here. It's only about 300 yards to the station." Another stab. "See what's there, draw a sketch map of the station and the buildings, and see if there's anything we can use. Don't make it obvious you were there. Don't bust up anything and try not to leave a lot of boondocker tracks." He looked at the patrol. "The main objective is to see if there's a waterwell, rain catchments, rain barrels, anything holding potable water."

"Portable water?" asked Spud.

"Potable water. Means you can drink it."

"Then why don't you—"

"Shut up, Spud."

"Just askin'. Thought you were going to tell me to drop."

"Wait until we get back. You're hitting the trail in ten minutes."

"Not even a cup of coffee for breakfast," grumbled Spud.

"Quit crying in your beer, jarhead."

"You have any?"

"I've got some figs," offered Lockler.

***

The patrol lineup was Snacks, Rankin, Henrik, and Spud. "Ten-foot intervals."

Rankin had told Spud, "Watch our ass." Snacks on point took it slow and easy, with a toe-heel gait feeling for sticks and leaves—the damp making for quiet footfalls. Rankin kept the pace count. Every hundred yards he'd move a pebble from his left pocket to the right. He'd count approximately 120 paces per 100 yards. Snacks halted and gave a good hard look at particularly deep shadow patches ahead.

There wasn't much to the trail, an indiscreet track one to two feet wide mostly hidden by fallen leaves and ferns overhung with drooping big-leafed plants. Snacks examined the rare patches lit by sunlight in search of footprints and scuffmarks. The rain-beaten sand revealed only a long disused trail.

Owing to the low-hanging vegetation, they were forced to crouch. Just feet away to the right were the open beach and the quietly surging surf. The trail was not far enough inside the jungle to muffle the surf.

Snacks suddenly dropped to a knee, staring at the ground. The patrol froze. With such halts the men dropped to a knee, rifles ready. Spud automatically faced to the rear.

Rankin crept forward at Snacks' summons. "Side trail to the left."

"I was just about to 700 yards in the count," said Rankin. "I don't see any sign. What do you see?"

"Just that two feet of broken limb dangling on that tree and three notch cuts on this one."

"Good goin', Snacks."

Rankin gestured to the others to follow down the side trail. They instinctively slowed, halting more often to listen. The winding, barely discernable trail led gradually downhill. Halfway down they found overgrown gardens, probably vegetable. They looked recently disturbed with dug-up mud and crushed plants. The patrol listened silently. There was only the breeze, no surf rush.

"Someone's been here," whispered Rankin.

"Henrik, give it a look."

"Nope, just hogs rooting around. That's all."

"Just like a farm boy."

"It's a gift."

"Hey," whispered Spud. "Maybe Lockler'll let us shoot a pig once we know we're not sharing this dirt pile."

"Maybe. Slower and quieter than we've been," ordered Rankin. "Nobody touch a thing, even if you find that Maltese Falcon statue, Spud. Move out." Mosquitos congregated whether they halted or were moving.

"What falcon?" said Spud, looking up.

"The one in that Bogart movie, you dunce," said Rankin.

"Oh, yeah. We could melt it down for the gold and diamonds maybe."

"The stuff that dreams are made of," muttered Snacks.

"I'd rather have a hamburger," said Rankin.

"I'd gladly pay you Tuesday for a hamburger today," Spud said in a singsong tone.

"Move out Wimpy and I'll give you a can of Kadota figs."

"Gag a maggot off a gut wagon."

They could see the shacks. Weather-worn, unpainted, wood-framed, corrugated tin-roofed, lots of windows, set up on stilts, maybe five or six feet off the ground. The grounds were overgrown with weeds and fledging shrubs. There were what looked like fishing-net drying racks and broad plank tables for sorting coconuts. Some were scattered on the tables and ground. It looked abandoned.

"Henrik, hang back and cover us. Keep an eye on windows and doors. Everybody keep an eye on the shadows under the buildings. Stay low. Let's go."

The three marines crept down the trail slowly, their rifles following their eyes.

The surf was barely audible now. A flock of gray pigeons fluttered over. *Green wings*, thought Henrik. *Everything wants to look like the jungle.*

A door slammed, sending everyone scrambling for the nearest cover and still trying to be silent. Henrik swung his rifle, trying to cover everyone. In two seconds there was no one to be seen. No one fired. A door slammed again, not as loudly.

Rankin came out from under a coconut table, knelt for a second, and then cautiously moved toward a house. Going up the steps, he paused at the door momentarily and came back down. Rankin gave the signal to pull back—two knuckle raps on the stock—and they fell back up the trail to Henrik. Rankin quickly backtracked them further before halting.

"Well, shit in my mess kit," said Spud. "Tell me that was just a damn screen door."

"Yeah, it was a damn screen door. Scared the pee out of me too," said Rankin. "Windblown. I wedged it shut. Henrik, go back to where you can see the layout and make a sketch. Make it fast. No Salvador Dali masterpieces." He glanced around. "Here's the rub. There were footprints on the steps of that house. A right foot."

"Were they recent?" asked Snacks.

"There was a little mud patch at the bottom of the steps. Looks like only part of the right foot stepped in it and made a few tracks on the stairs. No older than yesterday is my guess."

"Boot prints, bare feet?" asked Spud.

"Yeah, Size 10 Wide. I can't tell, you idiot," sputtered Rankin. "Just a small odd-shaped print, damp sand. The prints faded out halfway across the room. Let's go back. You can bet Lockler will send us to take another look-see. Hell, he'll probably want to check it out himself. There were some water drums, but I didn't check them out. And also a makeup kit."

"You didn't bring it with you?"

"Do you need one?"

Just as cautiously and quietly as their approach, even more so, they moved back to the OP's base.

***

"So this is what it looked like—a long oval with a cleft?" Lockler handed the notepad page back to Rankin.

"Bestest as I can draw it. Do the natives have funny-looking feet?"

Lockler pronounced, "It's a Jap split-toed shoe. They carry them as spares. Seen them in China."

"So I'm guessing we have unwanted guests," muttered Henrik.

Lockler said, "Maybe a boat patrol just checking out islands, or a castaway sailor or they saw us land and are looking for us." They had found a few fuel-soaked life vests, Japanese and American, on the beaches. "No surprise with all those ships sunk out there."

"You're just full of cheer, ain't you?"

Rankin described the station to Lockler. "I didn't see a well or catchments, but the place is grown over. Saw a few 55-gallon barrels under the building. They had 'WATER' painted on the sides. But the lids were off and the water looked funky."

Corporal Moscato, "Sparks," walked up. "Did I overhear we had company?" He squatted.

"Maybe so, maybe not," Lockler said. "You make radio contact yet?"

"We hear each other, the base station and us, but it's breaking up on both ends. They already knew that atmospherics are temperamental out here. We managed a weather report. We'll try every hour."

"Radio gear's okay, right?"

"Right as rain. You want us to keep it packed up in case we need to hightail out of here?"

"Good idea. Everyone keep their gear packed," said Lockler.

"What about all our supplies down by the beach?" asked Rankin.

Lockler said, "Okay, here's what we're doing. If there are Japs, the first thing I'll wager is that they'll run a patrol or two patrols around the island following the beaches. If they find the trail crossing the island from the station, they'll check it too. I don't think they'll be blindly crashing around in the jungle looking for anyone, especially at night. Too dense and rough."

He went on, "Discoll, go to the landing beach and move as much of the supplies as you can away from the trail, especially the water and at least part of the rations and ammo. Rankin, take your squad and Griff with the BAR and McKern down the west trail and set up an ambush at the best site you can find this side of the branch trail to the Aussie station. Handyman, guard the radio team with your life. Doc, go with Discoll. Nesto, take your Reising and you're now in Rankin's 1st Squad.

"Stay as quiet as a mouse fart. I'll make the rounds to you fellas and keep you posted. I may change it depending on how things go, but I figure that we'll hunker down for the night. In the morning at first light meet at the OP and go kill the Japs."

Everyone scurried off. Henrik sat on the edge on the "radio hole," as the commo men called it. "Guess I'm not to ask questions about your radio there."

Sparks looked over at him. "Oh, I think it'll be okay. It's not as secret as some folks make out. Katcher, think we can trust Handyman here with the black arts of radiotelegraphy?"

"Sure, don't see why not. He needs to understand the first rule of radiotelegraphy theory and practice though."

"What's that?" asked Henrik.

"Can't spell it, can you? Here goes. For any given piece of equipment, like this"—he held up a small microphone—"to the radio-transceiver"—he patted the radio's sheet steel shipping box—"it's gotta be as heavy as the designers can possibly make it."

"I thought that applied to anything a gyrene carries," said Henrik.

"You might be right, brother," said Sparks.

"The TBX is a box of dials, bulbs, condensers, and vacuum tubes with enough wire to run a telephone line to the moon."

"Imagine that," Katcher chuckled, "having Moon men and Mars men on the same party line."

"The TBX is complex 'cause the Navy designed it and it's not very waterproof as ya'd expect. The three loads are the receiver-transmitter, hand-cranked generator"—he pointed to a boxy device on a tripod with a pair of crank handles—"and an accessory box with the antenna wires, microphone, headphones, telegraph key, and seven batteries. The generator had a clamp and chain arrangement to fasten it to a tree and the cranker is on his knees to crank it."

"Must weigh a lot."

"Close to a hundred pounds."

"You said a telegraph key?" asked Henrik.

"Yeah, we can do voice," said Sparks, "but it's only a few miles' reach. For Continuous Wave—that's sending Morse code to you mud daubers untutored in the black arts—we can transmit further. We have to rig a long wire antenna like this." Sparks pointed to a lengthy wire disappearing into the tree limbs. "They have to be set at a certain angle 'aimed' in the direction of the other radio and set for a certain length depending on the frequency. Takes us at least fifteen minutes to set up, transmit a message, and break it down. If you need a response, then you'll have to wait a while."

"Wait, like on hold?"

"They have to decrypt the message, get it to the right officer, he has to process it, write an encrypted answer, and transmit it back to us. Then we decrypt it. That all takes time."

"I guess you get your nickel's worth for the call," said Henrik. "I see why Signal School's so long."

"Three months and another three weeks just to learn basic Morse code," said Sparks. "We have to send and receive at least fifteen words-a-minute."

"I hear you fellas use Morse code to chat about the bar chippies flirting with you."

"That is true. Dit-dit-dit-dit—da-dit-dit-dit is HOW-BAKER for 'Hot Babe.' In regular transmissions we use abbreviations for certain words and phrases. 'NAN-ITEM-LOVE' means 'I have nothing to send you' in normal use, but with the chippies it's a warning you'll get nutin' outta that gal."

"And I thought you fellas were stonewall serious."

"All work and no play, dit—dah—dah-dit-dah-dit," said Katcher.

"What was that?"

"Etcetera."

Katcher became serious. "You ground-pounders' main job is to protect us radio jockeys…at all costs." He grinned.

"Yeah, I guess we didn't do that too well for Julien."

"Couldn't be helped. If you're up to have your dog tags separated, well, it just happens."

Henrik couldn't help but think that going with a 500-pound bomb instantly disintegrating him would be better than a bullet in the belly mangling your bowels full of shit, burning like hell or punching a hole through your lungs to drown in your own blood.

There I go again, happy thoughts as funny as Tom and Jerry *cartoons.*

After a couple of hours Lockler picked up Henrik and took him to Rankin's trail block.

"Look," said Lockler, "we're moving down the trail to the branch junction so we can cover the west beach trail and the trail coming up from the Aussie station."

He wanted it done while it was still light so that every man knew the squad's layout and what the terrain was like in front of them. The seven of them took turns eating and moving into position.

"Two-man positions. No lighting cigs. You'd lose your night vision and no matter how small the glow, it'll give you away."

"What's eating you? You don't have to tell us that, okay?" said Snacks.

"I got an uncomfortable feeling about this," Lockler said. "Handyman and Nesto, left flank covering the branch trail. Griff and McKern, get in position across the junction where you can cover both the station branch and the main west trail as best you can. Priority to the main trail. I'll be on the other side of the trail with Snacks and Spud."

"Ahhh, you want me beside you, boss. I'm touched," said Spud.

"So I can keep my eye on you."

***

It was still light and they dug shallow prone slit trenches, what they called a fighting hole…or a grave. Fortunately, they dug in sand or it would have been difficult, even with the T-handle e-tool with a solid fixed blade. Once dark descended there was complete silence.

Nesto broke the quiet. "Where're you from Handyman, and how'd you get the Handyman handle?"

"Missouri, near St. Louis. My family name's Hahnemann."

"Lots of Kraut names in Texas. I've never been to Missouri. Never been out of Texas before the Corps. Been to Mexico a lot."

"What part of Texas? It's a big place."

"Harlingen, near the south tip of Texas, close to Brownsville."

"You speak Spanish?"

"You speak Missouri?"

"Not a word, except maybe 'Jeet'," said Henrik.

"Jeet?"

"It means 'did you eat?' mixing it into one word as in, 'Jeet this morning?'"

"*Sí, hablo español.*"

"Never heard Spanish before we went through Texas." Something popped into Henrik's mind. "Say, what's *mestizos* and *cholos* mean?"

"Where'd you hear *mestizo*? Means mixed breed. *Cholos* is a less kind word. What's that about?"

"Just something I heard on a railroad platform in West Texas." *They call people mixed breeds, like cattle?*

"Ahhh, West Texicans, they're different from us Rio Grande Valley Texicans."

"Why'd you join up, Nesto, being way down there in Texas?"

"You first," said Nesto.

"Simple, to get even with the Japs for Pearl Harbor. You?"

"Same here."

"I expected a different reason."

"I'm an American too," he said a little defensively. "And a *Tejano*," he quickly added.

"Sorry, I didn't mean—"

"I knew some Japanese dudes," Nesto said.

"You did, how so?"

"They lived in Mexico, immigrants. They said they're better treated in Mexico than the U.S., or even Jap-Land. They did fancy woodwork and there's another family with a beer brewery, good suds too."

"That's all a surprise to me."

"President Roosevelt asked the Mexican president to make the several thousand Japanese immigrants move 100 miles from the Mexico–U.S. border and 200 miles from the seacoasts."

"I learn something new every day."

***

They went quiet, pulling one-off and one-on peering at the unfathomable darkness and listening for movement through the trees and brush. There was barely a breeze. Any odd sounds caused a reaction. It was usually land crabs, rats too. "We can eat those crabs," Nesto pointed out. "Boil them in a No. 10 can."

Occasional rain showers made it worse, rattling on the leaves and dripping after it passed. They couldn't wear ponchos, as rain made a distinct patter on the rubberized material. At least the showers were brief and there were fewer ants. It didn't slow the mosquitos one bit. Sometime in the early morning hours, Henrik relieved Nesto. In moments, Nesto was breathing in soft gasps.

Henrik thought about how people's lives were turned upside down. A world war. All those people in Europe and Asia and just about everywhere else, even Aussies living out here and Japs in Mexico.

A thin rain band swept through the trees with a loud patter and it didn't sound right. He nudged Nesto.

"¿Qué?"

"Quiet," he whispered as softly as he could.

Nesto eased around into a sitting position. Henrik heard him fumble with the Reising's selector switch as its position couldn't be sensed by feel.

A rustle in the brush didn't sound like wind or rain, rats or crabs. There was a funny word shouted, something like "*utay!*"

A crackling bursting hell ripped loose.

Chapter Twenty-Four

For Lieutenant Kiyoshi's exploratory patrol to the Australian settlement, he summoned Corporal Masaichi, Obata, Takeo, Ikuo, and Saburo, his orderly. The platoon had discovered that Saburo accompanied the lieutenant wherever he went, with the exception of the latrine. Obata reasoned that he would probably follow him there if the lieutenant let him. Those left behind under Sergeant Toshio continued to move and hide supplies while the radio crew and the instrument man worked on the plotting station. The black-painted round-nosed shovels had detachable blades with a bracket into which the green wooden handle was inserted and bound by a wrapped cord.

The radio team made contact with a station on Shortland Island and another on New Georgia. They would relay traffic from Kombuana. They continued their efforts to contact the intended base station on Bougainville.

The lieutenant assembled his patrol, checking each man's equipment. He even had them jump up and down to see if they rattled or anything fell off. The patrol moved cautiously, making slower time to the settlement than before. The officer knew best, thought Obata. He assumed the lieutenant's much more advanced military training allowed him to anticipate what the Americans were up to.

The patrol started off confident, with the surf covering the sound of their footsteps. They all wore tabis. Their pace slowed as they got closer to the settlement. Even though the first patrol had sighted no enemy, they were cautious. The lieutenant and Takeo crept back to where the earlier patrol had first observed the settlement. The two men moved around to the building with the suspected waterwell. They crawled to it, confirming the pump was not connected and probably defective. They found no replacement pump. It was decided that when the Australians evacuated, they had been awaiting a new pump. After inspecting the six water drums under the building, the lieutenant declared, "The water is stagnant, overgrown with algae, and full of mosquito larvae."

They went to the front steps of the building, the lieutenant gripping his Nambu pistol. "What is this?" he asked, pointing at the faint partial tabi print on the wooden steps.

Takeo snapped to attention, rifle at his side, forgetting the need for silence. "I must have stepped in the mud without realizing it, Honorable Lieutenant."

The pistol slammed into the side of his face. Staggering, Takeo instinctively went back to attention, obviously in numbing pain. Blood trickled from his split lip.

"I will deal with you later," the lieutenant said, disregarding the need for silence. Returning to the waiting patrol, he had each man take a coconut from the sorting tables. "I will send men back later for more coconuts and salvage whatever we can use."

They continued to follow the edge of the settlement's clearing inland until they discovered the discreet path leading north. Takeo, in the lead, redeemed himself when he motioned all to halt. He was crouched over the path, pointing to a footprint—obviously a large man's boot print and much different than a hobnailed and cleated Japanese boot sole. American boots did not have hobnails or cleats. Australian boots had rows of small hobnails and horseshoe-shaped heel cleats.

"Americans have been here," said the lieutenant with an expression of incredulity.

Everyone dropped instantly, deploying in a ragged line facing north. The lieutenant went to the front, whispering to each man, "Absolute silence."

After listening for some time and scanning the trees ahead with binoculars, he signaled to advance. They crept forward, guiding on the path angling gradually uphill with the flanking jungle growing denser.

The path apparently ran into the north beach path. They could barely hear the surf from that side. The faint, overlapping boot prints could not tell them how many Americans had passed. In the lead was the lieutenant, followed by Saburo. The corporal brought up the rear. The lieutenant moved ever so slowly, causing Obata to wonder what lay ahead of them. If the Americans were still here, they might be waiting in ambush like crocodiles lurking in swamp-muck to snag rats, as they had been told on their New Britain lowland marches. Obata calmed down as he recalled that crocodiles hid in weeds along swamps or rivers. They would not be found on even low ridges away from the waters they hid in. Then he remembered it was not crocodiles they were concerned about.

Just as he cleared the distracting thoughts from his mind, guttural voices ahead whispered. The patrol stopped, paralyzed, not moving a muscle. After listening for some seconds, more muffled words were heard. Without having ever really heard American words, other than a little Pidgin-English in Rabaul,

Obata thought they must be Americans. They were separated by forty or fifty meters. The voices seemed to be receding, and then silence.

Did they leave? The lieutenant did not move, apparently listening. Minutes passed. Obata stifled a need to clear his throat. He swallowed instead, quietly.

Finally they began to move, with word passed to discard the coconuts. It must have occurred to the lieutenant they could not be cracked open quietly. In extreme quiet the lieutenant positioned the patrol forty meters west of the path junction. This covered the path in the direction the Americans had gone eastward plus covered the junction of the settlement path. He sent Obata and Takeo further down the path overlooking the settlement to cover that approach. Behind them was the north path leading west to their plotting station.

Much to their surprise they heard a quite shout and a short laugh. The lieutenant beckoned Obata and they crept forward under the low trees edging the beach to their left. They only approached close enough to confirm the Americans were digging in to cover the path. They could hear shovels scooping sand.

Apparently the Americans were dug in some sixty meters east of the junction of the north beach and settlement path. They probably were digging in facing both directions. Saburo was sent as a runner back to the plotting station to send five men to reinforce their position and to be especially quiet. This included the machine gun crew, rifleman Seiichi, and one of the grenade discharger crewmen, Akiyoshi. The lieutenant ascertained the Americans were only a small patrol scouting the island. He strongly felt the Americans would not move in the dark if they stayed on the island. He had been taught that Americans and British did not like to attack at night. They might attack at dawn, though, and he wanted to be ready if the Americans discovered they were there. Expecting to catch the Americans preparing to leave after dawn, he determined that he would attack them while they were still asleep and not expecting a Japanese pre-dawn attack. He pronounced that the Americans were lazy and lax about security, citing they had given themselves away with noise even if mostly silent. The Pearl Harbor attack had proved that along with other surprise attacks inflicted on the Americans and British during the Southern Operation. He ordered his men to cease digging and not to eat. They had full water bottles. Americans and British were trained to fight Germans in Europe. The lieutenant had read the translated German articles in the *Kaikosha Kiji—Officer's Association Journal*. The Imperial Army adapted German tactics, but they did not copy them verbatim. They were modified to the Japanese way.

They now had eleven men at the blockade, well hidden in case an American patrol ventured down the path during the night to protect their position.

The lieutenant told each soldier his plan. They would move up the path toward Americans at 04:00. He would personally position each man about forty meters from the Americans. If the Americans commenced to move out, regardless of direction, they would immediately open fire and charge into the enemy. He warned them not to use grenades among the trees. If the Americans had not yet started to move by the time they were ready to attack, the lieutenant would give the order to advance quietly. They were not to open fire until the Americans detected them and fired or shouted warnings. The machine gun would sweep the area where he suspected the Americans were concentrated. They would empty its 30-round magazine in one continuous burst and reload and again sweep the area.

What came next was a surprise to the men. The lieutenant very matter of factly announced that the Americans tortured prisoners with extreme cruelty. If captured, the Americans would cut off their ears, nose, and penis, and even blind them. It was said that if America was victorious in this war, they would send the mutilated soldiers back to Japan and to their families. They were reminded that they must do their duty and never dishonor their families, the Empire, or the Emperor. They were never to surrender.

Obata and Takeo were positioned near the path above the settlement in case other Americans patrolled up the path from the settlement. Being on slightly higher ground, even in the darkness, Obata could cover much of the settlement's grounds when the Moon peeked out.

It occurred to him that he could die on this small island. While every soldier's death proclaimed the glory of the Empire and Emperor, would his death in this dreary place mean anything? His parents, sister, and relatives would probably never know where he died, much less for what or how. His sacrifice would be for the Emperor of course—that is what they would be told. He thought of the hair and nail clippings he had left his family, knowing they would never receive his ashes in a little white-shrouded box as was customary. What he really died for was to keep a few of the enemy from walking up a path on a little island the enemy had not even bothered to defend when the Imperial Army and Navy came to take it for themselves the past May. He shook himself mentally. No, there were other things he should ponder, not his insignificant sacrifice to the Empire.

All he should ponder was doing things one special way—the Japanese way—the form and order of a process that cannot be changed or controlled, be it wrapping a gift or throwing a grenade, turning the earth on a farm, managing a factory, or navigating a fishing boat. There was naturally only one right way—the Japanese way. Perhaps the lieutenant pistol-striking Takeo on the face seemed overly severe, but he had disobeyed an officer's order, the same authority as if it was issued by the Emperor. It was not just an act of poorly judged disobedience or an awkward mistake. Obara's subconscious assumption was that the lieutenant possessed the authority to make such judgments. Takeo could have jeopardized their mission. An officer, with his superior education, family honor and traditions, military training, and authority granted by the Emperor, had access to what must be the one correct course of action. Therefore, it was the correct way, the Japanese way to punish Takeo. He had to dismiss any individual preference or inclination.

* * *

Nothing occurred during the night other than their battle to stay awake, preserve complete silence, ignore the drizzle, and quietly swat at mosquitos. The rain failed to hamper the mosquitos and ants. *Ants must sleep sometime!* Obata thought. They peered into the darkness for the extraordinarily camouflaged approaching enemy. Rare cloud breaks dimly illuminated patches of ground. For those brief displays, every bush looked like a creeping enemy. Muffled by the surf, Takeo periodically whispered his essential needs of the moment.

"I would like a cigarette.

"I would like a bottle of beer. No *sake*, instead.

"I would like a dose of *kampo* herbal powder for my head-bashing. It hurts.

"I would like a whole can of tuna fish.

"I would like that whore in Rabaul."

"Which one?" asked Obata."

"The eternally drunk one wearing the oversized British sailor's white jumper and shorts and always shouting, '*Buritania rue waves, boke.*'"

"I remember her," replied Obata. "She was very loud."

"Is there not something you wish for, Obata?"

"I would like to know what the Americans are doing, or better, when they are leaving."

"You are boring, Obata. I should have brought my blanket."

The day's fatiguing heat made any drop in night temperature feel chilly. They had food and Obata understood the lieutenant's desire to ration it, but they needed to eat. Their supper had been appreciated but proved to be inadequate for the long night. As with so many training exercises, it seemed nothing would happen. The main battle was simply to stay awake.

* * *

A pebble skipped through the weeds. Obata startled to attention and looked behind him. Another pebble. Someone hissed. It was still dark.

"*Tareka*"—Who are you? Obata asked, the standard challenge.

"*Hoshi*"—Star. *It is Ikuo*, thought Obata.

"*Tsuki*"—Moon, Obata replied.

Ikuo answered, "The lieutenant wants you to come up here. I think he is going to attack the Americans. Quickly, quietly."

Takeo had awakened and they followed Ikuo up the path, with Takeo rubbing his eyes. They moved up and were told to wait.

Takeo whispered, "I was having a dream about that noisy sailor girl. She had such big—"

"Think of something else and be quiet," whispered Obata.

"Hara Setsuko."

"Who?"

"I am thinking of something else like you ordered, comrade. She starred in *Priest of Darkness* and *The Daughter of the Samurai*."

"Ahhh, yes," agreed Obata. She is one of innocence and a humble beauty."

"Innocent? Did you sleep through those movies? When she peeled an apple with a dainty *kiridashi* knife, it was almost too—"

"Here," said Sergeant Toshio, surprising them with his unheard approach. "The Americans are stirring. The lieutenant says we outnumber them and we will soon attack. They are maybe sixty meters up the path heading east. No bayonets. They might make noise striking limbs." Toshio departed. "Silence." They heard not a sound other than the wet breeze through the trees.

Ikuo returned. Taking Obata by the hand, he led him up the path, with Takeo gripping his water bottle shoulder strap. It was that dark. Obata sensed there were others around him, on the path and in the brush. He had no idea of how they were deployed, how many were on either side, in front, or behind him. It was not a good time to ask.

He had not thought of it before, but now he wished he had a fixed bayonet. He knew it was more difficult to use among trees and in the dark. Two men bayonet fighting in total darkness stood little chance of success for either. All they achieved was to dance around and thrust, lunge, and slash blindly at one's opponent who was just as hampered as himself. To actually stab an enemy was luck. Maybe it was good to avoid using a bayonet in the dark after all. Grenades—he hoped no one started throwing grenades. It was impossible to determine the target's range. The grenade might bounce off a tree or hit a limb and come back at you.

How long will we have to wait? What if they have machine guns?

"*Ute*"—Fire!

Chapter Twenty-Five

A ripple of cracks exploded before Henrik and Nesto finished digging their position on the station trail. The Springfield muzzle blasts were bright flashes and the Jap rifles' faint flickers. Bullets cracked overhead and smacked into trees. Griff on the BAR was probably cracking off semi-auto shots to hide his position. He'd go to full-auto if the Japs rushed. Nesto simply swept the Reising gun right to left, emptying the magazine, and made a clatter of reloading. Snacks' Tommy gun rattled, firing a bit faster than the Reising. Henrik emptied his magazine, stripped in another five rounds and shot them off, reminding him to keep the fire low to the ground. *They're hugging the ground as hard as I am.*

The Jap rifles continued banging, with pauses of just seconds as individuals reloaded. Jap tracers flashed overhead. He heard garbled Jap shouts, bodies crashing through brush, then more chattering full-auto bursts as Griff emptied a BAR magazine. The shots tapered off, more shouts, running feet. *Theirs, ours?* Nesto hammered through another magazine. "Eat this *pendejos!*"

Silence fell in front of them. Birds made protesting noises. The Japs had bugged out...maybe. He hadn't expected that, the Japs pulling back. They hadn't charged them with bayonets and screams. Maybe they were waiting for them to come after them and charge into an ambush. Maybe a loner Jap had been left behind like a tripwire. Or were they coming again? You just never knew. They waited, quiet as they could, with panting breaths.

A sudden volley of Jap rifle shots cracked through the treetops.

Everyone dropped or crouched and held fire.

"Maybe it's a precautionary barrage to discourage pursuers," said Discoll.

Henrik expected Discoll to order a withdrawal. He didn't. It was normal to reposition to throw off the enemy if they came again.

"Anyone hit?" Driscoll loud-whispered. Silence. "Sound off your handles, left to right." All seven answered. It turned out the Greek and McKern had been hit by wood splinters or gravel. Mother O'Leary had lost his helmet running into a face-high limb. He couldn't find it in the dark brush down the trail.

"They'll dock your pay for sure, brother."

"Six bucks for the steel pot. About the same for boondockers."

"Wow, that was excitin'," someone said. "Can we do it again?"

"Just like you green jarheads—too young, too fearless, too patriotic, and too stupid," grumbled Lockler.

The surf rolled and the breeze whispered. For a few moments it seemed as if nothing of consequence had happened there.

With all that firing, Henrik was surprised they'd had only two men barely wounded. They were lucky or they had hugged the ground hard in graves they'd scraped. But that couldn't be it. Everyone was firing and that meant they'd had to expose themselves to some extent.

"Damn, we good," someone muttered. "They can't kill marines."

"Don't bet on it," came back Lockler. "Where's the corpsman?"

"Right here, boss."

"Check those fellas. Keep the noise down. Pull back fifty yards. Same deal; set up a firing line like before. If they come at us I want them charging into another ambush."

Pulling back quickly, they were completely quiet as they took up positions. Discoll positioned each man, making sure they covered the ground with interlocking fire. Lockler made sure both pairs of men on the line's flanks covered their side of the position. After half an hour Discoll said, "I don't think they're coming. If they're just scouting the island they may have left or they're waiting to ambush us, them being sneaky like."

"All right," said Lockler, "here's what we'll do." He'd cleared a patch of sand and it was light enough to stick-draw the island's outline.

"If they're waiting to jump us, they're probably further down the north beach trail like when we pulled back. They may have the trail to the station covered or maybe that's where they are and dug in. What we'll do is head down the north trail to the west. We'll leave four men at our OP. We'll send two men, Handyman and Nesto, down the station trail and check it out just to be safe. We'll scout the trail all the way around the island's west end and swing back to the Aussie station. We'll pick you two up there," he said, pointing at Henrik and Nesto. "Stay hidden once you get there and don't shoot us. If we're not back before dark, you two head back to the OP taking the station trail then the east trail along the north beach. That shouldn't happen. We've plenty of daylight to head around the west end and reach the station. If we get in a shootout, you two stay put at the station to cover us if we come a runnin'." He was trying to make light of it.

"If the Japs are still on the island we ought to catch up and we'll deal with them. Everyone got that?"

He was answered with growls of "They're dead," "Let's go get 'em," "Kill 'em Nips."

"Okay, get ready. Make sure you don't leave anything behind…like helmets." He scuffed over the sand sketch map.

"Sorry, Sarge," mumbled Mother O'Leary.

Before setting out, Lockler said, "Look boys. Let's be smart about this. We're on a little island with a bunch of Japs, we don't know how many, and we don't know when or even if we're getting picked up from this vacation resort. We need to take whatever we can use from the Japs. When one of you nail a Nip, at least take his rifle so they can't use it. If you got to ditch it, pull the bolt out just like on ours and chuck it into the brush. If you can, take his web gear too. It's got three ammo pouches, a canteen, and a bayonet. If he's got one of those German-looking mess pots, take it. Sometimes they carry chow in it."

"I don't wanna eat any of that Jap rice," said Patches.

"You will when you get hungry and you'll eat that canned crab too."

Henrik had never seen a real crab. He'd wait until he was hungry enough.

Look inside a dead Jap's left jacket pocket." He held up two paper-wrapped packets. "These are the Jap's field dressings. If you have time fetch them and give them to Doc, he might need them."

"Take their grenades too. We can really use them. Just no cooking them off. Don't trust their fuses. Supposed to be four-point-five-second delay. Pull the pin, smack the cap on a tree, rifle butt, your helmet, or your buddy's hard head, and throw it as quick as you can."

"Discoll, take two men and check out where we had that fight. See if they left any dead. See if they're Jap army or those special landing force guys."

Discoll took Henrik and Mother O'Leary. "See if you can find your pot, lug-head."

***

They crept quietly down the trail. The rising sun was dimming the jungle's shadows. Only the surf and occasional birds were heard.

They edged down the trail. "Holy crap," said Mother.

They went to prone. Henrik high-crawled through the brush and found the three scattered bodies. *Okay, I didn't expect that.*

After a quick search they rejoined the platoon.

Discoll reported to Lockler. "We found three dead Japs, no gear or weapons, they're army, only had that star on their helmets. No anchor badge. Nothing special about them that I could see. They were wearing those split-toe shoes." He took a swig from his canteen. "Two were shot. The other took a grenade blast full on, pretty messed up."

"That's not all," said Henrik with a head shake.

"What else, Handyman?"

"Well, the grenade gutted one, but they cut his head off. Why would they do that?"

"Who knows with them? I guess they wouldn't carry away someone that badly wounded."

"I didn't find my pot," reported O'Leary.

"One of them Nips heisted your pot for a keepsake," said Discoll with a laugh.

"Is that aiding and abetting the enemy?" said McKern.

"Nope, just stupid," replied Lockler.

"Why didn't you pick up one of those Jap piss pots?" suggested Nesto.

"I don't want any Jap cooties."

Henrik could tell some men were discouraged having inflicted so few casualties on the enemy.

Back at the trail block they formed up quietly, the sun peeking just over the trees. Lockler and Driscoll had a quick talk about leaving booby-trapped grenades, but decided they were too dangerous as they no doubt would travel this trail again.

The section filed down the trail heading for the island's west end. It would take the patrol at least four times as long to reach the station. Henrik wanted to get there quickly to make sure the area was clear of Japs.

Lockler hadn't mentioned which way the patrol would go once they arrived at the station. They could go back to the north trail and head east to the OP trail all the way around the east end to the OP. That was more likely, as they had not yet scouted the south trail.

"*Amigo*, I don't much like this."

"What's wrong?"

"It's just the two of us." Nesto was quiet for a spell. "I'd like it better if we were three."

"Oh, that would really stack the odds in our favor," responded Henrik.

"It would if we had Snacks and his Tommy gun."

"Maybe so. Hey! Come to think of it, why am I on point with a five-shot rifle? You take point with your bullet-spraying Reising gun."

"Reising gun? Hell it's a 'rusting gun.' Don't have enough oil to keep it from rusting. The Corps must have gone with the lowest bidder. Sand doesn't do it any good either. Damn brass thinks there's no sand on the beaches we run across."

"Still sprays bullets, right?"

"Okay, I'll take point," he said resignedly.

"Much thanks. I'll cover you with my long-range precision marksmanship."

"You're ten feet behind me."

"I wonder what the rest of the section at the OP's thinking?"

Henrik hadn't thought about that. The OP was not so far away on the island's northeast shore that they'd not hear the pre-dawn firefight.

"Yea, I can guess. Must have a hell of a pucker factor. I hope they have all the ammo, rats, and water hidden good."

As they worked their way down the trail, they were silent as they approached the station. Moving warily and slowly, they worked their way through the buildings and coconut-sorting tables. They checked each building's insides, looking for anything of use to themselves or that showed that Nips had been there. They didn't find anything of use, not even hand tools. Lockler had told them to hide any pioneer tools for later use.

"What's pioneer tools?" Patches had asked.

"Shovels, pick-mattocks, axes, and so forth in case we've got to dig in good."

They tried to crack open a coconut. They managed to shuck the husks but were befuddled as to how to crack the shell quietly.

"Damn," said Nesto, "how do those coconut-heads get these damn things open?"

"Don't know. I'll ask the next native who comes along."

"We brought the kitchen sink and no one thought to bring a machete."

"Wiseass."

A crackling sound from the northwest startled them to attention. The sound rose and fell, hesitated, and rose again, accompanied by muffled thumps.

"Grenades." The American grenades were obviously louder than the Japs'. These sounded like Jap grenades.

"I wonder who hit who?"

"No telling." It gave Henrik a helpless feeling.

"Should we go?" asked Nesto.

"No. No, I don't think so. They're going to be coming this way, and Lockler wants us here to cover them." Henrik thought a moment longer. "Plus, we don't need to walk straight into our folks or the Nips." He paused. "If ours make it."

"If they make it. Maybe it was an ambush and they're pinned. Or they're all dead."

"Then there's not much we can do, is there?" said Henrik.

"I guess not. Not just two of us, even if we clout them with hit-and-runs, sniping, maybe grenade booby-traps."

The firing tapered off, but in less than a minute it peaked, slowed, and rose again. Very abruptly it ceased. Birds circled the end of the island above the trees.

Henrik had a hollow feeling. He glanced hastily at Nesto. Unspoken, they both felt the same thing—a sense of helplessness. Guilt too.

Henrik grabbed his mind and shook it. *This isn't the time for weakness. We're Marines. We don't sit and dilly-dally. We take action.* That somehow sounded lame. But then Lockler had ordered them to stay at the settlement to back them if there was trouble.

"We'll hang here like Lockler wants us to, for, let's say for forty-five minutes," said Henrik. "Then we'll head down the trail running it to the west end." He thought for a few moments. "No, we'll go down the trail for a couple of hundred yards, and if we don't see anything we'll turn right and head across the narrow part to the north side trail and see what we can see."

"You mean cut straight through the jungle to the other side?" asked Nesto.

"Yeah," pondered Henrik. "That way we won't run straight into a crowd of Nips coming down the trail or our own people so we don't get shot up by them. If I'm going to get shot down I don't want my own people doing it." *What made me think that?*

"Does it really make much difference?"

"No, I guess not. Except maybe for my folks. It might make a difference to them."

"You're not afraid to go through that jungle? It's not that far and I've hunted deer in thicker Missouri woods."

A single shot popped in the distance. They both listened. Nothing more. "Someone's been put down," whispered Nesto.

They found a position near the beach giving a good field of vision on the beach trail and the trail down through the station. They were four or five yards apart on low mounds high enough to see over the brush within the station grounds. Weeds and small bushes screened them.

Henrik practiced sighting on possible spots Nips might use for cover if they showed up. Most shots were only at 100 to 150 yards. Nesto's Reising gun might reach that far firing short bursts, but it wasn't much good at over 100 yards. That wasn't much firepower against even a Nip squad. Henrik figured their best bet would be to fire them up by surprise, make them take cover, take off up the south beach trail, and make it around the island's east end to their OP.

Nesto again oiled the Reising and its magazines. "The only thing this piece of crap has on the Thompson is that it's about four pounds lighter."

The forty-five-minute self-imposed wait was agony. At forty-four minutes, Henrik said, "Let's go."

Chapter Twenty-Six

A ragged barrage of shots crackled, blinding flashes illuminating the darkness. Obata couldn't remember where the path was. He heard bolts working, and another rippling volley followed. Loud in the trees, but it was not a crippling barrage as he had envisioned. Bullets cracked and snapped. He felt twigs snapping, leaves falling. The Americans instantly returned fire, their dreaded machine guns clattering insanely. More muzzle flashes. Their own machine gun opened fire, spewing pale blue and pink tracers down the north path. The Nambu gun was firing twice as fast as the American guns, but there were more American machine guns. That, and the Nambu had a higher magazine capacity. Tracers ricocheted off trees. A tiny fire started but flickered out in the dampness. The rates of fire rose and fell as men reloaded, moved. Unseen voices shouted commands. It appeared the Americans were not firing tracers.

A grenade crashed, then another. Branches crashed around him. Obata reasoned that they must be American; they were much louder than their own. Ignition sparks; quick, startling explosive flashes, the zing of fragments. More shouts. Running feet, a stumbling fall. The firing tapered off. Shouts dwindled. Obata bumped into a tree—hard—and a limb smacked his face. A yellow flare rose into the sky and flickered out as he crouched trying not to look at it. Drifting shadows. He could hear men around him. Names were being called, followed by answering, "*Koko ni iru yo*"—Here I am.

There were low moans, an anguished cry. More groans. "Leave the dead," ordered the lieutenant. That was chilling. He had not thought about that—what to do with any dead. Who were the dead, who were wounded?

The path to the settlement was behind them. The Americans appeared to have fallen back to the east. *How many Americans can there be? A lot?*

"We will move down the path toward the plotting station." It was the sergeant.

Trees could be made out in the pre-dawn dimness. Men were moving through the trees.

A whispered "Withdraw down the settlement path," could be heard from Toshio.

Obata realized Takeo was still clutching his shoulder strap. He pulled Takeo's hand off. "Were you hit, Takeo?"

"I do not know, maybe my legs. It does not hurt much."

"Let down your pants."

"Maybe only some small grenade fragments, Obata."

"Hardly more than bug bites, Takeo. Pull your pants up."

Lieutenant Kiyoshi and Sergeant Toshio were giving orders and checking over men.

"Take the ammunition off the seriously wounded."

We have seriously wounded?

"Cover the path with the machine gun. How many dead and wounded are there?"

"We do not know yet," said Toshio.

The lieutenant ordered, "Corporal Masaichi and Obata, come with me to find the dead and recover their equipment. Look for American dead too and bring their weapons and equipment."

The sergeant was left with the rest of the patrol.

Obata hoped they were not walking into another fight. They moved slowly, approaching their own and the former American positions. There was a body, face down in the brush. It was Akiyoshi, the man from the grenade discharger crew; a couple of bullets had struck him in the back and exited his chest. "Coward," said the lieutenant with scorn. "He ran away."

Without warning, the corporal worked his rifle, quickly firing five rounds eastward up the path. No return fire. "I am letting the Americans know we are ready for them if they are planning a counterattack."

They found Ikuo, led to him by his muffled sobbing. Rolling him over, Obata and the lieutenant gagged. Ikuo's belly was torn open, his right forearm gone, mangled by a grenade. His left hand was clutching something bloody in his bowels. He knew not what gore the man held. Other wounds bloodied his uniform. His face was unmarked. The man gasped irregularly, drawing his legs up and groaning in agony. Then he would rock side-to-side, whimpering and dripping blood.

Masaichi returned. "There are no American dead unless they carried them away."

Obata could see the clouding anger in the lieutenant's face.

"There is no sense in us trying to carry him. He is barely alive." Looking grimly at the corporal, he ordered Masaichi, "Cut his throat." The corporal's expression was one of fearful revulsion. He involuntarily shook his head and backed away.

"I order you!"

Sergeant Toshio appeared from down the path.

"Why are you here?" the lieutenant demanded of the sergeant. He seemed muddled after the confused and less than victorious night fight, the loss of men, the stress of ordering a wounded soldier's death, and Toshio's unexpected appearance. Corporal Masaichi did not say anything.

The lieutenant shouted, "I again order you to execute that soldier, Honorable Corporal, immediately."

Toshio passed behind the lieutenant and swung a machete hatchet, lopping off the man's head. The body offered a final twitch and went limp. The head tumbled into the belly's gore.

The lieutenant was speechless but probably grateful that Toshio had dealt with it immediately, though he would never admit it. He still had to deal with Masaichi and his reluctance to follow an order.

"Honorable Lieutenant," said Sergeant Toshio, "I came up to ensure your security. We do not know where the Americans are or what they will do. We need to recover any equipment we have left."

"Thank you for your initiative and forethought." That was the only answer he could give with the loss of face the sergeant inflicted on him. Obata knew there would be retribution.

Takeo stood guard as they collected the dead's rifles, equipment, and identity tags. Obata felt fortunate that it was too dim within the trees to see their faces. What would he have done if that order had been given to him? He wanted to think that he would have been a dutiful soldier and immediately and diligently followed orders. But could he, even with the man unconscious and obviously doomed?

"We will bury the bodies later, after we have killed or driven off the Americans."

Back at the platoon, it was a confused sight. They had lost Rifleman Ikuo and Private Akiyoshi from the grenade discharger crew. Hajime, the instrument man, was nicked by a bullet across his back shoulder and what may have been a bullet fragment in his right thigh. The lieutenant chastised him for placing himself in danger. "It is essential to man the rangefinder and you are not to expose yourself again."

The corporal did what he could to clean and dress the wounds. He had a medical bag, but mostly all he could do was clean the wounds with water, painfully swab them with tincture of iodine, and wrap them with gauze. No one needed a tourniquet. The lieutenant believed a man was combat-capable so long as he did not need a tourniquet to staunch blood loss.

They moved back to a particularly dense stand of trees and brush. The machine gun covered the trail as did most of the other men. The lieutenant sent the signalman and the instrument man back to the plotting station. The discharger crew covered the trail behind them with their rifles as overhead vegetation prevented the high-angle launched grenades from being fired.

Takeo held up something. "Look at this. An American helmet I found beside the path. It is so big and heavy, heavier than ours."

It was passed around.

"Is there any blood on it?"

"No."

"Look, it has two parts, the steel shell and some kind of enameled inner-piece with the leather and web headband."

"Good workmanship," said Obata.

"They fear death," said the lieutenant, tossing it into the brush. "That is at least one casualty."

"How many machine guns were there?"

"Three, I think," said a machine gunner. Most had an opinion. "Three." "Two." "No, definitely three." "They were not trying to save ammunition."

"Three, there were three," finalized the lieutenant.

He paced about further down the path. Obata expected the officer to consult with the sergeant. He did not, other than, "Form up the platoon, Honorable Sergeant. We will move east to the plotting station. The enemy suffered few casualties. They may feel emboldened and follow the path to the plotting station. The radio crew and the instrument man will remain at the plotting station. We will ambush the Americans if they return and advance toward the plotting station, which we must protect."

He gave no orders regarding how they would prepare to meet the enemy.

"The sergeant ordered all to, "Replace your expended ammunition from the recovered belts and fill your water bottles from the dead's."

"Should we first bury our comrades, Honorable Lieutenant?" asked the corporal. "They will quickly decompose."

The lieutenant glared at him. "I ordered before that we would bury our men after we defeated the Americans. We have more urgent concerns than field sanitation. Battlefields stink by nature."

Takeo shoved himself off the sandstone pile and yanked his arm back, then peered at his hand.

"What is wrong?" asked Obata.

"This." He pointed to a black smear on a rock with a crushed tangle of legs and hairy fibers and then raised his hand. "This big spider bit me." There was a red spot as big as a ten *sen* coin on his left palm.

"Does it hurt much?" asked the corporal."

"Just a little. It itches."

"Show it to the sergeant, Takeo. Do not scratch it."

"How big?" asked the sergeant.

"Almost as big as my hand, eight centimeters across."

"There is nothing we can do until we wipe out the Americans." The sergeant nodded quickly at the lieutenant. "The corporal will clean it with alcohol and dab on tincture of iodine; maybe it will help."

The platoon formed up and moved out quietly, following the east path to the plotting station. The lieutenant shared nothing further about his plan. It was light enough now that they could see the deeper vegetation clearly, though in morning shadows.

It occurred to Obata that possibly the lieutenant had no plan without the location of the Americans being known. He dismissed his doubt; officers always had a plan, even for going to the latrine.

They moved down the path quickly in a shuffle march, covering ground with minimal noise. They halted with men aiming their rifles up and down the path and into the jungle on both flanks.

Obata took the lead. He closely looked over the retreating American boot tracks. They overstepped each other in opposite directions, making it impossible to determine how many there were. He stopped and listened frequently, in all likelihood irritating the impatient lieutenant. Faint breathing. Obata heard whispered words between the lieutenant and the sergeant. The sergeant left. Corporal Masaichi said the sergeant was going to the plotting station just a short distance away. They could hear the nearby surf, the island's north shore, near to where they had landed.

The lieutenant moved about the tense, crouching men. The machine gun crew had brought up the rear to cover their...withdrawal. The grenade discharger crew followed. No, the lieutenant would not consider a retreat or even a withdrawal. He took the machine gun crew down the path and positioned it in a clump of elephant ears on the path's south side, aiming it up the path. The grenade discharger crew were led further down the path and positioned out of sight. Obata assumed it was positioned in a scarce clear patch and prepared to fire grenades back up the trail. Obata could see that an ambush area was being set up. The rifles in the plotting station must be part of the plan covering the north flank and the shore.

A pair of men was positioned perpendicular to the path opposite the machine gun and firing parallel with the path. The rest of the men were positioned parallel with the path along its south side. There were not many available: Sergeant Toshio, Corporal Masaichi; Saburo the orderly; Shoichi the machine gun ammunition bearer; Rifleman Seiichi, and Takeo. Most were hidden ten to fifteen meters from the path. At first Obata thought they were too close to the path and that a walking enemy had only to look to the left and he would see them lying among the varied vegetation. However, the riflemen could see well enough from their prone positions under the plants while a walking enemy could only see the tops of the brush. A couple of men had small hand sickles like those used for rice harvesting. They cut some of the leaves under the larger plants. Obata and his comrades could make out the movement of their enemies on the path and take aim under the vegetation.

The sergeant led Obata back to the machine gun. On the way he told each man to ensure his rifle was fully loaded, a sixth round chambered, to remove their bayonet, take a drink, and make absolutely no noise or speak, or swat bugs. They were not to fire until the machine gun fired. They were to fire three clips as fast as they could even if they could not at that moment see the soon-to-be-vanquished enemy. "Aim low. Fix bayonets after you fired three clips, and charge into the dying enemy and bayonet them. Do not throw grenades." Slapping each man on the shoulder, he said, "We will obliterate the enemy and rally on the path."

The lieutenant, with Saburo following, pointed out their position, just two meters apart across from the machine gun. The lieutenant wanted to be assured that Obata could see up the trail, which sloped slightly uphill. The lieutenant had picked one of the few almost straight stretches, giving a good line of fire. "Do not worry about the enemy in the forefront. Fire further up the path and uphill even if so slight. I will accept only the complete annihilation of the enemy. If any escape, we will form into threes and track them down. Then we can complete our mission."

The sun beat down, warming the still air until it became stifling. The leafy plants over them did little to shield them from the heat. Mosquitos and gnats swarmed, being disturbed from their under-leaf hiding places. Their buzzing grew annoying. The birds quieted down, but the air grew thicker. *How long?* Obata's head grew heavier and he fought the urge to lay it in his arms. He forced himself to remain alert and steadfast. *The Americans will appear any minute.*

They didn't.

Trickles of sweat, buzzing insects, ants invading his body, thirst, and hunger all combined to tread on his morale and perseverance.

Did the lieutenant position us right? We did this in haste and the disturbed vegetation must look conspicuous. There had been too much movement along the path's margins. Occasionally, someone moved or cleared his throat. At one point someone dropped a rifle clip, a small, insignificant sound, but it shot a chill up his spine.

It seemed like day amplified noises, unlike night, which easily hid sounds. The night closed in on you. Daylight misled one. He peered up the path yet again. *When?* He would look up the trail where the dead air stilled the leaves. Any minute, any second, and any moment an American would appear. He knew it would be unnerving, to see the man glide quietly and ghostlike out of the Earth, already conscious and alert. He had already been tense and on guard after the early morning's brief fight. The enemy was bound to see one of our men attempting to hide in the leaves. All he had to do was make the slightest movement, and an elephant's ear would tremble. And then they would have to wait in agony under the muzzles of their rifles. They would have to wait as a file of Americans some meters apart agonizingly picked their way down the path until the lead enemy solider walked into the machine gun's muzzle.

It was firmly in his mind now—the lieutenant had chosen poorly. He could not envision the Americans, alert and tense, stumbling into this too quickly and poorly set ambush. They would be so close to the Americans, carefully stepping silently like tiger hunters. It would take but the slightest noise by one man just meters away for the Americans to open fire with all their machine guns and those big grenades. He resisted the urge to scratch at an ant bite; sweat trickled down his forehead, down his sides, his legs. His helmet baked his brains. He pictured a headless Ikuo blown open and his entrails spilled. He knew what was going to happen. Something, any moment now, was going to alert the Americans even before they entered the ambush site. The Americans would come down the path as they had done themselves and see the Japanese hobnailed boot prints. Something would alert them—a noise, he thought, some innocuous sound that would give them away. Their only hope was for the lieutenant to come to the realization that this was a trap, a trap for them, not the Americans.

A sound! He immediately recognized it as a parrot—no, several parrots—hopping from limb to limb. If only they would commence to squabble and frighten other birds. A rising cloud of birds might cause the Americans to falter, if they were still here. Sweat dripped off his nose. He realized he might have to shave his upper lip for the third time in his life…if they found deliverance from this island. Maybe they would become stranded here. He would have to remember what he could from *Robinson Crusoe*. He would give anything to experience a comfortable night's reading followed by a good sleep.

He needed to focus. He peered up the path and placed his rifle's crosshairs on the furthermost bit of the path's cleared route. An American's helmeted head and shoulders filled his telescope's ocular lens. His first thought. *Is that real? Is it really one of our men?*

He held a small weapon—some kind of machine gun? It was not a ruthless face, but alert, his eyes swinging with the short gun's muzzle; dirty and sweaty, like his own face perhaps. But young. Not what he expected. More men followed, just as slow and searching. He shifted to a far man up the path, keeping the crosshairs centered on the young face below the helmet's brim.

They drifted closer toward him. Some were looking at the ground. They no doubt saw the many tabi prints along this stretch of the path. They slowed to a crawl. Even the parrots slowed their hopping about and took interest in the humans below.

He had to make the slightest move to shift his telescope's image as the man moved closer.

He sensed all the ambushing men flanking the path just meters away, struggling to hold their fire until the enemy walked into their machine gun. He again shifted his aim to a young man, helmeted, holding a rifle at the ready. A memory returned, an instructor saying the Americans used a rifle called the Type 1903 and named after a town, Springfield, and not the inventor.

Obata carefully aimed to keep the telescope's crosshairs on the moving target just below the helmet's brim.

He waited, hoping none of their men would be detected at the final moment.

The Nambu gun ripped loose, hammering rounds down the path, lashing out tracers. Obata's rifle cracked as if remotely ordered to fire. The recoil lost his sight picture, something for which he was grateful—not having to see a face punctured and the exit spray of blood, brains, hair, skull fragments.

Men ran, shouted, stumbled, fired, reloaded. Obata fired as fast as possible. He did not know if he hit any other Americans. They had disappeared; fled from the path in seconds. Rifle shots continued, Japanese and American. More machine gun bursts rattled. Bullets cracked through branches. Birds protested and fled into the sky. Grenades burst, loud like American ones. Then from behind, a single pop. More followed amid the rifle cracks and the machine gun's long sweeping bursts. No attempt to conserve ammunition. *Fire until there is nothing, reload and keep firing.* More pops from behind, followed by muffled thumps further up the trail.

Obata operated instinctively, his training engrained in him. Hard-yank the bolt back to make certain the spent cartridge ejected. The bolt locked open when the last shot in the magazine was fired. Jam a five-round clip into the clip slot, thumb the cartridges into the magazine, slam the bolt forward, aim, fire, do it again.

There were no more clips on the rock next to him. He'd fired all sixteen rounds. What was he supposed to do? Bayonet, that was it; fix his bayonet, charge onto the path to skewer Americans, alive or even dead. He went to a crouch ready to lunge forward. Reluctance struck him. Shots were still cracking, twigs and leaves falling. He could be cut down in the continuing fire. It suddenly dwindled, stopped. He saw one of their own step out of the brush, and another. The lieutenant shouted, "*Totsugeki*"—Charge! There were grunting shouts. Bayonets jabbed and slashed. One man fumbled his blade, having forgotten to attach it before advancing on the path.

A few shots cracked. Someone moaned from up the trail and two men descended on a struggling shape, repeatedly jabbing it in spite of what sounded like pleads of mercy. It was not much of a bold charge.

The lieutenant appeared from near the machine gun. "Come with me to position the gun up the trail in case any Americans escaped." To the sergeant he ordered, "Assemble all the men and prepare to advance up the path when I order you to. Make certain all here are dead and throw the weapons into the brush." His orderly Saburo followed him of course. The lieutenant was excitedly speaking nineteen words to the dozen.

Obata followed the machine gun crew. They reported firing off four thirty-round magazines. They admitted having left an empty magazine behind. The lieutenant slapped the gunner, Superior Private Koji, and ordered him to send a man back to find it. The grenade discharger gunner, Superior Private Kazuo, accompanied them. He reported firing eight grenades further up the trail.

The American on the path before him was unquestionably dead. He lay face down, arms flung outward. Obata could see no wounds. His rifle lay beside him. Obata picked it up, slinging his own. Opening the bolt, the chambered round ejected. There were three rounds in the Type 1903's magazine. He had not fired a single shot before meeting death. Obata rapidly worked the action, ejecting the rounds, and flung the rifle into the brush.

More men emerged, gingerly poking the bodies before delivering death thrusts, whether they were needed or not. Some were more reluctant. There was little shouting as they thrust. The sergeant had to order some to throw the enemy's weapons away.

Obata, and obviously most others, experienced some degree of reluctance. "Finish the vanquished enemy!" ordered the sergeant. "You are soldiers!"

Some men found yellow-colored American grenades, twice as big as their own. Most kept them.

Obata took a kneeling position on the path opposite the machine gun. They found six more American bodies. Kazuo pointed out two obviously killed by grenades his crew had launched. The lieutenant was broadly smiling, a sight seldom seen.

The dead were pathetic—that was the only word Obata could use. Lifeless lumps sprawled about like discarded garbage, vulnerable, helpless, and if in such a state in life, embarrassed, humiliated. He understood for the first time why the dead from a street accident were so quickly hidden from view.

The lieutenant was rubbing his hands in glee. "Was anyone lost?" he disinterestedly asked the sergeant.

"One dead, Honorable Lieutenant, Corporal Masaichi."

The lieutenant shrugged.

The ambushers collected at the machine gun's position. The lieutenant, still verging on jovial, for once shared his plans.

"We will advance east on this path and go beyond the settlement path. We must determine if there are still any Americans here. If so, we will annihilate the survivors and continue our mission. If necessary, we will circumnavigate the entire island in search of them."

He sent the sergeant to the plotting station where the signalmen and the instrument man would remain. "Be especially cautious."

"Is anyone wounded?" asked the lieutenant.

Takeo reluctantly raised his hand. "The spider bite has become worse, Honorable Lieutenant." His left hand was inflamed and swollen, the palm tissue an angry red around the bite, which itself was blistered.

"You will remain with the plotting station." The sergeant cleaned the spider bite and rubbed in charcoal, a home remedy, along with ground turmeric spice which had accompanied the cooking supplies.

Obata felt saddened. The two men bowed.

"I hope you make a swift and speedy recovery, comrade."

"*Ko-un o inoru*"—Good luck! replied Takeo.

Obata would be the patrol's lead man along with Seiichi, the only other remaining rifleman. The machine gun crew followed, with the lieutenant behind it, and then the discharger crew. Sergeant Toshio brought up the rear. There were ten men in the patrol. They moved cautiously and as silently as possible.

"See you at *Yasukuni!*" Obata hoped he could avoid *Yasukuni Jinja*—the Peaceful Country Shrine honoring the Empire's war dead, dating back to 1869. He dreaded the idea of a black streamer floating in the breeze with the Empire's flag over his home. His mother might not be able to endure it.

Chapter Twenty-Seven

"It's been fifty minuets," said Henrik, glancing at his Hamilton watch. "Let's go." Henrik gripped Nesto's wrist and helped him up. He had to find out about that firefight. It nagged at him not knowing what had happened and that maybe they should have rushed to the sound of the guns. Besides, he'd had enough of rotting coconuts around the Aussie station. *Smells like spoiled blue cheese. Yuck.*

"They could have been here and halfway back by now. Let's go."

Nesto took the point with his Reising at the ready and Henrik four or five paces behind him. If shooting started he'd rapid-fire his rifle and start chucking grenades. *You're thinking like our boys may have been whacked bad. Don't. At any moment they'll come high-stepping down the trail little the worse for wear.*

They followed the beach-side trail to the island's west end. Their visibility in the shore-side vegetation let them see only feet ahead. After taking 200 yards slow and easy, Henrik became all the more antsy. *We could be walking into an ambush.*

"Nesto, hold a second."

"You have a bad feeling too?"

"I do. Let's cut across through the plantation to the north trail. We'll strike the trail about where we saw all those birds taking to wing."

"I'm with you."

"We'll take it slower than we did on the trail." Off the trail, Nesto took four or five paces, stopped, looked, and listened, then repeated the sequence.

A few birds fluttered and squawked over the trees, still reluctant to settle in the limbs. *Maybe there are still people there.*

Turning right into the plantation provided better visibility as there was little brush under the producing coconut palms. There was still plenty of vegetation further away to hide the enemy. There was little rise in the ground.

Henrik grew more anxious. *We have to do this. Our fellas no doubt need help.* He could feel it.

They pressed on with haste, but quietly. The birds had mostly settled down. It occurred to him the birds might again raise a ruckus and alert the Nips as they approached. He wished the birds would stay agitated for a spell.

They could hear the north side's surf, but fewer bird sounds. He reminded himself to keep an ear open if the birds were again disturbed by our boys or Japs.

Nesto went to a knee, his head scrunched down sighting the shouldered Reising. Did he see something? It crossed Henrik's mind, Nesto's complaint of the Reising's tendency to jam. *Don't fail us now, Buck Rogers gun.*

Three quiet knuckle raps on his butt stock alerted Nesto. Henrik motioned him to hold up. He'd go ahead himself. Nesto nodded. Creeping ever so slowly, Henrik eased into the thicker vegetation. The deeper he moved the fewer gnats there were, but as he approached the north trail more sunbeams penetrated and the gnats annoyingly increased.

He stopped and listened. Moved again on hand and knees. Listened. Nesto halted when he did. A voice. Two or three words maybe. Someone chuckled. Another word. All spoken quietly. *Got to be Jap talk.* He looked back at Nesto, who nodded.

They crept forward as silently as possible. The ground rose to a small knoll. Henrik noticed wilted leaves on the brush. They were cut limbs stuck in the sand. Finding a gap, he was among a patch of ground sheltered by a canopy of densely laced tree limbs. The branches sheltered two-foot-deep slit trenches. There were ammo and ration crates set about with camouflaging leaves. Nesto slipped up beside him.

"Gotta be their base camp," whispered Henrik.

Another quiet laugh. They could see moving shapes below them, on the knoll's north slope. The position was screened on its open north side, giving a view across the strait and screened it overhead as well. Observing the site for some minutes, Henrik decided they could close within twenty yards.

He whispered in Nesto's ear, "We'll crawl into those two slit trenches. When I get a clear shot on one of them, I'll take it and you burn up two or three magazines. I'll start throwing frags as fast as I can, so stay down. We'll take off up the trail inside the tree line, then upslope and back to the Aussie station. Just go there if we're separated. Got it?"

He nodded and they slipped through the shallow trenches and piled earth parapets. He noticed leaves were spread on the parapets and trench bottoms for extra aerial camouflage.

"¡*Mierda!*"—Shit! uttered Nesto.

"What?" The grip on his rifle tensed.

"Found their shitter."

He could smell the lime powder the Japs used. A few flies buzzed.

Henrik squirmed up next to a trench's parapet and used it as a rifle rest. He could indistinctly make out three men, sometimes four. They weren't moving much and they were mostly quiet and screened by leafy limbs and vines. One Jap was visible to the right and didn't move much. Next to him was some kind of thing like a telescope.

He set four grenades on the parapet and straightened the pins. He sighted the mostly sedentary man. The screening leaves shifted occasionally with the breeze. Henrik was acutely aware that he was about to start something of which the outcome was uncertain. It looked easy, but that was only an illusion. There was no telling what would happen in the coming seconds.

Nesto eased to a knee, shouldering the Reising, and nodded without turning to Henrik.

This was such a short-ranged shot that Henrik didn't adjust his rear sight.

The birds had settled down. Leaves rustled in the breeze.

One more good gust for a clear shot. He took a breath, let some out, kept his body rock steady, tightened the trigger's slack, and the leaves quivered and stilled to again obscure his view. Another breath. A feeble gust before he could let it out. He squeezed and took the recoil in his shoulder. The Reising rattled in spite of Nesto's lack of faith. Henrik gripped the yellow-painted grenade, yanked the cotter pin, and threw it straight like a softball, then grabbed another. The four grenades detonated with gouts of sand a second or two apart. He grabbed his Springfield, fired four rounds, and ran. The Reising hammered, another grenade thrown by Nesto, then a Jap grenade detonated. It wasn't close. Henrik heard Nesto behind him as he paralleled the trail and stumbled to a stop. Lying on the trail was an American, his body riddled with bullet holes. No rifle or web gear. He couldn't tell who it was, being face down and helmeted.

"Don't stop," shouted Nesto as a couple of rifle shots cracked behind him. "*¡Ándale!*" Henrik figured it meant, "Move your ass!"

He didn't hesitate.

Chapter Twenty-Eight

As the platoon moved slowly and cautiously eastward, the lieutenant had appointed Seiichi, a rifleman, to take the lead. The machine gun crew followed. In all there were nine in the group. To Obata's surprise he brought up the rear just ahead of Sergeant Toshio. He was to be prepared to provide covering fire in any direction. If they were engaged from the front, he was to rush forward to support the machine gun.

They moved a short distance after checking the path leading to the settlement. There were American boot prints turning off there, but not many. Other prints showed movement in both directions on the main north path, Japanese and American. As before they could not tell how many Americans there might be.

The lieutenant sounded apprehensive. "We will continue on this path and follow it around the island and back to the settlement. There, it will be decided to follow the path back to the north side or follow it around the west end and back to the plotting station. If the Americans are still on the island, we will locate and annihilate them."

Obata felt they were heading into another battle. It was disconcerting, not because of the expected fight, but because there was something confusing about this. Where were they going, where was the enemy going, how many Americans were there, and what were they planning? He felt like they might be running in circles.

The five or six grenade detonations boomed up the path, accented by machine gun bursts. Birds flocked into the sky filled with rumbling echoes. It was impossible to judge the distance.

They all dropped. The lieutenant yanked his pistol out and turned with a short-lived astonished expression. He rushed the machine gun to the column's rear and had them take up a position in the direction of the plotting station from which the explosions came. The grenade discharger crew set up as best they could further back on the path. The many overhanging trees restricted their fire down the path at a low angle. He next formed a rough perimeter with men covering the inland flank and peering into the jungle.

The American bodies still lay crumpled on the trail. It may mean the other Americans had not stayed long, or there were not enough men to remove the bodies. Did the Americans care enough to return and move the bodies to a more reverent place?

Obata felt a confining sensation of the patrol becoming trapped and perhaps outnumbered. There may be Americans closing in on them from both directions. He felt a sudden fear of American grenades and how many machine guns they appeared to have. It did not matter how rapidly one could fire one shot at a time with a bolt-action rifle when your enemy possessed machine guns able to spit out dozens of rounds.

They remained ready and silent. Ten, then fifteen, minutes ticked by. The lieutenant fidgeted and was soon glancing around as if the men were not remaining still and silent. Rising to a knee, he peered ahead with his binocular even though the vegetation allowed less than twenty meters' range.

He carefully rose to a crouch and crept ahead, passing the machine gun. Kneeling, he listened. He gestured to Obata to come here. He did the same for Seiichi. Crouching, the two soldiers hurried to the lieutenant.

"Use caution, move quietly to where you can see the plotting station. Look for live or dead Japanese and for Americans. Do not shoot if you are fired upon. If there is firing, fall to the ground and the machine gun will fire over your heads. Do you understand?"

They nodded.

"Go."

They looked at one another. Obata did not know Seiichi well, having barely spoken to him before they were sent on this mission.

Crouching as low as they could, almost a squat, they worked their way forward. Seiichi let Obata move ahead of him. More American dead littered the trail.

"*Takeo*," he said in a quiet voice.

Just bird noises and the breeze.

"*Takeo!*"

"*Tareka*"—Who are you? a voice asked.

"*Hoshi*"—Star.

"*Tsuki*"—Moon. It was Hajime, the instrument man.

"Are there Americans still here?" Obata asked.

The lieutenant arrived. "Tell me what happened."

Hajime was still distressed. He had a few small fragment injuries. "You had not been gone long and we were barraged by grenades and a machine gun. There must have been twice as many Americans as us. Many grenades exploded almost as one. They did not enter the position but retreated into the jungle." He pointed to the north side of the trail.

"Casualties?"

"There are three dead and one other wounded."

Obata sprang to his feet and ducked under the branches. Lance Corporal Isamu, the radio crew leader, and another signalman, Yukichi, were dead, hit by grenade blasts. They may have had bullet wounds.

Obata found Takeo doubled up near the radio, grenade-mangled and half-covered by sand and vegetation debris. The only way he could identify his comrade was by his bandaged hand.

Grief flashed through him, but he could not reveal his anguish, not now, maybe not ever. His parents…Takeo had two younger brothers. Unyielding sadness. Maybe Takeo's family could be found. He buried that thought, knowing it was unlikely that he would survive the war or even his days remaining on this virtually anonymous island. He drew his bayonet and cut a bit of Takeo's close-cropped hair and pushed it into a cardboard cartridge packet. For Takeo's parents, if he should live to find them.

Obata wanted revenge, but revenge was beneath a soldier. There was nothing that dictated mercy be conferred on the enemy. But there was something that might help them defeat the enemy. One did not make suggestions to superiors unless asked. *How does one make a suggestion to an officer?*

He emboldened himself. "Honorable Sergeant, I may have something the Honorable Lieutenant would approve of."

He looked at Obata with a hint of anger, but hesitated. "What have you to say, Honorable Private?" The lieutenant was standing three meters away.

"Honorable Lieutenant, would it be appropriate to perhaps carry some of the poison gas grenades? They may give us an advantage." He bowed, hoping tolerance for his impertinence.

The sergeant was thoughtful for a moment and turned to the lieutenant. He nodded to the sergeant. "That may prove to be useful. Take a man with you and find one of the boxes. Do be gentle with it."

He and Seiichi found the grenades in their metal container and hurried back to the platoon. They were not heavy, even if held in four individual cans and an outer metal box, but he still had to carry the 360-round box of extra 6.5mm cartridges along with bandoleers.

"Keep them in the containers and handle with caution," directed the sergeant.

Obata had hoped they would talk about how they would use them. He noticed too that some men had discarded their gasmasks.

The lieutenant ordered Kosaku, the remaining signalman, to test the radio set. The cabinet cover had been hit by a few small fragments.

"Someone needs to crank the generator for power."

"Obata, the generator. Kosaku will tell you what is necessary."

Obata had seen the crew operate the Model F generator with the radio. He sat on the ground and rigged the leather harness over his shoulders with the generator on his chest. He turned the single hand crank, building up speed to seventy rotations a minute. The moment Kosaku tapped the code key, the spinning handle locked to wrench Obata's right wrist.

"What happened?" shouted the lieutenant. Obata unharnessed the generator while Kosaku gave the radio a quick check over and then examined the generator.

He sprang to his feet and bowed. "The radio is operational, Honorable Lieutenant, but the generator is damaged by a grenade fragment. It cut through the copper coils."

"Can it be repaired?"

"No Honorable Lieutenant," he replied, obviously fearing a beating.

The lieutenant looked thoughtful for a time. "Destroy the radio so the Americans do not capture it. Burn the codebooks. Refill your cartridge pouches. Grenades, water, and rations. The Americans are fond of grenades. Every man must carry four. The mission now is only to find and annihilate the Americans."

The signalman opened the radio's case and removed its vacuum tubes; he put in an empty tin and hid it in piled leaves.

They formed into a column. The lieutenant moved them eastward. They passed the settlement path. The lieutenant did not feel any surviving Americans had retreated that way. They had visited the settlement several times and it was apparent the Americans were not operating from there. They had not explored the east end of the island and the Americans could be somewhere on the island's broader and hillier end with more places to hide.

They moved quickly with little caution. Obata reasoned that the lieutenant must feel there were few Americans left. Perhaps they were fleeing or hiding in the jungle after suffering the ambush. The brief fight after the ambush must have been executed by a small number of survivors. If that was true, they were in little danger.

Regardless, they gradually slowed as they moved toward what seemed to become the mysterious east end of the island.

The patrol began its move along the island's north side. They would frequently halt and listen. It was time consuming as they spread out in a defensive position.

Obata was still in the rear with the sergeant. It grew hotter, more humid. His mind dwelled on what the poison gas he carried would do to Takeo's murderers. He wanted to see them gag, choke, and vomit themselves to death. He hoped to soon have that opportunity.

Chapter Twenty-Nine

Henrik and Nesto overlooked the north shore trail. They did not know where they were in relation to the OP other than it was on the island's west end. They had to travel as fast up the island's hilly spine as the heavy air and vegetation allowed. Studded with brush and trees, the rough ground didn't allow a sprint by any means. Sweat soaked their uniforms, and they were almost out of water. They didn't know how many Japs there were, only that the Japs were ahead of them and heading toward their OP. They had no idea if the OP was alert and ready or how many marines manned the position.

Henrik was good on ammo, but out of grenades. Nesto had three Reising magazines, having filled two of his empties from his fifty-round carton. Nesto had a single grenade.

They couldn't overtake the Japs on the trail below to warn the OP. "I'm hoping the OP heard the ambush shootout and are ready for visitors," Henrik said. He was afraid too they may have responded to the sound of fire and then run into the Japs on the trail. The Japs might outnumber the marines at the OP. They, too, probably had no clear idea how many marines were left.

"The Nips are going to run into our boys sooner or later. Maybe we can at least hit the Nips from the rear," muttered Henrik, shaking his head, "and hope our boys don't shoot at us."

"I hope that too. Here, take my grenade. I'm going to be busy emptying Reising mags."

Henrik hung the frag grenade on his left harness. "Let's move closer to the trail. The Japs are ahead of us so we can ambush them if they fall back from the OP when they hit it. If they get in a standup fight, we can still hit the Nips from behind. Ready?"

"*Listo.*"

"What?"

"Yea, partner, ready."

A loud explosion detonated ahead to be immediately followed by a machine gun and then a rising crackle of rifles and submachine guns. Echoes rebounded through the trees.

Chapter Thirty

The eleven men in the patrol moved slowly up the path, rifles sweeping back and forth along with their eyes. The path was marred with American boot prints, spent cartridges, a cigarette butt, which Seiichi claimed, and a lid-top cut from a food tin.

"Smells like a fruit tin," said Koji, the machine gunner.

"Kadota figs."

The lieutenant had halted the spread-out group. Time trickled by, a longer wait than usual. Flies and gnats accumulated. Obata was in the rear and couldn't see up the path beyond its meandering route and drooping tree limbs and vines. From ahead he heard the meager sounds of men starting to move. He was ready when Sergeant Toshio in front of him rose from his crouch and crept forward.

An indiscreet shout from up ahead startled them. Then a thump, blending into a loud boom. Then another and another. Concussion waves rolled through the trees, shaking out leaves and twigs, and carrying away the mosquitoes and gnats. Machine guns ripped loose and more grenades burst. Their grenade discharger popped along with more hand grenades.

Obata forced himself to turn away from the action and face the rear. To his surprise, just meters from him crouched an American, his rifle to his shoulder aimed straight at him. Obata instinctively fired and rolled to the right off the path, toward the beach. He frantically worked the bolt and a burn streaked across his side below his left arm. He rolled through the low brush, rose to find the American again aiming at him. Their shots were virtually simultaneous and he was certain he'd hit the American in the head. Reloading, he pressed forward to stumble on ground vines and went down. He felt another burn, this one across his right shoulder blade. *I have been shot twice*, swirled through his mind. *Why does it not hurt?*

He came up again out of the brush. Anticipating being immediately shot, he urgently whipped the rifle from side-to-side. No one. He was oblivious while fully aware of the rattling shots and grenade bursts. Bark flew off a fallen tree trunk apparently fired blindly through the brush. He emptied his rifle and slid down a slight embankment. A grenade exploded on the spot he had knelt on moments before. He remembered his grenades and quickly threw two, guessing where the American might be. Ducking under the shore-side trees and ferns, he was on the narrow beach, feeling fully exposed. Blinding sunlight, seagulls, a stiffening breeze. No one shot at him. He turned and ran unhampered down the beach, the miniature waves sloshing ashore to wet his tabis. Another boom behind him. He wanted to get behind that American hunting him. *Obata is the sniper and thus the hunter, not the American*, he told himself. Why did his wounds not hurt? He pushed into the vegetation, desperately slashing his bayonet at the American barreling down on him. He butt-stroked at Obata's face, but he ducked to the right and the American only thumped his helmet. Obata slashed again, knocking off the American's own helmet to reveal short yellow hair, and then followed through with his own butt stroke. A discharger grenade exploded nearby and Obata ducked and ran. He found the path, crossed it, and worked his way uphill. A shot cracked over his head. He felt for a moment that he could not get away from this tenacious soldier. *Maybe the yellow-haired soldier is the hunter here after all.*

The firing died down. Shouts rent the air—in Japanese and English. He threw himself on the ground among dense ferns. Gasping for breath, he felt his heart would burst. According to the shouts it sounded like the Americans were on the higher ground and the Japanese on the lower. He was in the wrong place. He stayed mostly still and gingerly felt his wounds, which proved to be only bullet grazes. They burned, but were only a little annoying.

That American; he didn't think they would fight like that. He was fortunate; they had both been hampered by the tangled vegetation.

Then he remembered the perished Takeo and his solemn vow to avenge his death. He might have been able to fight more viciously if he had remembered it. Instead, he had momentarily forgotten his battle comrade and had fought only to save himself. He felt shame.

The firing had all but ceased. Someone shouted, "*Marīn you die!*"

Some American answering shots cracked. *We are fighting Marines?* thought Obata.

"Blood for Em-per-er!"

Obata had not realized any of their number spoke American.

"Blood for Eleanor!" a marine shouted from downhill.

There were quietly voiced orders. It seemed both sides were pulling back. No doubt both had suffered casualties and were reorganizing.

Rather than sneak back to his own side, Obata decided to stay hidden and let the Americans bypass him as they withdrew.

He heard a man creep past just meters away. He took only shallow breaths and stayed perfectly still. He could hear voices, but faint now. They were ahead of him on the island's low hill. Removing his helmet, he decided to leave it and keep his cap. The helmet was too predominant and made noise when low limbs brushed across it. Easing his head up, he saw there were higher and denser ferns ahead. Taking his time, he crawled forward, listening after each movement. A small but dense leafy bush offered good concealment. Patches of dead leaves swarmed with ants. He parted the leaves with his fingers. He saw shapes moving and heard the whisper of voices. He eased his rifle forward. The leaves were damp and they stuck in clumps as he pushed them open enough to slide the rifle through.

Squinting through the telescope, he saw three Americans. One was partially grizzled looking and older, a sergeant? Another's face in helmeted shadow was talking and handing something to the…sergeant. The third was a boy, yellow hair. Was he the one he had dueled with?

He had a clear shot and he knew the opportunity was fleeting. Ants were attacking his ankles. *Who to shoot?* The yellow hair had tried to kill him. The older may be the leader. *Decide now, do it now.* Obata took aim, setting the crosshairs on the boy's nose, inhaled slightly, and squeezed the trigger with it blurring though his mind that the trigger pull was too stiff.

Chapter Thirty-One

Henrik lay on his back, shaken and sucking in air. Forcing himself to sit up, he looked around for the insistent Nip. That was far too close of a hand-to-hand fight. Bullets, bayonet slashes, and butt strokes. He couldn't see worth a damn in the shore-side brush and trees. He heard Jap voices, babble in his mind. It sounded like they were receding, moving west. They were above the trail. They were soon quiet. He eased down to the trail and listened for a couple of minutes before venturing back on to it. That Nip was small, but quick and agile. Turning right, he moved quietly but stood erect so his men could see him.

"Lucky." A whispered password.

"Lollypop," he replied.

"Henrik, where you been?" It was Sergeant Lockler followed by Mother O'Leary.

"Did you all get ambushed? We heard the ruckus and followed the Japs here. Nesto and I were separated. Have you seen him?"

"He's here. Showed up a few minutes ago. He's okay and happy as can be that he can ammo up. You okay on ammo?"

"Just need grenades and water."

Lockler looked up and shoved Henrik to the side. His face jerked, contorted, blood spewed from his nostrils, and he fell forward.

Henrik and Mother fired in the direction of the shot, and others randomly but quickly opened fire. Someone let loose with a Reising. The firing quickly tapered off and no one moved except Doc Camphor who rushed up in a crouch, before anyone shouted for the corpsman.

"He's gone," Doc reported curtly. It was obvious. It took a couple of minutes though for comprehension to set in, for the word to spread. "Lockler bought it." There were curses and threats of vengeance. "Slant-eyed bastards." Everyone came by, what was left of the section. A neckerchief was laid over his destroyed face.

Mother O'Leary remorselessly gazed at his sergeant's body. "He must have seen that sniper taking a bead on you Handyman and pushed you away."

Corporal Rankin and Snacks with his Thompson gun searched for the sniper but found nothing. Rankin was now in charge. "Bet you didn't know he had a wife."

A wave of guilt washed through Henrik. *I wish he hadn't told me.*

"She lives in Bremerton, Washington state. He was stationed at the Puget Sound Navy Yard Marine Barracks. He was one of them barracks marines culled out and assigned to the infantry regiments. Claire Jane is her name."

I should be thinking, I wish it was me.

It took time to get everyone sorted out and the position organized. Everyone kept low owing to the sniper menace. They dug-in around the bivouac site and its slit trenches and the OP itself a short distance above the bivouac. They were maybe 150 yards inland from the island's northeast shore.

As they worked, Corporal Rankin filled in Henrik and Nesto on what had happened.

"They caught us cold. It was from the left flank and the front with a machine gun going off right in our faces. We lost six: Corporal Discoll, Patches, the Greek, McKern—the assistant BAR, and Katcher from commo.

Rubbing his chin, he added, "We don't even know how many of them we nailed. Two for sure. We're down to eight men. At least no one's wounded."

That struck Henrik. Scary having lost half their strength. It really didn't feel like they had actually lost that many. He hadn't witnessed it so it didn't feel like it. Losing half of the men—that made him feel they were losing. Better not to think about it. Henrik was adapting to the jungle's isolation though, a smothering shroud closing in around a man. Buddies could be just feet apart, but you seemed alone.

"We've got our supplies," said Rankin. "I guess you're good on ammo. Get some grenades. The Japs don't like them one little bit when we start chucking them. Careful though. I think Spud was killed by his own grenade. A bounce back. Any ideas on their strength since you were behind them part of the time, Handyman?"

"Not really, I had a feeling they're maybe ten, twelve. Just one of those damn Nambu machine guns."

Rankin was looking at his shoulder. "Is that blood on your shoulder?"

"A couple of grazes."

"Have Doc look at it. Most of us have nicks or grazes. They get infected easy."

"Will do. WILCO."

"Did you hear that grenade discharger of theirs? That got a few of us. When you hear it start rapid firing, hit the ground. They fast-fire six, eight rounds, and the next thing you know they're exploding all around you. Sometimes they get airbursts. That's really bad."

"What were the loud explosions at the beginning?" Henrik asked. "Sounded louder than even our frags."

"Lockler's idea, bless his heart," said Rankin. "We rigged three of those demolition grenades with tripwires. He taped rifle cartridges around the grenades for more fragmentation. Blew the shit out of them slant-eyes." He grinned.

Rankin unfixed his bayonet and sheathed it. "It's going to be dark soon. I'm thinking about moving out and hunkering down for the night where the Japs would make a lot of noise to get at us. Let's you and me look around. Find a place and then move into it after dark, so if the Nips have anyone watching, they'll lose us."

"We'll leave the radio," said Rankin.

Sparks nodded and admitted, "We seldom make contact. Sent some weather reports, but we've not sighted a single Jap garbage scowl." He showed everyone where it was hidden and well camouflaged. He left a couple of thermite grenades in case they needed to destroy it.

Henrik trusted Rankin, but he was already missing Lockler. The NCO knew a lot of things you didn't find in *The Marine's Handbook*. Things he'd learned the hard way.

Learned the hard way. Henrik had never heard the phrase before, but he understood it. He had learned a lot about farming and hunting the hard way. But when marines learned things the hard way, it meant that men had died.

He thought too about that Jap who'd kept coming at him. The thought of cold steel slicing though him—it troubled him more than ever.

They ate cold, greasy chow, cleaned weapons, loaded up on ammo, and Doc treated minor wounds, scrapes, and cuts. Gripping the pack on the man ahead of them, the eight remaining marines snaked to another location. It was dark when they finally reached a more or less level hummock on the hill's east side.

"We'll take a rest," said Rankin. "Sparks and I'll stay here as a base and you guys will go out in pairs, north, west, and south. See if we can shake the Nips out."

"How do we find our way back?" asked Griff.

"If you find the Nips, open fire and I want everyone to go to the gunfire. That means everyone. Immediately and fast. If you don't run into them, keep searching as long as you can manage. Hunker down for the night and we'll find each other in the morning. If nothing else, in the morning you should be able to find our OP. Moving out in an hour."

Chapter Thirty-Two

Obata set his case of spare 6.5mm ammunition and the gas grenades in a slit trench at their base. He was nearing exhaustion. Eating rice balls and little else was inadequate for energy. The tinned foods had barely been touched. He decided he would not need that much rifle ammunition. He had only fired a few shots during each engagement and it was much too heavy and bulky. He would hide it here and he could always recover it later, if he lived long enough to need it.

That young yellow-haired marine had given him a fright. Actually, his hair was like burnished bronze. He had not expected Americans to be that tenacious, not according to the lectures they had received. He pulled a couple of tins out of cartons. Two other men were looting as well, Kazuo and Shuzo. Empty tins lay scattered about. There was no time like the present. For once no one was telling him what to do. He was used to someone always ordering him exactly what to do and what not to do. Maybe he could hide out somewhere and avoid the lieutenant, the sergeant, and the corporal. He chastised himself for shirking his duties and honor, to even think about it. He shook that off. He could not avoid the duties expected of him. He needed to nourish himself to continue the fight.

His long bayonet was an awkward tool for cutting open tins. The small tin of crab and one of peas was filling enough. He took two more tins of crab and filed his water bottle from a near empty 25-liter can. The food rekindled his battle spirit.

He heard a sound behind him. Startled, he turned to find Lieutenant Kiyoshi emerging from the trees.

"Obata, have you seen anyone else?"

Springing to attention, he bowed and reported, "No one was seen, Honorable Lieutenant."

"Sit down, Obata. You need not beckon the enemy to shoot you."

Saburo, the orderly, and Kosaku, the surviving signalman, appeared behind the lieutenant. He ordered them to eat, fill their water bottles, and replenish their ammunition. "Each of you take three tins of food. We may not come back here."

That sounded ominous. Were they going to face and attack the enemy and perhaps never return? Were they leaving the island somehow?

Little was said as they ate. Obata found a tin of mandarin oranges, something he had never experienced. After tasting it, he took two more orange tins. *Mother would love these*, he thought, if he ever saw her again. He took two tins of fish too. It rained again. They had brought shelter-halves that could be used as rain capes, but they were not allowed as they were noisy passing through vegetation and restricted the use of a rifle. It rained off and on.

Eventually the lieutenant called them together. "It is not known how many of our men have died. We came here as this is the most likely place for our men to rally. We will wait here until dark. Then we will quietly move to the American position on the east end of the island. We can destroy them if we are stealthy, brave, audacious, and honorable."

Yes, thought Obata, *it is honorable to kill the Empire's enemies*. But what were they really achieving in this putrefying jungle, fighting like base animals to the death? What did the enemy think? It did not matter, he told himself.

In the jungle's gloom, they swatted at gnats. Ants had discovered their presence, drawn by the many empty tins. The lieutenant did not reveal his plan. It would be discussed before dark. Obata felt the lieutenant had or was making a plan. "Be alert for the sounds of movement in case the Americans approach or our own soldiers return."

Obata wondered what had happened to the other men—were they dead, lost, hiding? As far as they could agree on, the remainder of the men were dead or possibly some were simply lost in the jungle.

They rested, but one man remained awake and kept watch on the path below them. An hour before dark Sergeant Toshio arrived with machine gunner Koji. Obata was grateful the sergeant had returned because of his steadiness and battle knowledge. He was grateful for the machine gunner too, simply for the firepower, even though he had only six thirty-round magazines. He could reload the magazines with rifle ammunition. Koji knew his two crewmen had been caught by the explosives trap. Koji had been hit by gravel. Kazuo reported they had only six fragmentation grenades and two white phosphorus for the discharger. He had already found a rifle for his use once the grenades were expended.

They waited.

Obata watched a frog an arm's length before him. Its green mottled camouflage form had been revealed to him as he first watched a cricket perched on a twig. The frog, as large as his hand, had patiently awaited the cricket's cautious approach. Then, with a sudden, unexpected open-mouthed pounce, it gulped down the momentarily startled cricket. *We must do the same to the Americans—a fast unexpected attack.*

"Obata," said the lieutenant, startling him back to the immediate reality. He motioned with his hand when Obata began to spring to his feet. "Bring me the gas grenades." There was a note of finality in those crisp words.

He had hoped the grenades would slip the lieutenant's mind. Obata was not too excited about combat testing the grenades manufactured by his father's firm—even if they had come full circle from the home he was born in to this tiny corner of an island he might die on.

The lieutenant explained they would move quietly to the east end of the island, listening for the Americans. They enemy often made too much noise, and the lieutenant was confident they would hear the Americans, or even see lit cigarettes. They were careless. At least, that is what the lieutenant told them. Obata decided the lieutenant might not be so knowledgeable about the Americans. He had no more experience fighting them than Obata did. Still, the officer had been well schooled and served in China against a wily and crafty enemy.

Once they found the Americans, they would set the machine gun in a position from which they could spray their enemy as they fled from the barrage of poison gas grenades. Most of the men appeared uncomfortable with the idea. They said nothing though, nor did the lieutenant say anything about ensuring they had gasmasks.

"The glass grenades must be handled cautiously and kept in their sealed cans until needed. The cans are filled with sawdust treated with a neutralizing agent in case the glass sphere breaks. It releases a cloud of liquid hydrogen cyanide. When it comes in contact with air it vaporizes. It smells like bitter almonds and when breathed causes nausea, vomiting, and either increased or slowed breathing. Suffocation occurs in minutes."

He looked around at the wide-eyed men. "This will give us a prodigious and unexpected advantage over our enemies. Obata and Saburo will each carry four grenades."

Obata was momentarily gratified by the implicit trust. Then he saw the expression on the orderly's face. Maybe it was not such an honor after all. He noticed some of the men were searching slit trenches for masks discarded by their comrades. At least the grenades weren't too heavy, but they were bulky.

"When we find a suitable target, do not simply throw grenades at the target area like an explosive grenade; throw it at something that will cause it to break, such as trees or rock outcroppings. Of course throw it from upwind if possible." *If possible*, Obata thought.

"Have your mask ready to immediately pull over your face."

Obata pulled out his mask with its treated tan fabric face-piece. Soldiers joked about its Moon-shaped simpleton's face with two wide-eyed round lenses, a nubby nose-piece, and an elephant's snout in the place of a mouth. The snout's rubber hose was connected to an oval metal filter canister. Its many head straps gave it a deformed octopus-like grotesqueness. He donned and adjusted the head straps. Wearing the mask was suffocating in the hot, humid tropics. When running, one was gasping in no time. It also restricted the field of vision and the lens fogged. Wearing one at night just about blinded a man. That, and two men had to be face-to-face to speak in muffled voices. Obata found anti-fogging discs for the lens and anti-freeze for the inlet valve for China's bitter winters. *Little good would they do here.*

The sergeant checked each man. They tied their breathing canister to the mask bag's shoulder strap on their back and removed the inlet valve's bottom opening's rubber stopper. The mask was secured to their left shoulder strap. The sergeant led off with the machine gun crew. Obata brought up what was left of the platoon—eight men.

They moved out extremely slowly and cautiously, stopping and starting every few meters. It was difficult in the total darkness, hampered by vines, brush, trees, and limestone. A light rain fell. While miserable and making the mud and layered rotting leaves slick, the drizzle covered their movement and muffled the sound.

They crept downhill, causing more slips and sides. The rain continued to fall, and a lashing wind blew. The rush of the surf increased. Flares burst over the channel and fireballs billowed from dying ships. Those shadows and flickering lights made vision in the jungle more difficult. *How many sailors died right then? Was a dead soldier immediately taken by death or was the journey not made until his remains were enshrined at Yasukuni?*

Obata was soaked to the skin though his shirt, trousers, cap, and tabis. A chill was setting in, not like the freezing Nagoya parade ground, but a feverous sensation. Without orders, he unfixed his bayonet and sheathed it. The brush was too dense for a fixed blade. Illumination shells burst in the sky over the channel.

They halted again. Rather than moving on, after a brief wait they went into a crouch. Obata realized he was more than lost. He was disoriented. If he was ordered to make his way to the shore, he might manage to reach the lapping waves, but he would not know which side of the island he was one.

Voices, then sounds of movement almost hidden by the drizzle. The lieutenant appeared, or rather transmuted, beside him and Saburo. "Prepare two gas grenades each."

Obata heard some quiet English words. He could not make out a thing before him. The faintest of Moonbeams drifted through the trees. A machine gun opened fire—it was Japanese. Rifles fired seemingly in all directions. Other machine guns fired. No tracers; must be American.

Removing the grenade canister from the case, he had to do everything by feel. He wished he could have practiced this in the dark, not that he wished to handle the fragile grenades any more than necessary. He pried off the lid. The top, bottom, and sides of the canister were double-walled, and he knew it was filled with sawdust saturated with a neutralizing agent. The glass sphere was liquid-filled and sealed what felt like a beer bottle cap.

"Prepare to throw," whispered the lieutenant, his head close to theirs. He shifted Obata's arm, presumably in the desired direction. "Throw as hard as you can on order," he said, cupping both men's shoulders.

Obata envisioned himself throwing the glass sphere directly into a tree mere meters in front of him.

Someone ahead cleared his throat.

"In that direction, throw, now!"

He sensed Saburo throwing in unison. "Masks!" He heard the lieutenant donning his own. Two muffled pops, further in front of him than he expected. The officer shoved them both to the ground as rifles and machine guns crackled. The firing tapered off. There was little reaction.

"Throw again, same direction," the lieutenant ordered. Two pops and more gunfire. More shouts too as the Americans, and perhaps some Japanese, encountered the burning vapors. Their shouts grew into panic. Obata could smell the vapors, but that was all. "Follow me," shouted the lieutenant and they were running. The three of them tripped and ran into the scattered trees.

As they ran and stumbled, they gradually made their way to lower ground. In the tangled vegetation and darkness, they slowed to a crawl.

"We must rest," gasped the lieutenant. He said something to Saburo that he could not make out.

Obata recognized the sound of field dressing packaging being ripped open. "He is shot in the right calf," Saburo said. "It went through. Not deep." The orderly was obviously distressed. Obata had heard that if an officer was wounded and taken off the battlefield, his orderly did not accompany him. No surprise, but the former orderly seldom became the replacement officer's orderly. The replacement would select his own after interviewing men in his new platoon. It was a loss of face for the former orderly, who would revert to his previous duty position, usually as a rifleman.

"Obata," said the lieutenant, "we are somewhere on the island's north side. Go north to the shoreline and see if you can decide how far away the plotting station is. It should be to the left. If you find any of our men bring them back and we will move to the plotting station." The lieutenant had him repeat his orders. "Go, quickly."

***

Obata tried moving as slowly as one of his grandmother's lifelike ceramic snails. Working his way down the path, he had an overwhelming sensation he was being watched, no matter the solidity of the ink black night. He gingerly moved into the jungle, carefully pushing aside dangling vines and elephant ears. Voices. Very soft, barely heard. Just to his left front. He could tell they were American. No way of knowing how many. He decided three or four, maybe. He could let them go, or he could slip back to the lieutenant, or open fire with his rifle, or souvenir them a hand grenade.

In spite of his fear of throwing a grenade blindly at the Americans, he gripped one of the Type 97 grenades; a black segmented cylinder with its top painted red meant a high-explosive filler. With less confidence than he desired, he gripped the cord loop and pulled. He shook the safety cover off and struck the primer on his rifle's butt. The internal delay fuse sparked and fizzed a thin trail of smoke.

One second of a life. He flung his arm back.

Two seconds of a life. The fuse sizzled.

Three seconds of a life. He lofted his arm forward.

Four seconds of a life. It flew into the darkness, sparking.

Five seconds to end a life.

Chapter Thirty-Three

Henrik and Nesto had moved north only a short distance and paralleled the north shore trail west to the station cutoff trail. It was a dry hole, no recent sign of Japs. They moved to the south side of the north trail. They didn't move too far up the higher ground for fear of running into one of their own teams west of the main hill. They worked their way around the east side of the hill. The Japs could be in the area, increasing the likelihood of colliding in the dense vegetation and the on-and-off rain.

In the lowering darkness they literally stumbled over a couple of moss-covered fallen trunks crowned with gnarled and broken limbs. Hoping there were no bugs, snakes, or things with thorns in their nest, they quietly settled in back-to-back between the thick logs. Henrik liked Nesto. He seemed to be at home in the bush. Nesto had only shot .22 rifles at rabbits—never hit one—and tin cans, which he had more luck hitting if they stood still. He'd almost scored Sharpshooter. Of course the Reising gave him a better chance of mowing down Japs. He was exceedingly quiet, which could not be said of all marines. "This dump's a swindle. The roof leaks and there's rocks in the bed," Nesto whispered, holding up an offending stone.

"Wait until you see the John."

"Don't tell me, it's full of shit?"

"Shhhh!"

There was a swish of wet leaves, ever so faint. A rock rolled under someone's foot, for less than a moment. They could only guess who it might be.

In the pitch black, Henrik counted on Nesto to already be aiming his Reising at the faint sounds. A thin band of rain passed through shuddering leaves. Mosquitos were lively, disturbed by the rain and moving people.

A flash silhouetted the trees, lighting up the distant rolling surface of the channel and the underside of the damp clouds. A hollow boom swept across the channel. Star shells burst and an angry orange fireball blossomed, reaching for the glowing clouds.

Henrik probably couldn't count the number of sailors who died right then. Mentally, he slapped himself; he had better concentrate on what was going on around him right here and now.

A slipping sound in the wet leaves, faint. No oaths as one would expect. There was too much movement around them. He only hoped they would pass. More star shells, further away. Reflected beams of yellow-white star shells caused ever-changing bands and shadows crisscrossing on the water. The jungle created its own drifting shadows.

There was no doubt that there were men around them, but it was impossible to determine how far, their direction, and if friend or foe. No one dared a challenge. It became very quiet except for the faint booms across the channel.

Seconds later a submachine gun exploded into action and was immediately joined by others plus rifles and grenades. The Jap machine gun hammered out pink and blue tracers. The random bursts swept the hillside, with ricochets deflecting off trees and arching into the sky. *Maybe that's why they use two colors, to make it look like more weapons.*

Henrik didn't fire, as he couldn't see who was who. The Jap machine gun wasn't within his angle of fire.

Nesto belly-crawled between the pair of logs, wiggled into a good shooting position, and opened up on the muzzle flashes, spewing the colored tracers.

Something like "*nagadu*" was shouted. Had to be Jap-talk...for something.

The clouds cleared high up, revealing the moon and shapes darting through the jungle's shadows. A faint pop and another. The firing dwindled, picked up, and dwindled again. Garbled shouts. "*Gasu!*" *Was that Jap talk for gas?* The moon glowed through the trees to illuminate a drifting haze. A cough, another, and at least three men were coughing and gagging lower down the hillside.

The machine gun fired again. Henrik aimed at the origin of the tracers and the flicker of muzzle flash. He squeezed his trigger. The Nip machine gun kept firing. He emptied the magazine and yelled to Nesto to fire on the MG. He put two magazines into the gun position. It abruptly quieted.

More coughing. "That doesn't sound right, partner," said Nesto. "I've never heard anyone coughing and gagging like that."

"Sounds like a cousin who caught the whooping cough," said Henrik.

"Don't hardly ever hear of it in South Texas."

It grew quiet, but occasionally interrupted by a shot or shout; a deep moan.

That unknown word was shouted again. Two more pops and rifles cracked. A Reising went off. It wasn't Nesto's. A deeper rattle. Maybe Snacks' Tommy gun. Then another fit of coughing. Someone gagged out something in Jap-talk and someone else shouted, "Clear outta here!" in words so garbled Henrik couldn't recognize the voice.

"Hey, what's that smell? Like nuts. Shit, my throat's burning!"

Henrik too felt a stinging sensation in his mouth and throat gradually increasing. Nostrils too, and his eyes burned. By habit he tried to run and bounced off a tree to fall on his knees. He couldn't see and flailed his arms. Nesto crashed into him, knocking them both down.

"Wait, wait," Henrik gasped. "Canteens, eyes!"

They poured water over their eyes.

"Don't use it all. Wash your mouth out, don't swallow any." Henrik swished, gargled, and spit. "You okay?"

"Still burns in my throat, just a little," reported Nesto. "What the hell was that?"

"I don't know, maybe some war gas?"

"I remember history classes. Makes me wish I'd not slept through those classes."

They looked at one another. "Gasmasks!"

They'd almost forgotten their masks carried on the left side in a canvas case. The Army-designed mask had a green rubber face-piece with triangular lens, a vacuum-cleaner-style hose in the snout attached to a filter can inside the case. Their face-pieces were already glued to their bristly, sweaty faces. They sat, trying to take shallow breaths and fearing ghastly symptoms. Behind them were occasional faint shouts.

"We need to move," gasped Henrik. "To the water's edge without getting in the open. Need to catch the wind." They almost had to butt heads to speak with the masks.

They found the north trail and just beyond was the beach. A drifting ship burned to the east. They sat on the beach's edge under large-leaved plants.

"How you feel?" asked Henrik.

"Okay. What the hell was that?"

"Some kind of poison gas I guess," croaked Henrik.

"It sure sounded like it hit others—our fellas and Japs."

"It must have been Jap. We didn't load anything like that as far as I saw. How's your eyes?"

"Just stings a little. You?"

"Okay. How about you about-facing and watch our butts?"

They leaned against tree trunks, catching their breath.

"We only got a whiff of whatever it was." Nesto coughed up a gob of mucus.

After some minutes, Henrik grew aware of bobbing shapes among the two-foot waves. Rain sprinkled on the surface. Illuminated by distant flares, it was difficult to make out the bodies from life vests, life rings, and wreckage in vast oil slicks. The receding tide left bodies beached.

Now what?

He remembered reading about the Europeans in the Great War and their use of war gases causing thousands of casualties. The only gases he could remember were chlorine and mustard gas they were taught about at Camp Elliott. He thought probably neither smelled like nuts. No telling what they had breathed. At least it didn't feel like they had suffered any lasting ill effects.

"There's a good breeze here. I guess we can take a whiff of air."

There was a quiet spell.

"Well, flip you to see who goes first," muttered Henrik.

"You have a coin?"

"I spent my last change in the 'gedunk.' I don't wanta B-A-R, I just wanta candy bar."

"Some help you are, Nesto. Rock, paper, scissors."

"Damn, I always lose that one."

"Rock, paper, scissors, shoot. Stone breaks scissors," gleefully whispered Henrik, slamming his fist into his palm.

Nesto muttered, "*Hasta luego*—so long. Tell my mama I went bravely." He gingerly pulled the facemask's chin and gave an exaggerated sniff. He pulled the mask off over his head. "Smells like a rotting jungle."

Henrik removed his. It felt like he was peeling off a layer of skin with it. "Keep your mask ready." *I hope they're not using gas on Guadalcanal...but why wouldn't they?*

"Lucky," a muffled voice said.

"Lollypop."

Rankin came off the trail wearing a mask. Seeing Henrik and Nesto unmasked, he asked, "It's clear?"

"No one's clanged the gong to signal all clear. We're not dead yet," Henrik gibed, referring to the 105mm shell casing hung at Elliott to signal alarms. "What's with the gas—where is everybody?" he asked.

"I was separated from Doc when the gas hit near us. At least we were upwind. I heard someone else shout who sounded like Snacks and then it sounded like he was coughing to death. Heard some Japs too coughing up a storm 'til it died out."

"You heard Nips coughing like that? I'd of thought they'd have masks," said Henrik.

"I found one. Had all his gear and rifle, but no gasmask. Looked like a bad way to go. I checked him with my flashlight. Glazed eyes, mouth gaping open, like he'd died bad, coughing and gagging. His face and hands were discolored."

"No other Nips?" asked Henrik.

"Heard some, both shouting and coughing, like they were warning others. They quieted down too."

In the distance were sudden shots, a ragged shootout of both American and Jap rifles, a Reising gun, a couple of grenades.

"Someone's still kicking," said Nesto. "We're going after them?"

"Not until light," said Rankin. "Trying to move at night in this briar patch is a waste of time. Plus we'd be wearing masks. Can't see gas mist in the dark and trees."

"How'd they spread that gas?" asked Nesto.

They all struggled to stifle occasional raspy coughs.

"You got me. Maybe from that grenade discharger. Let's skate back to the OP and see if anyone's there."

Henrik heard a snap and a pop as the grenade detonated a foot behind the squatting Rankin.

Chapter Thirty-Four

In the grenade's flash Obata glimpsed a fleeting picture of a jungle of lit white tree limbs, branches, and leaves against a stark black sky. He threw himself rearward and rolled facedown, twigs and leaves raining down from the trees. There were no shots, no shouting voices. Had he missed, thrown the grenade too far, or had it bounced off a tree, or hung in a bush? He saw only a Sun-bright, black-rimmed spot. He rose to his feet, shaky and confused.

Where were the lieutenant and Saburo? He had left them someplace. He had to report back. Almost leaving his rifle on the ground, he retrieved it and felt his way through the grabbing brush like witches' skeletal arms. He heard an American voice, but it was some distance away.

After a few minutes of traveling, and knowing he was merely rambling about, he felt himself into a clump of elephant ears. He lay on his side, head in the crook of his arm. He kept his eyes closed, hoping that when he opened them he would have normal vision.

He dreamt of swarming ants on his hands and the bronze-haired American jamming an icepick into his forearm. He frantically swatted away the ants covering his blood-fouled hands and recognized the feel of a scorpion that stung his right forearm. Fully awake, he crab-crawled out of the big leaves. He may have swatted the scorpion, but it could still be alive, and the ants were spreading out in the defense of their mound. He wiped off the ants still on his rifle. The huge white spot had faded, but there was still a worrying smaller white spot hampering his vision. Humiliating himself yet again, he had had to again retrieve his rifle. He spit on the scorpion wound. It hurt no more than a bee sting and he felt only a little swelling.

It made him recall an ancient story. The Gautama Buddha was wandering about Paradise when he stopped at a lotus-filled pond. Through its crystal-clear water he saw the depths of Hell and spied a sinner named Kandata. He was a vicious immoral criminal. While walking through the forest, Kandata had decided not to kill a spider he was about to step on. Moved by Kandata's act of compassion, the Buddha took a spider's silvery thread to Paradise and lowered it into Hell.

In Hell, the Buddha found the many sinners struggling in the Pool of Blood in total darkness save for the light glinting off the Mountain of Spikes. All that could be heard was the screams of the damned. Kandata, in Hell, looked skyward above the pool. He saw the descending spider's thread lowered by the Buddha and grabbed hold with all his might. Climbing, he found the trip from Hell to Paradise was not a short one and tired quickly. Dangling from the middle of the thread, he looked downward to see how far he had come. Realizing he may actually escape from Hell, he laughed with joy. It was short-lived though as he realized others of the damned were climbing up the thread below him. Fearing the thread would snap from the weight of the others, he shouted that the spider's thread was his alone. At that moment the thread broke, and he and the other escaping sinners were cast back into the Pool of Blood.

Kandata condemned himself for being concerned only with his own salvation and not that of others. Sparing the spider had not saved him from Hell. Paradise continued on as it always had. Thus the Buddha continued his wanderings looking for the truly righteous.

Feeling his way, Obata found himself on a path. He squatted under the low tree branches on the beach's edge. There were still occasional flares to the south, but they did not bother him too much. Knowing it was dangerous, he continued on the path anyway. He moved slowly, frequently halting to listen. Once he heard muffled booms and saw more flashes beyond the trees. How far should he venture? The side trail to the settlement. He realized he was close to it. He had subconsciously absorbed terrain features from going this way so often. He listened for some time and then retraced his steps.

Unseen to the south he heard airplanes flying eastward. Not many and they were flying low. Fighters maybe. Who they were, he could only guess. He had lost all sense of time.

His leg bumped into a shin-high tree limb. He immediately stepped to the left and squatted. A flashing sensation of fear jolted through him.

"*Tareka*"—Who are you?

"*Hoshi*"—Star. *It is Kosaku*, thought Obata, *a signalman.*

"*Tsuki*"—Moon, Obata replied.

Kosaku sounded panicky. "I thought I was the only one left. That the rest of the platoon had been picked up and left me behind."

Obata grabbed Kosaku by the arm and dragged him off the trail. "Where is your rifle?" Obata was infuriated. He suddenly understood why corporals had such short tempers. "Stop it, Kosaku. No one has left you. Where is your rifle?"

"I do not know."

"How did you become separated—who were you with?"

"I do not know."

"Did they tell you to place this limb here to warn you of anyone's approach? Come with me and do not make any noise. Do you have any grenades?"

"Yes, two."

"Give them to me."

Kosaku did not argue or ask why.

Obata was afraid that he would fail to use them or throw them at the first sound they heard, to include their own men. "Do you have a bayonet?"

"It is on my rifle."

"You must look for a rifle. Let me know if you find one. Come with me, quietly."

They moved hastily, with Kosaku tripping on every ground root crossing the path. He asked several times where they were. Obata did not answer as he really did not know himself. Kosaku followed, with Obata hoping he might wander off.

Saburo challenged them right at the point where Obata estimated they would reach the spotting station.

They rested after the lieutenant severely chastised Kosaku for losing his rifle. He would be dealt with later.

They had found another water can and Obata refilled their water bottles. He ate another tin of mandarin oranges.

The lieutenant called the three men together. He seemed particularly solemn. "We are in a serious position."

That was something none of the men would have expected from any other officer. Besides seldom informing their soldiers of the actual situation, they never called them together like this.

"We have lost over half our strength and have lost contact with any still alive. We do not know how many are still able-bodied. We are no longer able to communicate with our radio and transmit information on enemy movements, our main mission."

Obata felt the lieutenant was giving them his steely look, but it was too dark to have any effect.

"Tonight, between 2200 and 2400, a Daihatsu landing barge will arrive to resupply us. Instead, we will withdraw from the island. Bring as many of the rations you can carry plus the radio, even if damaged." Obata did not understand how the lieutenant knew this. Maybe it had been in the original plan.

He did not mention that the amount the three of them could carry was minimal. "We will move to a position near the plotting station and avoid any Americans remaining here." Kosaku recovered the radio and other equipment and readied it for travel.

Obata was certainly not sorry about leaving this nightmarish island. He did wonder if he might be returning to be disciplined for failing to complete the mission. Most likely the lieutenant and he alone would invite any chastisement from his commander. Soldiers only followed orders and were not held to blame for their commander's shortcomings.

The lieutenant summoned Obata. "You will conduct a patrol around this position every hour in search of any signs of Americans. Be as silent and vigilant as you can. Find a rifle for Kosaku. Also, look for the sergeant."

Obata bowed, and after a short spell of simply listening, set out for his first circuit. He ventured up the path and found a rifle. A round was in the chamber and two in the magazine. He returned it to their position and Kosaku's battle spirit rose, even if it was not that of the Tokugawa Shogunate victors of the year 1600 Battle of Sekigahara.

He continued his creeping patrol. Further up the path he heard a faint noise and a change in the birds' chirping. He stepped to the path's side and assumed a crouch. It was Shuzo carrying his grenade discharger, as relaxed as a merchant man on his morning stroll. He was not even startled by Obata's challenge. He led him back to the position. At this rate they might recover enough stray soldiers to give a credible fight.

Again moving up the path, admittedly not as cautiously as he had previously, he decided to move into the trees and listen for a short time. The birds were still agitated, chirping and squawking. He would pick a site from which to watch the path and cover the surrounding jungle.

He continued forward slowly, three or four steps, then listened. Chirping increased. A slight bend in the trail. *Here comes yet another man.* He could see his rifle and it was whipped to the shoulder, and the man with bronze hair was aiming at him. The rifle cracked. Obata's helmet was clipped, momentarily stunning him. He flung himself to the right into a cluster of saplings. Before he could fire, the American fired two shots and was gone.

Obata reloaded, crouching low. Two more shots were fired, with one bullet snapping through the saplings. Minutes passed. No shots, no sounds of movement, and no one came to his support from their position just a short distance down the path.

The bronze-haired American was frightening. He seemed to be alone and was a persistent hunter. Maybe he actually was a hunter, like Ikuo, the sea lion hunter from Hokkaido. Unfortunately, Ikuo had been killed early on. Moving at first cautiously, Obata hurried back to their position and reported to the lieutenant. He ordered all of them to remain alert in all directions around their position.

"With the honorable lieutenant's permission, I will continue the patrol around the perimeter and hunt for the American."

"Very well. Return by sunset."

Obata took that as an order to pursue the bronzed hunter. The lieutenant did not have to remind him that the barge would not wait for him. The scorpion wound felt about the same but was swelling more.

Chapter Thirty-Five

At first Henrik didn't know if he'd been knocked unconscious, was dazed, or possibly dead. Gradually, his senses came back to him. Birds were still squawking. His head rang like out-of-tune chimes. His forehead ached where his rifle's forearm had hit, his entire body throbbing from the grenade's blast. He felt wetness on himself, especially his face. There wasn't any of the expected rifle fire or the sound of attackers busting through the brush. Sparks seemed to float inside his eyes.

Feeling about his head and torso, he concluded they were okay. Fragments may have hit his left leg and arm. Nothing serious, he assessed.

"Nesto. What the hell?"

"You okay?"

Rankin's gutted remains lay mangled in the mud. He'd been practically sitting on the grenade.

"Jesus, look at us." He didn't speak of the smell.

Blood-splattered Nesto teetered on his knees, his face contorted in anguish. He collapsed face forward.

"Get up, get up, Nesto! Don't do this now."

Henrik rolled him over, but remembered his rifle and searched through the leaves for it. Found! He looked around frantically for approaching Japs. "Where you hit, buddy?"

"Right leg, upper, and right side."

He ripped open the torn trousers and the shirt buttons. "Several fragment wounds. Can't tell but not too deep." Jap grenades mostly produced small fragments. He took out Nesto's and Rankin's field dressings, sprinkled all the sulfa powder, and tightly secured the dressings.

He made sure he had his rifle and found Nesto's Reising. He gingerly searched Rankin's torn remnants. The map was shredded and bloody—worthless. He found a half-dozen intact rifle clips and a grenade. The compass and canteen were destroyed, but the flashlight actually worked.

Slinging the rifle and Reising, he dragged the groaning Nesto some yards. "You really got it in for me dragging me like this, *pendejo*. I hope that corpsman shows up."

The only thing Henrik could do was leave Nesto in a hiding place and come back for him.

"*¡Qué cabrón!* You're going to leave me here alone?"

"We don't have a choice, buddy. There aren't any noncoms, we don't know how many of our boys are still kicking, and we don't know how many Japs there are and where they are."

He worked Nesto into a cluster of three trees in a dense patch of elephant ears. As best he could tell, one could walk right past him and not see him. He leaned a leafless limb against one of the trees as a marker.

"I'm going to find any of our people and be on the lookout for chow and water."

"Got it."

He set the Reising in Nesto's lap and took his spare pair of socks out of his haversack. "In case you start bleeding. You're not now, just a little. Don't move any more than you have to and don't do any one-man ambushes."

"Don't worry, man, I ain't starting no trouble. I plan on getting out of this if you don't forget me."

"I'm not leaving you here. I mean that, buddy."

"That's what I'm counting on. Look for some Reising mags and ammo while you're out there hunting cans of hash. I'm low."

"Will do. Maybe I can find some tacos."

"There'll be an extra tip if you do."

They firmly shook hands and Henrik slipped into the brush. He had something else to do. That Jap kid he kept running into. He actually had a telescope on his rifle. He'd not expected that. He didn't know the Nips had snipers, or at least ones with telescopes. That made him more dangerous. He'd be on the lookout for him.

Henrik had no idea of a plan or even in which direction to go. He decided to head to the island's east end, as slowly and quietly as possible. Hs eyes were tired. His feet felt like they'd never been removed from boots, like they were part of him.

I wonder if that Nip kid had been a hunter too. Do Nips even hunt? They mostly eat fish and rice.

***

Henrik spotted movement on the north trail two or three times. He kept his distance until he decided there was only one man, sometimes two, going back and forth. He knew not their destinations and he had no idea what they were up to. Since it was no more than two men at any one time, he decided to do something about it.

Soon after two more men passed, heading down the trail, he moved into a spread of three-foot ferns beside a thick-trunked tree. He was only a few feet off the trail and mostly hidden by a low pile of green moss-covered limbs. He felt secure enough in the darkness.

He soon heard a whispered voice. Then another. Two men were coming down the trail, maybe the same ones as before. He could take them. When they passed he'd rise up, taking cover behind a thick-trunked tree. They passed, one in front of the other. Both had bayonetted rifles. He stepped toward the tree, avoiding the piled limbs, then onto the trail around the tree. He rotated his rifle's silent safety lever, snap aimed, and squeezed the trigger. The bullet struck the trailing man between his shoulder blades. He didn't contemplate for a moment the "dishonor" of back-shooting a man and how underhanded it was considered in Western movies. His fleeting mind had considered that one bullet might take out both soldiers. As recruits, they'd argued if that was possible but had no sensible way of testing the theory.

The lead man spun, raising his rifle only to greet a bullet in the chest. The momentum of his rapid turn carried him into the trail-side brush. Henrik reloaded, slung his rifle, and rushed to the soldier's body. He plucked the field dressings from the tunic's inside pocket and unbuckled the belt to pull off the water bottle. He rolled the second body over and the man slashed a fighting knife, nicking his jaw and collarbone. Grabbing the man's right arm gripping the knife, Henrik jammed a knee into his crotch and reached back, pulling his Marble's knife to slash the Nip's left forearm. He twisted and slashed at the Nip's knife wrist, plunging the blade four times under the ribs. *His eyes...* The man went limp with a final raspy gasp, and quivered in death. He only now realized the Nip had fancy red collar tabs with a gold bar and two gold stars—no typical twenty-year-old rifleman. Henrik got the canteen off and found the field dressings plus three grenades. Yanking off the belt, a revolver fell out. It was a .38 Smith & Wesson like the corpsman carried. He didn't bother with the Jap haversacks.

Trying to stuff grenades into his utilities' big skirt pockets, he dropped one. He unslung his rifle to meet the gaze of the young sniper bursting out of the brush. The Nip fired the telescoped rifle from underarm and missed. In his left hand Henrik held his rifle, dropped it, fumbled the Nip grenade, and threw it under-armed as he tumbled off the trail. He ducked as the grenade boomed and twigs flew. He rolled to his feet, grabbing his rifle, and the Nip's rifle cracked. Birds screeched. He ran, bounding through the brush to the beach. It was high tide and he splashed through calf-deep water and shoved his way through hampering limbs overhanging the water. He saw Carley floats and life-jacketed bodies bobbing near shore and under the drooping limbs. After some yards he ducked into the brush like a kid chased by red wasps. Continuing uphill as fast as he could stumble, he ran until it felt as if his heart would burst. A panicked sensation swept through him. *Don't get caught!* Flopping onto his back, he gulped air at a startling rate. It seemed he'd never suck in enough air and that he'd suffocate. After many minutes he pushed himself up to rest on his elbows. What had just happened—had it really happened? It seemed dreamlike or more like a nightmare. He'd done everything by instinct and in some unfathomable manner he recalled. He'd done things correctly according to some molded training dictate, but at the same time he'd done something wrong, even evil. *When I put the blade into the Nip, the look in his eyes... Did he see his immediate death or was it simply the realized dread of what was happening to him? Was that sniper the same one as before? He had a scope. Is there more than one sniper? They all look alike.* His face cuts stung. Lots of blood. He reminded himself that face wounds bleed a lot.

He smeared swarming gnats off his sticky face and swallowed some water. *Nesto! Where did I leave him?*

His legs still wobbly and his lungs still wanting for air, he circled back in search of the three trees landmark he was previously so certain he could easily find. He tore open a Japanese dressing and wiped his face.

The sun was low and the shadows deep. He had come to expect this and knew he had to find Nesto soon. If he found his buddy, they might have to move to a new position and he didn't want to do that in the dark. Concealing oneself within vegetation in the dark was difficult and one couldn't tell if he was truly hidden.

He circled back to the trail, creeping slowly toward it, and found a position from which he could see the two bodies. He decided to briefly dry gulch anyone investigating. After half an hour, with time running out, he decided it was more important to find Nesto. He sneaked out of his position and back to the area he thought he'd left Nesto.

As he slogged his way up the low hill he heard a hiss and the standard challenge: "Lucky." Henrik crawled into the nest on hands and knees.

"Where you been, man?" whispered an anxious Nesto. "Someone's been snooping round. Thought it was you at first."

"You scared me half to death, buddy." Henrik didn't mention that it may not have been him, but a Jap passing through.

"You find anyone?" Nesto asked. "I heard shots and a grenade. Scared me you might not be coming back."

"I nailed two Nips and got this." Henrik pulled the S&W from a skirt pocket. It crossed his mind that he'd said, "nailed two Japs" with no more concern than "smushed two roaches."

"Doc's?"

"Most likely." He opened the cylinder. One of the six rounds had been fired. "Keep it, you're low on ammo."

"Bad luck to carry a dead man's weapon."

"Worse luck to be out of ammo. Take it, meathead." He gave him a Jap grenade too.

"What happened to your face?"

"I think it was a Jap noncom. He thought I was too pretty, I guess." He wiped off more blood. Sweat salt stung like mad.

They were silent for a spell until Henrik said, "Look, I think there are Japs still looking for us. We don't know what's happened to the rest of the section, there are no NCOs, and we're not reporting anything. We're done here. I've got an idea how to get out of here."

"I'm for that, pard," said Nesto, "but we're not abandoning our post, pulling out without orders?"

"We're not doing any good this way," mused Henrik. "We can at least bring back some intel."

"Yeah, I guess it's okay," said Nesto. "How do we do this surrounded by water?"

"We head for the beach."

"So it doesn't count anymore that I can walk further than I can swim?"

Chapter Thirty-Six

Sergeant Toshio and Private Shuzo of the grenade discharger crew lay dead before Obata's eyes. Shuzo had been shot in the back and Toshio partially disemboweled by the barbarians. They had been looted of their water bottles and, surprisingly, their field dressings too. Maybe they had wounded men. Their rifles had been thrown into the brush. He carried both back and gave one to Kosaku who accepted it gratefully. The lieutenant ordered him to immediately clean it.

Obata crept back up the path. He felt too exposed and decided to turn into the trees and search the higher ground. He did not like doing this on his own. He was no tracker, but he had seen enough footpaths on this island to at least know that someone had tracked through here. Probably both Japanese and Americans. He worked his way up the hill and then back down toward the path. It was a slow process. Once he thought he saw movement in the brush on the hillside. He watched and waited. Nothing. Then there was something. Movement. Not just the rare touch of breeze sneaking under the trees.

He crouched, his gaze fixed on where he thought he had seen something. He peered at the place though his telescope, then searched the fringe areas. It was not easy as the telescope had a narrow field of vision.

A rifle cracked, and bark flew from the tree he rested against. He dropped low and fired, unsure of his target's position. More rounds cracked back at him, a slight pause, and then five more. They smacked the tree and clipped through the brush, forcing him to hug the ground. He had waited too long. The American would have reloaded by now. He had lost his chance to climb to his feet and dart to better cover. He could see a thick-trunked tree just five or six meters to his right. Aiming roughly in the American's direction, he fired two shots, leapt to his feet, took three bounding strides, and hit the ground rolling. Then he fast low-crawled to the tree, his rifle held in the crook of his arms, digging his elbows in.

He was truly afraid to raise his head, even for a fraction of a second.

A grenade detonated, then another, both to his front. A red grenade landed a meter to his right. Death had caught him. He reached for the grenade and it sputtered vivid sparks of flaring molten particles of aluminum and iron. Some struck his arm. He rolled to the left. Even with damp vegetation, everything the sparks touched ignited. Flames rose, emitting streams of thin white smoke. The sparks spewed further. He thought it was a smoke grenade when it suddenly flared and thicker gray smoke spewed, along with more popping sparks.

Desperately hoping the smoke would screen him, Obata rose to his feet and ran downhill toward the north path in a near panic. Rifle shots cracked over his head. At the bottom of the rise, he slid in the damp leaves to a stop. Rolling over and peering up the slope, he saw only murky tress veiled by thin smoke. He threw a grenade upslope with no idea if he was at all close to the American. It only flew a scant short distance. The grenade banged and he reloaded. He laid there trying to catch his breath and listen for Americans coming down the hill. He had better watch the trail from both directions. Any sounds were drowned by the screeching and chirping of birds in flight.

Obata nested in a clump of brush on the trail's south side. Having waited over fifteen minutes, he decided the time had come to hunt for the American. Just then he heard a noise down the path. It was Kazuo of the grenade discharger crew. Besides the 5cm launcher, he carried a pistol and rifle.

"*Konnichi wa*"—Good afternoon. "I can use your help."

"The lieutenant sent me."

"Well armed, I see."

"I have only three fragmentation rounds and two white phosphorous for the discharger."

Obata told him that there were at least two Americans and the lieutenant had ordered him to find and kill them, if in not so many words.

Superior Private Kazuo outranked Obata, but he deferred to Obata as he was more familiar with the terrain and what the Americans were doing.

"What caused the fire?" he asked Obata.

"The American threw some type of fire grenade." From what they could see up the hill, through the trees was a rapidly creeping burn on one side. A branch of the fire was crawling downhill too where it made a turn onto a ridge. The wind currents were tricky around the island and the prevailing winds were mostly east-northeast. Obata was somewhat familiar with the behavior of winds around small islands and irregular coastlines from coastal fishing. He had seen and once even helped fight deliberately set brushfires, which farmers set for their burned-field agriculture. He knew too that fires travel uphill faster than downhill.

Looking at Kazuo, he asked, "Did the lieutenant tell you we are to be evacuated tonight?"

"Yes."

"I think the American sniper, a hunter, is on this end of the island. We can use the fire to trap him and hunt him down."

"Is that not dangerous?"

"We are soldiers and anticipate danger. It would be more dangerous allowing him to roam free and shoot at us as we board the landing barge."

Kazuo nodded.

"Kazuo, watch the right side of the hill and I will watch the left. Shoot immediately if you see an American. Maybe we cannot hit him, but we can keep him moving." They took up firing positions beside trees. "A man firing from behind a tree will shoot around its right side. When you fire at the tree hiding him, shoot at its left side—the side he is firing from. It is natural to shoot at the side opposite from which he is shooting."

After waiting and watching for a time, Obata motioned Kazuo for them to advance. Moving slowly, they worked their way up the north-side slope. The fire was spreading as the sun and wind dried the treetops.

There were a couple of false sightings owing to shifting limbs, shadows, and smoke. Then a man stood upright in the brush. A second man appeared. They were maybe fifty meters distant, a rare occurrence in the dense vegetation—two men together for just moments. Obata did not think they could see Kazuo and himself. They were moving downslope, probably from the north shore to avoid the flames. Its spread appeared to have slowed. Nonetheless, the fire was crawling toward the beach.

Obata and Kazuo kept moving until they reached the north shore trail. Obata covered its westward portion and Kazuo the eastward.

"I see one of them," shouted Kazuo. He had unslung the rifle and grenade discharger and crouched on a patch of sandy beach.

"Where?"

"Behind that two-by-four-meter raft five or six meters off the beach."

Why would he go out into the water and use a raft for cover? How did he get there? He did not know what it was made of. Certainly nothing that could stop a rifle bullet.

Kazuo readied the discharger.

"What are you doing?"

"Blasting him out from behind that raft. I have two white phosphorous rounds." He handed them to Obata. "When I am ready, arm the grenade and drop the round down the tube."

Obata had done this in training, but they were dummy projectiles dropped down the tube and not actually fired. The phosphorous rounds were black-painted round-nosed projectiles with white bands.

Kazuo perched on a knee, holding the discharger at a 45-degree angle with his boot bracing the curved base plate while his left hand held the barrel. He yanked the leather trigger strap, and with a pop the round arched into the sky to dive into the jungle behind the grounded raft. A flowering burst of dense white smoke sprayed particles of burning phosphorous. They would burn through human flesh and if, in panic, the sticky material was smeared, it would continue to burn on both the skin and palms. Particles hissed into the water, sizzling then burning out. Its smell was rotten-egg putrid. "We set the jungle aflame so he cannot escape by that route."

Obata dropped in the second round and it landed on the thin beach further behind the raft. Adjusting the elevation, a learned skill, Kazuo said, "We will fire the last three fragmentation rounds to kill or wound him."

The fragmentation rounds were simply hand grenades modified with a booster charge screwed into the base. Obata pulled the trigger loop to release the primer's safety cap and flicked it off. He did not strike the primer on a solid object to ignite the delay fuse. Instead, the round was dropped down the mortar tube and launched. The recoil activated the grenade's firing pin to ignite the eight- to nine-second delay. The explosion sent a thin column of sandy water four meters high. They fired two more rounds, making slight range adjustments. They did not manage to plant a round on the raft's far side where the American hid, but were close.

There was no movement beyond the raft except the smoldering jungle with hungry, leaping flames. The fires merged, flaring into a larger inferno. Obata readied his rifle, just in case.

Chapter Thirty-Seven

Henrik lay in a puddle of water, the sun warming his back, taking in the screams, splashes, shouts, and babbling voices. Everything slowed down. Kids shrieked, moms shouted for the little ones to stay off diving boards, and older kids goaded them to make the three-foot leap. Washington Municipal Swimming Pool was a luxury in Depression-troubled Missouri, the result of one of Roosevelt's Public Works Administration projects. Four years after it was built in 1936 Pastor Schäfer had approved Sunday school swimming trips. He justified it as a means of introducing youths to the wider modern world.

It had been the previous summer of 1940 that Karen Hathaway and her girlfriends showed up at the pool wearing the latest swimwear fashion straight from The Famous-Barr department store in St. Louis. The close-fitting suits were fringed with little short skirts displaying bare arms and legs. Karen's suit was a soft golden brown, highlighting her blonde locks. The girl's appearance turned things upside-down. The suits were startling in rural Missouri, but not all that much more revealing than the familiar looser-fitting suits with shorts-like thigh coverings rather than skirts.

"Well hi, Henrik!"

Startled by the perky voice, he sat up and was immediately taken by the flashy blonde through his chlorine-stung eyes. "Hello to you." She was wearing the same swimsuit as last year. Times were still tough, no new suits.

"I didn't expect you here today, being Sunday and all." She stood in the shallow end and was still otherwise dry as she tucked escaping strands under her close-fitting woven yellow bathing cap.

The manager had had a fit the first time they'd shown up declaring, "Hush my mouth, we forgot our caps." Girls had to wear caps for the manager's fear of hair clogging the filters. Henrik noticed the audience of fellas lining the poolside.

"Church trip. Happened because some parents wanted to visit the pool too. Karen, I've not seen you since the Fourth of July Festival," Henrik said, shading his eyes. "Your suit looks swell." He hoped that wasn't too forward. *Well, it does look swell, more than swell.*

She smiled brightly. "Race you," the golden girl shouted, turning to kick-off from the pool's side. She launched herself and he scrambled to his feet to dive in. He almost caught up with her, almost. He admired her gumption. He couldn't convince her he hadn't let her win.

If I ever make it home, I just may look her up anyway. I can't see how Clarence Baily can keep a spunky girl like Karen interested for long, the 4-F pogue.

The poolside screams, splashes, and shouts were a figment of Henrik's mind—a diversion from the awful reality he found himself in. Gobs of wet sand showered on him. It came to him that some kind of explosions had burst all about. He smelled seawater, cork, and the sour odor of some chemical—different from the poison gas they had experienced earlier.

He was lying on the shore. Folds in his damp utilities held clumped damp sand. The tide was out, and he was beached beside a seven-by-twelve-foot Carley float. The float was at the high-tide line and partly under the shore-edged tree and brush. How long had he been there? The cork float's doped canvas covering was peppered by tiny fragment holes. That didn't affect its flotation. A few small fragments had hit his legs and left arm. Just nicks. It gradually occurred that he was here for a reason. He wanted one of the floats, a smaller one, bobbing in the waves. They held rations, first aid gear, and water. Where was Nesto? He'd left him…someplace. Nesto could barely walk and irrationally dreaded Henrik abandoning him. *Not likely.*

He felt a thump strike the float. Okay, someone was shooting at him. From down the beach, he guessed. He started to take a look over the float, then decided that might not be a good ideal. He'd be an easy target. He had no idea how many Japs there were. He topped off his magazine. *Okay, why not?* he thought. He'd seen it done in Western movies. No sticks nearby. He unsheathed his bayonet and pulled his cover from a pocket. He set the cap on the end of the bayonet and slowly raised it just above the float. The wind was toward the Japs, he guessed, and he didn't hear the two answering shots. One made his cap jump, and the second knocked a chunk of cork off the float.

That first shot was dead on. Is it the same Jap sniper?

He thought about using the decoy cover again and darting into the vegetation after the Jap's shot. He didn't. Thinking it would take the Jap by surprise to get up and go, he launched himself into the brush. His legs were so stiff that he slipped and staggered as he took off. Another shot thumped the float.

He tripped on vines and rolled behind a tree. Under the drooping limbs he could just see the water's edge, and no further than three or four yards around him. The approaching jungle fire was some yards away. He'd not realized it had moved closer. Propelled by the breeze, the flames and smoke stung his eyes. He coughed. *Nesto!* He darted up the low slope and saw him waving from behind a fallen log. He thought he'd left Nesto further away.

"I can't move my legs, Handyman. Leave me here and you run for it!"

Henrik knew he didn't mean that—to leave him behind. He could hear the fear in his voice. No shame in that. No one in their right mind would want to be left on an island full of Japs. The wall of flames was avalanching down the slope, and the sun- and wind-dried treetops were bursting into fireballs. There had been barely any rain through the day. It was hard to breathe. The angry roar and crackling pops drowned their voices.

"Get up and get moving! Only thirty yards to the water." Henrik lifted Nesto and half-dragged him toward the shoreline. The burning trees seemed to dwindle. They were in a low area of soggy ground and taro pits. The blaze slowed, branched off to the southwest. He sat Nesto in a taro pit. Ducking under the limbs, he made his way to the shore and slid back into the water. On hands and knees, he made it to the float shrouded by dense smoke. He shoved and rocked the float across the wet sand. The water was only inches deep, with the tide beginning to flood. He had to get it away from the shore.

Nesto's Reising gun rattled repeated bursts. Henrik darted back through the trees. Between the smoke and long afternoon shadows, he could barely see anything.

He saw Nesto wave. The smoke and shadows made it difficult to stay oriented.

"I heard a shot and saw a shape running through the trees," shouted Nesto.

"Hang on. I'm getting some gear off the Carley float."

In the thickening gray smoke, he yanked releases and tossed the galvanized containers onto the narrow beach. They held all they needed except ammo. He didn't want the float to drift away with the tide or a wind change.

From the island's distant east end a faint crackle of shots and grenades arose. It dawned on him what it was. Their ammo and grenades, chow too, hidden there were being consumed by flames.

Henrik cleaned and bandaged their wounds while there was still light. They ate a couple of small cans of lifeboat rations, which were as bland as he'd been warned. The pemmican was okay. The Boy Scouts back at home had made it to show how Indians lived when traveling. It was made of dried venison and berries, and tallow. Dessert was chocolate tablets.

Scanning the burned-off hillside after sunset was heartening in that there were small spot fires, burning embers, and occasional flare ups scattered about. While there were significant burned swaths, most of the island was still smoky green. *Time to get outta this place.*

Chapter Thirty-Eight

§ Obata §

Obata had seen the American dart out of the trees and flop behind one of the two-by-four-meter rafts. *Why did he do that?* It was an exposed position. They had fired the remaining discharger rounds at the raft, but they saw occasional movement there. Kazuo, with the now useless discharger, had joined him. They fired a rifle shot once in a while to get a reaction. Kazuo had a 7.7mm rifle and it seemed to shoot through the raft's hull with ease, yet the raft did not appear to be sinking. Even the light 6.5mm bullet seemed to penetrate both sides. Obata had fired off a magazine, with the hits making an odd thump. He had started to tell Kazuo to abandon the discharger, but they had more ammunition in the base camp. It was not his place to give such an order. Kazuo would find his own way there. It was near the site where the evacuating barge was supposed to arrive. They needed to be back there before 2200; earlier to be safe.

Obata's position provided a view of much of the lower vegetated slopes as he was looking below much of the leafy portions.

The American was firing back, but cautiously, only a shot at a time. Obata kept an eye on the raft in case the American attempted to flee. There were other abandoned rafts, some damaged, what looked like bodies, and other floating debris.

Then there was movement from behind the raft. He nudged Kazuo. He made out a cap, took careful aim knowing the man's head would be exposed only for moments, and fired. The cap flew to the side. Something was left exposed—a stick? It too disappeared. *Was I fooled by a decoy?* He needed to be careful. Is it possible that he was again facing the bronze-haired sniper?

There was a great deal of smoke and the sinking sun cast long shadows. The fire began to die except for occasional flare-ups. He and Kazuo fired random shots. The Americans appeared to be moving and firing from different positions. There were even short machine gun bursts. Obata wondered if there might be more than two Americans.

Much to his surprise, in the gathering dusk it appeared one of the Americans had dashed onto the beach. He caught white splashes as the American ran and flopped into the water. He blindly fired to be answered by a machine gun burst.

Why did the American go back into the water? To escape aboard a raft? As far as he knew the abandoned rafts only had paddles and were slow going. It was so exposed, even in the growing darkness. Then it came to him that with the setting sun and darkness, they had to make it back to their own base camp and prepare for the landing barge's arrival in just a few hours.

Obata contemplated the meaning of their mission to this point. They had accomplished little, nothing really. A few Americans had been killed along with some Japanese. They had not reported the approach of enemy ships or airplane flights. What value were the few weather reports? Certainly others in the area were making such reports. Was it honorable to withdraw without having defeated the enemy? That had not been part of their mission. They had only injured the evasive enemy. According to the lieutenant they were now under orders to withdraw. He had no imaginable right to question an officer. As always, he decided to follow orders, precisely as demanded of a soldier of the Emperor.

The Americans fired a few more rifle shots along with sporadic machine gun bursts. They must have sufficient ammunition. He saw at least one shadowy man rushing through the dark trees and flickering embers. He disappeared. The increase in firing might mean they were going to attack or possibly withdraw.

Obata crawled to Kazuo. "We should return to the base camp and wait for the barge. Go on ahead. I will cover you and then check the area to ensure the enemy is not following. Take your rifle and the discharger," he added when he saw it lying on the ground.

Kazuo's farewell and "I will see you at Yasukuni" seemed not to be heartfelt. He trotted up the path, fading into the shadows. Maybe Obata would meet him at the Yasukuni, the fabled memorial of the war dead. He was not ready to be a national deity. Nor was he ready for what else he might have to do.

Obata was alone on the path in a darkening jungle. American marines were no doubt closing in on him. He should follow Kazuo. He wanted to run. Instead, he crouched and crept down the trail. He had to be quiet…and invisible. He wished to evaporate.

§ Henrik §

Henrik crouched to the side of the trail. He listened to the freshening breeze, muffled distant booms of naval cannonades, occasional cracks and pops of the nearby dying fires, errant star shells, and sweeping searchlight beams trying to silhouette opposing ships. Other than fleeting glimpses of a Jap or two, he had not seen anything ashore for almost an hour. There'd been no Nip shots either.

He had stayed beside the float to make sure it didn't drift off. The water's night-chill kept him awake. He kept a grip on the float's lifesaving rope and an eye on the trail. His eyes automatically swung in the direction of any flickering embers and flare-ups as potential sneaky Japs. He hoped Nesto wasn't too nervous, having not heard from him for so long. He was plainly concerned about being left behind or something happening to Henrik and stranding him there. Henrik would try not to let that happen. Down the trail he thought he spied movement, but it looked to be a breeze-blown batch of burning leaves. They fizzled out on reaching the ground.

Henrik decided to fetch Nesto once he had made a last circular patrol of his piece of the island. *His piece?* This would never be "his" island, but his mind told him it was the same as a piece of ground he'd staked out for a makeshift deer blind.

§ Obata §

Obata knelt on the path's edge. It was difficult to retain a sense of orientation in the smoky haze, flickering flares, and increasing ash as the breeze picked up. The sparks reminded him of fireflies, evoking feelings of nostalgia for the Japanese summer. It may be August in Japan, but here it was considered "winter," regardless of the ceaseless heat and humidity. Were there even fireflies here? He was surprised the lieutenant had not summoned him back to their base camp. The more he thought about it, the more concerned he became. Had he been forgotten? Had something happened to the lieutenant and the remaining soldiers? Possibly more Americans may have arrived.

Distant naval guns boomed and parachute flares drifted about, casting winking crisscrossing shadows over the hillside of burnt tree skeletons. He stooped beside the path, scanning the ruined landscape for movement. While mostly burned over, there were numerous unburned and partly burned brush and trees. Something moved. A limb tumbled off a big bush. Snapping his rifle to his shoulder, he relaxed. Peering through the telescope's narrow field of vision was difficult in the smoke and darkness. Something moved again—a hulked shape skulked slowly, hesitantly, on the same side of the path. Obata raised his rifle, shouldered it, and followed the drifting shape away from the path, not toward it as he had expected. He awaited the form's return.

§ Henrik §

Enough of this, thought Henrik. *It's time to get out of this place. Somehow.* A bus ride from Marthasville to Washington, Missouri, cost a dime. Of course, as luck would have it, he didn't have two nickels to rub together. Nothing looked right in the smoke, ash, and ruin. He didn't like it one bit snooping about the burnt area, stirring up a lot of ash. A faint hiss came from a scorched tree. He'd found Nesto quickly enough this time.

"I was half worried that if I found you, I'd be riddled by your Reising."

"Nothing to worry about. I shot it dry."

"You still have that .38?"

"Five rounds."

"Let's go," said Henrik. "Keep on the lookout for any stray rifles."

"How we doing this, partner?"

"I think I have a plan."

"I'm encouraged…"

"On your feet, marine." He pulled Nesto upright. "We've just got to reach the water. You can swim, can't you?"

"If I can't, I'm a fast learner."

"Maybe you shouldn't have told me that."

"For real, partner, I'm actually an Olympic swimmer, really."

"I bet. Where'd you swim in South Texas?"

"Irrigation canals after hurricane flooding."

He set Nesto down to sling his rifle across his back. This made him essentially weaponless. Hauling him up, Henrik draped Nesto's left arm over his shoulders. He dragged Nesto more than supported his effort to stumble along on his own.

"I don't wantta ask, but are we swimming home and can a Missouri farm boy even swim?" he managed, gritting his teeth.

"We've got three fishing ponds and a public pool. Just shut up and try and walk, meathead. I'm not carrying you."

They stepped onto the trail as a drifting star shell burned out and then fizzled into a burning gasp in its last moments. A shrub twenty feet away moved then morphed into a Jap, his telescoped rifle pointed at Henrik's face. An imagined bayonet plunged through his heart.

§ Obata §

Right before Obata a misshapen figure crouched, hideously displaying its malformed naked body. His mind yelled it was a sleep-deprived delusion. The green mottled creature, filthy shaggy hair, crept on clawed feet flicking its snaky tongue. An *akaname*—filth-licker—found lurking in ill-kept bathrooms and dilapidated public bathhouses. His mind was exhausted and fear lashed through him.

The creature became two—two humans, not an *akaname*. One was helping the other to his feet. A feebly burning star shell ember drifted over, casting enough light for Obata to make out the glisten of bronze hair. Both were unarmed; the bronze hunter, as he thought of him now, had slung his rifle across his back. No one moved. The hunter pulled his comrade to his feet but had to support the obviously wounded man. Obata's rifle was aimed, loaded, ready to fire. He merely had to squeeze the trigger. The flare's light revealed the wounded man held a pistol.

§ Henrik §

"Tell me your hand-cannon's out," whispered Henrik.
"It is."
"Well?"
"He's got us dead to rights, partner. We got ourselves in a Mexican standoff."
Henrik had never heard the phrase but knew exactly what it meant. He couldn't help but give a laugh of sorts, making the Jap uncomfortably shift his aim to Nesto. Was this the Jap sniper he'd stalked? He didn't look so fierce until the dwindling flare light illuminated his desperate eyes.

§ Obata §

With weapons aimed at each other at such close range, Obata felt the nausea of certain death. Then the sniper actually laughed at something the wounded, pistol-armed man said. Were the Americans that fearless?

The flare flickered out. Obata took a tentative step backwards, begging not to trip. He slid into a shallow gulley and was embraced in black gloom. He frantically looked back, and the two enemy soldier-creatures were gone. His mind still envisioned the grotesque *akaname* slithering in waste. He did not think of firing in their direction or throwing a grenade. Then it occurred to him they were only soldiers like him, one wounded with his comrade trying to save him, as he had done for Takeo.

He tottered down the path but had to slow as a sudden lightheadedness threatened to topple him. The ship battle in the channel must be over. There were fewer flares, flashes, and booms.

§ Henrik §

Reaching the chosen float, he dragged Nesto onto its slat bottom sloshing with water. As long as there was smoke mist to hide them in the overcast darkness, it was relatively safe. Henrik had drawn a smaller, five-by-eight-foot Carley float astern and tossed the gear he'd picked from the larger float. The smaller Carleys had little gear stowed.

"One man can't row this thing in a straight line," complained Nesto.

"Paddle, not row. Use a paddle as a rudder to keep me straight." He triple-looped the bow painter over his shoulders. It didn't work. He couldn't tow the float by swimming. Moving to the stern, he clung onto the lifesaving line and kicked to propel them. Nesto moved to the bow to guide Henrik. They would have to kick their way around the island and head south for over eight miles, passing Buena Vista Island. They covered over half the distance across an open channel with bursts of wind and sudden showers. "Let's hope I don't make a wrong turn," Henrik quipped.

"I'll beat you to death with a paddle," rasped Nesto.

Thankfully, the current was in their favor and the breeze feeble. Henrik periodically rested. A large fish bumped his leg. A very real terror of sharks plunged into him. At another point jelly fish caressing his legs inflicted stings, and a new fear took root.

All sense of time evaporated. Saltwater caused a ceaseless burn. Henrik tried to keep his eyes closed, but in spite of the unrelenting blackness, he could not. Closed eyes only served to disorient his sense of direction. At one point he panicked as the sensation they were propelling themselves into the endless open ocean seized him. They may well have, if not for the infrequent white Japanese flare shells and yellow-tinted American star shells to the east. His wounds and abrasions, crotch and armpits burned ceaselessly. His legs ached even when he simply drifted much less feebly kicked. The pain spread to his hips, back, and shoulders. His legs were numb, but at the same time cramping. Saltwater all but swelled shut his eyes. His face felt puffy and itchy.

At one point he could hear Nesto's befuddled voice sing-songing, *"Hut-Sut Rawlson on the rillerah...."*

Henrik threw up from ingesting saltwater. Parched, his throat screamed for freshwater. He drank from the water cans in the raft, but his churning stomach rejected it. At times he alternated between disoriented and nauseated, or both. His shoulders felt so knotted he had to resist the urge to let go the rope. He scanned the east sky for flares simply to convince himself which way was up. With his lips and eyes swollen shut, he struggled to see flares, which became less and less frequent. He realized that perhaps dawn was approaching as flares on the horizon were barely noticed.

Henrik came to, lying on his back. He resisted rolling over because of the belly pain, but he was forced to as he threw up brackish water. On forearms, he lifted himself from the wavelets washing pure white sand. The sun glared over the scattered rows of abandoned native huts nestled among the brush and palms. He heard the fresh breeze, waves, and the rustle of palm fronds.

The Carley float was some twenty feet behind him. He must have crawled to the surf's strand. A paddle leaned against the float's gray side.

Nesto! Henrik tried to rise to his feet, but nausea and light-headedness made him feel a stumbling, whirling sensation. Reaching the float on hands and knees, he found Nesto lying on the latticed bottom, still half-submerged in oily water.

"Hey, partner, I'm freezing my butt off. We on dry land?" croaked Nesto.

"We are." He dragged Nesto out of the Carley and they hands-and-kneed it to dry sand. Now they were thirsty. Henrik fetched water cans and used his sheath knife to cut two open. Restored, they dragged the float to the jungle's edge. Finding a portion for a ship's canvas deck awning, they were rigging it as a sunshade in a hulking shapeless form so as to appear like flotsam aground on the beach. They slumbered as time passed. Hunger caused Henrik to consider retrieving cans of pemmican.

The throb of a diesel engine arrived with the breeze. Ducking, Henrik saw its source and feebly waved a partly burnt sailor's jumper.

A bullhorn ordered, "Ahoy ashore. Cease hoppin' 'round if ya ain't Japs or I'll mow ya butts down like clover."

An LCR(L) bobbed at the narrow reef's edge. A pair of machine guns tracked them. The blunt bow swung about, and a Tommy-gun-armed bluejacket motioned. "How'd you seadogs make it way over here?"

"We're marines," corrected Nesto.

"We hitchhiked," muttered Henrik, as they stumbled up the lowered bow ramp.

"All we can offer are steerage class tickets," grinned the sailor. "Where ya bound? Maybe we can drop ya off."

Henrik and Nesto looked at one another. "Hawaii."

The searching LCR had plucked them off Mangalonga Island west of Guadalcanal. Henrik and Nesto spent two weeks in a Tulagi field hospital before returning to their units. Henrik was summoned to verify Nesto AWOL from the 2d Pioneer Battalion, after spouting what sounded as farfetched a tale as ever of having been Shanghaied to some small island. Henrik, as he climbed through staff NCO billets, managed to transfer Nesto to the battalion headquarters and later the regimental headquarters of the 2d Marines.

§ Obata §

Two hours after boarding, Lieutenant Kiyoshi, Obata, Kazuo, and Kosaku, the signalman, were aboard a landing barge backing away from the beach. It took two nights to reach some unnamed barge staging base on an island they never learned the name of. They seldom spoke, and certainly nothing of *Kombuana Jima*. Three weeks later Obata, Kazuo, and Kosaku were staged to Guadalcanal where they were eventually reassigned to different companies in the regiment. The wounded lieutenant was evacuated.

In the first week of February 1943, the three of them were evacuated to Shortland with 13,000 dilapidated Guadalcanal survivors. From there they were sent to Rabaul where they remained to the war's end. Lieutenant-General Vernon Sturdee commanding the First Australian Army accepted the surrender of 70,000 Japanese troops of the 8th Area Army and the Southern Area Fleet on 6 September 1945. They were repatriated to Japan soon after the year's end.

They did not suffer the humiliation and shame of Imperial soldiers and sailors captured or surrendered before the Imperial surrender. Most of the dishonored prisoners had been reported as having died in battle, died of illness, or starvation—"soldier's illness." Instead, months after V-J Day the returned soldiers began arriving at the doors of their homes, appearing as *yūrei*, a ruined and wasted spirit.

Epilogue

10 July 1951

Their common experiences in the "Kombuana Incident" bonded Obata, Kazuo, and Kosaku even though they were assigned to different 2nd Division units. They retained that friendship even when discharged and met in Nagoya two or three times a year. They were never able to locate Lieutenant Kiyoshi. Kosaku, the former signalman, studied electronics, while Kazuo gave up his grenade discharger to study engineering management. He attended a conference on coming business opportunities. America and the United Nations were fighting a war in Korea, formerly a Japanese colony. He discovered an aid program in which the occupying American armed forces based in Japan could contract for local products and services. American loans and technical advice could be provided to upgrade and produce a wide range of products.

Obata was taken by surprise when his mother introduced a *nakōdo*—matchmaker. It was a tradition that was fast disappearing in post-war Japan, but Mother was a traditionalist. Besides, the girl reminded him of someone at a place called the Sunflower.

The Nikko Special Glass Factory of course had to find a new product line. Glass fishing spheres were falling out of favor, and the former cork and new plastic net floats were becoming popular. Serious discussions were necessary to convince Obata's father that it was a changing world. Americans worked so quickly. Within weeks the company was granted a contract to produce glass vacuum tubes for American tactical radios.

22 December 1945

A vacant platform greeted Gunnery Sergeant Henrik C. Hahnemann stepping off the Pullman coach. After tipping the porter and shaking his hand, he canted his forest-green garrison cap. He picked up his seabag and a carton of Christmas gifts he'd bought in Nagasaki and Honolulu. Stenciled below the seabag's Globe and Anchor, hand-painted by a Japanese artist after V-J Day, were: "Fiji, Guadalcanal, Pombuana, New Zealand, Tarawa, Hawaii, Saipan, Tinian, Japan." He hadn't been home on leave for almost two years, before Saipan. He was more than ready for it.

But then the recurring image of him eventually taking over the farm emerged. Is that what he wanted? He'd done a lot, seen a lot, seen too much. *No, I'm not a farmer, not anymore.* Just about anything he decided would be new to him. Prompt decisions were his nature, and it was a relief standing alone in a biting wind to finally admit he's no farmer. Maybe once, but he had learned so much the hard way. A teacher, he could do that. Guiding kids. He liked that idea. He had steered many young men, some no longer present for duty. He could repay them by turning out upright stalwart young men to take their place.

It was colder than he'd expected. He'd dig out his gloves once inside the station.

"Well, howdy, Marine," said the stationmaster coming out onto the platform, rubbing his hands in the pre-dawn chill. "You're waiting for the next northbound train? It'll be just over three hours. Come on in for a cup of coffee, warm up a spell."

"I'd be obliged, sir." He faltered a moment. "Maybe you can help me. Is there a taxi or a car I can hire?"

"Well now, ol' Tim Briggs' got a pickup and does hauling; runs errands for folks. I can whistle him up in a flash. He'd be honored to tote a vet around. He won't charge you his usual dime-a-mile. I'll see to that."

Doffing his cap as they stepped into the coal stove's warmth, he glanced at the small Stars and Stripes flag now sewn into his cover's lining. "That sounds terrific," said Henrik. "Say, I'm looking for someone. I have a name, if I heard it right…"

The stationmaster looked at him quizzically. The depot sign over their heads proclaimed, "Sierra Blanca, Texas."

Abbreviations

The use of abbreviations is kept to a minimum. Some abbreviations have come into widespread common use and are provided here for convenience.

AA	antiaircraft
AT	antitank
BAR	Browning Automatic Rifle (Pronounced "B-A-R," not "Bar")
CO	commanding officer
GED	General Educational Development high school equivalency test
HQ	headquarters
KP	kitchen police
LCM	Landing Craft, Mechanized ("Mike boat")
LCP(L)	Landing Craft, Personnel (Large) ("Eureka boat")
LCV	Landing Craft, Vehicle ("Higgins boat")
LT	lieutenant (pronounced "El-Tee")
MG	machine gun
MP	Military Police
NCO	non-commissioned officer ("noncom"—corporals, sergeants)
OP	observation post
PA	public address system
ROTC	Reserve Officers' Training Corps
SP	Shore Patrol
XO	executive officer (2nd-in-command)
YP	Harbor [Yard] Patrol Boat ("yippee boat")

Japanese names are given in the traditional manner, family name (surname) first and given name second. Typically, family members addressed one by their surname.

Pombuana Island is pronounced "Pome-boo-anah" in English. The Japanese spell it *Kombuana Jima* and pronounced it "Kome-boo-anah Ji-ma." Its unconfirmed native meaning is "North Island."

The Marine terms Bn-2, R-2, and D-2 designate the Battalion, Regiment, and Division intelligence staff officers. Prior to 1945 the Marines used these terms instead of the Army's "S-" and "G-"; Staff and General Staff officers.